The Gospel in Tolstoy

Leo Tolstoy

The Gospel in Tolstoy

Selections from His Short Stories,
Spiritual Writings, and Novels

Leo Tolstoy

Edited by Miriam LeBlanc
With Artwork by Fritz Eichenberg

PLOUGH PUBLISHING HOUSE

Published by Plough Publishing House
Walden, New York
Robertsbridge, England
Elsmore, Australia
www.plough.com

ISBN: 978-0-87486-670-4

Cover woodcut by Karl Mahr, 1923 for Gemeinschafts-Verlag Eberhard Arnold, Sannerz / Leipzig

Artwork in the book interior is wood engravings by Fritz Eichenberg. The artwork on the frontispiece and on page 140 is from Eichenberg's illustrations for Tolstoy's *Resurrection* (New York: The Heritage Press, 1963). Eichenberg prepared the other engravings (on pages 2, 50, 106, 208, and 252) for the *Catholic Worker* newspaper. Artwork is copyright © 2015 by the Estate of Fritz Eichenberg. Used with permission.

Translations are by Louise and Aylmer Maude, Constance Garnett, and David Patterson, as described in "Note on the Translations" (page 326). The extract from David Patterson's translation of Tolstoy's *Confession* (W. W. Norton, 1983) is copyright © 1983 by David Patterson and used with permission.

A catalog record for this book is available from the British Library.
Library of Congress Cataloging-in-Publication Data

Tolstoy, Leo, graf, 1828-1910, author.
[Works. Selections. English]
The gospel in Tolstoy : selections from short stories, novels, and spiritual writings / Leo Tolstoy ; edited by Miriam Leblanc.
   pages ; cm
ISBN 978-0-87486-670-4 (paper)
I. LeBlanc, Miriam, editor. II. Title.
PG3366.A13L43 2015
891.73'3--dc23
                    2015032733

Contents

To the Reader

ALTHOUGH MORE THAN A CENTURY has passed since his death, for millions of readers the works of Leo Tolstoy (1828–1910) have only grown in their power and appeal. Virginia Woolf's verdict still rings as true as ever – Tolstoy is "the greatest of all novelists." Certainly, he ranks with Dostoyevsky in his probing insight into the workings of human nature, and with Shakespeare in his generous empathy with a startlingly broad array of people. What's more, his storytelling seems to have an effortless immediacy that, as Matthew Arnold said of *War and Peace*, leaves readers feeling they are experiencing not a piece of art, but simply life itself.

For such a writer, few justifications are needed for an anthology like this one, which includes much of what is widely regarded as Tolstoy's best work. For readers who are eager to explore Tolstoy but just don't have time for all eight hundred pages of *Anna Karenina,* this collection can serve as a tasting menu. Meanwhile, students and those who love classic literature will gain an appreciation of Tolstoy's remarkable range before they plunge into one of his major books. At the same time, serious Tolstoy enthusiasts will find in this selection a new lens through which to appreciate afresh the rich landscape of the author's work.

What, though, is "the gospel in Tolstoy" – is such a title even defensible? After all, this was a man who lost his traditional Christian faith as a teenager, and spent much of his career attacking the Russian church of his upbringing. Despite a sincere conversion and his self-description as a Christian, his views fell well outside the usual norms of Christian orthodoxy – after all, he rejected most articles of the Nicene Creed, and even compiled a version of the Gospels from which anything miraculous, including the resurrection, is left out.

Yet with all his rationalism, Tolstoy remained a man haunted by Jesus of Nazareth. Jesus' example and teachings – especially the Sermon on the Mount – loomed over the writer's life in ways large and small, from his ardent pacifism to his repeated attempts to divest himself of his inherited wealth and privilege. Even before Tolstoy's conversion (recounted in the selection from his *Confession* in chapter 4), the search for God and the meaning of life already formed a powerful impulse in his writings. In a Christendom all too comfortable with oppressive worldly power, Tolstoy issued a sharp challenge to return to the radical call of Jesus.

Ultimately, this was a call to a way of unreserved love toward others – love not as a feeling or theological concept but as action in everyday life. As Eberhard Arnold suggests in the "Afterword," this vision of love points to something beyond the rigid legalism to which Tolstoy was prone; it is a vision of a renewed world in which Jesus' promises have become reality.

At the beginning of the short story "What Men Live By" (Chapter 8), Tolstoy quotes the First Letter of John: "No man has ever seen God; if we love one another, God abides in us and his love is perfected in us." This is where the gospel is to be found in Tolstoy – delivered in a way that speaks to people of any religion or none. Whether or not we agree with the great Russian on anything else, it's a lesson we can learn from him, and one that we can strive, as he did, to practice.   —*The Editor*

Biographical Sketch

Charles Moore

BORN AUGUST 28, 1828, Lev "Leo" Nikolayevich Tolstoy was the fourth of five children in a family of the old Russian nobility; he lost his mother by the age of two. His first eight years were spent at Yasnaya Polyana, the family's large country estate southwest of Moscow. When he was eight, the family moved to Moscow, and shortly after, his father suddenly died. The loss was devastating, and ever after Tolstoy would be deeply pained by the inevitability of death.

After being tutored at home, he set out for the University of Kazan in 1844. Repelled at first by the coarseness of student life, he gradually fell in with his peers. He lost so much money gambling that his brother Sergei eventually had to bail him out; he began visiting brothels. After his excesses he always fell into moods of despair and self-accusation.

In 1847, he left the university without completing a degree, and returned to Yasnaya Polyana. The estate became his on his eighteenth birthday, with its four thousand acres and three hundred serfs. He made plans to better the lives of his serfs: school for the children, housing, more nourishing food, better sanitary conditions for all. But whatever he offered them was met with suspicion, and their children were usually absent from school. The young Tolstoy was soon frustrated.

Tolstoy sensed that his life was heading nowhere fast. Whenever he visited Moscow, he fell back into his old student ways.

To get away, he joined his brother Nicholas, volunteering on a military expedition in the Caucasus. Although he continued to womanize and gamble, something new began to emerge. His thoughts – meticulously recorded in his diary – were now interspersed with reflections about the mysteries of life and religion.

He also began to write. During this period he published *Childhood and Boyhood,* largely autobiographical fictional works, which were well received by the reading public. In November 1854 he joined the defense of Sevastopol during its year-long siege by the French and their allies. What he saw on the front inspired the writing of *Sevastopol Sketches,* accounts that documented war's brutality.

In 1856, Tolstoy left the army and moved into the apartment of the famed author, Ivan Turgenev, who introduced him to key figures of Russia's literary world. By 1860, Tolstoy had become disgusted with high society and with himself, and began to turn his energies to teaching in a village school in Yasnaya Polyana.

Two years later he married Sophia Andreyevna Behrs, "Sonya," an energetic and intelligent eighteen-year-old. Despite her own capabilities, she was young and intimidated by her new fiancé. Though at first harmony and joy prevailed between them, quarrels came, in part because Sonya, after reading Leo's diary the day before their wedding, found out that his most recent mistress was still living on the estate. Besides, moving to rural Yasnaya Polyana was frightening for a Europeanized city girl. Still, Sonya was committed to seeing that the Tolstoy style of life was one to be envied. Their house was enlarged and remodeled, with plenty of room for an endless stream of guests and visitors.

In the first ten years of marriage, Sonya gave birth to six children. In all, they had thirteen. One result of getting married was that Tolstoy had to abandon his educational work. Sonya demanded that he provide for her and for their expected family. Partly as a result, what had been brewing beneath the surface for years finally emerged in the form of what some consider the greatest novel ever written: *War and Peace.* For the next six years, the couple slaved together: he wrote, while Sonya plunged herself into the self-appointed task of protecting him from the outer world and copying and recopying the manuscript.

Upon completion of this masterpiece, Tolstoy was left inwardly exhausted. In *War and Peace,* he had grappled with the harsh and terrible fact of mortality. Generation after generation lives and dies – to what purpose? Leaving what behind? *War and Peace* ends in a series of unanswerable questions: what forces move the nations? Why do things happen? Why are we here?

Despite his inward alienation, or perhaps, because of it, Tolstoy, at his wife's persistence, managed in the 1870s to produce yet another great novel, *Anna Karenina,* which met with huge popular acclaim. The entire novel was written under the shadow of death. Of the 239 chapters, he gave a title to only one: the twentieth chapter of the Fifth Part, which he called, "Death." After *Anna Karenina* there would be no more great novels until *Resurrection,* published in 1899.

Though surrounded by success on all fronts, Tolstoy unraveled. He was plagued with suicidal thoughts, even to the point of hiding a rope, lest in a surge of sudden despair he take his own life. He consumed philosophy texts of every school of thought, hoping to find some explanation of the meaning of life. But neither the philosophers nor the sciences, not to mention his own contemporaries, helped him find what he was looking for.

Then it occurred to him to look beyond his own circle. He noticed that the peasants, despite their poverty, had an instinctive sense of life's purpose. Their faith in God and their simple labor propelled them to live. And then it dawned on him: he too only lived at those times when he believed in God. It was a decisive conversion experience, after which the light never left him.

To nurture his newfound faith, Tolstoy strove to enter into the spirit of the peasants and to overlook the contradictions of the Orthodox Church. But when the Holy Synod ordered prayers to be said in the churches for the success of the Russian armies, and when Tolstoy heard the priest, who had so often read the Gospel injunction to love your enemies, utter supplications in the name of Jesus that God might destroy the Turks with sword and bombshell, his soul revolted and he walked away from the church for good. He became an outspoken pacifist whose ideas influenced, among others, Gandhi, George Bernard Shaw, and Martin Luther King.

Tolstoy's conversion led to numerous visible signs of sacrifice. Worldly goods and all the surface attractions began to appear to him as shackles, and eventually became a cross he found hard to bear. At times he sought to break with his entire past, to reject the family life he had dreamed of in his youth, and finally to give up all the wealth he had acquired, renouncing his property and giving up the profits from the sales of his books. Sonya watched as her husband embarked on a religious warpath that would throw the two of them into one debilitating battle after another.

Sonya was particularly anxious about their finances and the future of his literary works. She argued bitterly with Chertkov, Tolstoy's assistant, who wanted some of the publication rights. She fought desperately for the funds she deemed necessary to sustain the family's standard of living. In 1891, Tolstoy finally managed to officially renounce the rights to virtually all his works published after 1881, allowing his earlier works to financially benefit the family. He also signed over all his property to her and the children.

In 1882 Tolstoy volunteered as an official to help with the 1882 municipal census in Moscow. It was here that he observed the moral deterioration that overtook those who had slipped down into society's slums. Unable to cope with the contradiction between his life and what he saw, Tolstoy poured everything out in his book, *What Then Must We Do?* In answer to the question of the book's title, Tolstoy came to a simple conclusion: repent, engage in manual labor, and live and eat simply. The privileged classes must no longer expect to be fed, clothed, and waited upon by others – they must "get off the backs of the poor" and obey the basic law of life.

He sought to put his own teachings in practice. In 1891 a drought brought famine to the provinces of central Russia, and Tolstoy successfully organized relief for the peasants, sometimes feeding thousands of people in a day. When the Doukhobors, a religious sect, were harshly persecuted, Tolstoy collected an enormous sum to help them emigrate to Canada, using the profits of his novel, *Resurrection*. This novel, in part a shocking indictment of the Russian Orthodox Church and the state with which it was intertwined, met with stern disapproval from the authorities. In 1901, the Orthodox Church excommunicated him.

Tolstoy continued his efforts to live out his convictions, leading to quarrels with his wife that would become legendary. Finally, one night while lying in bed, the eighty-two-year-old Tolstoy reached a decision. In the pre-dawn hours of October 28, 1910 he secretly left home, accompanied by his daughter and his doctor. He soon fell ill, and just over a week later, he died at the Astopovo railway station.

On the day before his death, Tolstoy called out to his son: "Sergei! Sergei! I love Truth . . . very much . . . I love Truth." And in many respects, this was Tolstoy's greatest legacy. Though never a saint, or even completely consistent, he sought to be ruth-lessly honest – both with himself and with those around him.

For Tolstoy, Truth was moral. It infuriated him that those who professed Jesus as being divine and infallible were also the very ones who neglected to do the things he actually taught. Although he replaces this inconsistency with one of his own – a Jesus who is not divine but whose words are – nevertheless, he rightly asked the question Jesus surely would have asked if he had been living during Tsarist Russia, and which perhaps could just as well be asked in our own day: how is it that self-professed Christians refuse to obey Christ?

In the end, Tolstoy's diatribes, whether against government, violence, property, or what have you, stem from his great under-standing of love – a reality that encompasses a fraternal order rooted in heartfelt sacrifice. The extracts from his works that follow, taken from a cross-section of his novels, short stories, and spiritual writings, must therefore be read against this back-drop, or else one risks taking Tolstoy's words out of context. It is love that ultimately matters. In the end, as Tolstoy writes,

> We can only unite with each other in God. We do not need to take steps toward each other; we need only to approach God. If there were a huge church in which the light from above fell only in the center, people would only have to go towards the light in the center to be gathered together. Be assured, if we all approach God, we will be drawn towards each other.

Finding God

For everyone who asks receives, and he who seeks finds, and to him who knocks it will be opened.
—Matthew 7:8

Illustration for Dorothy Day's The Long Loneliness

I.

The Three Hermits

An Old Legend Current in the Volga District

And in praying do not heap up empty phrases as the Gentiles do;
for they think that they will be heard for their many words. Do not
be like them, for your Father knows what you need before you ask
him. —Matthew 6:7–8

A BISHOP WAS SAILING from Arkhangelsk to the Solovetsky Monastery, and on the same vessel were a number of pilgrims on their way to visit the shrines at that place. The voyage was a smooth one. The wind favorable, and the weather fair. The pilgrims lay on deck, eating, or sat in groups talking to one another. The bishop, too, came on deck, and as he was pacing up and down, he noticed a group of men standing near the prow and listening to a fisherman who was pointing to the sea and telling them something. The bishop stopped, and looked in the direction in which the man was pointing. He could see nothing however, but the sea glistening in the sunshine. He drew nearer to listen, but when the man saw him, he took off his cap and was silent. The rest of the people also took off their caps, and bowed.

"Do not let me disturb you, friends," said the bishop. "I came to hear what this good man was saying."

"The fisherman was telling us about the hermits," replied one, a tradesman, rather bolder than the rest.

3

"What hermits?" asked the bishop, going to the side of the vessel and seating himself on a box. "Tell me about them. I should like to hear. What were you pointing at?"

"Why, that little island you can just see over there," answered the man, pointing to a spot ahead and a little to the right. "That is the island where the hermits live for the salvation of their souls."

"Where is the island?" asked the bishop. "I see nothing."

"There, in the distance, if you will please look along my hand. Do you see that little cloud? Below it and a bit to the left, there is just a faint streak. That is the island."

The bishop looked carefully, but his unaccustomed eyes could make out nothing but the water shimmering in the sun.

"I cannot see it," he said. "But who are the hermits that live there?"

"They are holy men," answered the fisherman. "I had long heard tell of them, but never chanced to see them myself till the year before last."

And the fisherman related how once, when he was out fishing, he had been stranded at night upon that island, not knowing where he was. In the morning, as he wandered about the island, he came across an earth hut, and met an old man standing near it. Presently two others came out, and after having fed him, and dried his things, they helped him mend his boat.

"And what are they like?" asked the bishop.

"One is a small man and his back is bent. He wears a priest's cassock and is very old; he must be more than a hundred, I should say. He is so old that the white of his beard is taking a greenish tinge, but he is always smiling, and his face is as bright as an angel's from heaven. The second is taller, but he also is very old. He wears a tattered peasant coat. His beard is broad, and of a yellowish grey color. He is a strong man. Before I had time to help him, he turned my boat over as if it were only a pail. He, too, is kindly and cheerful. The third is tall, and has a beard as white as snow and reaching to his knees. He is stern, with over-hanging eyebrows; and he wears nothing but a mat tied round his waist."

"And did they speak to you?" asked the bishop.

"For the most part they did everything in silence and spoke but little even to one another. One of them would just give a glance, and the others would understand him. I asked the tallest whether they had lived there long. He frowned, and muttered something as if he were angry; but the oldest one took his hand and smiled, and then the tall one was quiet. The oldest one only said: 'Have mercy upon us,' and smiled."

While the fisherman was talking, the ship had drawn nearer to the island.

"There, now you can see it plainly, if your Grace will please to look," said the tradesman, pointing with his hand.

The bishop looked, and now he really saw a dark streak – the island. Having looked at it a while, he left the prow of the vessel, and going to the stern, asked the helmsman:

"What island is that?"

"That one," replied the man, "has no name. There are many such in this sea."

"Is it true that there are hermits who live there for the salvation of their souls?"

"So it is said, your Grace, but I don't know if it's true. Fishermen say they have seen them; but of course they may only be spinning yarns."

"I should like to land on the island and see these men," said the bishop. "How could I manage it?"

"The ship cannot get close to the island," replied the helms-man, "but you might be rowed there in a boat. You had better speak to the captain."

The captain was sent for and came.

"I should like to see these hermits," said the bishop. "Could I not be rowed ashore?"

The captain tried to dissuade him.

"Of course it could be done," said he, "but we should lose much time. And if I might venture to say so to your Grace, the old men are not worth your pains. I have heard say that they are foolish old fellows, who understand nothing, and never speak a word, any more than the fish in the sea."

"I wish to see them," said the bishop, "and I will pay you for your trouble and loss of time. Please let me have a boat."

There was no help for it; so the order was given. The sailors trimmed the sails, the steersman put up the helm, and the ship's course was set for the island. A chair was placed at the prow for the bishop, and he sat there, looking ahead. The passengers all collected at the prow, and gazed at the island. Those who had the sharpest eyes could presently make out the rocks on it, and then a mud hut was seen. At last one man saw the hermits themselves. The captain brought a telescope and, after looking through it, handed it to the bishop.

"It's right enough. There are three men standing on the shore. There, a little to the right of that big rock."

The bishop took the telescope, got it into position, and he saw the three men: a tall one, a shorter one, and one very small and bent, standing on the shore and holding each other by the hand.

The captain turned to the bishop.

"The vessel can get no nearer in than this, your Grace. If you wish to go ashore, we must ask you to go in the boat, while we anchor here."

The cable was quickly let out, the anchor cast, and the sails furled. There was a jerk, and the vessel shook. Then, a boat having been lowered, the oarsmen jumped in, and the bishop descended the ladder and took his seat. The men pulled at their oars, and the boat moved rapidly towards the island. When they came within a stone's throw they saw three old men: a tall one with only a mat tied round his waist: a shorter one in a tattered peasant coat, and a very old one bent with age and wearing an old cassock – all three standing hand in hand.

The oarsmen pulled in to the shore, and held on with the boathook while the bishop got out.

The old men bowed to him, and he gave them his benediction, at which they bowed still lower. Then the bishop began to speak to them.

"I have heard," he said, "that you, godly men, live here saving your own souls, and praying to our Lord Christ for your fellow men. I, an unworthy servant of Christ, am called by God's mercy to keep and teach his flock. I wished to see you, servants of God, and to do what I can to teach you, also."

The old men looked at each other smiling, but remained silent.

"Tell me," said the bishop, "what you are doing to save your souls, and how you serve God on this island."

The second hermit sighed, and looked at the oldest, the very ancient one. The latter smiled, and said:

"We do not know how to serve God. We only serve and support ourselves, servant of God."

"But how do you pray to God?" asked the bishop.

"We pray in this way," replied the hermit. "Three are ye, three are we, have mercy upon us."

And when the old man said this, all three raised their eyes to heaven, and repeated:

"Three are ye, three are we, have mercy upon us!"

The bishop smiled.

"You have evidently heard something about the Holy Trinity," said he. "But you do not pray aright. You have won my affection, godly men. I see you wish to please the Lord, but you do not know how to serve him. That is not the way to pray; but listen to me, and I will teach you. I will teach you, not a way of my own, but the way in which God in the Holy Scriptures has commanded all people to pray to him."

And the bishop began explaining to the hermits how God had revealed himself to humankind; telling them of God the Father, and God the Son, and God the Holy Ghost.

"God the Son came down on earth," said he, "to save humankind, and this is how he taught us all to pray. Listen and repeat after me: 'Our Father.'"

And the first old man repeated after him, "Our Father," and the second said, "Our Father," and the third said, "Our Father."

"Which art in heaven," continued the bishop.

The first hermit repeated, "Which art in heaven," but the second blundered over the words, and the tall hermit could not say them properly. His hair had grown over his mouth so that he could not speak plainly. The very old hermit, having no teeth, also mumbled indistinctly.

The bishop repeated the words again, and the old men repeated them after him. The bishop sat down on a stone, and the old men stood before him, watching his mouth, and repeating the words as he uttered them. And all day long the bishop labored, saying a word twenty, thirty, a hundred times over, and the old men repeated it after him. They blundered, and he corrected them, and made them begin again.

The bishop did not leave off till he had taught them the whole of the Lord's Prayer so that they could not only repeat it after him, but could say it by themselves. The middle one was the first to know it, and to repeat the whole of it alone. The bishop made him say it again and again, and at last the others could say it too.

It was getting dark, and the moon was appearing over the water, before the bishop rose to return to the vessel. When he took leave of the old men, they all bowed down to the ground before him. He raised them, and kissed each of them, telling them to pray as he had taught them. Then he got into the boat and returned to the ship.

And as he sat in the boat and was rowed to the ship he could hear the three voices of the hermits loudly repeating the Lord's Prayer. As the boat drew near the vessel their voices could no longer be heard, but they could still be seen in the moonlight, standing as he had left them on the shore, the shortest in the middle, the tallest on the right, the middle one on the left. As soon as the bishop had reached the vessel and got on board, the anchor was weighed and the sails unfurled. The wind filled them, and the ship sailed away, and the bishop took a seat in the stern and watched the island they had left. For a time he could still see the hermits, but presently they disappeared from sight, though the island was still visible. At last it too vanished, and only the sea was to be seen, rippling in the moonlight.

The pilgrims lay down to sleep, and all was quiet on deck. The bishop did not wish to sleep, but sat alone at the stern, gazing at the sea where the island was no longer visible, and thinking of the good old men. He thought how pleased they had been to learn the Lord's Prayer; and he thanked God for having sent him to teach and help such godly men.

So the bishop sat thinking, and gazing at the sea where the island had disappeared. And the moonlight flickered before his eyes, sparkling, now here, now there, upon the waves. Suddenly he saw something white and shining, on the bright path which the moon cast across the sea. Was it a seagull, or the little gleaming sail of some small boat? The bishop fixed his eyes on it, wondering.

"It must be a boat sailing after us," thought he, "but it is overtaking us very rapidly. It was far, far away a minute ago, but now it is much nearer. It cannot be a boat, for I can see no sail; but whatever it may be, it is following us, and catching us up."

And he could not make out what it was. Not a boat, nor a bird, nor a fish! It was too large for a man, and besides a man could not be out there in the midst of the sea. The bishop rose, and said to the helmsman:

"Look there, what is that, my friend? What is it?" the bishop repeated, though he could now see plainly what it was – the three hermits running upon the water, all gleaming white, their grey beards shining, and approaching the ship as quickly as though it were not moving.

The steersman looked and let go the helm in terror.

"Oh Lord! The hermits are running after us on the water as though it were dry land!"

The passengers, hearing him, jumped up, and crowded to the stern. They saw the hermits coming along hand in hand, and the two outer ones beckoning the ship to stop. All three were gliding along upon the water without moving their feet. Before the ship could be stopped, the hermits had reached it, and raising their heads, all three as with one voice, began to say:

"We have forgotten your teaching, servant of God. As long as we kept repeating it we remembered, but when we stopped saying it for a time, a word dropped out, and now it has all gone to pieces. We can remember nothing of it. Teach us again."

The bishop crossed himself, and leaning over the ship's side, said:

"Your own prayer will reach the Lord, men of God. It is not for me to teach you. Pray for us sinners."

And the bishop bowed low before the old men; and they turned and went back across the sea. And a light shone until daybreak on the spot where they were lost to sight.

2.

Levin Looks for Miracles

From Anna Karenina

Konstantin Dmitrich Levin, a wealthy landowner, has long been plagued by doubts about faith, which are newly stirred up again after he watches his older brother die from tuberculosis.

EVER SINCE, by his beloved brother's deathbed, Levin had first glanced into the questions of life and death in the light of these new convictions, as he called them, which had during the period from his twentieth to his thirty-fourth year imperceptibly replaced his childish and youthful beliefs – he had been stricken with horror, not so much of death, as of life, without any knowledge of whence, and why, and how, and what it was. The physical organization, its decay, the indestructibility of matter, the law of the conservation of energy, evolution, were the words which usurped the place of his old belief. These words and the ideas associated with them were very well for intellectual purposes. But for life they yielded nothing, and Levin felt suddenly like a man who has changed his warm fur cloak for a muslin garment, and going for the first time into the frost is immediately convinced, not by reason, but by his whole nature that he is as good as naked, and that he must infallibly perish miserably.

From that moment, though he did not distinctly face it, and still went on living as before, Levin had never lost this sense of terror at his lack of knowledge.

He vaguely felt, too, that what he called his new convictions were not merely lack of knowledge, but that they were part of a whole order of ideas, in which no knowledge of what he needed was possible.

At first, marriage, with the new joys and duties bound up with it, had completely crowded out these thoughts. But of late, while he was staying in Moscow after his wife's confinement, with nothing to do, the question that clamored for solution had more and more often, more and more insistently, haunted Levin's mind.

The question was summed up for him thus: "If I do not accept the answers Christianity gives to the problems of my life, what answers do I accept?" And in the whole arsenal of his convictions, so far from finding any satisfactory answers, he was utterly unable to find anything at all like an answer. He was in the position of a man seeking food in toy shops and tool shops.

Instinctively, unconsciously, with every book, with every conversation, with every man he met, he was on the lookout for light on these questions and their solution.

What puzzled and distracted him above everything was that the majority of men of his age and circle had, like him, exchanged their old beliefs for the same new convictions, and yet saw nothing to lament in this, and were perfectly satisfied and serene. So that, apart from the principal question, Levin was tortured by other questions too. Were these people sincere, he asked himself, or were they playing a part? Or was it that they understood the answers science gave to these problems in some different, clearer sense than he did? And he assiduously studied both these people's opinions and the books which treated of these scientific explanations.

One fact he had found out since these questions had engrossed his mind, was that he had been quite wrong in supposing from the recollections of the circle of his young days at college, that religion had outlived its day, and that it was now practically non-existent. All the people nearest to him who were good in their lives were believers. The old prince, and Lvov, whom he liked so much, his brother Koznyshev, and all the women, believed. His wife had a childlike faith just like his as a small boy, and ninety-nine out of a hundred of the Russian people, all the working people for whose life he felt the deepest respect, believed.

Another fact of which he became convinced, after reading many scientific books, was that those who shared his views had no other construction to put on them, and that they gave no explanation of the questions which he felt he could not live without answering, but simply ignored their existence and attempted to explain other questions of no possible interest to him, such as the evolution of organisms, the materialistic theory of consciousness, and so forth.

Moreover, during his wife's confinement, something had happened that seemed extraordinary to him. He, an unbeliever, had fallen into praying, and at the moment he prayed, he believed. But that moment had passed, and he could not make his state of mind at that moment fit into the rest of his life.

He could not admit that at that moment he knew the truth, and that now he was wrong; for as soon as he began thinking calmly about it, it all fell to pieces. He could not admit that he was mistaken then, for his spiritual condition then was precious to him, and to admit that it was a proof of weakness would have been to desecrate those moments. He was miserably divided against himself, and strained all his spiritual forces to the utmost to escape from this condition.

✦ ✦ ✦

Making the rounds of his country estate, Levin speaks to one of his peasants about a local innkeeper who rents some land.

Levin, going up to the machine, moved Fyodor aside, and began feeding the corn in himself.

Working on till the peasants' dinner hour, which was not long in coming, he went out of the barn with Fyodor and fell into talk with him, stopping beside a neat yellow sheaf of rye laid on the threshing floor for seed.

Fyodor came from a village at some distance from the one in which Levin had once allotted land to his cooperative association. Now it had been let to a former house porter.

Levin talked to Fyodor about this land and asked whether Platon, a well-to-do peasant of good character belonging to the same village, would not take the land for the coming year.

"It's a high rent; it wouldn't pay Platon, Konstantin Dmitrich," answered the peasant, picking the ears off his sweat-drenched shirt.

"But how does Kirilov make it pay?"

"Oh, Mityuka" (as he contemptuously called the house porter), "you may be sure he'll make it pay, Konstantin Dmitrich! He'll get his share, however he has to squeeze to get it! He's no mercy on a Christian. But Uncle Fokanich" (so he called the old peasant Platon), "do you suppose he'd flay the skin off a man? He'll give credit, and sometimes he'll let a man off. And go short himself, too. He's that sort of person."

"But why will he let anyone off?"

"Oh, well, of course, folks are different. One man lives for his own wants and nothing else, like Mituh, he only thinks of filling his belly, but Fokanich is a righteous man. He lives for his soul. He does not forget God."

"How thinks of God? How does he live for his soul?" Levin almost shouted.

"Why, to be sure, in truth, in God's way. Folks are different. Take you now, you wouldn't wrong a man . . ."

"Yes, yes, goodbye!" said Levin, breathless with excitement, and turning round he took his stick and walked quickly away towards home.

A novel joyous feeling enveloped Levin. At the peasant's words about Platon living for his soul, rightly, in God's way, undefined but significant ideas crowded into his mind, as if they had broken loose from some place where they had been locked up, and all rushing forward towards one goal, whirled in his head, blinding him with their light.

✦ ✦ ✦

Levin strode along the highroad, absorbed not so much in his thoughts (he could not yet disentangle them) as in his spiritual condition, unlike anything he had experienced before.

The words uttered by the peasant had acted on his soul like an electric shock, suddenly transforming and combining into a single whole the whole swarm of disjointed, impotent, separate thoughts that incessantly occupied his mind. These thoughts had unconsciously been in his mind even when he was talking to Fyodor about letting the land.

He was aware of something new in his soul and took a delight in probing it, not yet knowing what this new something was.

"Not living for his own wants, but for God? For what God? And could anything be more senseless than what he said? He said that we must not live for our own wants, that is, we must not live for what we understand, what we are attracted by, what we desire, but must live for something incomprehensible, for God, whom no one can understand nor even define. What of it? Didn't I understand those senseless words of Fyodor's? And understanding them, did I doubt of their truth? Did I think them stupid, obscure, inexact?

"No, I understood him, and exactly as he understands the words. I understood them more fully and clearly than I understand anything in life, and never in my life have I doubted nor can I doubt about it. And not only I, but everyone, the whole world understands nothing fully but this, and about this only they have no doubt and are always agreed.

"And I looked out for miracles, complained that I did not see a miracle which would convince me. A material miracle would have persuaded me. And here is a miracle, the sole miracle possible, continually existing, surrounding me on all sides, and I never noticed it!

"Fyodor says that Kirilov lives for his belly. That's comprehensible and rational. All of us as rational beings can't do anything else but live for our belly. And all of a sudden the same Fyodor says that one mustn't live for one's belly, but must live for truth, for God, and at a hint I understand him! And I and millions of people, people who lived ages ago and people living now – peasants, the poor in spirit and the learned, who have thought and written about it, in their obscure words saying the same thing – we are all agreed about this one thing: what we must live for and what is good. I and all people have only one firm, incontestable, clear knowledge, and that knowledge cannot be explained by the reason – it is outside it, and has no causes and can have no effects.

"If goodness has causes, it is not goodness; if it has effects, a reward, it is not goodness either. So goodness is outside the chain of cause and effect.

"And yet I know it, and we all know it.

"What could be a greater miracle than that?

"Can I have found the solution of it all? Can my sufferings be over?" thought Levin, striding along the dusty road, not noticing the heat nor his weariness, and experiencing a sense of relief from prolonged suffering. This feeling was so delicious that it seemed to him incredible. He was breathless with emotion and incapable of going farther; he turned off the road into the forest and lay down in the shade of an aspen on the uncut grass. He took his hat off his hot head and lay propped on his elbow in the lush, feathery, woodland grass.

"Yes, I must make it clear to myself and understand," he thought, looking intently at the untrampled grass before him, and following the movements of a green beetle, advancing along a blade of couch grass and lifting up in its progress a leaf of goatweed. "What have I discovered?" he asked himself, bending aside the leaf of goatweed out of the beetle's way and twisting another blade of grass above for the beetle to cross over onto it. "What is it makes me glad? What have I discovered?

"I have discovered nothing. I have simply opened my eyes to what I knew. I have come to the recognition of that Power that not only in the past gave me life but now too gives me life. I have been set free from fallacy, I have found the Master."

3.

The Death of Ivan Ilyich

A Selection from the Novella

Ivan Ilyich, an ambitious and conventionally successful judge, moves to St. Petersburg to pursue his career. While helping his wife arrange the décor in their new house, he slips from a ladder and injures himself. Bedridden after the accident, he is cared for by the young peasant Gerasim.

HIS WIFE RETURNED late at night. She came in on tiptoe, but he heard her, opened his eyes, and made haste to close them again. She wished to send Gerasim away and to sit with him herself, but he opened his eyes and said: "No, go away."

"Are you in great pain?"

"Always the same."

"Take some opium."

He agreed and took some. She went away.

Till about three in the morning he was in a state of stupefied misery. It seemed to him that he and his pain were being thrust into a narrow, deep black sack, but though they were pushed further and further in, they could not be pushed to the bottom. And this, terrible enough in itself, was accompanied by suffering. He was frightened yet wanted to fall through the sack, he struggled but yet cooperated. And suddenly he broke through, fell, and regained consciousness. Gerasim was sitting at the foot of the bed dozing quietly and patiently, while he himself lay with his emaciated stockinged legs resting on Gerasim's shoulders; the same shaded candle was there and the same unceasing pain.

"Go away, Gerasim," he whispered.

"It's all right, sir. I'll stay a while."

"No. Go away."

He removed his legs from Gerasim's shoulders, turned sideways onto his arm, and felt sorry for himself. He only waited till Gerasim had gone into the next room and then restrained himself no longer but wept like a child. He wept on account of his helplessness, his terrible loneliness, the cruelty of man, the cruelty of God, and the absence of God.

"Why hast Thou done all this? Why hast Thou brought me here? Why, why dost Thou torment me so terribly?"

He did not expect an answer and yet wept because there was no answer and could be none. The pain again grew more acute, but he did not stir and did not call. He said to himself: "Go on! Strike me! But what is it for? What have I done to Thee? What is it for?"

Then he grew quiet and not only ceased weeping but even held his breath and became all attention. It was as though he were listening not to an audible voice but to the voice of his soul, to the current of thoughts arising within him.

"What is it you want?" was the first clear conception capable of expression in words that he heard.

"What do you want? What do you want?" he repeated to himself.

"What do I want? To live and not to suffer," he answered.

And again he listened with such concentrated attention that even his pain did not distract him.

"To live? How?" asked his inner voice.

"Why, to live as I used to – well and pleasantly."

"As you lived before, well and pleasantly?" the voice repeated.

And in imagination he began to recall the best moments of his pleasant life. But strange to say none of those best moments of his pleasant life now seemed at all what they had then seemed – none of them except the first recollections of childhood. There, in childhood, there had been something really pleasant with which it would be possible to live if it could return. But the child who had experienced that happiness existed no longer; it was like a reminiscence of somebody else.

As soon as the period began which had produced the present Ivan Ilyich, all that had then seemed joys now melted before his sight and turned into something trivial and often nasty.

And the further he departed from childhood and the nearer he came to the present the more worthless and doubtful were the joys. This began with the School of Law. A little that was really good was still found there – there was lightheartedness, friendship, and hope. But in the upper classes there had already been fewer of such good moments. Then during the first years of his official career, when he was in the service of the governor, some pleasant moments again occurred: they were the memories of love for a woman. Then all became confused and there was still less of what was good; later on again there was still less that was good, and the further he went the less there was. His marriage, a mere accident, then the disenchantment that followed it, his wife's bad breath and the sensuality and hypocrisy: then that deadly official life and those preoccupations about money, a year of it, and two, and ten, and twenty, and always the same thing. And the longer it lasted the more deadly it became. "It is as if I had been going downhill while I imagined I was going up. And that is really what it was. I was going up in public opinion, but to the same extent life was ebbing away from me. And now it is all done and there is only death.

"Then what does it mean? Why? It can't be that life is so senseless and horrible. But if it really has been so horrible and senseless, why must I die and die in agony? There is something wrong! "Maybe I did not live as I ought to have done," it suddenly occurred to him. "But how could that be, when I did everything properly?" he replied, and immediately dismissed from his mind this, the sole solution of all the riddles of life and death, as something quite impossible.

"Then what do you want now? To live? Live how? Live as you lived in the law courts when the usher proclaimed 'The judge is coming!' The judge is coming, the judge!" he repeated to himself. "Here he is, the judge. But I am not guilty!" he exclaimed angrily. "What is it for?" And he ceased crying, but turning his face to the wall continued to ponder on the same question: Why, and for what purpose, is there all this horror? But however much he pondered he found no answer. And whenever the thought occurred to him, as it often did, that it all resulted from his not having lived as he ought to have done, he at once recalled the correctness of his whole life and dismissed so strange an idea.

✦ ✦ ✦

Another fortnight passed. Ivan Ilyich now no longer left his sofa. He would not lie in bed but lay on the sofa, facing the wall nearly all the time. He suffered ever the same unceasing agonies and in his loneliness pondered always on the same insoluble question: "What is this? Can it be that it is Death?" And the inner voice answered: "Yes, it is Death."

"Why these sufferings?" And the voice answered, "For no reason – they just are so." Beyond and besides this there was nothing.

From the very beginning of his illness, ever since he had first been to see the doctor, Ivan Ilyich's life had been divided between two contrary and alternating moods: now it was despair and the expectation of this uncomprehended and terrible death, and now hope and an intently interested observation of the functioning of his organs. Now before his eyes there was only a kidney or an intestine that temporarily evaded its duty, and now only that incomprehensible and dreadful death from which it was impossible to escape.

These two states of mind had alternated from the very beginning of his illness, but the further it progressed the more doubtful and fantastic became the conception of the kidney, and the more real the sense of impending death.

He had but to call to mind what he had been three months before and what he was now, to call to mind with what regularity he had been going downhill, for every possibility of hope to be shattered.

Lately during the loneliness in which he found himself as he lay facing the back of the sofa, a loneliness in the midst of a populous town and surrounded by numerous acquaintances and relations but that yet could not have been more complete anywhere – either at the bottom of the sea or under the earth – during that terrible loneliness Ivan Ilyich had lived only in memories of the past. Pictures of his past rose before him one after another. They always began with what was nearest in time and then went back to what was most remote – to his childhood – and rested there. If he thought of the stewed prunes that had been offered him that day, his mind went back to the raw shriveled French plums of his childhood, their peculiar flavor and the flow of saliva when he sucked their stones, and along with the memory of that taste came a whole series of memories of those days: his nurse, his brother, and their toys. "No, I mustn't think of that. . . . It is too painful," Ivan Ilyich said to himself, and brought himself back to the present – to the button on the back of the sofa and the creases in its morocco. "Morocco is expensive, but it does not wear well: there had been a quarrel about it. It was a different kind of quarrel and a different kind of morocco that time when we tore father's portfolio and were punished, and mamma brought us some tarts . . ." And again his thoughts dwelt on his childhood, and again it was painful and he tried to banish them and fix his mind on something else.

Then again, together with that chain of memories, another series passed through his mind – of how his illness had progressed and grown worse. There also the further back he looked the more life there had been. There had been more of what was good in life and more of life itself. The two merged together. "Just as the pain went on getting worse and worse, so my life grew worse and worse," he thought. "There is one bright spot there at the back, at the beginning of life, and afterwards all becomes blacker and blacker and proceeds more and more rapidly – in inverse ratio to the square of the distance from death," thought Ivan Ilyich. And the example of a stone falling downwards with increasing velocity entered his mind. Life, a series of increasing sufferings, flies further and further towards its end – the most terrible suffering. "I am flying . . ." He shuddered, shifted himself, and tried to resist, but was already aware that resistance was impossible, and again with eyes weary of gazing but unable to cease seeing what was before them, he stared at the back of the sofa and waited – awaiting that dreadful fall and shock and destruction.

"Resistance is impossible!" he said to himself. "If I could only understand what it is all for! But that too is impossible.

An explanation would be possible if it could be said that I have not lived as I ought to. But it is impossible to say that," and he remembered all the legality, correctitude, and propriety of his life. "That at any rate can certainly not be admitted," he thought, and his lips smiled ironically as if someone could see that smile and be taken in by it. "There is no explanation! Agony, death . . . what for?"

✦ ✦ ✦

When his wife came into the room the next morning, she found him still lying on the sofa but in a different position. He lay on his back, groaning and staring fixedly straight in front of him.

She began to remind him of his medicines, but he turned his eyes towards her with such a look that she did not finish what she was saying; so great an animosity, to her in particular, did that look express.

"For Christ's sake let me die in peace!" he said.

She would have gone away, but just then their daughter came in and went up to say good morning. He looked at her as he had done at his wife, and in reply to her inquiry about his health said dryly that he would soon free them all of himself. They were both silent and after sitting with him for a while went away.

"Is it our fault?" Lisa said to her mother. "It's as if we were to blame! I am sorry for papa, but why should we be tortured?"

The doctor came at his usual time. Ivan Ilyich answered "Yes" and "No," never taking his angry eyes from him, and at last said: "You know you can do nothing for me, so leave me alone."

"We can ease your sufferings."

"You can't even do that. Let me be."

The doctor went into the drawing room and told Praskovya Fedorovna that the case was very serious and that the only resource left was opium to allay her husband's sufferings, which must be terrible.

It was true, as the doctor said, that Ivan Ilyich's physical sufferings were terrible, but worse than the physical sufferings were his mental sufferings which were his chief torture.

His mental sufferings were due to the fact that that night, as he looked at Gerasim's sleepy, good-natured face with its prominent cheek-bones, the question suddenly occurred to him: "What if my whole life has been wrong?"

It occurred to him that what had appeared perfectly impossible before, namely that he had not spent his life as he should have done, might after all be true. It occurred to him that his scarcely perceptible attempts to struggle against what was considered good by the most highly placed people, those scarcely noticeable impulses which he had immediately suppressed, might have been the real thing, and all the rest false. And his professional duties and the whole arrangement of his life and of his family, and all his social and official interests, might all have been false. He tried to defend all those things to himself and suddenly felt the weakness of what he was defending. There was nothing to defend.

"But if that is so," he said to himself, "and I am leaving this life with the consciousness that I have lost all that was given me and it is impossible to rectify it – what then?"

He lay on his back and began to pass his life in review in quite a new way. In the morning when he saw first his footman, then his wife, then his daughter, and then the doctor, their every word and movement confirmed to him the awful truth that had been revealed to him during the night. In them he saw himself – all that for which he had lived – and saw clearly that it was not real at all, but a terrible and huge deception which had hidden both life and death. This consciousness intensified his physical suffering tenfold. He groaned and tossed about, and pulled at his clothing, which choked and stifled him. And he hated them on that account.

He was given a large dose of opium and became unconscious, but at noon his sufferings began again. He drove everybody away and tossed from side to side.

His wife came to him and said:

"Jean, my dear, do this for me. It can't do any harm and often helps. Healthy people often do it."

He opened his eyes wide.

"What? Take communion? Why? It's unnecessary! However . . ."

She began to cry.

"Yes, do, my dear. I'll send for our priest. He is such a nice man."

"All right. Very well," he muttered.

When the priest came and heard his confession, Ivan Ilyich was softened and seemed to feel a relief from his doubts and consequently from his sufferings, and for a moment there came a ray of hope. He again began to think of the vermiform appendix and the possibility of correcting it. He received the sacrament with tears in his eyes.

When they laid him down again afterwards he felt a moment's ease, and the hope that he might live awoke in him again. He began to think of the operation that had been suggested to him. "To live! I want to live!" he said to himself. His wife came in to congratulate him after his communion, and when uttering the usual conventional words she added:

"You feel better, don't you?"

Without looking at her he said, "Yes."

Her dress, her figure, the expression of her face, the tone of her voice, all revealed the same thing. "This is wrong; it is not as it should be. All you have lived for and still live for is false-hood and deception, hiding life and death from you." And as soon as he admitted that thought, his hatred and his agoniz-ing physical suffering again sprang up, and with that suffering a consciousness of the unavoidable, approaching end. And to this was added a new sensation of grinding shooting pain and a feeling of suffocation.

The expression of his face when he uttered that "Yes" was dreadful. Having uttered it, he looked her straight in the eyes, turned on his face with a rapidity extraordinary in his weak state and shouted:

"Go away! Go away and leave me alone!"

From that moment the screaming began that continued for three days, and was so terrible that one could not hear it through two closed doors without horror. At the moment he answered, his wife realized that he was lost, that there was no return, that the end had come, the very end, and his doubts were still unsolved and remained doubts.

"Oh! Oh! Oh!" he cried in various intonations. He had begun by screaming, "I won't!" and continued screaming on the letter O.

For three whole days, during which time did not exist for him, he struggled in that black sack into which he was being thrust by an invisible, resistless force. He struggled as a man condemned to death struggles in the hands of the executioner, knowing that he cannot save himself. And every moment he felt that despite all his efforts he was drawing nearer and nearer to what terrified him. He felt that his agony was due to his being thrust into that black hole and still more to his not being able to get right into it. He was hindered from getting into it by his conviction that his life had been a good one. That very justification of his life held him fast and prevented his moving forward, and it caused him the most torment of all.

Suddenly some force struck him in the chest and side, making it still harder to breathe, and he fell through the hole and there at the bottom was a light. What had happened to him was like the sensation one sometimes experiences in a railway carriage when one thinks one is going backwards while one is really going forwards and suddenly becomes aware of the real direction.

"Yes, it was not the right thing," he said to himself, "but that's no matter. It can be done. But what is the right thing? He asked himself, and suddenly grew quiet.

This occurred at the end of the third day, two hours before his death. Just then his schoolboy son had crept softly in and gone up to the bedside. The dying man was still screaming desperately and waving his arms. His hand fell on the boy's head, and the boy caught it, pressed it to his lips, and began to cry.

At that very moment Ivan Ilyich fell through and caught sight of the light, and it was revealed to him that though his life had not been what it should have been, this could still be rectified. He asked himself, "What is the right thing?" and grew still, listening. Then he felt that someone was kissing his hand. He opened his eyes, looked at his son, and felt sorry for him. His wife came up to him and he glanced at her. She was gazing at him open-mouthed, with undried tears on her nose and cheek and a despairing look on her face. He felt sorry for her too.

"Yes, I am making them wretched," he thought. "They are sorry, but it will be better for them when I die." He wished to say this but had not the strength to utter it. "Besides, why speak? I must act," he thought. With a look at his wife he indicated his son and said: "Take him away . . . sorry for him . . . sorry for you too. . . ." He tried to add, "Forgive me," but said "Forego" and waved his hand, knowing that He whose understanding mattered would understand.

And suddenly it grew clear to him that what had been oppressing him and would not leave him was all dropping away at once from two sides, from ten sides, and from all sides. He was sorry for them; he must act so as not to hurt them: release them and free himself from these sufferings. "How good and how simple!" he thought. "And the pain?" he asked himself. "What has become of it? Where are you, pain?"

He turned his attention to it.

"Yes, here it is. Well, what of it? Let the pain be."

"And death . . . where is it?"

He sought his former accustomed fear of death and did not find it. "Where is it? What death?" There was no fear because there was no death.

In place of death there was light.

"So that's what it is!" he suddenly exclaimed aloud. "What joy!"

To him all this happened in a single instant, and the meaning of that instant did not change. For those present his agony continued for another two hours. Something rattled in his throat, his emaciated body twitched, then the gasping and rattle became less and less frequent.

"It is finished!" said someone near him.

He heard these words and repeated them in his soul.

"Death is finished," he said to himself. "It is no more!"

He drew in a breath, stopped in the midst of a sigh, stretched out, and died.

4.

My Way to Faith

From Confession

I WAS BAPTIZED AND EDUCATED in the Orthodox Christian faith. Even as a child and throughout my adolescence and youth I was schooled in the Orthodox beliefs. But when at the age of eighteen I left my second year of studies at the university, I had lost all belief in what I had been taught. Judging from what I can remember, I never really had a serious belief. I simply trusted in what I had been taught and in the things my elders adhered to. But even this trust was very shaky.

I remember that when I was eleven years old a high school boy visited us one Sunday with an announcement of the latest discovery made at school. The discovery was that there is no God and that the things they were teaching us were nothing but fairy tales (this was in 1838). I remember how this news captured the interest of my older brothers; they even let me in on their discussions. I remember that we were all very excited and that we took this news to be both quite engaging and entirely possible. . . .

The teachings of faith instilled in me since childhood left me, just as they have left others; the only difference is that since I began reading and thinking a great deal at an early age, I became aware of my renunciation of the teachings of faith very early in life. From the age of sixteen I gave up praying and on my own accord quit going to church and fasting. I ceased to believe in what had been instilled in me since childhood, yet

I did believe in something, though I could not say what. I even believed in God – or rather I did not deny God – but what kind of God I could not say; nor did I deny Christ and his teachings, but I could not have said what those teachings consisted of. As I now look back at that time I clearly see that apart from animal instincts, the faith that affected my life, the only real faith I had, was faith in perfection. But I could not have said what perfection consisted of or what its purpose might be. I tried to achieve intellectual perfection; I studied everything I could, everything that life gave me a chance to study. I tried to perfect my will and set up rules for myself that I endeavored to follow. I strove for physical perfection by doing all the exercises that develop strength and agility and by undergoing all the hardships that discipline the self in endurance and perseverance. I took all this to be perfection. The starting point of it all was, of course, moral perfection, but this was soon replaced by a belief in overall perfection, that is, a desire to be better not in my own eyes or in the eyes of God, but rather a desire to be better in the eyes of other people. And this effort to be better in the eyes of other people was very quickly displaced by a longing to be stronger than other people, that is, more renowned, more important, wealthier than others.

✦ ✦ ✦

I think that many, very many, have had the same experiences. With all my soul I longed to be good; but I was young, I had passions, and I was alone, utterly alone, whenever I sought what was good. Every time I tried to express my most heartfelt desires to be morally good I met with contempt and ridicule; and as soon as I would give in to vile passions I was praised and encouraged. Ambition, love of power, self-interest, lechery, pride, anger, vengeance – all of it was highly esteemed. As I gave myself over to these passions I became like my elders, and I felt that they were pleased with me. A kindhearted aunt of mine with whom I lived, one of the finest of women, was forever telling me that her fondest desire was for me to have an affair with a married woman: *"Rien ne forme un jeune homme comme une liaison avec une femme comme il faut."* Another happiness she wished for me was that I become an adjutant, preferably to the emperor. And the greatest happiness of all would be for me to marry a very wealthy young lady who could bring me as many serfs as possible.

I cannot recall those years without horror, loathing, and heartrending pain. I killed people in war, challenged men to duels with the purpose of killing them, and lost at cards; I squandered the fruits of the peasants' toil and then had them executed; I was a fornicator and a cheat. Lying, stealing, promiscuity of every kind, drunkenness, violence, murder – there was not a crime I did not commit; yet in spite of it all I was praised, and my colleagues considered me and still do consider me a relatively moral man.

Thus I lived for ten years. . . .

✦ ✦ ✦

My belief assumed a form that it commonly assumes among the educated people of our time. This belief was expressed by the word "progress." At the time it seemed to me that this word had meaning. Like any living individual, I was tormented by questions of how to live better. I still had not understood that in answering that one must live according to progress, I was talking just like a person being carried along in a boat by the waves and the wind; without really answering, such a person replies to the only important question – "Where are we to steer?"– by saying, "We are being carried somewhere."

I did not notice this at the time. Only now and then would my feelings, and not my reason, revolt against this commonly held superstition of the age, by means of which people hide from themselves their own ignorance of life. Thus during my stay in Paris the sight of an execution revealed to me the feebleness of my superstitious belief in progress. When I saw how the head was severed from the body and heard the thud of each part as it fell into the box, I understood, not with my intellect but with my whole being, that no theories of the rationality of existence or of progress could justify such an act; I realized that even if all the people in the world from the day of creation found this to be necessary according to whatever theory, I knew that it was not necessary and that it was wrong. Therefore, my judgments must be based on what is right and necessary and not on what people say and do; I must judge not according to progress but according to my own heart. The death of my brother was another instance in which I realized the inadequacy of the superstition of progress in regard to life. A good, intelligent, serious man, he was still young when he fell ill. He suffered for over a year and died an agonizing death without ever understanding why he lived and understanding even less why he was dying. No theories could provide any answers to these questions, either for him or for me, during his slow and painful death.

But these were only rare instances of doubt; on the whole I continued to live, embracing only a faith in progress. "Everything is developing, and I am developing; the reason why I am developing in this way will come to light, along with everything else." Thus I was led to formulate my faith at the time. . . .

✦ ✦ ✦

And so I lived. But five years ago something very strange began to happen to me. At first I began having moments of bewilderment, when my life would come to a halt, as if I did not know how to live or what to do; I would lose my presence of mind and fall into a state of depression. But this passed, and I continued to live as before. Then the moments of bewilderment recurred more frequently, and they always took the same form. Whenever my life came to a halt, the questions would arise: Why? And what next?

At first I thought these were pointless and irrelevant questions. I thought that the answers to them were well known and that if I should ever want to resolve them, it would not be too hard for me; it was just that I could not be bothered with it now, but if I should take it upon myself, then I would find the answers. But the questions began to come up more and more frequently, and their demands to be answered became more and more urgent. And like points concentrated into one spot, these questions without answers came together to form a single black stain.

It happened with me as it happens with everyone who contracts a fatal internal disease. At first there were the insignificant symptoms of an ailment, which the patient ignores; then these symptoms recur more and more frequently, until they merge into one continuous duration of suffering. The suffering increases, and before he can turn around the patient discovers what he already knew: the thing he had taken for a mere indisposition is in fact the most important thing on earth to him, is in fact death.

This is exactly what happened to me. I realized that this was not an incidental ailment but something very serious, and that if the same questions should continue to recur, I would have to answer them. And I tried to answer them. The questions seemed to be such foolish, simple, childish questions. But as soon as I laid my hands on them and tried to resolve them, I was immediately convinced, first of all, that they were not childish and foolish questions but the most vital and profound questions in life, and, secondly, that no matter how much I pondered them, there was no way I could resolve them. . . . In the middle of thinking about the fame that my works were bringing me I would say to myself, "Very well, you will be more famous than Gogol, Pushkin, Shakespeare, Molière – more famous than all the writers in the world – so what?"

And I could find absolutely no reply.

✦ ✦ ✦

I grew sick of life; some irresistible force was leading me to somehow get rid of it. It was not that I wanted to kill myself. The force that was leading me away from life was more powerful, more absolute, more all-encompassing than any desire. With all my strength I struggled to get away from life. The thought of suicide came to me as naturally then as the thought of improving life had come to me before. . . .

And this was happening to me at a time when, from all indications, I should have been considered a completely happy man; this was when I was not yet fifty years old. I had a good, loving, and beloved wife, fine children, and a large estate that was growing and expanding without any effort on my part. More than ever before I was respected by friends and acquaintances, praised by strangers, and I could claim a certain renown without really deluding myself. Moreover, I was not physically and mentally unhealthy; on the contrary, I enjoyed a physical and mental vigor such as I had rarely encountered among others my age. Physically, I could keep up with the peasants working in the fields; mentally, I could work eight and ten hours at a stretch without suffering any aftereffects from the strain. And in such a state of affairs I came to a point where I could not live; and even though I feared death, I had to employ ruses against myself to keep from committing suicide.

I described my spiritual condition to myself in this way: my life is some kind of stupid and evil practical joke that someone is playing on me. In spite of the fact that I did not acknowledge the existence of any "Someone" who might have created me, the notion that someone brought me into the world as a stupid and evil joke seemed to be the most natural way to describe my condition.

I could not help imagining that somewhere there was someone who was now amusing himself, laughing at me and at the way I had lived for thirty or forty years, studying, developing, growing in body and soul; laughing at how I had now completely matured intellectually and had reached that summit from which life reveals itself only to stand there like an utter fool, clearly seeing that there is nothing in life, that there never was and never will be. And it makes him laugh.

But whether or not there actually was someone laughing at me did not make it any easier for me. I could not attach a rational meaning to a single act in my entire life. The only thing that amazed me was how I had failed to realize this in the very beginning. All this had been common knowledge for so long. If not today, then tomorrow sickness and death will come (indeed, they were already approaching) to everyone, to me, and nothing will remain except the stench and the worms. My deeds, whatever they may be, will be forgotten sooner or later, and I myself will be no more. Why, then, do anything? How can anyone fail to see this and live? That's what is amazing! It is possible to live only as long as life intoxicates us; once we are sober we cannot help seeing that it is all a delusion, a stupid delusion! Nor is there anything funny or witty about it; it is only cruel and stupid.

✦ ✦ ✦

I was now prepared to accept any faith, as long as it did not demand of me a direct denial of reason, for such a denial would be a lie. So I studied the texts of Buddhism and Islam; and more than ever those of Christianity and the lives of Christians who lived around me. . . .

In spite of the fact that I made every possible concession and avoided all arguments, I could not accept the faith of these people. I saw that what they took to be faith did not explain the meaning of life but only obscured it, and that they themselves professed their faith not in response to the question of life that had drawn me to faith but for some purpose that was alien to me.

I remember the agonizing feeling of horror upon returning to my original despair, which followed the hope I had felt so many times in my relations with these people. The more they laid their teachings before me in ever-increasing detail, the more clearly I could see their error, until I lost all hope of discovering in their faith any explanation of the meaning of life.

I was not alienated so much by the fact that in present-ing their beliefs they would mix the Christian truths that had always been so dear to me with much that was superfluous and irrational. Rather, it was that their lives were so much like my own, but with this one difference: they did not live according to the principles they professed. I felt very strongly that they were deceiving themselves and that, like myself, they had no sense of life's meaning other than to live while they lived and to lay their hands on everything they could. This was clear to me because if they harbored any meaning that might destroy all fear of privation, suffering, and death, they would not be frightened of these things. But these believers from our class lived a life of plenty, just as I did; they endeavored to increase and preserve their wealth and were afraid of privation, suffering, and death. Like myself and all the rest of us unbelievers, they lived only to satisfy their lusts, lived just as badly as, if not worse than, those who did not believe.

No rationalization could convince me of the truth of their faith, though one thing might have: actions proving that these people held the key to a meaning of life that would eliminate in them the fear of poverty, sickness, and death that haunted me. But I saw no trace of such actions among the various believers in our class. On the contrary, I saw such actions among people in our class who were not believers but never among the so-called believers. . . .

And I began to grow closer to the believers from among the poor, the simple, the uneducated folk, from among the pilgrims, the monks, the Raskolniks,* the peasants. The beliefs of those from among the people, like those of the pretentious believers from our class, were Christian. Here too there was much superstition mixed in with the truths of Christianity, but with this difference: the superstitions of the believers from our class were utterly unnecessary to them, played no role in their lives, and were only a kind of epicurean diversion, while the superstitions of the believers from the laboring people were intertwined with their lives to such a degree that their lives could not be conceived

---

* Raskolniks were "dissenters" from the Russian Orthodox Church and members of any one of several groups, including the Doukhobors and the Khlysty, which arose as a result of the schism of the seventeenth century in protest against liturgical reforms; they are sometimes referred to as Old Believers.

without them: their superstitions were a necessary condition for their lives. The whole life of the believers from our class was in opposition to their faith, while the whole life of the believers from the working people was a confirmation of that meaning of life which was the substance of their faith. So I began to examine the life and the teachings of these people, and the closer I looked, the more I was convinced that theirs was the true faith, that their faith was indispensable to them, and that this faith alone provided them with the meaning and possibility of life. . . .

I grew to love these people. The more I learned about the lives of those living and dead about whom I had read and heard, the more I loved them and the easier it became for me to live. I lived this way for about two years, and a profound transformation came over me, one that had been brewing in me for a long time and whose elements had always been a part of me. The life of our class, of the wealthy and the learned, was not only repulsive to me but had lost all meaning. The sum of our action and thinking, of our science and art, all of it struck me as the over-indulgences of a spoiled child. I realized that meaning was not to be sought here. The actions of the laboring people, of those who create life, began to appear to me as the one true way. I realized that the meaning provided by this life was truth, and I embraced it.

✦ ✦ ✦

Recognizing the errors of rational knowledge helped me to free myself from the temptations of idle reflection. The conviction that a knowledge of the truth can be found only in life led me to doubt that my own life was as it should be; and the one thing that saved me was that I was able to tear myself from my isolation, look at the true life of the simple working people, and realize that this alone is the true life. I realized that if I wanted to understand life and its meaning, I would have to live not the life of a parasite but the genuine life; and once I had accepted the meaning that is given to life by the real humanity that makes up life, I would have to test it out.

This is what happened to me at the time: in the course of a whole year, when almost every minute I was asking myself whether I should end it all with a rope or a bullet, when I was occupied with the thoughts and observations I have described, my heart was tormented with an agonizing feeling. This feeling I can only describe as a search for God.

I say that this search for God was born not of reason but of an emotion because it was a search that arose not from my thought process – indeed, it was in direct opposition to my thinking – but from my heart. It was a feeling of dread, of loneliness, of forlornness in the midst of all that was alien to me; and it was a feeling of hope for someone's help.

In spite of the fact that I was convinced of the impossibility of proving the existence of God, I nonetheless searched for God in the hope that I might find him, and according to an old habit of prayer, I addressed the one for whom I searched and could not find. . . . I began to pray to the one whom I sought, that he might help me. And the more I prayed, the more clear it became to me that he did not hear me and that there was absolutely no one I could turn to. My heart full of despair over the fact that there is no God, I cried, "Lord, have mercy on me, save me! O Lord, my God, show me the way!" But no one had mercy on me, and I felt that my life had come to a stop.

But again and again and from various directions I kept coming back to the conviction that I could not have come into the world without any motive, cause, or meaning, that I could not be the fledgling fallen from a nest that I felt myself to be. If I lie on my back in the tall grass and cry out like a fallen fledgling, it is because my mother brought me into the world, kept me warm, fed me, and loved me. But where is my mother now? If I have been cast out, then who has cast me out? I cannot help but feel that someone who loved me gave birth to me. Who is this someone? Again, God.

"He sees and knows of my search, my despair, my struggle," I would say to myself. "He exists." And as soon as I acknowledged this for an instant, life immediately rose up within me, and I could sense the possibility and even the joy of being. But again I would shift from the acknowledgment of the existence of God to a consideration of my relation to him, and again there arose before me the God who is our creator, the God of the Trinity, who sent his son, our Redeemer. And again, isolated from me and from the world, God would melt away before my eyes like a piece of ice; again nothing remained, again the source of life withered away. I was overcome with despair and felt that there was nothing for me to do but kill myself. And, worst of all, I felt that I could not bring myself to go through with it.

I slipped into these situations not two or three times but tens and hundreds of times – now joy and vitality, now despair and a consciousness of the impossibility of life.

I remember one day in early spring when I was alone in the forest listening to the sounds of the woods. I listened and thought about the one thing that had constantly occupied me for the last three years. Again I was searching for God.

"Very well," I said to myself. "So there is no God like the one I have imagined; the only reality is my life. There is no such God.

And nothing, no miracle of any kind, can prove there is, because miracles exist only in my irrational imagination.

"But where does my notion of God, of the one whom I seek, come from?" I asked myself. And again with this thought there arose in me joyous waves of life. Everything around me came to life, full of meaning. But my joy did not last long. My mind continued its work. "The concept of God," I told myself, "is not God. A concept is something that occurs within me; the concept of God is something I can conjure up inside myself at will. This is not what I seek. I am seeking that without which there could be no life." Once again everything within me and around me began to die; again I felt the longing to kill myself.

But at that point I took a closer look at myself and at what had been happening within me; and I remembered the hundreds of times I had gone through these deaths and revivals. I remembered that I had lived only when I believed in God. Then, as now, I said to myself, "As long as I know God, I live; when I forget, when I do not believe in him, I die." What are these deaths and revivals? It is clear that I do not live whenever I lose my faith in the existence of God, and I would have killed myself long ago if I did not have some vague hope of finding God. I truly live only whenever I am conscious of him and seek him. "What, then, do I seek?" a voice cried out within me. "He is there, the one without whom there could be no life." To know God and to live come to one and the same thing. God is life.

"Live, seeking God, for there can be no life without God." And more powerfully than ever a light shone within me and all around me, and this light has not abandoned me since.

Thus I was saved from suicide. When and how this transformation within me was accomplished, I could not say. Just as the life force within me was gradually and imperceptibly destroyed, and I encountered the impossibility of life, the halting of life, and the need to murder myself, so too did this life force return to me gradually and imperceptibly. And the strange thing is that the life force which returned to me was not new but very old; it was the same force that had guided me during the early periods of my life. In essence I returned to the first things, to the things of childhood and youth. I returned to a faith in that will which gave birth to me and which asked something of me; I returned to the conviction that the single most important purpose in my life was to be better, to live according to this will. I returned to the conviction that I could find the expression of this will in something long hidden from me, something that all of humanity had worked out for its own guidance; in short, I returned to a belief in God, in moral perfection, and in a tradition that instills life with meaning. The only difference was that I had once accepted all this on an unconscious level, while now I knew that I could not live without it.

✦ ✦ ✦

I wrote the above three years ago.*

The other day, as I was looking over this printed portion and returning to the thoughts and feelings that went through me when I was experiencing all this, I had a dream. This dream expressed for me in a condensed form everything I lived through and wrote about; therefore I think that for those who have understood me, a description of the dream will refresh, clarify, and gather into one piece what has been discussed at length in these pages. Here is the dream: I see that I am lying in

---

* This last portion of the *Confession* was written in 1882.

bed. Feeling neither good nor bad, I am lying on my back. But I begin to wonder whether it is a good thing for me to be lying there; and it seems to me that there is something wrong with my legs; whether they are too short or uneven, I do not know, but there is something awkward about them. As I start to move my legs, I begin to wonder how and on what I am lying, something that up till now had not entered my mind. Looking about my bed, I see that I am lying on some cords woven together and attached to the sides of the bed. My heels are resting on one of the cords and my lower legs on another in an uncomfortable way. Somehow I know that these cords can be shifted. Moving one leg, I push away the furthest cord. It seems to me that it will be more comfortable that way. But I have pushed it too far away; I try to catch it, but this movement causes another cord to slip out from under my legs, leaving them hanging down. I rearrange my whole body, quite certain I will be settled now; but this movement causes still other cords to shift and slip out from under me, and I see that the whole situation is getting worse: the whole lower part of my body is sinking and hanging down, and my feet are not touching the ground. I am supported only along the upper part of my back, and for some reason I begin to feel not only uncomfortable but terrified. Only now do I ask myself what had not yet occurred to me: where am I and what am I lying on? I begin to look around, and the first place I look is down toward where my body is dangling, in the direction where I feel I must soon fall. I look below, and I cannot believe my eyes. I am resting on a height such as I could never have imagined, a height altogether unlike that of the highest tower or mountain.

I cannot even tell whether I can see anything down below in the bottomless depths of the abyss over which I am hanging and into which I am drawn. My heart stops, and I am overcome with horror. It is horrible to look down there. I feel that if I look down, I will immediately slip from the last cord and perish. I do not look, yet not looking is worse, for now I am thinking about what will happen to me as soon as the last cord breaks. I feel that I am losing the last ounce of my strength from sheer terror and that my back is slowly sinking lower and lower. Another instant and I shall break away. And then a thought occurs to me: this cannot be real. It is just a dream. I will wake up. I try to wake up, but I cannot. "What am I to do, what am I to do?" I ask myself, looking up. Above me there is also an abyss. I gaze into this abyss of sky and try to forget about the one below, and I actually do forget. The infinity below repels and horrifies me; the infinity above attracts me and gives me strength. Thus I am hanging over the abyss suspended by the last of the cords that have not yet slipped out from under me. I know I am hanging there, but I am only looking upward, and my terror passes. As it happens in a dream, a voice is saying, "Mark this, this is it!" I gaze deeper and deeper into the infinity above me, and I seem to grow calm. I recall everything that has happened, and I remember how it all came about: how I moved my legs, how I was dangling there, the horror that came over me, and how I was saved from the horror by looking up. And I ask myself, "Well, am I still hanging here?" And as soon as I glance around, I feel with my whole body a support that is holding me up. I can see that I am no longer dangling or falling but am firmly supported. I ask myself how I am being supported; I touch myself, look around, and see that there is a single cord underneath the center of my body, that when I look up I am lying on it firmly balanced, and that it alone has supported me all along. As it happens in a dream, the mechanism by which I am supported seems quite natural, understandable, and beyond doubt, in spite of the fact that when I am awake the mechanism is completely incomprehensible. In my sleep I am even astonished that I had not understood this before. It seems that there is a pillar beside me and that there is no doubt of the solidity of the pillar, even though it has nothing to stand on. The cord is somehow very cleverly yet very simply attached to the pillar, leading out from it, and if you place the middle of your body on the cord and look up, there cannot even be a question of falling.

All this was clear to me, and I was glad and at peace. Then it is as if someone is saying to me, "See that you remember." And I awoke.

Love of Neighbor

Greater love has no man than this, that a man lay down his life for his friends. —John 15:13

The Light (detail)

5.

Three Questions

A Story

IT ONCE OCCURRED TO A CERTAIN KING, that if he always knew the right time to begin everything; if he knew who were the right people to listen to, and whom to avoid, and, above all, if he always knew what was the most important thing to do, he would never fail in anything he might undertake.

And this thought having occurred to him, he had it proclaimed throughout his kingdom that he would give a great reward to anyone who would teach him what was the right time for every action, and who were the most necessary people, and how he might know what was the most important thing to do.

And learned men came to the king, but they all answered his questions differently.

In reply to the first question, some said that to know the right time for every action, one must draw up in advance, a table of days, months and years, and must live strictly according to it. Only thus, said they, could everything be done at its proper time. Others declared that it was impossible to decide beforehand the right time for every action; but that, not letting oneself be absorbed in idle pastimes, one should always attend to all that was going on, and then do what was most needful. Others, again, said that however attentive the king might be to what was going on, it was impossible for one man to decide correctly the right time for every action, but that he should have a Council of wise

51

men, who would help him to fix the proper time for everything.

But then again others said there were some things which could not wait to be laid before a Council, but about which one had at once to decide whether to undertake them or not. But in order to decide that, one must know beforehand what was going to happen. It is only magicians who know that; and, therefore, in order to know the right time for every action, one must consult magicians.

Equally various were the answers to the second question. Some said the people the king most needed were his councilors; others, the priests; others, the doctors; while some said the warriors were the most necessary.

To the third question, as to what was the most important occupation: some replied that the most important thing in the world was science. Others said it was skill in warfare; and others, again, that it was religious worship.

All the answers being different, the king agreed with none of them, and gave the reward to none. But still wishing to find the right answers to his questions, he decided to consult a hermit, widely renowned for his wisdom.

The hermit lived in a wood which he never quitted, and he received none but common folk. So the king put on simple clothes, and before reaching the hermit's cell dismounted from his horse, and, leaving his bodyguard behind, went on alone.

When the king approached, the hermit was digging the ground in front of his hut. Seeing the king, he greeted him and went on digging. The hermit was frail and weak, and each time he stuck his spade into the ground and turned a little earth, he breathed heavily.

The king went up to him and said: "I have come to you, wise hermit, to ask you to answer three questions: How can I learn to do the right thing at the right time? Who are the people I most need, and to whom should I, therefore, pay more attention than to the rest? And, what affairs are the most important and need my first attention?"

The hermit listened to the king, but answered nothing. He just spat on his hand and recommenced digging.

"You are tired," said the king, "let me take the spade and work awhile for you."

"Thanks!" said the hermit, and, giving the spade to the king, he sat down on the ground.

When he had dug two beds, the king stopped and repeated his questions. The hermit again gave no answer, but rose, stretched out his hand for the spade, and said:

"Now rest awhile–and let me work a bit."

But the king did not give him the spade, and continued to dig. One hour passed, and another. The sun began to sink behind the trees, and the king at last stuck the spade into the ground, and said:

"I came to you, wise man, for an answer to my questions. If you can give me none, tell me so, and I will return home."

"Here comes someone running," said the hermit, "let us see who it is."

The king turned round, and saw a bearded man come running out of the wood. The man held his hands pressed against his stomach, and blood was flowing from under them. When he reached the king, he fell fainting on the ground moaning feebly. The king and the hermit unfastened the man's clothing. There was a large wound in his stomach. The king washed it as best he could, and bandaged it with his handkerchief and with a towel the hermit had. But the blood would not stop flowing, and the king again and again removed the bandage soaked with warm blood, and washed and re-bandaged the wound. When at last the blood ceased flowing, the man revived and asked for something to drink. The king brought fresh water and gave it to him. Meanwhile the sun had set, and it had become cool. So the king, with the hermit's help, carried the wounded man into the hut and laid him on the bed. Lying on the bed the man closed his eyes and was quiet; but the king was so tired with his walk and with the work he had done, that he crouched down on the threshold, and also fell asleep–so soundly that he slept all through the short summer night. When he awoke in the morning, it was long before he could remember where he was, or who was the strange bearded man lying on the bed and gazing intently at him with shining eyes.

"Forgive me!" said the bearded man in a weak voice, when he saw that the king was awake and was looking at him.

"I do not know you, and have nothing to forgive you for," said the king.

"You do not know me, but I know you. I am that enemy of yours who swore to revenge himself on you, because you executed his brother and seized his property. I knew you had gone alone to see the hermit, and I resolved to kill you on your way back. But the day passed and you did not return. So I came out from my ambush to find you, and I came upon your bodyguard, and they recognized me, and wounded me. I escaped from them, but should have bled to death had you not dressed my wound. I wished to kill you, and you have saved my life. Now, if I live, and if you wish it, I will serve you as your most faithful slave, and will bid my sons do the same. Forgive me!"

The king was very glad to have made peace with his enemy so easily, and to have gained him for a friend, and he not only forgave him, but said he would send his servants and his own physician to attend him, and promised to restore his property.

Having taken leave of the wounded man, the king went out into the porch and looked around for the hermit. Before going away he wished once more to beg an answer to the questions he had put. The hermit was outside, on his knees, sowing seeds in the beds that had been dug the day before.

The king approached him, and said:

"For the last time, I pray you to answer my questions, wise man."

"You have already been answered!" said the hermit, still crouching on his thin legs, and looking up at the king, who stood before him.

"How answered? What do you mean?" asked the king.

"Do you not see," replied the hermit. "If you had not pitied my weakness yesterday, and had not dug these beds for me, but had gone your way, that man would have attacked you, and you would have repented of not having stayed with me. So the most important time was when you were digging the beds; and I was the most important man; and to do me good was your most important business. Afterwards, when that man ran to us, the most important time was when you were attending to him, for if you had not bound up his wounds he would have died without having made peace with you. So he was the most important man, and what you did for him was your most important business. Remember then: there is only one time that is important – now! It is the most important time because it is the only time when we have any power. The most necessary man is he with whom you are, for no man knows whether he will ever have dealings with anyone else: and the most important affair is to do him good, because for that purpose alone was man sent into this life."

6.

Where Love Is, God Is

A Story

IN A CERTAIN TOWN there lived a cobbler, Martin Avdéitch by name. He had a tiny room in a basement, the one window of which looked out on to the street. Through it one could only see the feet of those who passed by, but Martin recognized the people by their boots. He had lived long in the place and had many acquaintances. There was hardly a pair of boots in the neighborhood that had not been once or twice through his hands, so he often saw his own handiwork through the window. Some he had re-soled, some patched, some stitched up, and to some he had even put fresh uppers. He had plenty to do, for he worked well, used good material, did not charge too much, and could be relied on. If he could do a job by the day required, he undertook it; if not, he told the truth and gave no false promises; so he was well known and never short of work.

Martin had always been a good man, but in his old age he began to think more about his soul and to draw nearer to God. While he still worked for a master, before he set up on his own account, his wife had died, leaving him with a three-year-old son. None of his elder children had lived; they had all died in infancy. At first Martin thought of sending his little son to his sister's in the country, but then he felt sorry to part with the boy, thinking: "It would be hard for my little Kapitón to have to grow up in a strange family; I will keep him with me."

56

Martin left his master and went into lodgings with his little son. But he had no luck with his children. No sooner had the boy reached an age when he could help his father and be a support as well as a joy to him, than he fell ill and, after being laid up for a week with a burning fever, died. Martin buried his son, and gave way to despair so great and overwhelming that he murmured against God. In his sorrow he prayed again and again that he too might die, reproaching God for having taken the son he loved, his only son while he, old as he was, remained alive. After that Martin left off going to church.

One day an old man from Martin's native village who had been a pilgrim for the last eight years, called in on his way from Troitsa Monastery. Martin opened his heart to him, and told him of his sorrow.

"I no longer even wish to live, holy man," he said. "All I ask of God is that I soon may die. I am now quite without hope in the world."

The old man replied: "You have no right to say such things, Martin. We cannot judge God's ways. Not our reasoning, but God's will, decides. If God willed that your son should die and you should live, it must be best so. As to your despair – that comes because you wish to live for your own happiness."

"What else should one live for?" asked Martin.

"For God, Martin," said the old man. "He gives you life, and you must live for him. When you have learnt to live for him, you will grieve no more, and all will seem easy to you."

Martin was silent awhile, and then asked: "But how is one to live for God?"

The old man answered: "How one may live for God has been shown us by Christ. Can you read? Then buy the Gospels, and read them: there you will see how God would have you live. You have it all there."

These words sank deep into Martin's heart, and that same day he went and bought himself a Testament in large print, and began to read.

At first he meant only to read on holidays, but having once begun he found it made his heart so light that he read every day. Sometimes he was so absorbed in his reading that the oil in his lamp burnt out before he could tear himself away from the book. He continued to read every night, and the more he read the more clearly he understood what God required of him and how he might live for God. And his heart grew lighter and lighter. Before, when he went to bed he used to lie with a heavy heart, moaning as he thought of his little Kapitón; but now he only repeated again and again: "Glory to Thee, glory to Thee, O Lord! Thy will be done!"

From that time Martin's whole life changed. Formerly, on holidays he used to go and have tea at the public house, and did not even refuse a glass or two of vodka. Sometimes, after having had a drop with a friend, he left the public house not drunk, but rather merry, and would say foolish things: shout at a man, or abuse him. Now, all that sort of thing passed away from him. His life became peaceful and joyful. He sat down to his work in the morning, and when he had finished his day's work he took the lamp down from the wall, stood it on the table, fetched his book from the shelf, opened it, and sat down to read. The more he read the better he understood, and the clearer and happier he felt in his mind.

It happened once that Martin sat up late, absorbed in his book. He was reading Luke's Gospel; and in the sixth chapter he came upon the verses:

To him who strikes you on the cheek, offer the other also; and from him who takes away your coat do not withhold even your shirt. Give to everyone who begs from you; and of him who takes away your goods do not ask them again. And as you wish that others would do to you, do so to them.

He also read the verses where our Lord says:

Why do you call me "Lord, Lord," and not do what I tell you? Everyone who comes to me and hears my words and does them, I will show you what he is like: he is like a man building a house, who dug deep, and laid the foundation upon rock; and when a flood arose, the stream broke against that house, and could not shake it, because it had been well built. But he who hears and does not do them is like a man who built a house on the ground without a foundation; against which the stream broke, and immediately it fell, and the ruin of that house was great.

When Martin read these words his soul was glad within him. He took off his spectacles and laid them on the book, and leaning his elbows on the table pondered over what he had read. He tried his own life by the standard of those words, asking himself:

"Is my house built on the rock, or on sand? If it stands on the rock, it is well. It seems easy enough while one sits here alone, and one thinks one has done all that God commands; but as soon as I cease to be on my guard, I sin again. Still I will persevere. It brings such joy. Help me, O Lord!"

He thought all this, and was about to go to bed, but was loath to leave his book. So he went on reading the seventh chapter – about the centurion, the widow's son, and the answer to John's disciples – and he came to the part where a rich Pharisee invited the Lord to his house; and he read how the woman who was a sinner, anointed his feet and washed them with her tears, and how he justified her. Coming to the forty-fourth verse, he read:

Then turning toward the woman he said to Simon, "Do you see this woman? I entered your house, you gave me no water for my feet, but she has wet my feet with her tears and wiped them with her hair. You gave me no kiss, but from the time I came in she has not ceased to kiss my feet. You did not anoint my head with oil, but she has anointed my feet with ointment."

He read these verses and thought: "He gave no water for his feet, gave no kiss, his head with oil he did not anoint . . ." And Martin took off his spectacles once more, laid them on his book, and pondered.

"He must have been like me, that Pharisee. He too thought only of himself – how to get a cup of tea, how to keep warm and comfortable; never a thought of his guest. He took care of himself, but for his guest he cared nothing at all. Yet who was the guest? The Lord himself! If he came to me, should I behave like that?"

Then Martin laid his head upon both his arms and, before he was aware of it, he fell asleep.

"Martin!" he suddenly heard a voice, as if someone had breathed the word above his ear.

He started from his sleep. "Who's there?" he asked.

He turned round and looked at the door; no one was there. He called again. Then he heard quite distinctly: "Martin, Martin! Look out into the street tomorrow, for I shall come."

Martin roused himself, rose from his chair and rubbed his eyes, but did not know whether he had heard these words in a dream or awake. He put out the lamp and lay down to sleep.

Next morning he rose before daylight, and after saying his prayers he lit the fire and prepared his cabbage soup and buckwheat porridge. Then he lit the samovar, put on his apron, and sat down by the window to do his work. As he sat working

Martin thought over what had happened the night before. At times it seemed to him like a dream, and at times he thought that he had really heard the voice. "Such things have happened before now," thought he.

So he sat by the window, looking out into the street more than he worked, and whenever anyone passed in unfamiliar boots he would stoop and look up, so as to see not the feet only but the face of the passer-by as well. A house-porter passed in new felt boots; then a water-carrier. Presently an old soldier of Nicholas' reign came near the window, spade in hand. Martin knew him by his boots, which were shabby old felt ones, galoshed with leather. The old man was called Stepanich: a neighboring tradesman kept him in his house for charity, and his duty was to help the house-porter. He began to clear away the snow before Martin's window. Martin glanced at him and then went on with his work.

"I must be growing crazy with age," said Martin, laughing at his fancy. "Stepanich comes to clear away the snow, and I must needs imagine it's Christ coming to visit me. Old dotard that I am!"

Yet after he had made a dozen stitches he felt drawn to look out of the window again. He saw that Stepanich had leaned his spade against the wall, and was either resting himself or trying to get warm. The man was old and broken down, and had evidently not enough strength even to clear away the snow.

"What if I called him in and gave him some tea?" thought Martin. "The samovar is just on the boil."

He stuck his awl in its place, and rose; and putting the samovar on the table, made tea. Then he tapped the window with his fingers. Stepanich turned and came to the window. Martin beckoned to him to come in, and went himself to open the door.

"Come in," he said, "and warm yourself a bit. I'm sure you must be cold."

"May God bless you!" Stepanich answered. "My bones do ache to be sure." He came in, first shaking off the snow, and lest he should leave marks on the floor he began wiping his feet; but as he did so he tottered and nearly fell.

"Don't trouble to wipe your feet," said Martin. "I'll wipe up the floor – it's all in the day's work. Come, friend, sit down and have some tea."

Filling two tumblers, he passed one to his visitor, and pouring his own out into the saucer, began to blow on it.

Stepanich emptied his glass, and, turning it upside down, put the remains of his piece of sugar on the top. He began to express his thanks, but it was plain that he would be glad of some more.

"Have another glass," said Martin, refilling the visitor's tumbler and his own. But while he drank his tea Martin kept looking out into the street.

"Are you expecting anyone?" asked the visitor.

"Am I expecting anyone? Well, now, I'm ashamed to tell you. It isn't that I really expect anyone; but I heard something last night which I can't get out of my mind. Whether it was a vision, or only a fancy, I can't tell. You see, friend, last night I was reading the Gospel, about Christ the Lord, how he suffered, and how he walked on earth. You have heard tell of it, I dare say."

"I have heard tell of it," answered Stepanich; "but I'm an ignorant man and not able to read."

"Well, you see, I was reading of how he walked on earth. I came to that part, you know, where he went to a Pharisee who did not receive him well. Well friend, as I read about it, I thought, now that man did not receive Christ the Lord with proper honor. Suppose such a thing could happen to such a man as myself, I thought, what would I not do to receive him! But that man gave him no reception at all. Well, friend, as I was thinking of this, I began to doze, and as I dozed I heard someone call me by name. I got up, and thought I heard someone whispering, 'Expect me; I will come tomorrow.' This happened twice over. And to tell you the truth, it sank so into my mind that, though I am ashamed of it myself, I keep on expecting him, the dear Lord!"

Stepanich shook his head in silence, finished his tumbler and laid it on its side; but Martin stood it up again and refilled it for him.

"Here drink another glass, bless you! And I was thinking too, how he walked on earth and despised no one, but went mostly among common folk. He went with plain people, and chose his disciples from among the likes of us, from workmen like us, sinners that we are. 'He who raises himself,' he said, 'shall be humbled and he who humbles himself shall be raised.' 'You call me Lord,' he said, 'and I will wash your feet.' 'He who would be first,' he said, 'let him be the servant of all; because,' he said, 'blessed are the poor, the humble, the meek, and the merciful.'"

Stepanich forgot his tea. He was an old man easily moved to tears, and as he sat and listened the tears ran down his cheeks.

"Come, drink some more," said Martin. But Stepanich crossed himself, thanked him, moved away his tumbler, and rose.

"Thank you, Martin Avdéitch," he said, "you have given me food and comfort both for soul and body."

"You're very welcome. Come again another time. I am glad to have a guest," said Martin.

Stepanich went away; and Martin poured out the last of the tea and drank it up. Then he put away the tea things and sat down to his work, stitching the back seam of a boot. And as he stitched he kept looking out of the window, waiting for Christ, and thinking about him and his doings. And his head was full of Christ's sayings.

Two soldiers went by: one in government boots, the other in boots of his own; then the master of a neighboring house, in shining galoshes; then a baker carrying a basket. All these passed on. Then a woman came up in worsted stockings and peasant-made shoes. She passed the window, but stopped by the wall. Martin glanced up at her through the window, and saw that she was a stranger, poorly dressed, and with a baby in her arms. She stopped by the wall with her back to the wind, trying to wrap the baby up though she had hardly anything to wrap it in. The woman had only summer clothes on, and even they were shabby and worn. Through the window Martin heard the baby crying, and the woman trying to soothe it, but unable to do so. Martin rose and going out of the door and up the steps he called to her.

"My dear, I say, my dear!"

The woman heard, and turned round.

"Why do you stand out there with the baby in the cold? Come inside. You can wrap him up better in a warm place. Come this way!"

The woman was surprised to see an old man in an apron, with spectacles on his nose, calling to her, but she followed him in.

They went down the steps, entered the little room, and the old man led her to the bed.

"There, sit down, my dear, near the stove. Warm yourself, and feed the baby."

"Haven't any milk. I have eaten nothing myself since early morning," said the woman, but still she took the baby to her breast.

Martin shook his head. He brought out a basin and some bread. Then he opened the oven door and poured some cabbage soup into the basin. He took out the porridge pot also but the porridge was not yet ready, so he spread a cloth on the table and served only the soup and bread.

"Sit down and eat, my dear, and I'll mind the baby. Why, bless me, I've had children of my own; I know how to manage them."

The woman crossed herself, and sitting down at the table began to eat, while Martin put the baby on the bed and sat down by it. He chucked and chucked, but having no teeth he could not do it well and the baby continued to cry. Then Martin tried poking at him with his finger; he drove his finger straight at the baby's mouth and then quickly drew it back, and did this again and again. He did not let the baby take his finger in its mouth, because it was all black with cobbler's wax. But the baby first grew quiet watching the finger, and then began to laugh. And Martin felt quite pleased.

The woman sat eating and talking, and told him who she was, and where she had been.

"I'm a soldier's wife," said she. "They sent my husband somewhere, far away, eight months ago, and I have heard nothing of him since. I had a place as cook till my baby was born, but then they would not keep me with a child. For three months now I have been struggling, unable to find a place, and I've had to sell all I had for food. I tried to go as a wet-nurse, but no one would have me; they said I was too starved-looking and thin. Now I have just been to see a tradesman's wife (a woman from our village is in service with her) and she has promised to take me. I thought it was all settled at last, but she tells me not to come till next week. It is far to her place, and I am exhausted, and baby is quite starved, poor mite. Fortunately our landlady has pity on us, and lets us lodge free, else I don't know what we should do."

Martin sighed. "Haven't you any warmer clothing?" he asked.

"How could I get warm clothing?" said she. "Why, I pawned my last shawl for sixpence yesterday."

Then the woman came and took the child, and Martin got up. He went and looked among some things that were hanging on the wall, and brought back an old cloak.

"Here," he said. "Though it's a worn-out old thing, it will do to wrap him up in."

The woman looked at the cloak, then at the old man, and taking it, burst into tears. Martin turned away, and groping under the bed brought out a small trunk. He fumbled about in it, and again sat down opposite the woman. And the woman said:

"The Lord bless you, friend. Surely Christ must have sent me to your window, else the child would have frozen. It was mild when I started, but now see how cold it has turned. Surely it must have been Christ who made you look out of your window and take pity on me, poor wretch!"

Martin smiled and said, "It is quite true; it was he made me do it. It was no mere chance made me look out."

And he told the woman his dream, and how he had heard the Lord's voice promising to visit him that day.

"Who knows? All things are possible," said the woman. And she got up and threw the cloak over her shoulders, wrapping it round herself and round the baby. Then she bowed, and thanked Martin once more.

"Take this for Christ's sake," said Martin, and gave her six-pence to get her shawl out of pawn. The woman crossed herself, and Martin did the same, and then he saw her out.

After the woman had gone, Martin ate some cabbage soup, cleared the things away, and sat down to work again. He sat and worked, but did not forget the window, and every time a shadow fell on it he looked up at once to see who was passing. People he knew and strangers passed by, but no one remarkable.

After a while Martin saw an apple woman stop just in front of his window. She had a large basket, but there did not seem to be many apples left in it; she had evidently sold most of her stock. On her back she had a sack full of chips, which she was taking home. No doubt she had gathered them at some place where building was going on. The sack evidently hurt her, and she wanted to shift it from one shoulder to the other, so she put it down on the footpath and, placing her basket on a post, began to shake down the chips in the sack. While she was doing this a boy in a tattered cap ran up, snatched an apple out of the basket, and tried to slip away; but the old woman noticed it, and turning, caught the boy by his sleeve. He began to struggle, trying to free himself, but the old woman held on with both hands, knocked his cap off his head, and seized hold of his hair. The boy screamed and the old woman scolded. Martin dropped his awl, not waiting to stick it in its place, and rushed out of the door. Stumbling up the steps, and dropping his spectacles in his hurry, he ran out into the street. The old woman was pulling the boy's hair and scolding him, and threatening to take him to the police. The lad was struggling and protesting, saying, "I did not take it. What are you beating me for? Let me go!"

Martin separated them. He took the boy by the hand and said, "Let him go, Granny. Forgive him for Christ's sake."

"I'll pay him out, so that he won't forget it for a year! I'll take the rascal to the police!"

Martin began entreating the old woman.

"Let him go, Granny. He won't do it again. Let him go for Christ's sake!"

The old woman let go, and the boy wished to run away, but Martin stopped him.

"Ask the Granny's forgiveness!" said he. "And don't do it another time. I saw you take the apple."

The boy began to cry and to beg pardon.

"That's right. And now here's an apple for you," and Martin took an apple from the basket and gave it to the boy, saying, "I will pay you, Granny."

"You will spoil them that way, the young rascals," said the old woman. "He ought to be whipped so that he should remember it for a week."

"Oh, Granny, Granny," said Martin, "that's our way – but it's not God's way. If he should be whipped for stealing an apple, what should be done to us for our sins?"

The old woman was silent.

And Martin told her the parable of the lord who forgave his servant a large debt, and how the servant went out and seized his debtor by the throat. The old woman listened to it all, and the boy, too, stood by and listened.

"God bids us forgive," said Martin, "or else we shall not be forgiven. Forgive everyone; and a thoughtless youngster most of all."

The old woman wagged her head and sighed.

"It's true enough," said she, "but they are getting terribly spoilt."

"Then we old ones must show them better ways," Martin replied.

"That's just what I say," said the old woman. "I have had seven of them myself, and only one daughter is left." And the old woman began to tell how and where she was living with her daughter, and how many grandchildren she had. "There now," she said, "I have but little strength left, yet I work hard for the sake of my grandchildren; and nice children they are, too. No one comes out to meet me but the children. Little Annie, now, won't leave me for anyone. 'It's Grandmother, dear Grandmother, darling Grandmother.'" And the old woman completely softened at the thought.

"Of course, it was only his childishness, God help him," said she, referring to the boy.

As the old woman was about to hoist her sack on her back, the lad sprang forward to her, saying, "Let me carry it for you, Granny. I'm going that way."

The old woman nodded her head, and put the sack on the boy's back, and they went down the street together, the old woman quite forgetting to ask Martin to pay for the apple. Martin stood and watched them as they went along talking to each other.

When they were out of sight Martin went back to the house. Having found his spectacles unbroken on the steps, he picked up his awl and sat down again to work. He worked a little, but could soon not see to pass the bristle through the holes in the leather; and presently he noticed the lamplighter passing on his way to light the street lamps.

"Seems it's time to light up," thought he. So he trimmed his lamp, hung it up, and sat down again to work. He finished off one boot and, turning it about, examined it. It was all right. Then he gathered his tools together, swept up the cuttings, put away the bristles and the thread and the awls, and, taking down the lamp, placed it on the table. Then he took the Gospels from the shelf. He meant to open them at the place he had marked the day before with a bit of morocco, but the book opened at another place. As Martin opened it, his yesterday's dream came back to his mind, and no sooner had he thought of it than he seemed to hear footsteps, as though someone were moving behind him. Martin turned round, and it seemed to him as if people were standing in the dark corner, but he could not make out who they were. And a voice whispered in his ear: "Martin, Martin, don't you know me?"

"Who is it?" muttered Martin.

"It is I," said the voice. And out of the dark corner stepped Stepanich, who smiled and, vanishing like a cloud, was seen no more.

"It is I," said the voice again. And out of the darkness stepped the woman with the baby in her arms and the woman smiled and the baby laughed, and they too vanished.

"It is I," said the voice once more. And the old woman and the boy with the apple stepped out and both smiled, and then they too vanished.

And Martin's soul grew glad. He crossed himself, put on his spectacles, and began reading the Gospel just where it had opened; and at the top of the page he read:

"For I was hungry and you gave me food, I was thirsty and you gave me drink, I was a stranger and you welcomed me."

And at the bottom of the page he read:

"Truly, I say to you, as you did it to one of the least of these, you did it to me."

And Martin understood that his dream had come true; and that the Savior had really come to him that day, and he had welcomed him.

7.

Master and Man

A Selection from the Story

The merchant and church elder Vasili Andreevich Brekhunov is so intent on building a fortune that, ignoring warnings, he heads out into a December snowstorm with his serf Nikita to buy a piece of land before any competitors. When the two are caught in the blizzard, Vasili takes the horse and abandons his serf to freeze. The horse, however, goes in circles, and to Vasili's horror he finds himself back where he started.

HAVING STUMBLED back to the sledge, Vasili Andreevich caught hold of it and for a long time stood motionless, trying to calm himself and recover his breath. Nikita was not in his former place, but something, already covered with snow, was lying in the sledge and Vasili Andreevich concluded that this was Nikita. His terror had now quite left him, and if he felt any fear it was lest the dreadful terror should return that he had experienced when on the horse and especially when he was left alone in the snowdrift. At any cost he had to avoid that terror, and to keep it away he must do something – occupy himself with something. And the first thing he did was to turn his back to the wind and open his fur coat. Then, as soon as he recovered his breath a little, he shook the snow out of his boots and out of his left-hand glove (the right-hand glove was hopelessly lost and by this time probably lying somewhere under a dozen inches of snow); then as was his custom when going out of his shop to buy grain from the peasants, he pulled his girdle low down and tightened it and prepared for action. The first thing that occurred to him was to free Mukhorty's leg from the rein. Having done that, and tethered him to the iron cramp at the front of the sledge where he had been before, he was going round the horse's quarters to put the breeching and pad straight and cover him with the cloth, but at that moment he noticed that something was moving in the sledge and Nikita's head rose up out of the snow that covered it. Nikita, who was half frozen, rose with great difficulty and sat up, moving his hand before his nose in a strange manner just as if he were driving away flies. He waved his hand and said something, and seemed to Vasili Andreevich to be calling him. Vasili Andreevich left the cloth unadjusted and went up to the sledge.

"What is it?" he asked. "What are you saying?"

"I'm dy . . . ing, that's what," said Nikita brokenly and with difficulty. "Give what is owing to me to my lad, or to my wife, no matter."

"Why, are you really frozen?" asked Vasili Andreevich.

"I feel it's my death. Forgive me for Christ's sake . . ." said Nikita in a tearful voice, continuing to wave his hand before his face as if driving away flies.

Vasili Andreevich stood silent and motionless for half a minute. Then suddenly, with the same resolution with which he used to strike hands when making a good purchase, he took a step back and turning up his sleeves began raking the snow off Nikita and out of the sledge. Having done this he hurriedly undid his girdle, opened out his fur coat, and having pushed Nikita down, lay down on top of him, covering him not only with his fur coat but with the whole of his body, which glowed with warmth. After pushing the skirts of his coat between Nikita and the sides of the sledge, and holding down its hem with his knees, Vasili Andreevich lay like that face down, with his head pressed against the front of the sledge. Here he no longer heard the horse's movements or the whistling of the wind, but only Nikita's breathing. At first and for a long time Nikita lay motionless, then he sighed deeply and moved.

"There, and you say you are dying! Lie still and get warm, that's our way . . ." began Vasili Andreevich.

But to his great surprise he could say no more, for tears came to his eyes and his lower jaw began to quiver rapidly. He stopped speaking and only gulped down the risings in his throat. "Seems I was badly frightened and have gone quite weak," he thought. But this weakness was not only unpleasant, but gave him a peculiar joy such as he had never felt before.

"That's our way!" he said to himself, experiencing a strange and solemn tenderness. He lay like that for a long time, wiping his eyes on the fur of his coat and tucking under his knee the right skirt, which the wind kept turning up.

But he longed so passionately to tell somebody of his joyful condition that he said: "Nikita!"

"It's comfortable, warm!" came a voice from beneath.

"There, you see, friend, I was going to perish. And you would have been frozen, and I should have . . ."

But again his jaws began to quiver and his eyes to fill with tears, and he could say no more.

"Well, never mind," he thought. "I know about myself what I know."

He remained silent and lay like that for a long time.

Nikita kept him warm from below and his fur coats from above. Only his hands, with which he kept his coat-skirts down round Nikita's sides, and his legs which the wind kept uncovering, began to freeze, especially his right hand which had no glove. But he did not think of his legs or of his hands but only of how to warm the peasant who was lying under him. He looked out several times at Mukhorty and could see that his back was uncovered and the drugget and breeching lying on the snow, and that he ought to get up and cover him, but he could not bring himself to leave Nikita and disturb even for a moment the joyous condition he was in. He no longer felt any kind of terror.

"No fear, we shan't lose him this time!" he said to himself, referring to his getting the peasant warm with the same boastfulness with which he spoke of his buying and selling.

Vasili Andreevich lay in that way for one hour, another, and a third, but he was unconscious of the passage of time. At first impressions of the snow-storm, the sledge-shafts, and the horse with the shaft-bow shaking before his eyes, kept passing through his mind, then he remembered Nikita lying under him, then recollections of the festival, his wife, the police officer, and the box of candles, began to mingle with these; then again Nikita, this time lying under that box, then the peasants, customers and traders, and the white walls of his house with its iron roof with Nikita lying underneath, presented themselves to his imagination. Afterwards all these impressions blended into one nothingness. As the colors of the rainbow unite into one white light, so all these different impressions mingled into one, and he fell asleep.

For a long time he slept without dreaming, but just before dawn the visions recommenced. It seemed to him that he was standing by the box of tapers and that Tikhon's wife was asking for a five kopek taper for the Church fete. He wished to take one out and give it to her, but his hands would not lift up, being held tight in his pockets. He wanted to walk round the box but his feet would not move and his new clean galoshes had grown to the stone floor, and he could neither lift them nor get his feet out of the galoshes. Then the taper-box was no longer a box but a bed, and suddenly Vasili Andreevich saw himself lying in his bed at home. He was lying in his bed and could not get up. Yet it was necessary for him to get up because Ivan Matveich, the police officer, would soon call for him and he had to go with him – either to bargain for the forest or to put Mukhorty's breeching straight.

He asked his wife: "Nikolaevna, hasn't he come yet?"

"No, he hasn't," she replied. He heard someone drive up to the front steps. "It must be him." "No, he's gone past." "Nikolaevna! I say, Nikolaevna, isn't he here yet?" "No." He was still lying on his bed and could not get up, but was always waiting. And this waiting was uncanny and yet joyful. Then suddenly his joy was completed. He whom he was expecting came; not Ivan Matveich the police officer, but someone else – yet it was he whom he had been waiting for. He came and called him; and it was he who had called him and told him to lie down on Nikita. And Vasili Andreevich was glad that that one had come for him.

"I'm coming!" he cried joyfully, and that cry awoke him, but woke him up not at all the same person he had been when he fell asleep. He tried to get up but could not, tried to move his arm and could not, to move his leg and also could not, to turn his head and could not. He was surprised but not at all disturbed by this. He understood that this was death, and was not at all disturbed by that either. He remembered that Nikita was lying under him and that he had got warm and was alive, and it seemed to him that he was Nikita and Nikita was he, and that his life was not in himself but in Nikita. He strained his ears and heard Nikita breathing and even slightly snoring. "Nikita is alive, so I too am alive!" he said to himself triumphantly.

And he remembered his money, his shop, his house, the buying and selling, and Mironov's millions, and it was hard for him to understand why that man, called Vasili Brekhunov, had troubled himself with all those things with which he had been troubled.

"Well, it was because he did not know what the real thing was," he thought, concerning that Vasili Brekhunov. "He did not know, but now I know and know for sure. Now I know!" And again he heard the voice of the one who had called him before. "I'm coming! Coming!" he responded gladly, and his whole being was filled with joyful emotion. He felt himself free and that nothing could hold him back any longer.

After that Vasili Andreevich neither saw, heard, nor felt anything more in this world.

All around the snow still eddied. The same whirlwinds of snow circled about, covering the dead Vasili Andreevich's fur coat, the shivering Mukhorty, the sledge, now scarcely to be seen, and Nikita lying at the bottom of it, kept warm beneath his dead master.

8.

What Men Live By

A Story

We know that we have passed out of death into life, because we love the brethren. He who does not love abides in death.

But if anyone has the world's goods and sees his brother in need, yet closes his heart against him, how does God's love abide in him? Little children, let us not love in word or speech but in deed and in truth.

Love is of God, and he who loves is born of God and knows God. He who does not love does not know God; for God is love.

No man has ever seen God; if we love one another, God abides in us.

God is love, and he who abides in love abides in God, and God abides in him.

If anyone says, "I love God," and hates his brother, he is a liar; for he who does not love his brother whom he has seen, cannot love God whom he has not seen.   —*from 1 John 3–4*

I

A SHOEMAKER NAMED SIMON, who had neither house nor land of his own, lived with his wife and children in a peasant's hut, and earned his living by his work. Work was cheap but bread was dear, and what he earned he spent for food. The man and his wife had but one sheepskin coat between them for winter wear, and even that was worn to tatters, and this was the second year he had been wanting to buy sheepskins for a new coat. Before winter Simon saved up a little money: a three-ruble note lay hidden in his wife's box, and five rubles and twenty kopeks were owed him by customers in the village.

So one morning he prepared to go to the village to buy the sheepskins. He put on over his shirt his wife's wadded nankeen jacket, and over that he put his own cloth coat. He took the three-ruble note in his pocket, cut himself a stick to serve as a staff, and started off after breakfast. "I'll collect the five rubles that are due to me," thought he, "add the three I have got, and that will be enough to buy sheepskins for the winter coat."

He came to the village and called at a peasant's hut, but the man was not at home. The peasant's wife promised that the money should be paid next week, but she would not pay it herself. Then Simon called on another peasant, but this one swore he had no money, and would only pay twenty kopeks which he owed for a pair of boots Simon had mended. Simon then tried to buy the sheepskins on credit, but the dealer would not trust him.

"Bring your money," said he, "then you may have your pick of the skins. We know what debt collecting is like."

So all the business the shoemaker did was to get the twenty kopeks for boots he had mended, and to take a pair of felt boots a peasant gave him to sole with leather.

Simon felt downhearted. He spent the twenty kopeks on vodka, and started homewards without having bought any skins. In the morning he had felt the frost; but now, after drinking the vodka, he felt warm even without a sheepskin coat. He trudged along, striking his stick on the frozen earth with one hand, swinging the felt boots with the other, and talking to himself.

"I'm quite warm," said he, "though I have no sheepskin coat. I've had a drop, and it runs through all my veins. I need no sheepskins. I go along and don't worry about anything. That's the sort of man I am! What do I care? I can live without sheepskins. I don't need them. My wife will fret, to be sure. And, true enough, it's a shame; one works all day long, and then does not get paid. Stop a bit! If you don't bring that money along, sure enough I'll skin you, blessed if I don't. How's that? He pays twenty kopeks at a time! What can I do with twenty kopeks: Drink it–that's all one can do! Hard up, he says he is! So he may be–but what about me? You have house, and cattle, and everything; I've only what I stand up in! You have corn of your own growing; I have to buy every grain. Do what I will, I must spend three rubles every week for bread alone. I come home and find the bread all used up, and I have to fork out another ruble and a half. So just you pay up what you owe, and no nonsense about it!"

By this time he had nearly reached the shrine at the bend of the road. Looking up, he saw something whitish behind the shrine. The daylight was fading, and the shoemaker peered at the thing without being able to make out what it was. "There was no white stone here before. Can it be an ox? It's not like an ox. It has a head like a man, but it's too white; and what could a man be doing there?"

He came closer, so that it was clearly visible. To his surprise it really was a man, alive or dead, sitting naked, leaning motionless against the shrine. Terror seized the shoemaker, and he thought, "Someone has killed him, stripped him, and left him here. If I meddle I shall surely get into trouble."

So the shoemaker went on. He passed in front of the shrine so that he could not see the man. When he had gone some way, he looked back, and saw that the man was no longer leaning against the shrine, but was moving as if looking towards him. The shoemaker felt more frightened than before, and thought, "Shall I go back to him, or shall I go on? If I go near him something dreadful may happen. Who knows who the fellow is? He has not come here for any good. If I go near him he may jump up and throttle me, and there will be no getting away. Or if not, he'd still be a burden on one's hands. What could I do with a naked man? I couldn't give him my last clothes. Heaven only help me to get away!"

So the shoemaker hurried on, leaving the shrine behind him – when suddenly his conscience smote him and he stopped in the road.

"What are you doing, Simon?" said he to himself. "The man may be dying of want, and you slip past afraid. Have you grown so rich as to be afraid of robbers? Ah, Simon, shame on you!"

So he turned back and went up to the man.

II

Simon approached the stranger, looked at him, and saw that he was a young man, fit, with no bruises on his body, only evidently freezing and frightened, and he sat there leaning back without looking up at Simon, as if too faint to lift his eyes. Simon went close to him, and then the man seemed to wake up. Turning his head, he opened his eyes and looked into Simon's face. That one look was enough to make Simon fond of the man. He threw the felt boots on the ground, undid his sash, laid it on the boots, and took off his cloth coat.

"It's not a time for talking," said he. "Come, put this coat on at once!" And Simon took the man by the elbows and helped him to rise. As he stood there, Simon saw that his body was clean and in good condition, his hands and feet shapely, and his face good and kind. He threw his coat over the man's shoulders but the latter could not find the sleeves. Simon guided his arms into them, and drawing the coat well on wrapped it closely about him, tying the sash round the man's waist.

Simon even took off his torn cap to put it on the man's head, but then his own head felt cold, and he thought: "I'm quite bald, while he has long curly hair." So he put his cap on his own head again. "It will be better to give him something for his feet," thought he; and he made the man sit down, and helped him to put on the felt boots, saying, "There, friend, now move about and warm yourself. Other matters can be settled later on. Can you walk?"

The man stood up and looked kindly at Simon, but could not say a word.

"Why don't you speak?" said Simon. "It's too cold to stay here; we must be getting home. There now, take my stick, and if you're feeling weak, lean on that. Now step out!"

The man started walking, and moved easily, not lagging behind.

As they went along, Simon asked him, "And where do you belong to?"

"I'm not from these parts."

"I thought as much. I know the folks hereabouts. But how did you come to be there by the shrine?"

"I cannot tell."

"Has someone been ill-treating you?"

"No one has ill-treated me. God has punished me."

"Of course God rules all. Still, you'll have to find food and shelter somewhere. Where do you want to go to?"

"It is all the same to me."

Simon was amazed. The man did not look like a rogue, and he spoke gently, but yet he gave no account of himself. Still Simon thought, "Who knows what may have happened?" And he said to the stranger: "Well then, come home with me, and at least warm yourself awhile."

So Simon walked towards his home, and the stranger kept up with him, walking at his side. The wind had risen and Simon felt it cold under his shirt. He was getting over his tipsiness by now, and began to feel the frost. He went along sniffling and wrapping his wife's coat round him, and he thought to himself: "There now–talk about sheepskins! I went out for sheepskins and come home without even a coat to my back and what is more, I'm bringing a naked man along with me. Matryóna won't be pleased!" And when he thought of his wife he felt sad; but when he looked at the stranger and remembered how he had looked up at him at the shrine, his heart was glad.

III

Simon's wife had everything ready early that day. She had cut wood, brought water, fed the children, eaten her own meal, and now she sat thinking. She wondered when she ought to make bread: now or tomorrow? There was still a large piece left.

"If Simon has had some dinner in town," thought she, "and does not eat much for supper, the bread will last out another day."

She weighed the piece of bread in her hand again and again, and thought: "I won't make any more today. We have only enough flour left to bake one batch. We can manage to make this last out till Friday."

So Matryóna put away the bread, and sat down at the table to patch her husband's shirt. While she worked she thought how her husband was buying skins for a winter coat.

"If only the dealer does not cheat him. My good man is much too simple; he cheats nobody, but any child can take him in. Eight rubles is a lot of money – he should get a good coat at that price. Not tanned skins, but still a proper winter coat. How difficult it was last winter to get on without a warm coat. I could neither get down to the river, nor go out anywhere. When he went out he put on all we had, and there was nothing left for me. He did not start very early today, but still it's time he was back. I only hope he has not gone on the spree!"

Hardly had Matryóna thought this, when steps were heard on the threshold, and someone entered. Matryóna stuck her needle into her work and went out into the passage. There she saw two men: Simon, and with him a man without a hat, and wearing felt boots.

Matryóna noticed at once that her husband smelt of spirits. "There now, he has been drinking," thought she. And when she saw that he was coatless, had only her jacket on, brought no parcel, stood there silent, and seemed ashamed, her heart was ready to break with disappointment. "He has drunk the money," thought she, "and has been on the spree with some good-for-nothing fellow whom he has brought home with him."

Matryóna let them pass into the hut, followed them in, and saw that the stranger was a young, slight man, wearing her husband's coat. There was no shirt to be seen under it, and he had no hat. Having entered, he stood neither moving nor raising his eyes, and Matryóna thought: "He must be a bad man – he's afraid."

Matryóna frowned, and stood beside the oven looking to see what they would do.

Simon took off his cap and sat down on the bench as if things were all right.

"Come, Matryóna; if supper is ready, let us have some."

Matryóna muttered something to herself and did not move, but stayed where she was, by the oven. She looked first at the one and then at the other of them, and only shook her head. Simon saw that his wife was annoyed, but tried to pass it off. Pretending not to notice anything, he took the stranger by the arm.

"Sit down, friend," said he, "and let us have some supper."

The stranger sat down on the bench.

"Haven't you cooked anything for us?" said Simon.

Matryóna's anger boiled over. "I've cooked, but not for you. It seems to me you have drunk your wits away. You went to buy a sheepskin coat, but come home without so much as the coat you had on, and bring a naked vagabond home with you. I have no supper for drunkards like you."

"That's enough, Matryóna. Don't wag your tongue without reason! You had better ask what sort of man – "

"And you tell me what you've done with the money?"

Simon found the pocket of the jacket, drew out the three-ruble note, and unfolded it.

"Here is the money. Trífonof did not pay, but promises to pay soon."

Matryóna got still more angry; he had bought no sheepskins, but had put his only coat on some naked fellow and had even brought him to their house.

She snatched up the note from the table, took it to put away in safety, and said: "I have no supper for you. We can't feed all the naked drunkards in the world."

"There now, Matryóna, hold your tongue a bit. First hear what a man has to say!"

"Much wisdom I shall hear from a drunken fool. I was right in not wanting to marry you – a drunkard. The linen my mother gave me you drank; and now you've been to buy a coat – and have drunk it too!"

Simon tried to explain to his wife that he had only spent twenty kopeks; tried to tell how he had found the man – but Matryóna would not let him get a word in. She talked nineteen to the dozen, and dragged in things that had happened ten years before.

Matryóna talked and talked, and at last she flew at Simon and seized him by the sleeve.

"Give me my jacket! It is the only one I have and you must needs take it from me and wear it yourself. Give it here, you mangy dog, and may the devil take you."

Simon began to pull off the jacket, and turned a sleeve of it inside out; Matryóna seized the jacket and it burst its seams. She snatched it up, threw it over her head and went to the door. She meant to go out, but stopped undecided – she wanted to work off her anger, but she also wanted to learn what sort of a man the stranger was.

IV

Matryóna stopped and said: "If he were a good man he would not be naked. Why, he hasn't even a shirt on him. If he were all right, you would say where you came across the fellow."

"That's just what I am trying to tell you," said Simon. "As I came to the shrine I saw him sitting all naked and frozen. It isn't quite the weather to sit about naked! God sent me to him, or he would have perished. What was I to do? How do we know what may have happened to him? So I took him, clothed him, and brought him along. Don't be so angry, Matryóna. It is a sin. Remember, we all must die one day."

Angry words rose to Matryóna's lips, but she looked at the stranger and was silent. He sat on the edge of the bench, motionless, his hands folded on his knees, his head drooping on his breast, his eyes closed, and his brows knit as if in pain. Matryóna was silent, and Simon said: "Matryóna, have you no love of God?"

Matryóna heard these words, and as she looked at the stranger, suddenly her heart softened towards him. She came back from the door, and going to the oven she got out the supper. Setting a cup on the table, she poured out some kvass. Then she brought out the last piece of bread, and set out a knife and spoons.

"Eat, if you want to," said she.

Simon drew the stranger to the table.

"Take your place, young man," said he.

Simon cut the bread, crumbled it into the broth, and they began to eat. Matryóna sat at the corner of the table, resting her head on her hand and looking at the stranger.

And Matryóna was touched with pity for the stranger, and began to feel fond of him. And at once the stranger's face lit up; his brows were no longer bent, he raised his eyes and smiled at Matryóna.

When they had finished supper, the woman cleared away the things and began questioning the stranger. "Where are you from?" said she.

"I am not from these parts."

"But how did you come to be on the road?"

"I may not tell."

"Did someone rob you?"

"God punished me."

"And you were lying there naked?"

"Yes, naked and freezing. Simon saw me and had pity on me. He took off his coat, put it on me and brought me here. And you have fed me, given me drink, and shown pity on me. God will reward you!"

Matryóna rose, took from the window Simon's old shirt she had been patching, and gave it to the stranger. She also brought out a pair of trousers for him.

"There," said she, "I see you have no shirt. Put this on, and lie down where you please, in the loft or on the oven."

The stranger took off the coat, put on the shirt, and lay down in the loft. Matryóna put out the candle, took the coat, and climbed to where her husband lay on the oven.

Matryóna drew the skirts of the coat over her and lay down, but could not sleep; she could not get the stranger out of her mind.

When she remembered that he had eaten their last piece of bread and that there was none for tomorrow and thought of the shirt and trousers she had given away, she felt grieved; but when she remembered how he had smiled, her heart was glad.

Long did Matryóna lie awake, and she noticed that Simon also was awake – he drew the coat towards him.

"Simon!"

"Well?"

"You have had the last of the bread, and I have not put any to rise. I don't know what we shall do tomorrow. Perhaps I can borrow some of neighbor Martha."

"If we're alive we shall find something to eat."

The woman lay still awhile, and then said, "He seems a good man, but why does he not tell us who he is?"

"I suppose he has his reasons."

"Simon!"

"Well?"

"We give; but why does nobody give us anything?"

Simon did not know what to say; so he only said, "Let us stop talking," and turned over and went to sleep.

V

In the morning Simon awoke. The children were still asleep; his wife had gone to the neighbor's to borrow some bread. The stranger alone was sitting on the bench, dressed in the old shirt and trousers, and looking upwards. His face was brighter than it had been the day before.

Simon said to him, "Well, friend; the belly wants bread and the naked body clothes. One has to work for a living. What work do you know?"

"I do not know any."

This surprised Simon, but he said, "Men who want to learn can learn anything."

"Men work, and I will work also."

"What is your name?"

"Michael."

"Well Michael, if you don't wish to talk about yourself that is your own affair; but you'll have to earn a living for yourself. If you will work as I tell you, I will give you food and shelter."

"May God reward you! I will learn. Show me what to do."

Simon took yarn, put it round his thumb and began to twist it.

"It is easy enough – see!"

Michael watched him, put some yarn round his own thumb in the same way, caught the knack, and twisted the yarn also.

Then Simon showed him how to wax the thread. This also Michael mastered. Next Simon showed him how to twist the bristle in, and how to sew, and this, too, Michael learned at once.

Whatever Simon showed him he understood at once, and after three days he worked as if he had sewn boots all his life. He worked without stopping, and ate little. When work was over he sat silently, looking upwards. He hardly went into the street, spoke only when necessary, and neither joked nor laughed. They never saw him smile, except that first evening when Matryóna gave them supper.

VI

Day by day and week by week the year went round. Michael lived and worked with Simon. His fame spread till people said that no one sewed boots so neatly and strongly as Simon's workman, Michael; and from all the district round people came to Simon for their boots, and he began to be well off.

One winter day, as Simon and Michael sat working, a carriage on sledge-runners with three horses and with bells, drove up to the hut. They looked out of the window; the carriage stopped at their door and a fine servant jumped down from the box and opened the door. A gentleman in a fur coat got out and walked up to Simon's hut. Up jumped Matryóna and opened the door wide. The gentleman stooped to enter the hut, and when he drew himself up again his head nearly reached the ceiling, and he seemed quite to fill his end of the room.

Simon rose, bowed, and looked at the gentleman with astonishment. He had never seen anyone like him. Simon himself was lean, Michael was thin, and Matryóna was dry as a bone, but this man was like someone from another world: red-faced, burly, with a neck like a bull's, and looking altogether as if he were cast in iron.

The gentleman puffed, threw off his fur coat, sat down on the bench, and said, "Which of you is the master boot maker?"

"I am, your Excellency," said Simon, coming forward.

Then the gentleman shouted to his lad, "Hey, Fédka, bring the leather!"

The servant ran in, bringing a parcel. The gentleman took the parcel and put it on the table.

"Untie it," said he. The lad untied it.

The gentleman pointed to the leather.

"Look here, shoemaker," said he, "do you see this leather?"

"Yes, your honor."

"But do you know what sort of leather it is?"

Simon felt the leather and said, "It is good leather."

"Good, indeed! Why, you fool, you never saw such leather before in your life. It's German, and cost twenty rubles."

Simon was frightened, and said, "Where should I ever see leather like that?"

"Just so! Now, can you make it into boots for me?"

"Yes, your Excellency, I can."

Then the gentleman shouted at him: "You can, can you? Well, remember whom you are to make them for, and what the leather is. You must make me boots that will wear for a year, neither losing shape nor coming unsewn. If you can do it, take the leather and cut it up; but if you can't, say so. I warn you now, if your boots come unsewn or lose shape within a year, I will have you put in prison. If they don't burst or lose shape for a year, I will pay you ten rubles for your work."

Simon was frightened, and did not know what to say. He glanced at Michael and nudging him with his elbow, whispered: "Shall I take the work?"

Michael nodded his head as if to say, "Yes, take it."

Simon did as Michael advised, and undertook to make boots that would not lose shape or split for a whole year.

Calling his servant, the gentleman told him to pull the boot off his left leg, which he stretched out.

"Take my measure!" said he.

Simon stitched a paper measure seventeen inches long, smoothed it out, knelt down, wiped his hands well on his apron so as not to soil the gentleman's sock, and began to measure. He measured the sole, and round the instep, and began to measure the calf of the leg, but the paper was too short. The calf of the leg was as thick as a beam.

"Mind you don't make it too tight in the leg."

Simon stitched on another strip of paper. The gentleman twitched his toes about in his sock, looking round at those in the hut, and as he did so he noticed Michael.

"Whom have you there?" asked he.

"That is my workman. He will sew the boots."

"Mind," said the gentleman to Michael, "remember to make them so that they will last me a year."

Simon also looked at Michael, and saw that Michael was not looking at the gentleman, but was gazing into the corner behind the gentleman, as if he saw someone there. Michael looked and looked, and suddenly he smiled, and his face became brighter.

"What are you grinning at, you fool?" thundered the gentleman. "You had better look to it that the boots are ready in time."

"They shall be ready in good time," said Michael.

"Mind it is so," said the gentleman, and he put on his boots and his fur coat, wrapped the latter round him, and went to the door. But he forgot to stoop and struck his head against the lintel.

He swore and rubbed his head. Then he took his seat in the carriage and drove away.

When he had gone, Simon said: "There's a figure of a man for you! You could not kill him with a mallet. He almost knocked out the lintel, but little harm it did him."

And Matryóna said: "Living as he does, how should he not grow strong? Death itself can't touch such a rock as that."

VII

Then Simon said to Michael: "Well, we have taken the work, but we must see we don't get into trouble over it. The leather is dear, and the gentleman hot-tempered. We must make no mistakes. Come, your eye is truer and your hands have become nimbler than mine, so you take this measure and cut out the boots. I will finish off the sewing of the vamps."

Michael did as he was told. He took the leather, spread it out on the table, folded it in two, took a knife, and began to cut out.

Matryóna came and watched him cutting, and was surprised to see how he was doing it. Matryóna was accustomed to seeing boots made, and she looked and saw that Michael was not cutting the leather for boots, but was cutting it round.

She wished to say something, but she thought to herself: "Perhaps I do not understand how gentlemen's boots should be made. I suppose Michael knows more about it – and I won't interfere."

When Michael had cut up the leather, he took a thread and began to sew not with two ends, as boots are sewn, but with a single end, as for soft slippers.

Again Matryóna wondered, but again she did not interfere. Michael sewed on steadily till noon. Then Simon rose for dinner, looked around, and saw that Michael had made slippers out of the gentleman's leather.

"Ah!" groaned Simon, and he thought, "How is it that Michael, who has been with me a whole year and never made a mistake before, should do such a dreadful thing? The gentleman ordered high boots, welted, with whole fronts, and Michael has made soft slippers with single soles, and has wasted the leather. What am I to say to the gentleman? I can never replace leather such as this."

And he said to Michael, "What are you doing, friend? You have ruined me! You know the gentleman ordered high boots, but see what you have made!"

Hardly had he begun to rebuke Michael, when "rat-tat" went the iron ring that hung at the door. Someone was knocking. They looked out of the window; a man had come on horseback, and was fastening his horse. They opened the door, and the servant who had been with the gentleman came in.

"Good day," said he.

"Good day," replied Simon. "What can we do for you?"

"My mistress has sent me about the boots."

"What about the boots?"

"Why, my master no longer needs them. He is dead."

"Is it possible?"

"He did not live to get home after leaving you, but died in the carriage. When we reached home and the servants came to help him alight he rolled over like a sack. He was dead already, and so stiff that he could hardly be got out of the carriage. My mistress sent me here, saying: 'Tell the boot maker that the gentleman who ordered boots from him and left the leather for them no longer needs the boots, but that he must quickly make soft slippers for the corpse. Wait till they are ready, and bring them back with you.' That is why I have come."

Michael gathered up the remnants of the leather; rolled them up, took the soft slippers he had made, slapped them together, wiped them down with his apron, and handed them and the roll of leather to the servant, who took them and said: "Goodbye, masters, and good day to you!"

VIII

Another year passed, and another, and Michael was now living his sixth year with Simon. He lived as before. He went nowhere, only spoke when necessary, and had only smiled twice in all those years – once when Matryóna gave him food, and a second time when the gentleman was in their hut. Simon was more than pleased with his workman. He never now asked him where he came from, and only feared lest Michael should go away.

They were all at home one day. Matryóna was putting iron pots in the oven, the children were running along the benches and looking out of the window; Simon was sewing at one window, and Michael was fastening on a heel at the other.

One of the boys ran along the bench to Michael, leant on his shoulder, and looked out of the window.

"Look, Uncle Michael! There is a lady with little girls! She seems to be coming here. And one of the girls is lame."

When the boy said that, Michael dropped his work, turned to the window, and looked out into the street.

Simon was surprised. Michael never used to look out into the street, but now he pressed against the window, staring at something. Simon also looked out, and saw that a well-dressed woman was really coming to his hut, leading by the hand two little girls in fur coats and woolen shawls. The girls could hardly be told one from the other, except that one of them was crippled in her left leg and walked with a limp.

The woman stepped into the porch and entered the passage. Feeling about for the entrance she found the latch, which she lifted, and opened the door. She let the two girls go in first, and followed them into the hut.

"Good day, good folk!"

"Pray come in," said Simon. "What can we do for you?"

The woman sat down by the table. The two little girls pressed close to her knees, afraid of the people in the hut.

"I want leather shoes made for these two little girls, for spring."

"We can do that. We never have made such small shoes, but we can make them; either welted or turnover shoes, linen lined. My man, Michael, is a master at the work."

Simon glanced at Michael and saw that he had left his work and was sitting with his eyes fixed on the little girls. Simon was surprised. It was true the girls were pretty, with black eyes, plump, and rosy-cheeked, and they wore nice kerchiefs and fur coats, but still Simon could not understand why Michael should look at them like that – just as if he had known them before. He was puzzled, but went on talking with the woman and arranging the price. Having fixed it, he prepared the measure. The woman lifted the lame girl onto her lap and said: "Take two measures from this little girl. Make one shoe for the lame foot and three for the sound one. They both have the same sized feet. They are twins."

Simon took the measure and, speaking of the lame girl, said: "How did it happen to her? She is such a pretty girl. Was she born so?"

"No, her mother crushed her leg."

Then Matryóna joined in. She wondered who this woman was, and whose the children were, so she said: "Are not you their mother, then?"

"No, my good woman, I am neither their mother nor any relation to them. They were quite strangers to me, but I adopted them."

"They are not your children and yet you are so fond of them?"

"How can I help being fond of them? I fed them both at my own breasts. I had a child of my own, but God took him. I was not so fond of him as I now am of these."

"Then whose children are they?"

IX

The woman, having begun talking, told them the whole story.

"It is about six years since their parents died, both in one week: their father was buried on the Tuesday, and their mother died on the Friday. These orphans were born three days after their father's death, and their mother did not live another day. My husband and I were then living as peasants in the village. We were neighbors of theirs, our yard being next to theirs. Their father was a lonely man; a woodcutter in the forest. When felling trees one day, they let one fall on him. It fell across his body and crushed his bowels out. They hardly got him home before his soul went to God; and that same week his wife gave birth to twins – these little girls. She was poor and alone; she had no one, young or old, with her. Alone she gave them birth, and alone she met her death.

"The next morning I went to see her, but when I entered the hut, she, poor thing, was already stark and cold. In dying she had rolled on to this child and crushed her leg. The village folk came to the hut, washed the body, laid her out, made a coffin, and buried her. They were good folk. The babies were left alone. What was to be done with them? I was the only woman there who had a baby at the time. I was nursing my first-born – eight weeks old. So I took them for a time. The peasants came together, and thought and thought what to do with them, and at last they said to me: 'For the present, Mary, you had better keep the girls, and later on we will arrange what to do for them.' So I nursed the sound one at my breast, but at first I did not feed this crippled one. I did not suppose she would live. But then I thought to myself, why should the poor innocent suffer? I pitied her, and began to feed her. And so I fed my own boy and these two – the three of them – at my own breast. I was young and strong, and had good food, and God gave me so much milk that at times it even overflowed. I used sometimes to feed two at a time, while the third was waiting. When one had had enough I nursed the third. And God so ordered it that these grew up, while my own was buried before he was two years old. And I had no more children, though we prospered. Now my husband is working for the corn merchant at the mill. The pay is good and we are well off. But I have no children of my own, and how lonely I should be without these little girls! How can I help loving them! They are the joy of my life!"

She pressed the lame little girl to her with one hand while with the other she wiped the tears from her cheeks.

And Matryóna sighed, and said: "The proverb is true that says, 'One may live without father or mother, but one cannot live without God.'"

So they talked together, when suddenly the whole hut was lighted up as though by summer lightning from the corner where Michael sat. They all looked towards him and saw him sitting, his hands folded on his knees, gazing upwards and smiling.

X

The woman went away with the girls. Michael rose from the bench, put down his work, and took off his apron. Then, bowing low to Simon and his wife, he said: "Farewell, masters. God has forgiven me. I ask your forgiveness, too, for anything done amiss."

And they saw that a light shone from Michael. And Simon rose, bowed down to Michael, and said: "I see, Michael, that you are no common man, and I can neither keep you nor question you. Only tell me this: how is it that when I found you and brought you home, you were gloomy, and when my wife gave you food you smiled at her and became brighter? Then when the gentleman came to order the boots, you smiled again and became brighter still? And now, when this woman brought the little girls, you smiled a third time, and have become as bright as day? Tell me, Michael, why does your face shine so, and why did you smile those three times?"

And Michael answered: "Light shines from me because I have been punished, but now God has pardoned me. And I smiled three times, because God sent me to learn three truths, and I have learnt them. One I learnt when your wife pitied me and that is why I smiled the first time. The second I learnt when the rich man ordered the boots and then I smiled again. And now, when I saw those little girls, I learnt the third and last truth, and I smiled the third time."

And Simon said, "Tell me, Michael, what did God punish you for? And what were the three truths, that I, too, may know them?"

And Michael answered: "God punished me for disobeying him. I was an angel in heaven and disobeyed God. God sent me to fetch a woman's soul. I flew to earth, and saw a sick woman lying alone, who had just given birth to twin girls. They moved feebly at their mother's side, but she could not lift them to her breast. When she saw me, she understood that God had sent me for her soul, and she wept and said: 'Angel of God! My husband has just been buried, killed by a falling tree. I have neither sister, nor aunt, nor mother: no one to care for my orphans. Do not take my soul! Let me nurse my babes, feed them, and set them on their feet before I die. Children cannot live without father or mother.' And I hearkened to her. I placed one child at her breast and gave the other into her arms, and returned to the Lord in heaven. I flew to the Lord, and said: 'I could not take the soul of the mother. Her husband was killed by a tree; the woman has twins, and prays that her soul may not be taken. She says: "Let me nurse and feed my children, and set them on their feet. Children cannot live without father or mother." I have not taken her soul.' And God said: 'Go – take the mother's soul, and learn three truths: Learn *What dwells in man*, *What is not given to man*, and *What men live by*. When thou hast learnt these things, thou shalt return to heaven.' So I flew again to earth and took the mother's soul. The babes dropped from her breasts. Her body rolled over on the bed and crushed one babe, twisting its leg. I rose above the village, wishing to take her soul to God; but a wind seized me, and my wings drooped and dropped off. Her soul rose alone to God, while I fell to earth by the roadside."

XI

And Simon and Matryóna understood who it was that had lived with them, and whom they had clothed and fed. And they wept with awe and with joy. And the angel said: "I was alone in the field, naked. I had never known human needs, cold and hunger, till I became a man. I was famished, frozen, and did not know what to do. I saw, near the field I was in, a shrine built for God, and I went to it hoping to find shelter. But the shrine was locked, and I could not enter. So I sat down behind the shrine to shelter myself at least from the wind. Evening drew on. I was hungry, frozen, and in pain. Suddenly I heard a man coming along the road. He carried a pair of boots, and was talking to himself. For the first time since I became a man I saw the mortal face of a man, and his face seemed terrible to me and I turned from it. And I heard the man talking to himself of how to cover his body from the cold in winter, and how to feed wife and children. And I thought: 'I am perishing of cold and hunger, and here is a man thinking only of how to clothe himself and his wife, and how to get bread for themselves. He cannot help me.' When the man saw me he frowned and became still more terrible, and passed me by on the other side. I despaired, but suddenly I heard him coming back. I looked up, and did not recognize the same man: before, I had seen death in his face; but now he was alive, and I recognized in him the presence of God. He came up to me, clothed me, took me with him, and brought me to his home. I entered the house; a woman came to meet us and began to speak. The woman was still more terrible than the man had been; the spirit of death came from her mouth; I could not breathe for the stench of death that spread around her. She wished to drive me out into the cold, and I knew that if she did so she would die. Suddenly her husband spoke to her of God, and the woman changed at once. And when she brought me food and looked at me, I glanced at her and saw that death no longer dwelt in her; she had become alive, and in her too I saw God.

"Then I remembered the first lesson God had set me: 'Learn what dwells in man.' And I understood that in man dwells love! I was glad that God had already begun to show me what he had promised, and I smiled for the first time. But I had not yet learnt all. I did not yet know *What is not given to man,* and *What men live by.*

"I lived with you, and a year passed. A man came to order boots that should wear for a year without losing shape or cracking. I looked at him, and suddenly, behind his shoulder, I saw my comrade – the angel of death. None but me saw that angel; but I knew him, and knew that before the sun set he would take that rich man's soul. And I thought to myself, 'The man is making preparations for a year, and does not know that he will die before evening.' And I remembered God's second saying, 'Learn what is not given to man.'

"What dwells in man I already knew. Now I learnt what is not given him. It is not given to man to know his own needs. And I smiled for the second time. I was glad to have seen my comrade angel – glad also that God had revealed to me the second saying.

"But I still did not know all. I did not know *What men live by.* And I lived on, waiting till God should reveal to me the last lesson. In the sixth year came the girl-twins with the woman; and I recognized the girls, and heard how they had been kept alive. Having heard the story, I thought, 'Their mother besought me for the children's sake, and I believed her when she said that children cannot live without father or mother; but a stranger has nursed them, and has brought them up.' And when the woman showed her love for the children that were not her own, and wept over them, I saw in her the living God, and understood *What men live by.* And I knew that God had revealed to me the last lesson, and had forgiven my sin. And then I smiled for the third time."

XII

And the angel's body was bared, and he was clothed in light so that eye could not look on him; and his voice grew louder, as though it came not from him but from heaven above. And the angel said:

"I have learnt that all people live not by care for themselves, but by love.

"It was not given to the mother to know what her children needed for their life. Nor was it given to the rich man to know what he himself needed. Nor is it given to any man to know whether, when evening comes, he will need boots for his body or slippers for his corpse.

"I remained alive when I was a man, not by care of myself, but because love was present in a passerby, and because he and his wife pitied and loved me. The orphans remained alive, not because of their mother's care, but because there was love in the heart of a woman, a stranger to them, who pitied and loved them. And all people live not by the thought they spend on their own welfare, but because love exists in man.

"I knew before that God gave life to humankind and desires that they should live; now I understood more than that.

"I understood that God does not wish people to live apart, and therefore he does not reveal to them what each one needs for himself; but he wishes them to live united, and therefore reveals to each of them what is necessary for all.

"I have now understood that though it seems to people that they live by care for themselves, in truth it is love alone by which they live. He who has love is in God, and God is in him, for God is love."

And the angel sang praise to God, so that the hut trembled at his voice. The roof opened, and a column of fire rose from earth to heaven. Simon and his wife and children fell to the ground. Wings appeared upon the angel's shoulders, and he rose into the heavens.

And when Simon came to himself the hut stood as before, and there was no one in it but his own family.

Peace and Nonviolence

Love your enemies and pray for those who persecute you, so that you may be sons of your Father who is in heaven. —Matthew 5:44–45

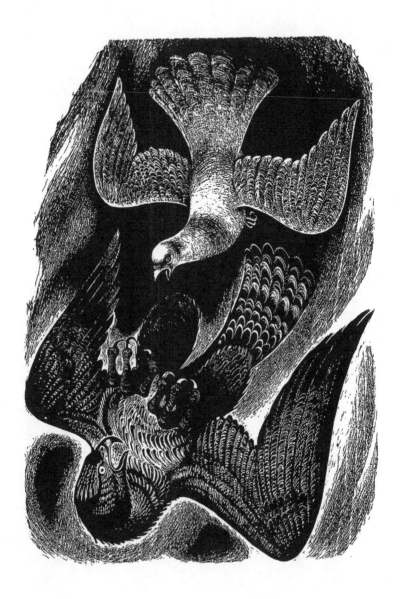

The Dove and the Hawk

9.

The Empty Drum

A Folk Tale from the Volga Region

EMELYÁN WAS A LABORER and worked for a master. Crossing the meadows one day on his way to work, he nearly trod on a frog that jumped right in front of him, but he just managed to avoid it. Suddenly he heard someone calling to him from behind.

Emelyán looked round and saw a lovely lassie, who said to him: "Why don't you get married, Emelyán?"

"How can I marry, my lass?" said he. "I have but the clothes I stand up in, nothing more, and no one would have me for a husband."

"Take me for a wife," said she.

Emelyán liked the maid. "I should be glad to," said he, "but where and how could we live?"

"Why trouble about that?" said the girl. "One only has to work more and sleep less, and one can clothe and feed oneself anywhere."

"Very well then, let us marry," said Emelyán. "Where shall we go to?"

"Let us go to town."

So Emelyán and the lass went to town, and she took him to a small hut on the very edge of the town, and they married and began housekeeping.

One day the king, driving through the town, passed by Emelyán's hut. Emelyán's wife came out to see the king. The king noticed her and was quite surprised.

"Where did such a beauty come from?" said he, and stopping his carriage he called Emelyán's wife and asked her: "Who are you?"

"The peasant Emelyán's wife," said she.

"Why did you, who are such a beauty, marry a peasant?" said the king. "You ought to be a queen!"

"Thank you for your kind words," said she, "but a peasant husband is good enough for me."

The king talked to her awhile and then drove on. He returned to the palace, but could not get Emelyán's wife out of his head. All night he did not sleep, but kept thinking how to get her for himself. He could think of no way of doing it, so he called his servants and told them they must find a way.

The king's servants said: "Command Emelyán to come to the palace to work, and we will work him so hard that he will die. His wife will be left a widow, and then you can take her for yourself."

The king followed their advice. He sent an order that Emelyán should come to the palace as a workman and that he should live at the palace, and his wife with him.

The messengers came to Emelyán and gave him the king's message. His wife said, "Go, Emelyán; work all day, but come back home at night."

So Emelyán went, and when he got to the palace the king's steward asked him, "Why have you come alone, without your wife?"

"Why should I drag her about?" said Emelyán. "She has a house to live in."

At the king's palace they gave Emelyán work enough for two. He began the job not hoping to finish it; but when evening came, lo and behold! It was all done. The steward saw that it was finished, and set him four times as much for next day.

Emelyán went home. Everything there was swept and tidy; the oven was heated, his supper was cooked and ready, and his wife sat by the table sewing and waiting for his return. She greeted him, laid the table, gave him to eat and drink, and then began to ask him about his work.

"Ah!" said he, "it's a bad business: they give me tasks beyond my strength, and want to kill me with work."

"Don't fret about the work," said she, "don't look either before or behind to see how much you have done or how much there is left to do; only keep on working and all will be right."

So Emelyán lay down and slept. Next morning he went to work again and worked without once looking round. And, lo and behold! by the evening it was all done, and before dark he came home for the night.

Again and again they increased Emelyán's work, but he always got through it in good time and went back to his hut to sleep. A week passed, and the king's servants saw they could not crush him with rough work so they tried giving him work that required skill. But this, also, was of no avail. Carpentering, and masonry, and roofing, whatever they set him to do, Emelyán had it ready in time, and went home to his wife at night. So a second week passed.

Then the king called his servants and said: "Am I to feed you for nothing? Two weeks have gone, and I don't see that you have done anything. You were going to tire Emelyán out with work, but I see from my windows how he goes home every evening – singing cheerfully! Do you mean to make a fool of me?"

The king's servants began to excuse themselves. "We tried our best to wear him out with rough work," they said, "but nothing was too hard for him; he cleared it all off as though he had swept it away with a broom. There was no tiring him out. Then we set him to tasks needing skill, which we did not think he was clever enough to do, but he managed them all. No matter what one sets him, he does it all, no one knows how. Either he or his wife must know some spell that helps them. We ourselves are sick of him, and wish to find a task he cannot master. We have now thought of setting him to build a cathedral in a single day. Send for Emelyán, and order him to build a cathedral in front of the palace in a single day. Then, if he does not do it, let his head be cut off for disobedience."

The king sent for Emelyán. "Listen to my command," said he: "build me a new cathedral on the square in front of my palace, and have it ready by tomorrow evening. If you have it ready I will reward you, but if not I will have your head cut off."

When Emelyán heard the king's command he turned away and went home. "My end is near," thought he. And coming to his wife, he said: "Get ready, wife, we must fly from here, or I shall be lost by no fault of my own."

"What has frightened you so?" said she, "and why should we run away?"

"How can I help being frightened? The king has ordered me, tomorrow, in a single day, to build him a cathedral. If I fail he will cut my head off. There is only one thing to be done: we must fly while there is yet time."

But his wife would not hear of it. "The king has many soldiers," said she. "They would catch us anywhere. We cannot escape from him, but must obey him as long as strength holds out."

"How can I obey him when the task is beyond my strength?"

"Eh, good man, don't be downhearted. Eat your supper now, and go to sleep. Rise early in the morning and all will get done." So Emelyán lay down and slept. His wife roused him early next day. "Go quickly," said she, "and finish the cathedral. Here are nails and a hammer; there is still enough work there for a day."

Emelyán went into the town, reached the palace square, and there stood a large cathedral not quite finished. Emelyán set to work to do what was needed, and by the evening all was ready.

When the king awoke he looked out from his palace and saw the cathedral, and Emelyán going about driving in nails here and there. And the king was not pleased to have the cathedral – he was annoyed at not being able to condemn Emelyán and take his wife. Again he called his servants. "Emelyán has done this task also," said the king, "and there is no excuse for putting him to death. Even this work was not too hard for him. You must find a more cunning plan, or I will cut off your heads as well as his."

So his servants planned that Emelyán should be ordered to make a river round the palace, with ships sailing on it. And the king sent for Emelyán and set him this new task.

"If," said he, "you could build a cathedral in one night, you can also do this. Tomorrow all must be ready. If not, I will have your head off."

Emelyán was more downcast than before, and returned to his wife sad at heart.

"Why are you so sad?" said his wife. "Has the king set you a fresh task?"

Emelyán told her about it. "We must fly," said he.

But his wife replied: "There is no escaping the soldiers; they will catch us wherever we go. There is nothing for it but to obey."

"How can I do it?" groaned Emelyán.

"Eh! Eh! Good man," said she, "don't be downhearted. Eat your supper now, and go to sleep. Rise early, and all will get done in good time."

So Emelyán lay down and slept. In the morning his wife woke him. "Go," said she "to the palace – all is ready. Only, near the wharf in front of the palace, there is a mound left; take a spade and level it."

When the king awoke he saw a river where there had not been one; ships were sailing up and down, and Emelyán was leveling a mound with a spade. The king wondered, but was pleased neither with the river nor with the ships, so vexed was he at not being able to condemn Emelyán. "There is no task," thought he, "that he cannot manage. What is to be done?" And he called his servants and again asked their advice.

"Find some task," said he, "which Emelyán cannot compass. For whatever we plan he fulfills, and I cannot take his wife from him."

The king's servants thought and thought, and at last devised a plan. They came to the king and said: "Send for Emelyán and say to him: 'Go to there, don't know where,' and bring back 'that, don't know what.' Then he will not be able to escape you. No matter where he goes, you can say that he has not gone to the right place, and no matter what he brings, you can say it is not the right thing. Then you can have him beheaded and can take his wife."

The king was pleased. "That is well thought of," said he. So the king sent for Emelyán and said to him: "Go to 'there, don't know where,' and bring back 'that, don't know what.' If you fail to bring it, I will have you beheaded."

Emelyán returned to his wife and told her what the king had said. His wife became thoughtful.

"Well," said she, "they have taught the king how to catch you. Now we must act warily." So she sat and thought, and at last said to her husband: "You must go far, to our grandmother – the old peasant woman, the mother of soldiers – and you must ask her aid. If she helps you to anything, go straight to the palace with it, I shall be there: I cannot escape them now. They will take me by force, but it will not be for long. If you do everything as Grandmother directs, you will soon save me."

So the wife got her husband ready for the journey. She gave him a wallet, and also a spindle. "Give her this," said she. "By this token she will know that you are my husband." And his wife showed him his road.

Emelyán set off. He left the town behind, and came to where some soldiers were being drilled. Emelyán stood and watched them. After drill the soldiers sat down to rest. Then Emelyán went up to them and asked: "Do you know, brothers, the way to 'there, don't know where?' and how I can get 'that, don't know what'?"

The soldiers listened to him with surprise. "Who sent you on this errand?" said they.

"The king," said he.

"From the day we became soldiers," said they, "we go 'don't know where,' and never yet have we got there; and we seek we 'don't know what,' and cannot find it. We cannot help you."

Emelyán sat a while with the soldiers and then went on again. He trudged many a mile, and at last came to a wood. In the wood was a hut, and in the hut sat an old, old woman, the mother of peasant soldiers, spinning flax and weeping. And as she spun she did not put her fingers to her mouth to wet them with spittle, but to her eyes to wet them with tears. When the old woman saw Emelyán she cried out at him: "Why have you come here?" Then Emelyán gave her the spindle, and said his wife had sent it.

The old woman softened at once, and began to question him. And Emelyán told her his whole life: how he married the lass; how they went to live in the town; how he had worked, and what he had done at the palace; how he built the cathedral, and made a river with ships on it, and how the king had now told him to go to "there, don't know where," and bring back "that, don't know what."

The grandmother listened to the end, and ceased weeping. She muttered to herself: "The time has surely come," and said to him: "All right, my lad. Sit down now, and I will give you something to eat."

Emelyán ate, and then the grandmother told him what to do. "Here," said she, "is a ball of thread; roll it before you, and follow where it goes. You must go far till you come right to the sea. When you get there you will see a great city. Enter the city and ask for a night's lodging at the furthest house. There look out for what you are seeking."

"How shall I know it when I see it, Granny?" said he.

"When you see something men obey more than father or mother, that is it. Seize that, and take it to the king. When you bring it to the king, he will say it is not right, and you must answer: 'If it is not the right thing it must be smashed,' and you must beat it, and carry it to the river, break it in pieces, and throw it into the water. Then you will get your wife back and my tears will be dried."

Emelyán bade farewell to the grandmother and began rolling his ball before him. It rolled and rolled until at last it reached the sea. By the sea stood a great city, and at the further end of the city was a big house. There Emelyán begged for a night's lodging, and was granted it. He lay down to sleep, and in the morning awoke and heard a father rousing his son to go and cut wood for the fire. But the son did not obey. "It is too early," said he, "there is time enough." Then Emelyán heard the mother say, "Go, my son, your father's bones ache; would you have him go himself? It is time to be up!"

But the son only murmured some words and fell asleep again. Hardly was he asleep when something thundered and rattled in the street. Up jumped the son and quickly putting on his clothes ran out into the street. Up jumped Emelyán, too, and ran after him to see what it was that a son obeys more than father or mother. What he saw was a man walking along the street carrying, tied to his stomach, a thing which he beat with sticks, and that it was that rattled and thundered so, and that the son had obeyed. Emelyán ran up and had a look at it. He saw it was round, like a small tub, with a skin stretched over both ends, and he asked what it was called.

He was told, "A drum."

"And is it empty?"

"Yes, it is empty."

Emelyán was surprised. He asked them to give the thing to him, but they would not. So Emelyán left off asking, and followed the drummer. All day he followed, and when the drummer at last lay down to sleep, Emelyán snatched the drum from him and ran away with it.

He ran and ran, till at last he got back to his own town. He went to see his wife, but she was not at home. The day after he went away, the king had taken her. So Emelyán went to the palace, and sent in a message to the king: "He has returned who went to 'there, don't know where,' and he has brought with him 'that, don't know what.'"

They told the king, and the king said he was to come again next day.

But Emelyán said, "Tell the king I am here today, and have brought what the king wanted. Let him come out to me, or I will go in to him!"

The king came out. "Where have you been?" said he.

Emelyán told him.

"That's not the right place," said the king. "What have you brought?"

Emelyán pointed to the drum, but the king did not look at it. "That is not it."

"If it is not the right thing," said Emelyán, "it must be smashed, and may the devil take it!"

And Emelyán left the palace, carrying the drum and beating it. And as he beat it all the king's army ran out to follow Emelyán, and they saluted him and waited his commands.

The king, from his window, began to shout at his army telling them not to follow Emelyán. They did not listen to what he said, but all followed Emelyán.

When the king saw that, he gave orders that Emelyán's wife should be taken back to him, and he sent to ask Emelyán to give him the drum.

"It can't be done," said Emelyán. "I was told to smash it and to throw the splinters into the river."

So Emelyán went down to the river carrying the drum, and the soldiers followed him. When he reached the river bank Emelyán smashed the drum to splinters, and threw the splinters into the stream. And then all the soldiers ran away.

Emelyán took his wife and went home with her. And after that the king ceased to trouble him; and so they lived happily ever after.

10.

Nikolai Meets the Enemy

From War and Peace

Napoleon Bonaparte, having conquered most of Europe, leads the French army into Russia in 1812. Nikolai Ilyich Rostov, a young Russian cavalryman in a hussar unit, is eager to join the fight against the invading French. He finally encounters the French dragoons (light cavalry) in the Battle of Ostrovno.

ROSTOV, WITH HIS KEEN SPORTSMAN'S EYE, was one of the first to catch sight of these blue French dragoons pursuing our uhlans [Russian cavalry]. Nearer and nearer in disorderly crowds came the uhlans and the French dragoons pursuing them. He could already see how these men, who looked so small at the foot of the hill, jostled and overtook one another, waving their arms and their sabers in the air.

Rostov gazed at what was happening before him as at a hunt. He felt instinctively that if the hussars struck at the French dragoons now, the latter could not withstand them, but if a charge was to be made it must be done now, at that very moment, or it would be too late. He looked around. A captain, standing beside him, was gazing like himself with eyes fixed on the cavalry below them.

"Andrei Sevastyanych!" said Rostov. "You know, we could crush them . . ."

"A fine thing too!" replied the captain, "and really . . ."

Rostov, without waiting to hear him out, touched his horse, galloped to the front of his squadron, and before he had time to finish giving the word of command, the whole squadron, sharing his feeling, was following him. Rostov himself did not know how or why he did it. He acted as he did when hunting, without reflecting or considering. He saw the dragoons near and that they were galloping in disorder; he knew they could not withstand an attack – knew there was only that moment and that if he let it slip it would not return. The bullets were whining and whistling so stimulatingly around him and his horse was so eager to go that he could not restrain himself. He touched his horse, gave the word of command, and immediately, hearing behind him the tramp of the horses of his deployed squadron, rode at full trot downhill toward the dragoons. Hardly had they reached the bottom of the hill before their pace instinctively changed to a gallop, which grew faster and faster as they drew nearer to our uhlans and the French dragoons who galloped after them. The dragoons were now close at hand. On seeing the hussars, the foremost began to turn, while those behind began to halt. With the same feeling with which he had galloped across the path of a wolf, Rostov gave rein to his Donets horse and galloped to intersect the path of the dragoons' disordered lines. One uhlan stopped, another who was on foot flung himself to the ground to avoid being knocked over, and a riderless horse fell in among the hussars. Nearly all the French dragoons were galloping back. Rostov, picking out one on a gray horse, dashed after him. On the way he came upon a bush, his gallant horse cleared it, and almost before he had righted himself in his saddle he saw that he would immediately overtake the enemy he had selected. That Frenchman, by his uniform an officer, was going at a gallop, crouching on his gray horse and urging it on with his saber. In another moment Rostov's horse dashed its breast against the hindquarters of the officer's horse, almost knocking it over, and at the same instant Rostov, without knowing why, raised his saber and struck the Frenchman with it.

The instant he had done this, all Rostov's animation vanished. The officer fell, not so much from the blow – which had but slightly cut his arm above the elbow – as from the shock to his horse and from fright. Rostov reined in his horse, and his eyes sought his foe to see whom he had vanquished. The French dragoon officer was hopping with one foot on the ground, the other being caught in the stirrup. His eyes, screwed up with fear as if he every moment expected another blow, gazed up at Rostov with shrinking terror. His pale and mud-stained face – fair and young, with a dimple in the chin and light blue eyes – was not an enemy's face at all suited to a battlefield, but a most ordinary, homelike face. Before Rostov had decided what to do with him, the officer cried, "I surrender!" He hurriedly but vainly tried to get his foot out of the stirrup and did not remove his frightened blue eyes from Rostov's face. Some hussars who galloped up disengaged his foot and helped him into the saddle. On all sides, the hussars were busy with the dragoons; one was wounded, but though his face was bleeding, he would not give up his horse; another was perched up behind a hussar with his arms round him; a third was being helped by a hussar to mount his horse. In front, the French infantry were firing as they ran. The hussars galloped hastily back with their prisoners. Rostov galloped back with the rest, aware of an unpleasant feeling of depression in his heart. Something vague and confused, which he could not at all account for, had come over him with the capture of that officer and the blow he had dealt him.

Count Ostermann-Tolstoy met the returning hussars, sent for Rostov, thanked him, and said he would report his gallant deed to the Emperor and would recommend him for a Saint George's Cross. When sent for by Count Ostermann, Rostov, remembering that he had charged without orders, felt sure his commander was sending for him to punish him for breach of discipline. Ostermann's flattering words and promise of a reward should therefore have struck him all the more pleasantly, but he still felt that same vaguely disagreeable feeling of moral nausea. "But what on earth is worrying me?" he asked himself as he rode back from the general. "Ilyin? No, he's safe. Have I disgraced myself in any way? No, that's not it." Something else, resembling remorse, tormented him. "Yes, oh yes, that French officer with the dimple. And I remember how my arm paused when I raised it."

Rostov saw the prisoners being led away and galloped after them to have a look at his Frenchman with the dimple on his chin. He was sitting in his foreign uniform on a hussar pack-horse and looked anxiously about him; the sword cut on his arm could scarcely be called a wound. He glanced at Rostov with a feigned smile and waved his hand in greeting. Rostov still had the same indefinite feeling, as of shame.

All that day and the next his friends and comrades noticed that Rostov, without being dull or angry, was silent, thoughtful, and preoccupied. He drank reluctantly, tried to remain alone, and kept turning something over in his mind.

Rostov was always thinking about that brilliant exploit of his, which to his amazement had gained him the Saint George's Cross and even given him a reputation for bravery, and there was something he could not at all understand. "So others are even more afraid than I am!" he thought. "So that's all there is in what is called heroism! And did I do it for my country's sake?

And how was he to blame, with his dimple and blue eyes? And how frightened he was! He thought that I should kill him. Why should I kill him? My hand trembled. And they have given me a Saint George's Cross . . . I can't make it out at all."

But while Nicholas was considering these questions and still could reach no clear solution of what puzzled him so, the wheel of fortune in the service, as often happens, turned in his favor. After the Battle of Ostrovno he was brought into notice, received command of a hussar battalion, and when a brave officer was needed he was chosen.

How to Resist Evil

From The Kingdom of God Is Within You

Tolstoy, a military veteran who had seen action as a Russian officer fighting in the Caucasus, later became an ardent advocate of nonviolent resistance. In this selection from an essay that influenced Albert Schweitzer, Mohandas Gandhi, and Martin Luther King Jr., he gives his reasons: the teaching and example of Jesus of Nazareth.

PEOPLE ARE ASTONISHED that every year there are sixty thousand cases of suicide in Europe, and those only the recognized and recorded cases – and excluding Russia and Turkey; but one ought rather to be surprised that there are so few. Every person of the present day, if we go deep enough into the contradiction between his conscience and his life, is in a state of despair.

Not to speak of all the other contradictions between modern life and the conscience, the permanently armed condition of Europe together with its profession of Christianity is alone enough to drive anyone to despair, to doubt of the sanity of humankind, and to terminate an existence in this senseless and brutal world. This contradiction, which is a quintessence of all the other contradictions, is so terrible that to live and to take part in it is only possible if one does not think of it – if one is able to forget it.

What! All of us, Christians, not only profess to love one another, but do actually live one common life; we whose social existence beats with one common pulse – we aid one another, learn from one another, draw ever closer to one another to our mutual happiness, and find in this closeness the whole meaning of life! – and tomorrow some crazy ruler will say some stupidity, and another will answer in the same spirit, and then I must go expose myself to being murdered, and murder people – who have done me no harm – and more than that, whom I love. And this is not a remote contingency, but the very thing we are all preparing for, which is not only probable, but an inevitable certainty.

To recognize this clearly is enough to drive people out of their senses or to make them shoot themselves. And this is just what does happen, and especially often in the military. People need only come to themselves for an instant to be impelled inevitably to such an end.

And this is the only explanation of the dreadful intensity with which people of modern times strive to stupefy themselves, with spirits, tobacco, opium, cards, reading newspapers, traveling, and all kinds of spectacles and amusements. These pursuits are followed up as an important, serious business. And indeed they are a serious business. If there were no external means of dulling their sensibilities, half of humankind would shoot themselves without delay, for to live in opposition to one's reason is the most intolerable condition. And that is the condition of all people of the present day. All people of the modern world exist in a state of continual and flagrant antagonism between their conscience and their way of life. This antagonism is apparent in economic as well as political life. But most striking of all is the contradiction between the Christian law of the brotherhood of all people existing in the conscience and the necessity under which all men are placed by compulsory military service of being prepared for hatred and murder – of being at the same time a Christian and a gladiator.

✦ ✦ ✦

Just as in a wicker basket all the ends are so hidden away that it is hard to find them, in the state organization the responsibility for the crimes committed is so hidden away that people will commit the most atrocious acts without seeing their responsibility for them.

In ancient times tyrants got credit for the crimes they committed, but in our day the most atrocious infamies, inconceivable under the Neros, are perpetrated and no one gets blamed for them.

One set of people have suggested, another set have proposed, a third have reported, a fourth have decided, a fifth have confirmed, a sixth have given the order, and a seventh set have carried it out. They hang, they flog to death women, old men, and innocent people, as was done recently among us in Russia at the Yuzovsky factory, and is always being done everywhere in Europe and America in the struggle with the anarchists and all other rebels against the existing order; they shoot and hang people by hundreds and thousands, or massacre millions in war, or break their hearts in solitary confinement, and ruin their souls in the corruption of a soldier's life, and no one is responsible.

At the bottom of the social scale soldiers, armed with guns, pistols, and sabers, injure and murder people, and compel people through these means to enter the army, and are absolutely convinced that the responsibility for the actions rests solely on the officers who command them.

At the top of the scale – the tsars, presidents, ministers, and parliaments decree these tortures and murders and military conscription, and are fully convinced that since they are either placed in authority by the grace of God or by the society they govern, which demands such decrees from them, they cannot be held responsible.

Between these two extremes are the intermediary personages who superintend the murders and other acts of violence, and are fully convinced that the responsibility is taken off their shoulders partly by their superiors who have given the order, partly by the fact that such orders are expected from them by all who are at the bottom of the scale.

The authority who gives the orders and the authority who executes them at the two extreme ends of the state organization, meet together like the two ends of a ring; they support and rest on one another and enclose all that lies within the ring.

Without the conviction that there is a person or persons who will take the whole responsibility of his acts, not one soldier would ever lift a hand to commit a murder or other deed of violence. Without the conviction that it is expected by the whole people, not a single king, emperor, president, or parliament would order murders or acts of violence. Without the conviction that there are persons of a higher grade who will take the responsibility, and people of a lower grade who require such acts for their welfare, not one of the intermediate class would superintend such deeds.

✦ ✦ ✦

Christianity is at once a doctrine of truth and a prophecy. Eighteen centuries ago Christianity revealed to people the truth in which they ought to live, and at the same time foretold what human life would become if they would not live by it but continued to live by their previous principles, and what it would become if they accepted the Christian doctrine and carried it out in their lives.

Laying down in the Sermon on the Mount the principles by which to guide people's lives, Christ said:

> Everyone then who hears these words of mine and does them will be like a wise man who built his house upon the rock; and the rain fell, and the floods came, and the winds blew and beat upon that house, but it did not fall, because it had been founded on the rock. And everyone who hears these words of mine and does not do them will be like a foolish man who built his house upon the sand; and the rain fell, and the floods came, and the winds blew and beat against that house, and it fell; and great was the fall of it. (Matt. 7:24–27)

And now after eighteen centuries the prophecy has been fulfilled. Not having followed Christ's teaching generally and its application to social life in nonresistance to evil, we have been brought in spite of ourselves to the inevitable destruction foretold by Christ for those who do not fulfill his teaching.

People often think the question of nonresistance to evil by force is a theoretical one, which can be neglected. Yet this question is presented by life itself to all people, and calls for some answer from every thinking person. Ever since Christianity has been outwardly professed, this question is for people in their social life like the question which presents itself to a traveler when the road on which he has been journeying divides into two branches. He must go on and he cannot say: I will not think about it, but will go on just as I did before. There was one road, now there are two, and he must make his choice.

In the same way, since Christ's teaching has been known by people they cannot say: I will live as before and will not decide the question of resistance or nonresistance to evil by force. At every new struggle that arises one must inevitably decide; am I, or am I not, to resist by force what I regard as evil.

12

What Pierre Learned from Platon the Peasant

From War and Peace

Following the Battle of Borodino in September 1812, the French army under Napoleon seizes control of Moscow. The young Russian officer Pierre (also known as Pyotr Kirillovich Bezukhov), a wealthy aristocrat married to an unfaithful wife, is taken prisoner by the French. He witnesses the execution of a group of Russian prisoners of war, allegedly for starting the fires that burned down much of Moscow.

PIERRE WAS NO LONGER ABLE to turn away and close his eyes. His curiosity and agitation, like that of the whole crowd, reached the highest pitch at this fifth murder. . . .

Probably a word of command was given and was followed by the reports of eight muskets; but try as he would Pierre could not afterwards remember having heard the slightest sound of the shots. He only saw how the workman suddenly sank down on the cords that held him, how blood showed itself in two places, how the ropes slackened under the weight of the hanging body, and how the workman sat down, his head hanging unnaturally and one leg bent under him. Pierre ran up to the post. No one hindered him. Pale, frightened people were doing something around the workman. The lower jaw of an old Frenchman with a thick mustache trembled as he untied the ropes. The body collapsed. The soldiers dragged it awkwardly from the post and began pushing it into the pit.

They all plainly and certainly knew that they were criminals who must hide the traces of their guilt as quickly as possible.

Pierre glanced into the pit and saw that the factory lad was lying with his knees close up to his head and one shoulder higher than the other. That shoulder rose and fell rhythmically and convulsively, but spadefuls of earth were already being thrown over the whole body. One of the soldiers, evidently suffering, shouted gruffly and angrily at Pierre to go back. But Pierre did not understand him and remained near the post, and no one drove him away.

When the pit had been filled up a command was given. Pierre was taken back to his place, and the rows of troops on both sides of the post made a half turn and went past it at a measured pace. The twenty-four sharpshooters with discharged muskets, standing in the center of the circle, ran back to their places as the companies passed by.

Pierre gazed now with dazed eyes at these sharpshooters who ran in couples out of the circle. All but one rejoined their companies. This one, a young soldier, his face deadly pale, his shako pushed back, and his musket resting on the ground, still stood near the pit at the spot from which he had fired. He swayed like a drunken man, taking some steps forward and back to save himself from falling. An old, noncommissioned officer ran out of the ranks and taking him by the elbow dragged him to his company. The crowd of Russians and Frenchmen began to disperse. They all went away silently and with drooping heads.

"That will teach them to start fires," said one of the Frenchmen.

Pierre glanced round at the speaker and saw that it was a soldier who was trying to find some relief after what had been done, but was not able to do so. Without finishing what he had begun to say he made a hopeless movement with his arm and went away.

✦ ✦ ✦

After the execution Pierre was separated from the rest of the prisoners and placed alone in a small, ruined, and befouled church.

Toward evening a noncommissioned officer entered with two soldiers and told him that he had been pardoned and would now go to the barracks for the prisoners of war. Without understanding what was said to him, Pierre got up and went with the soldiers. They took him to the upper end of the field, where there were some sheds built of charred planks, beams, and battens, and led him into one of them. In the darkness some twenty different men surrounded Pierre. He looked at them without understanding who they were, why they were there, or what they wanted of him. He heard what they said, but did not understand the meaning of the words and made no kind of deduction from or application of them. He replied to questions they put to him, but did not consider who was listening to his replies, nor how they would understand them. He looked at their faces and figures, but they all seemed to him equally meaningless.

From the moment Pierre had witnessed those terrible murders committed by men who did not wish to commit them, it was as if the mainspring of his life, on which everything depended and which made everything appear alive, had suddenly been wrenched out and everything had collapsed into a heap of meaningless rubbish. Though he did not acknowledge it to himself, his faith in the right ordering of the universe, in humanity, in his own soul, and in God, had been destroyed. He had experienced this before, but never so strongly as now. When similar doubts had assailed him before, they had been the result of his own wrongdoing, and at the bottom of his heart he had felt that relief from his despair and from those doubts was to be found within himself. But now he felt that the universe had crumbled before his eyes and only meaningless ruins remained, and this not by any fault of his own. He felt that it was not in his power to regain faith in the meaning of life.

Around him in the darkness men were standing and evidently something about him interested them greatly. They were telling him something and asking him something. Then they led him away somewhere, and at last he found himself in a corner of the shed among men who were laughing and talking on all sides.

"Well, then, my brothers . . . that very prince who . . ." some voice at the other end of the shed was saying, with a strong emphasis on the word who.

Sitting silent and motionless on a heap of straw against the wall, Pierre sometimes opened and sometimes closed his eyes. But as soon as he closed them he saw before him the dreadful face of the factory lad – especially dreadful because of its simplicity – and the faces of the murderers, even more dreadful because of their disquiet. And he opened his eyes again and stared vacantly into the darkness around him. Beside him in a stooping position sat a small man of whose presence he was first made aware by a strong smell of perspiration which came from him every time he moved. This man was doing something to his legs in the darkness, and though Pierre could not see his face he felt that the man continually glanced at him. On growing used to the darkness Pierre saw that the man was taking off his leg bands, and the way he did it aroused Pierre's interest.

Having unwound the string that tied the band on one leg, he carefully coiled it up and immediately set to work on the other leg, glancing up at Pierre. While one hand hung up the first string the other was already unwinding the band on the second leg. In this way, having carefully removed the leg bands by deft circular motions of his arms following one another uninterruptedly, the man hung the leg bands up on some pegs fixed above his head. Then he took out a knife, cut something, closed the knife, placed it under the head of his bed, and, seating himself comfortably, clasped his arms round his lifted knees and fixed his eyes on Pierre. The latter was conscious of something pleasant, comforting, and well-rounded in these deft movements, in the man's well-ordered arrangements in his corner, and even in his very smell, and he looked at the man without taking his eyes from him.

"You've seen a lot of trouble, sir, eh?" the little man suddenly said.

And there was so much kindliness and simplicity in his singsong voice that Pierre tried to reply, but his jaw trembled and he felt tears rising to his eyes. The little fellow, giving Pierre no time to betray his confusion, instantly continued in the same pleasant tones:

"Eh, little falcon, don't grieve!" said he, in the tender singsong caressing voice old Russian peasant women employ. "Don't grieve, dear little friend – 'suffer an hour, live for an age!' that's how it is, my dear fellow. And here we live, thank heaven, without offense. Among these folk, too, there are good men as well as bad," said he, and still speaking, he turned on his knees with a supple movement, got up, coughed, and went off to another part of the shed.

"Eh, you rascal!" Pierre heard the same kind voice saying at the other end of the shed. "So you've come, you rascal? She remembers . . . Now, now, that'll do!"

And the soldier, pushing away a little dog that was jumping up at him, returned to his place and sat down. In his hands he had something wrapped in a rag.

"Here, eat a bit, master," said he, resuming his former respectful tone as he unwrapped and offered Pierre some baked potatoes. "We had soup for dinner and the potatoes are the grandest!"

Pierre had not eaten all day and the smell of the potatoes seemed extremely pleasant to him. He thanked the soldier and began to eat.

"Well, are they all right?" said the soldier with a smile. "You should do like this."

He took a potato, drew out his clasp knife, cut the potato into two equal halves on the palm of his hand, sprinkled some salt on it from the rag, and handed it to Pierre.

"The potatoes are the grandest!" he said once more. "Eat some like that!"

Pierre thought he had never eaten anything that tasted better.

"Oh, I'm all right," said he, "but why did they shoot those poor fellows? The last one was hardly twenty."

"Tss, tt . . !" said the little man. "Ah, what a sin . . . what a sin!" he added quickly, and as if his words were always waiting ready in his mouth and flew out involuntarily he went on: "How was it, master, that you stayed in Moscow?"

"I didn't think they would come so soon. I stayed accidentally," replied Pierre.

"And how did they arrest you, little falcon? At your house?"

"No, I went to look at the fire, and they arrested me there, and tried me as an incendiary."

"Where there's law there's injustice," put in the little man.

"And have you been here long?" Pierre asked as he munched the last of the potato.

"Me? It was last Sunday they took me, out of a hospital in Moscow."

"Why, are you a soldier then?"

"Yes, we are soldiers of the Apsheron regiment. I was dying of fever. We weren't told anything. There were some twenty of us lying there. We had no idea, never guessed at all."

"And do you feel sad here?" Pierre inquired.

"How can you help it, little falcon? My name is Platon, and the surname is Karataev," he added, evidently wishing to make it easier for Pierre to address him. "They call me 'little falcon' in the regiment. How can one help feeling sad, little falcon? Moscow – she's the mother of cities. How can you not feel sad with what you've seen? But 'the maggot gnaws the cabbage, yet dies first'; that's what the old folks used to tell us," he added rapidly.

"What? What did you say?" asked Pierre.

"Who? Me?" said Karataev. "I say things happen not as we plan but as God judges," he replied, thinking that he was repeating what he had said before, and immediately continued:

"Well, and you, have you a family estate, sir? And a house? So you have abundance, then? And a wife? And your old parents, are they still living?" he asked.

And though it was too dark for Pierre to see, he felt that a suppressed smile of kindliness puckered the soldier's lips as he put these questions. He seemed grieved that Pierre had no parents, especially that he had no mother.

"A wife for counsel, a mother-in-law for welcome, but there's none as dear as one's own mother!" said he. "Well, and do you have little ones?" he went on asking.

Again Pierre's negative answer seemed to distress him, and he hastened to add:

"Never mind! You're young folks yet, and God may yet grant, there will be some. Only be sure to live in harmony . . ."

"But it's all the same now," Pierre could not help saying.

"Ah, my dear fellow!" rejoined Karataev, "Never decline a prison or a beggar's sack!"

He seated himself more comfortably and coughed, evidently preparing to tell a long story.

"Well, my kind friend, I was still living at home," he began. "We had a well-to-do homestead, plenty of land, we peasants lived well and our house was one to thank God for. When father and we went out mowing there were seven of us. We lived well. We were real peasants. It so happened . . ."

And Platon Karataev told a long story of how he had gone into someone's copse to take wood, how he had been caught by the keeper, had been tried, flogged, and sent to serve as a soldier.

"Well, little falcon," and a smile changed the tone of his voice, "we thought it was a misfortune but it turned out a blessing! If it had not been for my sin, my brother would have had to go as a soldier. But he, my younger brother, had five little ones, while I, you see, only left a wife behind. We had a little girl, but God took her before I went as a soldier. I come home on leave and I'll tell you how it was, I look and see that they are living better than before. The yard full of cattle, the women at home, two brothers away earning wages, and only Michael, the youngest, at home. Father, he says, 'All my children are the same to me: it hurts the same whichever finger gets bitten. But if Platon hadn't been shaved for a soldier, Michael would have had to go.' He called us all to him and, will you believe it, placed us in front of the icons. 'Michael,' he says, 'come here and bow down to his feet;

and you, young woman, you bow down too; and you, grandchildren, also bow down before him! Do you understand?' he says. That's how it is, dear fellow. Fate looks for a head. But we are always judging, 'that's not well – that's not right!' Our luck is like water in a dragnet: you pull at it and it bulges, but when you've drawn it out it's empty! That's how it is."

And Platon shifted his seat on the straw.

After a short silence he rose.

"Well, I think you must be sleepy," said he, and began rapidly crossing himself and repeating:

"Lord Jesus Christ, holy Saint Nicholas, Frola and Lavra! Lord Jesus Christ, holy Saint Nicholas, Frola and Lavra! Lord Jesus Christ, have mercy on us and save us!" he concluded, then bowed to the ground, got up, sighed, and sat down again on his heap of straw. "That's the way. Lay me down like a stone, O God, and raise me up like a loaf," he muttered as he lay down, pulling his coat over him.

"What prayer was that you were saying?" asked Pierre.

"Eh?" murmured Platon, who had almost fallen asleep. "What was I saying? I was praying. Don't you pray?"

"Yes, I do," said Pierre. "But what was that you said: Frola and Lavra?"

"Well, of course," replied Platon quickly, "the horses' saints. One must pity the animals too. Eh, the rascal! Now you've curled up and got warm, you daughter of a bitch!" said Karataev, touching the dog that lay at his feet, and again turning over he fell asleep immediately.

Sounds of crying and screaming came from somewhere in the distance outside, and flames were visible through the cracks of the shed, but inside it was quiet and dark. For a long time Pierre did not sleep, but lay with eyes open in the darkness, listening to the regular snoring of Platon who lay beside him, and he felt that the world that had been shattered was once more stirring in his soul with a new beauty and on new and unshakable foundations.

Forgiveness

Forgive, and you will be forgiven. . . . For the
measure you give will be the measure you get back.

—*Luke 6:37–38*

Katusha on trial (detail), illustration for Resurrection. *See page 169.*

13.

God Sees the Truth, but Waits

A Story

IN THE TOWN OF VLADIMIR lived a young merchant named Ivan Dmitrich Aksyónof. He had two shops and a house of his own.

Aksyónof was a handsome, fair-haired, curly-headed fellow, full of fun, and very fond of singing. When quite a young man he had been given to drink, and was riotous when he had had too much, but after he married he gave up drinking, except now and then.

One summer Aksyónof was going to the Nizhny Fair, and as he bade goodbye to his family his wife said to him, "Ivan Dmitrich, do not start today; I have had a bad dream about you."

Aksyónof laughed, and said, "You are afraid that when I get to the fair I shall go on the spree."

His wife replied: "I do not know what I am afraid of; all I know is that I had a bad dream. I dreamt you returned from the town, and when you took off your cap I saw that your hair was quite grey."

Aksyónof laughed. "That's a lucky sign," said he. "See if I don't sell out all my goods, and bring you some presents from the fair."

So he said goodbye to his family, and drove away.

When he had traveled halfway, he met a merchant whom he knew, and they put up at the same inn for the night. They had some tea together, and then went to bed in adjoining rooms.

It was not Aksyónof's habit to sleep late, and, wishing to travel while it was still cool, he aroused his driver before dawn, and told him to put in the horses.

Then he made his way across to the landlord of the inn (who lived in a cottage at the back), paid his bill, and continued his journey.

When he had gone about twenty-five miles, he stopped for the horses to be fed. Aksyónof rested awhile in the passage of the inn, then he stepped out into the porch and, ordering a samovar to be heated, got out his guitar and began to play.

Suddenly a troika drove up with tinkling bells, and an official alighted, followed by two soldiers. He came to Aksyónof and began to question him, asking him who he was and whence he came. Aksyónof answered him fully, and said, "Won't you have some tea with me?" But the official went on cross-questioning him and asking him, "Where did you spend last night? Were you alone, or with a fellow merchant? Did you see the other merchant this morning? Why did you leave the inn before dawn?"

Aksyónof wondered why he was asked all these questions, but he described all that had happened, and then added, "Why do you cross-question me as if I were a thief or a robber? I am travelling on business of my own, and there is no need to question me."

Then the official, calling the soldiers, said, "I am the police officer of this district, and I question you because the merchant with whom you spent last night has been found with his throat cut. We must search your things."

They entered the house. The soldiers and the police officer unstrapped Aksyónof's luggage and searched it. Suddenly the officer drew a knife out of a bag, crying, "Whose knife is this?" Aksyónof looked, and seeing a bloodstained knife taken from his bag, he was frightened.

"How is it there is blood on this knife?"

Aksyónof tried to answer, but could hardly utter a word, and only stammered: "I – I don't know – not mine."

Then the police officer said, "This morning the merchant was found in bed with his throat cut. You are the only person who could have done it. The house was locked from inside, and no one else was there. Here is this bloodstained knife in your bag, and your face and manner betray you! Tell me how you killed him, and how much money you stole?"

Aksyónof swore he had not done it; that he had not seen the merchant after they had had tea together; that he had no money except eight thousand rubles of his own, and that the knife was not his. But his voice was broken, his face pale, and he trembled with fear as though he were guilty.

The police officer ordered the soldiers to bind Aksyónof and to put him in the cart. As they tied his feet together and flung him into the cart, Aksyónof crossed himself and wept. His money and goods were taken from him, and he was sent to the nearest town and imprisoned there. Enquiries as to his character were made in Vladimir. The merchants and other inhabitants of that town said that in former days he used to drink and waste his time, but that he was a good man. Then the trial came on: he was charged with murdering a merchant from Ryazan, and robbing him of twenty thousand rubles.

His wife was in despair, and did not know what to believe. Her children were all quite small; one was a baby at her breast.

Taking them all with her, she went to the town where her husband was in jail. At first she was not allowed to see him; but, after much begging, she obtained permission from the officials, and was taken to him. When she saw her husband in prison dress and in chains, shut up with thieves and criminals, she fell down, and did not come to her senses for a long time. Then she drew her children to her, and sat down near him. She told him of things at home, and asked about what had happened to him. He told her all, and she asked, "What can we do now?"

"We must petition the tsar not to let an innocent man perish."

His wife told him that she had sent a petition to the tsar, but that it had not been accepted.

Aksyónof did not reply, but only looked downcast.

Then his wife said, "It was not for nothing I dreamt your hair had turned grey. You remember? You should not have started that day." And passing her fingers through his hair, she said: "Vanya dearest, tell your wife the truth; was it not you who did it?"

"So you, too, suspect me!" said Aksyónof, and hiding his face in his hands, he began to weep. Then a soldier came to say that the wife and children must go away; and Aksyónof said goodbye to his family for the last time.

When they were gone, Aksyónof recalled what had been said, and when he remembered that his wife also had suspected him, he said to himself, "It seems that only God can know the truth, it is to him alone we must appeal, and from him alone expect mercy."

And Aksyónof wrote no more petitions, gave up all hope, and only prayed to God.

Aksyónof was condemned to be flogged and sent to the mines. So he was flogged with a knout, and when the wounds made by the knout were healed, he was driven to Siberia with other convicts.

For twenty-six years Aksyónof lived as a convict in Siberia. His hair turned white as snow and his beard grew long, thin, and grey. All his mirth went; he stooped; he walked slowly, spoke little, and never laughed, but he often prayed.

In prison Aksyónof learnt to make boots, and earned a little money, with which he bought *The Lives of the Saints*. He read this book when there was light enough in the prison; and on Sundays in the prison church he read the lessons and sang in the choir, for his voice was still good.

The prison authorities liked Aksyónof for his meekness, and his fellow prisoners respected him: they called him "Grandfather," and "The Saint." When they wanted to petition the prison authorities about anything, they always made Aksyónof their spokesman, and when there were quarrels among the prisoners they came to him to put things right and to judge the matter.

No news reached Aksyónof from his home, and he did not even know if his wife and children were still alive.

One day a fresh gang of convicts came to the prison. In the evening the old prisoners collected round the new ones and asked them what towns or villages they came from, and what they were sentenced for. Among the rest Aksyónof sat down near the newcomers, and listened with downcast air to what was said.

One of the new convicts, a tall, strong man of sixty, with a closely cropped grey beard, was telling the others what he had been arrested for.

"Well, friends," he said, "I only took a horse that was tied to a sledge, and I was arrested and accused of stealing. I said I had only taken it to get home quicker, and had then let it go; besides, the driver was a personal friend of mine. So I said, 'It's all right.' 'No,' said they, 'you stole it.' But how or where I stole it they could not say. I once really did something wrong, and ought by rights to have come here long ago, but that time I was not found out. Now I have been sent here for nothing at all . . . Eh, but it's lies I'm telling you; I've been to Siberia before, but I did not stay long."

"Where are you from?" asked someone.

"From Vladimir. My family are of that town. My name is Makár, and they also call me Semyónich."

Aksyónof raised his head and said: "Tell me, Semyónich, do you know anything of the merchants Aksyónof, of Vladimir? Are they still alive?"

"Know them? Of course I do. The Aksyónofs are rich, though their father is in Siberia: a sinner like ourselves, it seems! As for you, Gran'dad, how did you come here?"

Aksyónof did not like to speak of his misfortune. He only sighed, and said, "For my sins I have been in prison these twenty-six years."

"What sins?" asked Makár Semyónich.

But Aksyónof only said, "Well, well – I must have deserved it!" He would have said no more, but his companions told the newcomer how Aksyónof came to be in Siberia: how someone had killed a merchant and had put a knife among Aksyónof's things, and Aksyónof had been unjustly condemned.

When Makár Semyónich heard this, he looked at Aksyónof, slapped his own knee, and exclaimed, "Well this is wonderful! Really wonderful! But how old you've grown, Gran'dad!"

The others asked him why he was so surprised, and where he had seen Aksyónof before; but Makár Semyónich did not reply. He only said: "It's wonderful that we should meet here, lads!"

These words made Aksyónof wonder whether this man knew who had killed the merchant; so he said, "Perhaps, Semyónich, you have heard of that affair or maybe you've seen me before?"

"How could I help hearing? The world's full of rumors. But it's long ago, and I've forgotten what I heard."

"Perhaps you heard who killed the merchant?" asked Aksyónof.

Makár Semyónich laughed, and replied, "It must have been him in whose bag the knife was found! If someone else hid the knife there, 'He's not a thief till he's caught,' as the saying is. How could anyone put a knife into your bag while it was under your head? It would surely have woken you up?"

When Aksyónof heard these words, he felt sure this was the man who had killed the merchant. He rose and went away. All that night Aksyónof lay awake. He felt terribly unhappy, and all sorts of images rose in his mind. There was the image of his wife as she was when he parted from her to go to the fair. He saw her as if she were present; her face and her eyes rose before him; he heard her speak and laugh. Then he saw his children, quite little, as they were at that time: one with a little cloak on, another at his mother's breast. And then he remembered himself as he used to be – young and merry. He remembered how he sat playing the guitar in the porch of the inn where he was arrested, and how free from care he had been. He saw, in his mind, the place where he was flogged, the executioner, and the people standing around; the chains, the convicts, all the twenty-six years of his prison life, and his premature old age. The thought of it all made him so wretched that he was ready to kill himself.

"And it's all that villain's doing!" thought Aksyónof. And his anger was so great against Makár Semyónich that he longed for vengeance, even if he himself should perish for it. He kept repeating prayers all night, but could get no peace. During the day he did not go near Makár Semyónich, nor even look at him.

A fortnight passed in this way. Aksyónof could not sleep at nights, and was so miserable that he did not know what to do.

One night as he was walking about the prison he noticed some earth that came rolling out from under one of the shelves on which the prisoners slept. He stopped to see what it was. Suddenly Makár Semyónich crept out from under the shelf, and looked up at Aksyónof with frightened face. Aksyónof tried to pass without looking at him, but Makár seized his hand and told him that he had dug a hole under the wall, getting rid of the earth by putting it into his high-boots, and emptying it out every day on the road when the prisoners were driven to their work.

"Just you keep quiet, old man, and you shall get out too. If you blab they'll flog the life out of me, but I will kill you first."

Aksyónof trembled with anger as he looked at his enemy. He drew his hand away, saying, "I have no wish to escape, and you have no need to kill me; you killed me long ago! As to telling of you – I may do so or not, as God shall direct."

Next day, when the convicts were led out to work, the convoy soldiers noticed that one or other of the prisoners emptied some earth out of his boots. The prison was searched, and the tunnel found. The governor came and questioned all the prisoners to find out who had dug the hole. They all denied any knowledge of it. Those who knew would not betray Makár Semyónich, knowing he would be flogged almost to death. At last the governor turned to Aksyónof, whom he knew to be a just man, and said:

"You are a truthful old man; tell me, before God, who dug the hole?"

Makár Semyónich stood as if he were quite unconcerned, looking at the governor and not so much as glancing at Aksyónof. Aksyónof's lips and hands trembled, and for a long time he could not utter a word. He thought, "Why should I screen him who ruined my life? Let him pay for what I have suffered. But if I tell, they will probably flog the life out of him and maybe I suspect him wrongly. And, after all, what good would it be to me?"

"Well, old man," repeated the governor, "tell us the truth: who has been digging under the wall?"

Aksyónof glanced at Makár Semyónich, and said "I cannot say, your honor. It is not God's will that I should tell! Do what you like with me; I am in your hands."

However much the governor tried, Aksyónof would say no more, and so the matter had to be left.

That night, when Aksyónof was lying on his bed and just beginning to doze, someone came quietly and sat down on his bed. He peered through the darkness and recognized Makár.

"What more do you want of me?" asked Aksyónof. "Why have you come here?"

Makár Semyónich was silent. So Aksyónof sat up and said, "What do you want? Go away, or I will call the guard!"

Makár Semyónich bent close over Aksyónof, and whispered, "Ivan Dmitrich, forgive me!"

"What for?" asked Aksyónof.

"It was I who killed the merchant and hid the knife among your things. I meant to kill you too, but I heard a noise outside; so I hid the knife in your bag and escaped out of the window."

Aksyónof was silent, and did not know what to say. Makár Semyónich slid off the bed-shelf and knelt upon the ground. "Ivan Dmitrich," said he, "forgive me! For the love of God, forgive me! I will confess that it was I who killed the merchant, and you will be released and can go to your home."

"It is easy for you to talk," said Aksyónof, "but I have suffered for you these twenty-six years. Where could I go to now? . . . My wife is dead, and my children have forgotten me. I have nowhere to go . . ."

Makár Semyónich did not rise, but beat his head on the floor. "Ivan Dmitrich, forgive me!" he cried. "When they flogged me with the knout it was not so hard to bear as it is to see you now . . . yet you had pity on me, and did not tell. For Christ's sake forgive me, wretch that I am!" And he began to sob.

When Aksyónof heard him sobbing he, too, began to weep.

"God will forgive you!" said he. "Maybe I am a hundred times worse than you." And at these words his heart grew light, and the longing for home left him. He no longer had any desire to leave the prison, but only hoped for his last hour to come.

In spite of what Aksyónof had said, Makár Semyónich confessed his guilt. But when the order for his release came, Aksyónof was already dead.

14.

A Spark Neglected Burns the House

A Story

Then Peter came up and said to him, "Lord, how often shall my brother sin against me, and I forgive him? As many as seven times?" Jesus said to him, "I do not say to you seven times, but seventy times seven.

"Therefore the kingdom of heaven may be compared to a king who wished to settle accounts with his servants. When he began the reckoning, one was brought to him who owed him ten thousand talents; and as he could not pay, his lord ordered him to be sold, with his wife and children and all that he had, and payment to be made. So the servant fell on his knees, imploring him, 'Lord, have patience with me, and I will pay you everything.' And out of pity for him the lord of that servant released him and forgave him the debt. But that same servant, as he went out, came upon one of his fellow servants who owed him a hundred denarii; and seizing him by the throat he said, 'Pay what you owe.' So his fellow servant fell down and besought him, 'Have patience with me, and I will pay you.' He refused and went and put him in prison till he should pay the debt. When his fellow servants saw what had taken place, they were greatly distressed, and they went and reported to their lord all that had taken place. Then his lord summoned him and said to him, 'You wicked servant! I forgave you all that debt

*because you besought me; and should not you have had mercy
on your fellow servant, as I had mercy on you?' And in anger his
lord delivered him to the jailers, till he should pay all his debt. So
also my heavenly Father will do to every one of you, if you do not
forgive your brother from your heart."* —Matthew 18:21–35

THERE ONCE LIVED IN A VILLAGE a peasant named Ivan
Stcherbakóf. He was comfortably off, in the prime of life, the
best worker in the village, and had three sons all able to work.
The eldest was married, the second about to marry, and the third
was a big lad who could mind the horses and was already beginning to plow. Ivan's wife was an able and thrifty woman, and they
were fortunate in having a quiet, hardworking daughter-in-law.
There was nothing to prevent Ivan and his family from living
happily. They had only one idle mouth to feed; that was Ivan's
old father, who suffered from asthma and had been lying ill on
the top of the brick oven for seven years. Ivan had all he needed:
three horses and a colt, a cow with a calf, and fifteen sheep. The
women made all the clothing for the family, besides helping in
the fields, and the men tilled the land. They always had grain
enough of their own to last over beyond the next harvest and
sold enough oats to pay the taxes and meet their other needs. So
Ivan and his children might have lived quite comfortably had
it not been for a feud between him and his next-door neighbor,
Limping Gabriel, the son of Gordéy Ivanof.

As long as old Gordéy was alive and Ivan's father was still
able to manage the household, the peasants lived as neighbors
should. If the women of either house happened to want a sieve
or a tub, or the men required a sack, or if a cartwheel got broken
and could not be mended at once, they used to send to the other
house, and helped each other in neighborly fashion. When a calf

strayed into the neighbor's thrashing ground they would just drive it out, and only say, "Don't let it get in again; our grain is lying there." And such things as locking up the barns and outhouses, hiding things from one another, or backbiting were never thought of in those days.

That was in the fathers' time. When the sons came to be at the head of the families, everything changed.

It all began about a trifle.

Ivan's daughter-in-law had a hen that began laying rather early in the season, and she started collecting its eggs for Easter. Every day she went to the cart shed, and found an egg in the cart; but one day the hen, probably frightened by the children, flew across the fence into the neighbor's yard and laid its egg there. The woman heard the cackling, but said to herself: "I have no time now; I must tidy up for Sunday. I'll fetch the egg later on." In the evening she went to the cart, but found no egg there. She went and asked her mother-in-law and brother-in-law whether they had taken the egg. "No," they had not; but her youngest brother-in-law, Tarás, said: "Your Biddy laid its egg in the neighbor's yard. It was there she was cackling, and she flew back across the fence from there."

The woman went and looked at the hen. There she was on the perch with the other birds, her eyes just closing ready to go to sleep. The woman wished she could have asked the hen and got an answer from her.

Then she went to the neighbor's, and Gabriel's mother came out to meet her.

"What do you want, young woman?"

"Why, Granny, you see, my hen flew across this morning. Did she not lay an egg here?"

"We never saw anything of it. The Lord be thanked, our own hens started laying long ago. We collect our own eggs and have no need of other people's! And we don't go looking for eggs in other people's yards, lass!"

The young woman was offended, and said more than she should have done. Her neighbor answered back with interest, and the women began abusing each other. Ivan's wife, who had been to fetch water, happening to pass just then, joined in too. Gabriel's wife rushed out, and began reproaching the young woman with things that had really happened and with other things that never had happened at all. Then a general uproar commenced, all shouting at once, trying to get out two words at a time, and not choice words either.

"You're this!" and "You're that!" "You're a thief!" and "You're a slut!" and "You're starving your old father-in-law to death!" and "You're a good-for-nothing!" and so on.

"And you've made a hole in the sieve I lent you, you jade! And it's our yoke you're carrying your pails on – you just give back our yoke!"

Then they caught hold of the yoke, and spilt the water, snatched off one another's shawls, and began fighting. Gabriel, returning from the fields, stopped to take his wife's part. Out rushed Ivan and his son and joined in with the rest. Ivan was a strong fellow, he scattered the whole lot of them, and pulled a handful of hair out of Gabriel's beard. People came to see what was the matter, and the fighters were separated with difficulty.

That was how it all began.

Gabriel wrapped the hair torn from his beard in a paper, and went to the district court to have the law on Ivan. "I didn't grow my beard," said he, "for pockmarked Ivan to pull it out!" And his wife went bragging to the neighbors, saying they'd have Ivan condemned and sent to Siberia. And so the feud grew.

The old man, from where he lay on the top of the oven, tried from the very first to persuade them to make peace, but they would not listen. He told them, "It's a stupid thing you are after, children, picking quarrels about such a paltry matter. Just think! The whole thing began about an egg. The children may have taken it – well, what matter? What's the value of one egg? God sends enough for all! And suppose your neighbor did say an unkind word – put it right; show her how to say a better one! If there has been a fight – well, such things will happen; we're all sinners, but make it up, and let there be an end of it! If you nurse your anger it will be worse for you yourselves."

But the younger folk would not listen to the old man. They thought his words were mere senseless dotage. Ivan would not humble himself before his neighbor.

"I never pulled his beard," he said. "He pulled the hair out himself. But his son has burst all the fastenings on my shirt, and torn it. . . . Look at it!"

And Ivan also went to law. They were tried by the justice of the peace and by the district court. While all this was going on, the coupling pin of Gabriel's cart disappeared. Gabriel's womenfolk accused Ivan's son of having taken it. They said: "We saw him in the night go past our window, towards the cart; and a neighbor says he saw him at the pub, offering the pin to the landlord."

So they went to law about that. And at home not a day passed without a quarrel or even a fight. The children, too, abused one another, having learnt to do so from their elders; and when the women happened to meet by the riverside, where they went to rinse the clothes, their arms did not do as much wringing as their tongues did nagging, and every word was a bad one.

At first the peasants only slandered one another; but afterwards they began in real earnest to snatch anything that lay handy, and the children followed their example. Life became harder and harder for them. Ivan Stcherbakóf and Limping Gabriel kept suing one another at the Village Assembly, and at the district court, and before the justice of the peace until all the judges were tired of them. Now Gabriel got Ivan fined or imprisoned; then Ivan did as much to Gabriel; and the more they spited each other the angrier they grew–like dogs that attack one another and get more and more furious the longer they fight. You strike one dog from behind, and it thinks it's the other dog biting him, and gets still fiercer. So these peasants: they went to law, and one or other of them was fined or locked up, but that only made them more and more angry with each other. "Wait a bit," they said, "and I'll make you pay for it." And so it went on for six years. Only the old man lying on the top of the oven kept telling them again and again: "Children, what are you doing? Stop all this paying back; keep to your work, and don't bear malice–it will be better for you. The more you bear malice, the worse it will be."

But they would not listen to him.

In the seventh year, at a wedding, Ivan's daughter-in-law held Gabriel up to shame, accusing him of having been caught horse stealing. Gabriel was tipsy, and unable to contain his anger, gave the woman such a blow that she was laid up for a week; and she was pregnant at the time. Ivan was delighted. He went to the magistrate to lodge a complaint. "Now I'll get rid of my neighbor! He won't escape imprisonment, or exile to Siberia." But Ivan's wish was not fulfilled. The magistrate dismissed the case. The woman was examined, but she was up and about and showed no sign of any injury. Then Ivan went to the justice of the peace, but he referred the business to the district court. Ivan bestirred himself: treated the clerk and the elder of the district court to a gallon of liquor and got Gabriel condemned to be flogged. The sentence was read out to Gabriel by the clerk: "The court decrees that the peasant Gabriel Gordéyef shall receive twenty lashes with a birch rod at the district court."

Ivan too heard the sentence read, and looked at Gabriel to see how he would take it. Gabriel grew as pale as a sheet, and turned round and went out into the passage. Ivan followed him, meaning to see to the horse, and he overheard Gabriel say, "Very well! He will have my back flogged: that will make it burn; but something of his may burn worse than that!"

Hearing these words, Ivan at once went back into the Court, and said: "Upright judges! He threatens to set my house on fire! Listen: he said it in the presence of witnesses!"

Gabriel was recalled. "Is it true that you said this?"

"I haven't said anything. Flog me, since you have the power. It seems that I alone am to suffer, and all for being in the right, while he is allowed to do as he likes."

Gabriel wished to say something more, but his lips and his cheeks quivered, and he turned towards the wall. Even the officials were frightened by his looks. "He may do some mischief to himself or to his neighbor," thought they.

Then the old Judge said: "Look here, my men; you'd better be reasonable and make it up. Was it right of you, friend Gabriel, to strike a pregnant woman? It was lucky it passed off so well, but think what might have happened! Was it right? You had better confess and beg his pardon, and he will forgive you, and we will alter the sentence."

The clerk heard these words, and remarked: "That's impossible under Statute 117. An agreement between the parties not having been arrived at, a decision of the Court has been pronounced and must be executed."

But the Judge would not listen to the clerk.

"Keep your tongue still, my friend," said he. "The first of all laws is to obey God, who loves peace." And the Judge began again to persuade the peasants, but could not succeed. Gabriel would not listen to him.

"I shall be fifty next year," said he, "and have a married son, and have never been flogged in my life, and now that pockmarked Ivan has had me condemned to be flogged, and am I to go and ask his forgiveness? No; I've borne enough . . . Ivan shall have cause to remember me!"

Again Gabriel's voice quivered, and he could say no more, but turned round and went out.

It was seven miles from the Court to the village, and it was getting late when Ivan reached home. He unharnessed his horse, put it up for the night, and entered the cottage. No one was there. The women had already gone to drive the cattle in, and the young fellows were not yet back from the fields. Ivan went in, and sat down, thinking. He remembered how Gabriel had listened to the sentence, and how pale he had become, and how he had turned to the wall; and Ivan's heart grew heavy. He thought how he himself would feel if he were sentenced, and he pitied Gabriel. Then he heard his old father up on the oven cough, and saw him sit up, lower his legs, and scramble down. The old man dragged himself slowly to a seat, and sat down. He was quite tired out with the exertion, and coughed a long time till he had cleared his throat. Then, leaning against the table, he said: "Well, has he been condemned?"

"Yes, to twenty strokes with the rods," answered Ivan.

The old man shook his head.

"A bad business," said he. "You are doing wrong, Ivan! Ah! it's very bad – not for him so much as for yourself! . . . Well, they'll flog him: but will that do you any good?"

"He'll not do it again," said Ivan.

"What is it he'll not do again? What has he done worse than you?"

"Why, think of the harm he has done me!" said Ivan. "He nearly killed my son's wife, and now he's threatening to burn us up. Am I to thank him for it?"

The old man sighed, and said: "You go about the wide world, Ivan, while I am lying on the oven all these years, so you think you see everything, and that I see nothing . . . Ah, lad! It's you that don't see; malice blinds you. Others' sins are before your eyes, but your own are behind your back. 'He's acted badly!' What a thing to say! If he were the only one to act badly, how could strife exist? Is strife among men ever bred by one alone? Strife is always between two. His badness you see, but your own you don't. If he were bad, but you were good, there would be no strife. Who pulled the hair out of his beard? Who spoilt his haystack? Who dragged him to the law court? Yet you put it all on him! You live a bad life yourself, that's what is wrong! It's not the way I used to live, lad, and it's not the way I taught you. Is that the way his old father and I used to live? How did we live? Why, as neighbors should! If he happened to run out of flour, one of the women would come across: 'Uncle Trol, we want some flour.' 'Go to the barn, dear,' I'd say: 'take what you need.' If he'd no one to take his horses to pasture, 'Go, Ivan,' I'd say, 'and look after his horses.' And if I was short of anything, I'd go to him. 'Uncle Gordéy,' I'd say, 'I want so-and-so!' 'Take it Uncle Trol!' That's how it was between us, and we had an easy time of it. But now? . . . That soldier the other day was telling us about the fight at Plevna. Why, there's war between you worse than at Plevna! Is that living? . . . What a sin it is! You are a man and master of the house; it's you who will have to answer. What are you teaching the women and the children? To snarl and snap? Why, the other day your Taráska – that greenhorn – was swearing at neighbor Irena, calling her names; and his mother listened and laughed. Is that right? It is you will have to answer. Think of your soul. Is this all as it should be? You throw a word at me, and I give you two in return; you give me a blow, and I give you two. No, lad! Christ, when he walked on earth, taught us fools something very different . . . If you get a hard word from anyone, keep silent, and his own conscience will accuse him. That is what our Lord taught. If you get a slap, turn the other cheek. 'Here, beat me, if that's what I deserve!' And his own conscience will rebuke him. He will soften, and will listen to you. That's the way He taught us, not to be proud! . . . Why don't you speak? Isn't it as I say?"

Ivan sat silent and listened.

The old man coughed, and having with difficulty cleared his throat, began again: "You think Christ taught us wrong? Why, it's all for our own good. Just think of your earthly life; are you better off, or worse, since this Plevna began among you? Just reckon up what you've spent on all this law business – what the driving backwards and forwards and your food on the way have cost you! What fine fellows your sons have grown; you might live and get on well; but now your means are lessening. And why? All because of this folly; because of your pride. You ought to be plowing with your lads, and do the sowing yourself; but the fiend carries you off to the judge, or to some pettifogger or other. The plowing is not done in time, nor the sowing, and mother earth can't bear properly. Why did the oats fail this year? When did you sow them? When you came back from town! And what did you gain? A burden for your own shoulders . . . Eh, lad, think of your own business! Work with your boys in the field and at home, and if someone offends you, forgive him, as God wished you to. Then life will be easy, and your heart will always be light."

Ivan remained silent.

"Ivan, my boy, hear your old father! Go and harness the roan, and go at once to the Government office; put an end to all this affair there; and in the morning go and make it up with Gabriel in God's name, and invite him to your house for tomorrow's holiday (It was the eve of the Virgin's Nativity). Have tea ready, and get a bottle of vodka and put an end to this wicked business, so that there should not be any more of it in future, and tell the women and children to do the same."

Ivan sighed, and thought, "What he says is true," and his heart grew lighter. Only he did not know how to begin to put matters right.

But again the old man began, as if he had guessed what was in Ivan's mind.

"Go, Ivan, don't put it off! Put out the fire before it spreads, or it will be too late."

The old man was going to say more, but before he could do so the women came in, chattering like magpies. The news that Gabriel was sentenced to be flogged, and of his threat to set fire to the house, had already reached them. They had heard all about it and added to it something of their own, and had again had a row, in the pasture, with the women of Gabriel's household. They began telling how Gabriel's daughter-in-law threatened a fresh action: Gabriel had got the right side of the examining magistrate, who would now turn the whole affair upside down; and the schoolmaster was writing out another petition, to the Tsar himself this time, about Ivan; and everything was in the petition – all about the coupling-pin and the kitchen garden – so that half of Ivan's homestead would be theirs soon. Ivan heard what they were saying, and his heart grew cold again, and he gave up the thought of making peace with Gabriel.

In a farmstead there is always plenty for the master to do. Ivan did not stop to talk to the women, but went out to the threshing floor and to the barn. By the time he had tidied up there, the sun had set and the young fellows had returned from the field. They had been plowing the field for the winter crops with two horses. Ivan met them, questioned them about their work, helped to put everything in its place, set a torn horse collar aside to be mended, and was going to put away some stakes under the barn, but it had grown quite dusk, so he decided to leave them where they were till next day. Then he gave the cattle their food, opened the gate, let out the horses Tarás was to take to pasture for the night, and again closed the gate and barred it. "Now," thought he, "I'll have my supper, and then to bed." He took the horse collar and entered the hut. By this time he had forgotten about Gabriel and about what his old father had been saying to him. But, just as he took hold of the door handle to enter the passage, he heard his neighbor on the other side of the fence cursing somebody in a hoarse voice: "What the devil is he good for?" Gabriel was saying. "He's only fit to be killed!" At these words all Ivan's former bitterness towards his neighbor re-awoke. He stood listening while Gabriel scolded, and, when he stopped, Ivan went into the hut.

There was a light inside; his daughter-in-law sat spinning, his wife was getting supper ready, his eldest son was making straps for bark shoes, his second sat near the table with a book, and Tarás was getting ready to go out to pasture the horses for the night. Everything in the hut would have been pleasant and bright, but for that plague – a bad neighbor!

Ivan entered, sullen and cross; threw the cat down from the bench, and scolded the women for putting the slop pail in the wrong place. He felt despondent, and sat down, frowning, to mend the horse collar. Gabriel's words kept ringing in his ears: his threat at the law court, and what he had just been shouting in a hoarse voice about someone who was "only fit to be killed."

His wife gave Tarás his supper, and, having eaten it, Tarás put on an old sheepskin and another coat, tied a sash round his waist, took some bread with him, and went out to the horses. His eldest brother was going to see him off, but Ivan himself rose instead, and went out into the porch. It had grown quite dark outside, clouds had gathered, and the wind had risen. Ivan went down the steps, helped his boy to mount, started the foal after him, and stood listening while Tarás rode down to the village and was there joined by other lads with their horses. Ivan waited until they were all out of hearing. As he stood there by the gate he could not get Gabriel's words out of his head: "Mind that something of yours does not burn worse!"

"He is desperate," thought Ivan. "Everything is dry, and it's windy weather besides. He'll come up at the back somewhere, set fire to something, and be off. He'll burn the place and escape scot free, the villain! . . . There now, if one could but catch him in the act, he'd not get off then!" And the thought fixed itself so firmly in his mind that he did not go up the steps but went out into the street and round the corner. "I'll just walk round the buildings; who can tell what he's after?" And Ivan, stepping softly, passed out of the gate. As soon as he reached the corner, he looked round along the fence, and seemed to see something suddenly move at the opposite corner, as if someone had come out and disappeared again. Ivan stopped, and stood quietly, listening and looking. Everything was still; only the leaves of the willows fluttered in the wind, and the straws of the thatch rustled. At first it seemed pitch dark, but, when his eyes had grown used to the darkness, he could see the far corner, and a plow that lay there, and the eaves. He looked a while, but saw no one.

"I suppose it was a mistake," thought Ivan, "but still I will go round," and Ivan went stealthily along by the shed. Ivan stepped so softly in his bark shoes that he did not hear his own footsteps. As he reached the far corner, something seemed to flare up for a moment near the plow and to vanish again. Ivan felt as if struck to the heart; and he stopped. Hardly had he stopped, when something flared up more brightly in the same place, and he clearly saw a man with a cap on his head, crouching down, with his back towards him, lighting a bunch of straw he held in his hand. Ivan's heart fluttered within him like a bird. Straining every nerve, he approached with great strides, hardly feeling his legs under him. "Ah," thought Ivan, "now he won't escape! I'll catch him in the act!"

Ivan was still some distance off, when suddenly he saw a bright light, but not in the same place as before, and not a small flame. The thatch had flared up at the eaves, the flames were reaching up to the roof, and, standing beneath it, Gabriel's whole figure was clearly visible.

Like a hawk swooping down on a lark, Ivan rushed at Limping Gabriel. "Now I'll have him; he shan't escape me!" thought Ivan. But Gabriel must have heard his steps, and (however he managed it) glancing round, he scuttled away past the barn like a hare.

"You shan't escape!" shouted Ivan, darting after him.

Just as he was going to seize Gabriel, the latter dodged him; but Ivan managed to catch the skirt of Gabriel's coat. It tore right off, and Ivan fell down. He recovered his feet, and shouting, "Help! Seize him! Thieves! Murder!" ran on again. But meanwhile Gabriel had reached his own gate. There Ivan overtook him and was about to seize him, when something struck Ivan a

stunning blow, as though a stone had hit his temple, quite deaf-
ening him. It was Gabriel who, seizing an oak wedge that lay
near the gate, had struck out with all his might.

Ivan was stunned; sparks flew before his eyes, then all grew
dark and he staggered. When he came to his senses Gabriel was
no longer there: it was as light as day, and from the side where his
homestead was something roared and crackled like an engine
at work. Ivan turned round and saw that his back shed was all
ablaze, and the side shed had also caught fire, and flames and
smoke and bits of burning straw mixed with the smoke, were
being driven towards his hut.

"What is this, friends? . . ." cried Ivan, lifting his arms and
striking his thighs." Why, all I had to do was just to snatch it out
from under the eaves and trample on it! What is this, friends? . . ."
he kept repeating. He wished to shout, but his breath failed him;
his voice was gone. He wanted to run, but his legs would not
obey him, and got in each other's way. He moved slowly, but
again staggered and again his breath failed. He stood still till
he had regained breath, and then went on. Before he had got
round the back shed to reach the fire, the side shed was also all
ablaze; and the corner of the hut and the covered gateway had
caught fire as well. The flames were leaping out of the hut, and it
was impossible to get into the yard. A large crowd had collected,
but nothing could be done. The neighbors were carrying their
belongings out of their own houses, and driving the cattle out
of their own sheds. After Ivan's house, Gabriel's also caught fire,
then, the wind rising, the flames spread to the other side of the
street and half the village was burnt down.

At Ivan's house they barely managed to save his old father;
and the family escaped in what they had on; everything else,
except the horses that had been driven out to pasture for the

night, was lost; all the cattle, the fowls on their perches, the carts, plows, and harrows, the women's trunks with their clothes, and the grain in the granaries – all were burnt up!

At Gabriel's, the cattle were driven out, and a few things saved from his house.

The fire lasted all night. Ivan stood in front of his homestead and kept repeating, "What is this? . . . Friends! . . . One need only have pulled it out and trampled on it!" But when the roof fell in, Ivan rushed into the burning place, and seizing a charred beam, tried to drag it out. The women saw him, and called him back; but he pulled out the beam, and was going in again for another when he lost his footing and fell among the flames. Then his son made his way in after him and dragged him out. Ivan had singed his hair and beard and burnt his clothes and scorched his hands, but he felt nothing. "His grief has stupefied him," said the people. The fire was burning itself out, but Ivan still stood repeating: "Friends! . . . What is this? . . . One need only have pulled it out!"

In the morning the village elder's son came to fetch Ivan.

"Daddy Ivan, your father is dying! He has sent for you to say goodbye."

Ivan had forgotten about his father, and did not understand what was being said to him.

"What father?" he said. "Whom has he sent for?"

"He sent for you, to say goodbye; he is dying in our cottage! Come along, daddy Ivan," said the elder's son, pulling him by the arm; and Ivan followed the lad.

When he was being carried out of the hut, some burning straw had fallen on to the old man and burnt him, and he had been taken to the village elder's in the farther part of the village, which the fire did not reach.

When Ivan came to his father, there was only the elder's wife in the hut, besides some little children on the top of the oven. All the rest were still at the fire. The old man, who was lying on a bench holding a wax candle in his hand, kept turning his eyes towards the door. When his son entered, he moved a little. The old woman went up to him and told him that his son had come. He asked to have him brought nearer. Ivan came closer.

"What did I tell you, Ivan?" began the old man. "Who has burnt down the village?"

"It was he, father!" Ivan answered. "I caught him in the act. I saw him shove the firebrand into the thatch. I might have pulled away the burning straw and stamped it out, and then nothing would have happened."

"Ivan," said the old man, "I am dying, and you in your turn will have to face death. Whose is the sin?"

Ivan gazed at his father in silence, unable to utter a word.

"Now, before God, say whose is the sin? What did I tell you?"

Only then Ivan came to his senses and understood it all. He sniffed and said, "Mine, father!" And he fell on his knees before his father, saying, "Forgive me, father; I am guilty before you and before God."

The old man moved his hands, changed the candle from his right hand to his left, and tried to lift his right hand to his forehead to cross himself, but could not do it, and stopped.

"Praise the Lord! Praise the Lord!" said he, and again he turned his eyes towards his son.

"Ivan! I say, Ivan!"

"What, father?"

"What must you do now?"

Ivan was weeping.

"I don't know how we are to live now, father!" he said.

The old man closed his eyes, moved his lips as if to gather strength, and opening his eyes again, said: "You'll manage. If you obey God's will, you'll manage!" He paused, then smiled, and said: "Mind, Ivan! Don't tell who started the fire! Hide another man's sin, and God will forgive two of yours!" And the old man took the candle in both hands and, folding them on his breast, sighed, stretched out, and died.

Ivan did not say anything against Gabriel, and no one knew what had caused the fire.

And Ivan's anger against Gabriel passed away, and Gabriel wondered that Ivan did not tell anybody. At first Gabriel felt afraid, but after a while he got used to it. The men left off quarrelling, and then their families left off also. While rebuilding their huts, both families lived in one house; and when the village was rebuilt and they might have moved farther apart, Ivan and Gabriel built next to each other, and remained neighbors as before.

They lived as good neighbors should. Ivan Stcherbakóf remembered his old father's command to obey God's law, and quench a fire at the first spark; and if anyone does him an injury he now tries not to revenge himself, but rather to set matters right again; and if anyone gives him a bad word, instead of giving a worse in return, he tries to teach the other not to use evil words; and so he teaches his womenfolk and children. And Ivan Stcherbakóf has got on his feet again, and now lives better even than he did before.

15

Nekhlyudov Seeks Redemption

From Resurrection

Ten years after seducing Katusha Maslova, a serf girl adopted by his aunts, the nobleman Dmitri Ivanovich Nekhlyudov is summoned to jury duty. In the courtroom, he discovers that Maslova, now a prostitute, is the defendant in one of the cases being tried; she faces charges of theft and murder. Nekhlyudov's first response is fear that his former relations with her will be discovered.

THE PRESIDENT OF THE COURT spoke and the members on either side of him listened with deeply attentive expressions, but looked from time to time at the clock, for they considered the speech too long though very good – i.e., such as it ought to be. The public prosecutor, the lawyers, and, in fact, everyone in the court, shared the same impression. The president finished the summing up.

From the moment the president commenced his speech, Maslova watched him without moving her eyes as if afraid of losing a single word; so that Nekhlyudov was not afraid of meeting her eyes and kept looking at her all the time. And his mind's eye suffered the familiar sequence in which at first we only notice the changes in a face that we have not seen for a long time, and then gradually the beloved face begins to look exactly as it was those many years ago: the changes all disappear until our spiritual eyes see only the one unique inimitable spiritual personality.

This was what happened with Nekhlyudov.

Yes, though dressed in a prison cloak, and in spite of the developed figure, the fullness of the bosom and lower part of the face, in spite of a few wrinkles on the forehead and temples and the swollen eyes, this was certainly the same Katusha who, on that Easter eve, had so innocently looked up to him whom she loved, with her fond, laughing eyes full of joy and life.

"What a strange coincidence that after ten years, during which I never saw her, this case should have come up today when I am on the jury, and that it is in the prisoners' dock that I see her again! And how will it end? Oh, dear, if they would only get on quicker."

Still he would not give in to the feelings of repentance which began to arise within him. He tried to consider it all as a coincidence which would pass without infringing his manner of life. He felt himself in the position of a puppy, when its master, taking it by the scruff of its neck, rubs its nose in the mess it has made. The puppy whines, draws back, and wants to get away as far as possible from the effects of its misdeed, but the pitiless master does not let go.

And so, Nekhlyudov, feeling all the repulsiveness of what he had done, felt also the powerful hand of the Master, but he did not feel the whole significance of his action yet and would not recognize the Master's hand. He did not wish to believe that it was the effect of his deed that lay before him, but the pitiless hand of the Master held him and he felt he could not get away. He was still keeping up his courage and sat on his chair in the first row in his usual self-possessed pose, one leg carelessly

thrown over the other, and playing with his pince-nez. Yet all
the while, in the depths of his soul, he felt the cruelty, coward-
ice, and baseness, not only of this particular action of his, but of
his whole self-willed, depraved, cruel, idle life; and that dreadful
veil which had in some unaccountable manner hidden from him
this sin of his and the whole of his subsequent life was beginning to shake, and he caught glimpses of what was covered by
that veil.

✦ ✦ ✦

Though Katusha Maslova is acquitted of murder, she is never-
theless sentenced to hard labor in Siberia as a result of the jury's
careless wording of the verdict. Nekhlyudov visits her in prison,
seeking to atone for his guilt toward her.

The jailer who had brought Maslova in sat on a windowsill at
some distance from them. The decisive moment had come for
Nekhlyudov. He had been incessantly blaming himself for not
having told her the principal thing at the first interview, and
was now determined to tell her that he would marry her. She
was sitting at the further side of the table. Nekhlyudov sat down
opposite her. It was light in the room, and Nekhlyudov for the
first time saw her face quite near. He distinctly saw the wrinkles
round her eyes and mouth, and the swollen eyelids. And he felt
more pity for her than ever.

Leaning over the table so as not to be heard by the jailer,
Nekhlyudov said:

"Should this petition come to nothing we shall appeal to the
Emperor. All that is possible shall be done."

"There, now, if we had had a proper advocate from the first,"
she interrupted him. "As it was, the lawyer I had was nothing but

an old fool. He did nothing but pay me compliments," she said, and burst into a laugh. "If it had then been known that I was acquainted with you, it would have been another matter. They think everyone's a thief."

"How strange she is today," Nekhlyudov thought, and was just going to say what he had on his mind when she began again:

"There's something I want to say. We have here an old woman; such a fine one, d'you know, she just surprises everyone; she is imprisoned for nothing, and her son, too, and everybody knows they are innocent, though they are accused of having set fire to a house. D'you know, hearing I was acquainted with you, she says: 'Tell him to ask to see my son; he'll tell him all about it.'" Thus spoke Maslova, turning her head from side to side, and glancing at Nekhlyudov. "Their name's Menshov. Well, will you do it? Such a fine old thing, you know; you can see at once she's innocent. You'll do it, there's a dear," and she smiled, glanced up at him, and then cast down her eyes.

"All right. I'll find out about them," Nekhlyudov said, more and more astonished by her free-and-easy manner. "But I was going to speak to you about myself. Do you remember what I told you last time?"

"You said a lot last time. What was it you told me?" she said, continuing to smile and to turn her head from side to side.

"I said I had come to ask you to forgive me," he began.

"What's the use of that? Forgive, forgive, where's the good of–"

"To atone for my sin, not by mere words, but in deed. I have made up my mind to marry you."

An expression of fear suddenly came over her face. Her squinting eyes remained fixed on him, and yet seemed not to be looking at him.

"Why should that be necessary?" she said with an angry frown.

"I feel that it is my duty before God to do it."

"What God have you found now? You are not saying what you ought to. God, indeed! What God? You ought to have remembered God then," she said, and stopped with her mouth open. It was only now that Nekhlyudov noticed that her breath smelled of spirits, and that he understood the cause of her excitement.

"Try and be calm," he said.

"I'm calm enough. You think I'm tipsy? So I am, but I know what I'm saying." She began speaking fast, her face scarlet. "I am a convict, a whore . . . but you are a gentleman and a prince. There's no need for you to soil yourself by touching me. You go to your princesses; my price is a ten-ruble note."

"Say all the cruel things you like, you cannot express what I myself am feeling," he said, trembling all over; "you cannot imagine to what extent I feel myself guilty towards you."

"Feel yourself guilty?" she said, angrily mimicking him. "You did not feel so then, but threw me one hundred rubles. That's your price."

"I know, I know; but what can we do about it now?" said Nekhlyudov. "I have decided not to leave you, and what I have said I shall do."

"And I say you shan't," she said, and laughed aloud.

"Katusha!" he began, touching her hand.

"Go away from me! I am a convict and you a prince, and you've no business here," she cried, pulling away her hand, her whole appearance transformed by her wrath. "You've got pleasure out of me in this life, and want to save yourself through me in the life to come. You disgust me – with your spectacles and your fat ugly mug. Go, go!" she screamed, starting to her feet.

The jailer came up to them.

"What are you kicking up this row for? That won't – "

"Let her alone, please," said Nekhlyudov.

"She must not forget herself," said the jailer.

"Please wait a little," said Nekhlyudov, and the jailer returned to the window. Maslova sat down again, dropping her eyes and firmly clasping her small hands.

Nekhlyudov stooped over her, not knowing what to do.

"You do not believe me?" he said.

"That you mean to marry me? It will never be. I'll rather hang myself. So there!"

"Well, still I shall devote myself to you."

"That's your affair, only I don't want anything from you. I am telling you the plain truth," she said. "Oh, why did I not die then?" she added, and began to cry piteously.

Nekhlyudov could not speak; her tears infected him.

She lifted her eyes, looked at him in surprise, and began to wipe her tears with her kerchief.

The jailer came up again and reminded them that it was time to part. Maslova rose.

"You are upset now. If it is possible, I shall come again tomorrow; you think it over," said Nekhlyudov.

She gave him no answer and, without looking up, followed the jailer out of the room.

"Well, lass, you'll have rare times now," a fellow prisoner said, when Maslova returned to the cell. "Seems he's mighty sweet on you; make the most of it while he's after you. He'll help you out. Rich people can do anything."

"Yes, that's so," remarked the watchman's wife, with her musical voice. "When a poor man thinks of getting married, there's many a slip 'twixt the cup and the lip; but a rich man need only make up his mind and it's done. We knew a toff like that, duckie. What d'you think he did?"

"Well, have you spoken about my affairs?" the old woman asked.

But Maslova gave her fellow-prisoners no answer; she lay down on the shelf bedstead, her squinting eyes fixed on a corner of the room, and lay there until the evening. A painful struggle went on in her soul. What Nekhlyudov had told her called up the memory of that world in which she had suffered and which she had left without having understood, hating it. She now feared to wake from the trance in which she was living. Not having arrived at any conclusion when evening came, she again bought some vodka and drank with her companions.

"So this is what it means, this," thought Nekhlyudov as he left the prison, only now fully understanding his crime. If he had not tried to expiate his guilt he would never have found out how great his crime was. Nor was this all; she, too, would never have felt the whole horror of what had been done to her. He only now saw what he had done to the soul of this woman; only now she saw and understood what had been done to her. Up to this time Nekhlyudov had played with a sensation of self-admiration, had admired his own remorse; now he was simply filled with horror. To cast her off – that, he felt, he could never do now, and yet he could not imagine what would come of their relations to one another.

✦ ✦ ✦

Though snubbed by Katusha, Nekhlyudov does everything in his power to save her, following her into a series of horrific prisons. He is present when she, together with a group of fellow convicts, is marched to the railway station for transport to Siberia. On the way, two of the prisoners succumb to heatstroke.

The heat in the large third-class carriage, which had been standing in the burning sun all day, was so great that Nekhlyudov did not go in, but stopped on the little platform behind the carriage which formed a passage to the next one. But there was not a breath of fresh air here either, and Nekhlyudov breathed freely only when the train had passed the buildings and the draught blew across the platform.

"Yes, killed," he repeated to himself, the words he had used to his sister. And in his imagination in the midst of all other impressions there arose with wonderful clearness the beautiful face of the second dead convict, with the smile of the lips, the severe expression of the brows, and the small, firm ear below the shaved bluish skull.

And what seemed terrible was that he had been murdered, and no one knew who had murdered him. Yet he had been murdered. He was led out like all the rest of the prisoners by Maslennikov's orders. Maslennikov had probably given the order in the usual manner, had signed with his stupid flourish the paper with the printed heading, and most certainly would not consider himself guilty. Still less would the careful doctor who examined the convicts consider himself guilty. He had performed his duty accurately, and had separated the weak. How could he have foreseen this terrible heat, or the fact that they would start so late in the day and in such crowds? The prison inspector? But the inspector had only carried into execution the order that on a given day a certain number of exiles and convicts – men and women – had to be sent off. The convoy officer could not be guilty either, for his business was to receive a certain number of persons in a certain place, and to deliver up the same number. He conducted them in the usual manner, and could not foresee that two such strong men as those Nekhlyudov saw would not be able to stand it and would die. No one is guilty, and yet the men have been murdered by these people who are not guilty of their murder.

"All this comes," Nekhlyudov thought, "from the fact that all these people, governors, inspectors, police officers, and men, consider that there are circumstances in which human relations are not necessary between human beings. All these men, Maslennikov, and the inspector, and the convoy officer, if they were not governor, inspector, officer, would have considered twenty times before sending people in such heat in such a mass – would have stopped twenty times on the way, and, seeing that a man was growing weak, gasping for breath, would have led him into the shade, would have given him water and let him rest, and if an accident had still occurred they would have expressed pity. But they not only did not do it, but hindered others from doing it, because they considered not men and their duty towards them but only the office they themselves filled, and held what that office demanded of them to be above human relations. "That's what it is," Nekhlyudov went on in his thoughts. "If one acknowledges but for a single hour that anything can be more important than love for one's fellowmen, even in some one exceptional case, any crime can be committed without a feeling of guilt."

Nekhlyudov was so engrossed by his thoughts that he did not notice how the weather changed. The sun was covered over by a low-hanging, ragged cloud. A compact, light grey cloud was rapidly coming from the west, and was already falling in heavy, driving rain on the fields and woods far in the distance.

Moisture, coming from the cloud, mixed with the air. Now and then the cloud was rent by flashes of lightning, and peals of thunder mingled more and more often with the rattling of the train. The cloud came nearer and nearer, the raindrops driven by the wind began to spot the platform and Nekhlyudov's coat; and he stepped to the other side of the little platform, and, inhaling the fresh, moist air – filled with the smell of corn and wet earth that had long been waiting for rain – he stood looking at the gardens, the woods, the yellow rye fields, the green oat fields, the dark-green strips of potatoes in bloom, that glided past. Everything looked as if covered over with varnish – the green turned greener, the yellow yellower, the black blacker.

"More! more!" said Nekhlyudov, gladdened by the sight of gardens and fields revived by the beneficent shower. The shower did not last long. Part of the cloud had come down in rain, part passed over, and the last fine drops fell straight onto the earth. The sun reappeared, everything began to glisten, and in the east – not very high above the horizon – appeared a bright rainbow, with the violet tint very distinct and broken only at one end.

"Why, what was I thinking about?" Nekhlyudov asked himself when all these changes in nature had come to an end, and the train ran into a cutting between two high banks. "Ah, yes, I remember – I was thinking that all those people: the inspector, the convoy soldiers, and all the others in official positions, most of them gentle kindly people, have become bad only because of their office."

He recalled Maslennikov's indifference when he told him about what was being done in the prison, the inspector's severity, the cruelty of the convoy officer when he refused places on the carts to those who asked for them, and paid no attention to the fact that there was a woman in travail in the train. All these people were evidently invulnerable and impregnable to the simplest feelings of compassion only because they held offices. "As officials they were impermeable to the feelings of humanity, as this paved ground is impermeable to the rain." Thus thought Nekhlyudov as he looked at the railway embankment paved with stones of different colors, down which the water was running in streams instead of soaking into the earth. "Perhaps it is necessary to pave the banks with stones, but it is sad to look at the ground, which might be yielding corn, grass, bushes, or trees in the same way as the ground visible up there is doing – deprived of vegetation, and so it is with people," thought Nekhlyudov. "Perhaps these governors, inspectors, police officers are needed, but it is terrible to see people deprived of the chief human attribute, that of love and sympathy for one another.

"This is what it comes to," thought Nekhlyudov, "these people consider lawful what is not lawful, and do not consider the eternal, immutable law, written in the hearts of human beings by God, as law. . . . It is only necessary that these people should be governors, inspectors, policemen; that they should be fully convinced that there is a kind of business, called government service, which allows people to treat other people as things, without human brotherly relations with them, and also that these people should be so linked together by this government service that the responsibility for the results of their actions should not fall on any one of them separately. Without these conditions, the terrible acts I witnessed today would be impossible in our times. It all lies in the fact that people think there are circumstances in which one may deal with human beings without love; and there are no such circumstances. One may deal with things without love. One may cut down trees, make bricks, hammer iron without love; but you cannot deal with people without it, just as one cannot deal with bees without being careful. If you deal carelessly with bees you will injure them, and will yourself be injured. And so with human beings. It cannot be otherwise, because natural love is the fundamental law of human life. It is true that a man cannot force another to love him, as he can force him to work for him; but it does not follow that a man may deal with others without love, especially to demand anything from them. If you feel no love, leave people alone," thought Nekhlyudov, addressing himself. "Occupy yourself with things, with yourself, with anything you like, only not with human beings. Just as one can eat without harm and profitably only when one is hungry, so one can usefully and without injury deal with people only when one loves them. Only let yourself deal with a man without love, as I did yesterday with my brother-in-law, and there are no limits to the suffering you will bring on yourself, as all my life proves. Yes, yes, it is so," thought Nekhlyudov. "It is good; yes, it is good," he repeated to himself again and again, enjoying the two-fold delight of refreshing coolness after the torturing heat and the assurance of having arrived at the clearest possible understanding of a problem that had occupied him for a long time.

✦ ✦ ✦

Despite his tireless efforts, Nekhlyudov comes to the end of what he can do for Katusha. Her suffering, and the suffering of the prisoners he has seen along the way, drives him to look for an answer to humankind's evil.

"And is this all?" Nekhlyudov suddenly exclaimed aloud, and the inner voice of the whole of his being said, "Yes, it is all." And it happened to Nekhlyudov, as it often happens to those who are living a spiritual life. The thought that seemed strange at first and paradoxical or even to be only a joke, being confirmed more and more often by life's experience, suddenly appeared as the simplest, truest certainty. In this way the idea that the only certain means of salvation from the terrible evil from which human beings were suffering was that they should always acknowledge themselves to be sinning against God, and therefore unable to punish or correct others, because they were dear to him. It became clear to him that all the dreadful evil he had been witnessing in prisons and jails and the quiet self-satisfaction of the perpetrators of this evil were the consequences of people trying to do what was impossible; trying to correct evil while being evil themselves; vicious men were trying to correct other vicious men, and thought they could do it by using mechanical means, and the only consequence of all this was that the needs and the cupidity of some people induced them to take up this so-called punishment and correction as a profession, and have themselves become utterly corrupt, and go on unceasingly depraving those whom they torment. Now he saw clearly what all the terrors he had seen came from, and what ought to be done to put a stop to them. The answer he could not find was the same that Christ gave to Peter. It was that we should forgive always an infinite number of times because there are none who have not sinned themselves, and therefore none can punish or correct others.

"But surely it cannot be so simple," thought Nekhlyudov, and yet he saw with certainty, strange as it had seemed at first, that it was not only a theoretical but also a practical solution of the question. The usual objection, "What is one to do with the evil-doers? Surely not let them go unpunished?" no longer confused him. This objection might have a meaning if it were proved that punishment lessened crime, or improved the criminal, but when the contrary was proved, and it was evident that it was not in people's power to correct each other, the only reasonable thing to do is to leave off doing the things which are not only useless, but harmful, immoral, and cruel.

For many centuries people who were considered criminals have been tortured. Well, and have they ceased to exist? No; their numbers have been increased not alone by the criminals corrupted by punishment but also by those lawful criminals, the judges, prosecutors, magistrates, and jailers, who judge and punish. Nekhlyudov now understood that society and order in general exists not because of these lawful criminals who judge and punish others, but because in spite of people being thus depraved, they still pity and love one another.

In hopes of finding a confirmation of this thought in the Gospel, Nekhlyudov began reading it from the beginning. When he had read the Sermon on the Mount, which had always touched him, he saw in it for the first time today not beautiful abstract thoughts, setting forth for the most part exaggerated and impossible demands, but simple, clear, practical laws. If these laws were carried out in practice (and this was quite possible) they would establish perfectly new and surprising conditions of social life, in which the violence that filled Nekhlyudov with such indignation would cease of itself. Not only this, but the greatest blessing that is obtainable to humankind – the kingdom of heaven on earth – would be established. There were five of these laws.

The first (Matt. 5:21–26), that man should not only do no murder, but not even be angry with his brother, should not consider anyone worthless: "Raca," and if he has quarreled with anyone he should make it up with him before bringing his gift to God – i.e., before praying.

The second (Matt. 5:27–32), that man should not only not commit adultery but should not even seek for enjoyment in a woman's beauty, and if he has once come together with a woman he should never be faithless to her.

The third (Matt. 5:33–37), that man should never bind himself by oath.

The fourth (Matt. 5:38–42), that man should not only not demand an eye for an eye, but when struck on one cheek should hold out the other, should forgive an offence and bear it humbly, and never refuse the service others demand of him.

The fifth (Matt. 5:43–48), that man should not only not hate his enemy and not fight him, but love him, help him, serve him.

Nekhlyudov sat staring at the lamp and his heart stood still. Recalling the monstrous confusion of the life we lead, he distinctly saw what that life could be if people were brought up to obey these rules, and rapture such as he had long not felt filled his soul, just as if after long days of weariness and suffering he had suddenly found ease and freedom.

He did not sleep all night, and as it happens to vast numbers who read the Gospels, he understood for the first time the full meaning of the words read and passed over innumerable times in the past. He imbibed all these necessary, important, and joyful revelations as a sponge imbibes water. And all he read seemed so familiar and seemed to confirm, to form into a conception, what he had known long ago, but had never realized and never quite believed. Now he realized and believed it, and not only realized and believed that if people would obey these laws they would obtain the highest blessing they can attain to, he also realized and believed that the only duty of every man is to fulfill these laws; that in this lies the only reasonable meaning of life, that

every stepping aside from these laws is a mistake which is immediately followed by retribution. This flowed from the whole of
the teaching, and was most strongly and clearly illustrated in the
parable of the vineyard.

The husbandmen imagined that the vineyard in which they
were sent to work for their master was their own, that all that
was in it was made for them, and that their business was to
enjoy life in this vineyard, forgetting the Master and killing all
those who reminded them of his existence. "Are we not doing
the same," Nekhlyudov thought, "when we imagine ourselves to
be masters of our lives, and that life is given us for enjoyment?
This evidently is an incongruity. We were sent here by someone's
will and for some reason. And we have concluded that we live
only for our own joy, and of course we feel unhappy as laborers
do when not fulfilling their Master's orders. The Master's will is
expressed in these commandments. If human beings will only
fulfill these laws, the kingdom of heaven will be established on
earth, and people will receive the greatest good that they can
attain to.

"'Seek first the kingdom of God and his righteousness, and all
these things shall be yours as well.'

"And so here it is, the business of my life. Scarcely have I finished one, and another has commenced." And a perfectly new
life dawned that night for Nekhlyudov, not because he had
entered into new conditions of life, but because everything he
did after that night had a new and quite different significance
than before. How this new period of his life will end time alone
will prove.

16.

The Healing of Prince Andrei

From War and Peace

The Battle of Borodino in September 1812 is the Russian army's last doomed attempt to prevent Napoleon from occupying Moscow. During the fighting, a shell injures Prince Andrei Bolkonsky, a Russian regimental commander. As Andrei lies in a field hospital, he sees nearby a man whose leg is being amputated. On closer inspection, he recognizes the patient as Anatole Kuragin, who in Andrei's absence has attempted to seduce his fiancée Natasha, prompting her to break off the engagement. Andrei has vowed to avenge himself on Anatole.

ONE OF THE DOCTORS came out of the tent in a bloodstained apron, holding a cigar between the thumb and little finger of one of his small bloodstained hands, so as not to smear it. He raised his head and looked about him, but above the level of the wounded men. He evidently wanted a little respite. After turning his head from right to left for some time, he sighed and looked down.

"All right, immediately," he replied to a dresser who pointed Prince Andrei out to him, and he told them to carry him into the tent.

Murmurs arose among the wounded who were waiting.

"It seems that even in the next world only the gentry are to have a chance!" remarked one.

Prince Andrei was carried in and laid on a table that had only just been cleared and which a dresser was washing down. Prince Andrei could not make out distinctly what was in that tent. The pitiful groans from all sides and the torturing pain in his thigh, stomach, and back distracted him. All he saw about him merged into a general impression of naked, bleeding human bodies that seemed to fill the whole of the low tent, as a few weeks previously, on that hot August day, such bodies had filled the dirty pond beside the Smolensk road. Yes, it was the same flesh, the same cannon-fodder, the sight of which had even then filled him with horror, as by a presentiment.

There were three operating tables in the tent. Two were occupied, and on the third they placed Prince Andrei. For a little while he was left alone and involuntarily witnessed what was taking place on the other two tables. On the nearest one sat a Tartar, probably a Cossack, judging by the uniform thrown down beside him. Four soldiers were holding him, and a spectacled doctor was cutting into his muscular brown back.

"Ooh, ooh, ooh!" grunted the Tartar, and suddenly lifting up his swarthy snub-nosed face with its high cheekbones, and baring his white teeth, he began to wriggle and twitch his body and utter piercing, ringing, and prolonged yells. On the other table, round which many people were crowding, a tall well-fed man lay on his back with his head thrown back. His curly hair, its color, and the shape of his head seemed strangely familiar to Prince Andrei. Several dressers were pressing on his chest to hold him down. One large, white, plump leg twitched rapidly all the time with a feverish tremor. The man was sobbing and choking convulsively. Two doctors – one of whom was pale and trembling – were silently doing something to this man's other, gory leg. When he had finished with the Tartar, whom they covered with an overcoat, the spectacled doctor came up to Prince Andrei, wiping his hands.

He glanced at Prince Andrei's face and quickly turned away. "Undress him! What are you waiting for?" he cried angrily to the dressers.

His very first, remotest recollections of childhood came back to Prince Andrei's mind when the dresser with sleeves rolled up began hastily to undo the buttons of his clothes and undressed him. The doctor bent down over the wound, felt it, and sighed deeply. Then he made a sign to someone, and the torturing pain in his abdomen caused Prince Andrei to lose consciousness. When he came to himself the splintered portions of his thigh-bone had been extracted, the torn flesh cut away, and the wound bandaged. Water was being sprinkled on his face. As soon as Prince Andrei opened his eyes, the doctor bent over, kissed him silently on the lips, and hurried away.

After the sufferings he had been enduring, Prince Andrei enjoyed a blissful feeling such as he had not experienced for a long time. All the best and happiest moments of his life – especially his earliest childhood, when he used to be undressed and put to bed, and when leaning over him his nurse sang him to sleep and he, burying his head in the pillow, felt happy in the mere consciousness of life – returned to his memory, not merely as something past but as something present.

The doctors were busily engaged with the wounded man the shape of whose head seemed familiar to Prince Andrei: they were lifting him up and trying to quiet him.

"Show it to me . . . Oh, ooh . . . Oh! Oh, ooh!" his frightened moans could be heard, subdued by suffering and broken by sobs.

Hearing those moans Prince Andrei wanted to weep. Whether because he was dying without glory, or because he was sorry to part with life, or because of those memories of a childhood that could not return, or because he was suffering and others were suffering and that man near him was groaning so piteously – he felt like weeping childlike, kindly, and almost happy tears.

The wounded man was shown his amputated leg stained with clotted blood and with the boot still on.

"Oh! Oh, ooh!" he sobbed, like a woman.

The doctor who had been standing beside him, preventing Prince Andrei from seeing his face, moved away.

"My God! What is this? Why is he here?" said Prince Andrei to himself.

In the miserable, sobbing, enfeebled man whose leg had just been amputated, he recognized Anatole Kuragin. Men were supporting him in their arms and offering him a glass of water, but his trembling, swollen lips could not grasp its rim. Anatole was sobbing painfully. "Yes, it is he! Yes, that man is somehow closely and painfully connected with me," thought Prince Andrei, not yet clearly grasping what he saw before him. "What is the connection of that man with my childhood and life?" he asked himself without finding an answer. And suddenly a new unexpected memory from that realm of pure and loving childhood presented itself to him. He remembered Natasha as he had seen her for the first time at the ball in 1810, with her slender neck and arms and with a frightened happy face ready for rapture, and love and tenderness for her, stronger and more vivid than ever, awoke in his soul. He now remembered the connection that existed between himself and this man who was dimly gazing at him through tears that filled his swollen eyes. He remembered everything, and ecstatic pity and love for that man overflowed his happy heart.

Prince Andrei could no longer restrain himself and wept tender loving tears for his fellow men, for himself, and for his own and their errors.

"Compassion, love of our brothers, for those who love us and for those who hate us, love of our enemies; yes, that love which God preached on earth and which Princess Marya taught me and I did not understand – that is what made me sorry to part with life, that is what remained for me had I lived. But now it is too late. I know it!"

✦ ✦ ✦

Seven days had passed since Prince Andrei found himself in the ambulance station on the field of Borodino. His feverish state and the inflammation of his bowels, which were injured, were in the doctor's opinion sure to carry him off. But on the seventh day he ate with pleasure a piece of bread with some tea, and the doctor noticed that his temperature was lower. He had regained consciousness that morning. The first night after they left Moscow had been fairly warm and he had remained in the calash, but at Mytishchi the wounded man himself asked to be taken out and given some tea. The pain caused by his removal into the hut had made him groan aloud and again lose consciousness. When he had been placed on his camp bed he lay for a long time motionless with closed eyes. Then he opened them and whispered softly: "And the tea?" His remembering such a small detail of everyday life astonished the doctor. He felt Prince Andrei's pulse, and to his surprise and dissatisfaction found it had improved. He was dissatisfied because he knew by experience that if his patient did not die now, he would do so a little later with greater suffering. Timokhin, the red-nosed major of

Prince Andrei's regiment, had joined him in Moscow and was being taken along with him, having been wounded in the leg at the battle of Borodino. They were accompanied by a doctor, Prince Andrei's valet, his coachman, and two orderlies.

They gave Prince Andrei some tea. He drank it eagerly, looking with feverish eyes at the door in front of him as if trying to understand and remember something.

"I don't want any more. Is Timokhin here?" he asked.

Timokhin crept along the bench to him.

"I am here, your excellency."

"How's your wound?"

"Mine, sir? All right. But how about you?"

Prince Andrei again pondered as if trying to remember something. "Couldn't one get a book?" he asked.

"What book?"

"The Gospels. I haven't one."

The doctor promised to procure it for him and began to ask how he was feeling. Prince Andrei answered all his questions reluctantly but reasonably, and then said he wanted a bolster placed under him as he was uncomfortable and in great pain. The doctor and valet lifted the cloak with which he was covered and, making wry faces at the noisome smell of mortifying flesh that came from the wound, began examining that dreadful place. The doctor was very much displeased about something and made a change in the dressings, turning the wounded man over so that he groaned again and grew unconscious and delirious from the agony. He kept asking them to get him the book and put it under him.

"What trouble would it be to you?" he said. "I have not got one. Please get it for me and put it under for a moment," he pleaded in a piteous voice.

The doctor went into the passage to wash his hands.

"You fellows have no conscience," said he to the valet who was pouring water over his hands. "For just one moment I didn't look after you . . . It's such pain, you know, that I wonder how he can bear it."

"By the Lord Jesus Christ, I thought we had put something under him!" said the valet.

The first time Prince Andrei understood where he was and what was the matter with him and remembered being wounded and how was when he asked to be carried into the hut after his calash had stopped at Mytishchi. After growing confused from pain while being carried into the hut he again regained consciousness, and while drinking tea once more recalled all that had happened to him, and above all vividly remembered the moment at the ambulance station when, at the sight of the sufferings of a man he disliked, those new thoughts had come to him which promised him happiness. And those thoughts, though now vague and indefinite, again possessed his soul. He remembered that he had now a new source of happiness and that this happiness had something to do with the Gospels. That was why he asked for a copy of them. The uncomfortable position in which they had put him and turned him over again confused his thoughts, and when he came to himself a third time it was in the complete stillness of the night. Everybody near him was sleeping. A cricket chirped from across the passage; someone was shouting and singing in the street; cockroaches rustled on the table, on the icons, and on the walls, and a big fly flopped at the head of the bed and around the candle beside him, the wick of which was charred and had shaped itself like a mushroom.

His mind was not in a normal state. A healthy man usually thinks of, feels, and remembers innumerable things simultaneously, but has the power and will to select one sequence of thoughts or events on which to fix his whole attention. A healthy man can tear himself away from the deepest reflections to say a civil word to someone who comes in and can then return again to his own thoughts. But Prince Andrei's mind was not in a normal state in that respect. All the powers of his mind were more active and clearer than ever, but they acted apart from his will. Most diverse thoughts and images occupied him simultaneously. At times his brain suddenly began to work with a vigor, clearness, and depth it had never reached when he was in health, but suddenly in the midst of its work it would turn to some unexpected idea and he had not the strength to turn it back again.

"Yes, a new happiness was revealed to me of which man cannot be deprived," he thought as he lay in the semi-darkness of the quiet hut, gazing fixedly before him with feverish wide open eyes. "A happiness lying beyond material forces, outside the material influences that act on man – a happiness of the soul alone, the happiness of loving. Every man can understand it, but to conceive it and enjoin it was possible only for God. But how did God enjoin that law? And why was the Son . . . ?"

And suddenly the sequence of these thoughts broke off, and Prince Andrei heard (without knowing whether it was a delusion or reality) a soft whispering voice incessantly and rhythmically repeating "piti-piti-piti," and then "titi," and then again "piti-piti-piti," and "titi" once more. At the same time he felt that above his face, above the very middle of it, some strange airy structure was being erected out of slender needles or splinters, to the sound of this whispered music. He felt that he had to balance carefully (though it was difficult) so that this airy structure should not collapse; but nevertheless it kept collapsing and again slowly rising to the sound of whispered rhythmic music – "it stretches, stretches, spreading out and stretching," said Prince Andrei to himself. While listening to this whispering and feeling the sensation of this drawing out and the construction of this edifice of needles, he also saw by glimpses a red halo round the candle, and heard the rustle of the cockroaches and the buzzing of the fly that flopped against his pillow and his face. Each time the fly touched his face it gave him a burning sensation and yet to his surprise it did not destroy the structure, though it knocked against the very region of his face where it was rising. But besides this there was something else of importance. It was something white by the door – the statue of a sphinx, which also oppressed him.

"But perhaps that's my shirt on the table," he thought, "and that's my legs, and that is the door, but why is it always stretching and drawing itself out, and 'piti-piti-piti' and 'ti-ti' and 'piti-piti-piti' . . . ? That's enough, please leave off!" Prince Andrei painfully entreated someone. And suddenly thoughts and feelings again swam to the surface of his mind with peculiar clearness and force.

"Yes – love," he thought again quite clearly. "But not love which loves for something, for some quality, for some purpose, or for some reason, but the love which I – while dying – first experienced when I saw my enemy and yet loved him. I experienced that feeling of love which is the very essence of the soul and does not require an object. Now again I feel that bliss. To love one's neighbors, to love one's enemies, to love everything, to love God in all his manifestations. It is possible to love someone dear to you with human love, but an enemy can only be loved by divine love. That is why I experienced such joy when I felt that I loved that man. What has become of him? Is he alive? . . .

"When loving with human love one may pass from love to hatred, but divine love cannot change. No, neither death nor anything else can destroy it. It is the very essence of the soul."

✦ ✦ ✦

Transported home from the battlefield, Prince Andrei is cared for by his sister Marya. When it becomes clear he is dying, his son Nikolushka – born to Andrei's deceased wife – is brought to say goodbye.

When little Nikolushka was brought into Prince Andrei's room he looked at his father with frightened eyes, but did not cry, because no one else was crying. Prince Andrei kissed him and evidently did not know what to say to him.

When Nikolushka had been led away, Princess Marya again went up to her brother, kissed him, and unable to restrain her tears any longer began to cry.

He looked at her attentively.

"Is it about Nikolushka?" he asked.

Princess Marya nodded her head, weeping.

"Marya, you know the Gosp . . . " but he broke off.

"What did you say?"

"Nothing. You mustn't cry here," he said, looking at her with the same cold expression.

When Princess Marya began to cry, he understood that she was crying at the thought that Nikolushka would be left without a father. With a great effort he tried to return to life and to see things from their point of view.

"Yes, to them it must seem sad!" he thought. "But how simple it is."

"Look at the birds of the air: they neither sow nor reap nor gather into barns, and yet your heavenly Father feeds them," he said to himself and wished to say to Princess Marya. "But no, they will take it their own way, they won't understand! They can't understand that all those feelings they prize so – all our feelings, all those ideas that seem so important to us, are unnecessary. We cannot understand one another," and he remained silent.

✦ ✦ ✦

Prince Andrei's little son was seven. He could scarcely read, and knew nothing. After that day he lived through many things, gaining knowledge, observation, and experience, but had he possessed all the faculties he afterwards acquired, he could not have had a better or more profound understanding of the meaning of the scene he had witnessed between his father, Marya, and Natasha, than he had then. He understood it completely, and, leaving the room without crying, went silently up to Natasha who had come out with him and looked shyly at her with his beautiful, thoughtful eyes. Then his uplifted, rosy upper lip trembled and leaning his head against her he began to cry.

✦ ✦ ✦

Not only did Prince Andrei know he would die, but he felt that he was dying and was already half dead. He was conscious of an aloofness from everything earthly and a strange and joyous lightness of existence. Without haste or agitation he awaited what was coming. That inexorable, eternal, distant, and unknown – the presence of which he had felt continually all his life – was now near to him and, by the strange lightness he experienced, almost comprehensible and palpable . . .

Formerly he had feared the end. He had twice experienced that terribly tormenting fear of death – the end – but now he no longer understood that fear.

He had felt it for the first time when the shell spun like a top before him, and he looked at the fallow field, the bushes, and the sky, and knew that he was face to face with death. When he came to himself after being wounded and the flower of eternal, unfettered love had instantly unfolded itself in his soul as if freed from the bondage of life that had restrained it, he no longer feared death and ceased to think about it.

During the hours of solitude, suffering, and partial delirium he spent after he was wounded, the more deeply he penetrated into the new principle of eternal love revealed to him, the more he unconsciously detached himself from earthly life. To love everything and everybody and always to sacrifice oneself for love meant not to love anyone, not to live this earthly life. And the more imbued he became with that principle of love, the more he renounced life and the more completely he destroyed that dreadful barrier which – in the absence of such love – stands between life and death. When during those first days he remembered that he would have to die, he said to himself: "Well, what of it? So much the better!"

But after the night in Mytishchi when, half delirious, he had seen her for whom he longed appear before him and, having pressed her hand to his lips, had shed gentle, happy tears, love for a particular woman again crept unobserved into his heart and once more bound him to life. And joyful and agitating thoughts began to occupy his mind. Recalling the moment at the ambulance station when he had seen Kuragin, he could not now regain the feeling he then had, but was tormented by the question whether Kuragin was alive. And he dared not inquire.

His illness pursued its normal physical course, but what Natasha referred to when she said: "This suddenly happened," had occurred two days before Princess Marya arrived. It was the last spiritual struggle between life and death, in which death gained the victory. It was the unexpected realization of the fact that he still valued life as presented to him in the form of his love for Natasha, and a last, though ultimately vanquished, attack of terror before the unknown.

It was evening. As usual after dinner he was slightly feverish, and his thoughts were preternaturally clear. Sonya [Natasha's cousin] was sitting by the table. He began to doze. Suddenly a feeling of happiness seized him.

"Ah, she has come!" thought he.

And so it was: in Sonya's place sat Natasha who had just come in noiselessly.

Since she had begun looking after him, he had always experienced this physical consciousness of her nearness. She was sitting in an armchair placed sideways, screening the light of the candle from him, and was knitting a stocking. She had learned to knit stockings since Prince Andrei had casually mentioned that no one nursed the sick so well as old nurses who knit stockings, and that there is something soothing in the knitting of stockings. The needles clicked lightly in her slender, rapidly moving hands, and he could clearly see the thoughtful profile of her drooping face. She moved, and the ball rolled off her knees. She started, glanced round at him, and screening the candle with her hand stooped carefully with a supple and exact movement, picked up the ball, and regained her former position.

He looked at her without moving and saw that she wanted to draw a deep breath after stooping, but refrained from doing so and breathed cautiously.

At the Troitsa Monastery they had spoken of the past, and he had told her that if he lived he would always thank God for his wound which had brought them together again, but after that they never spoke of the future.

"Can it or can it not be?" he now thought as he looked at her and listened to the light click of the steel needles. "Can fate have brought me to her so strangely only for me to die? . . . Is it possible that the truth of life has been revealed to me only to show me that I have spent my life in falsity? I love her more than anything in the world! But what am I to do if I love her?" he thought, and he involuntarily groaned, from a habit acquired during his sufferings.

On hearing that sound Natasha put down the stocking, leaned nearer to him, and suddenly, noticing his shining eyes, stepped lightly up to him and bent over him.

"You are not asleep?"

"No, I have been looking at you a long time. I felt you come in. No one else gives me that sense of soft tranquility that you do . . . that light. I want to weep for joy."

Natasha drew closer to him. Her face shone with rapturous joy.

"Natasha, I love you too much! More than anything in the world."

"And I!" She turned away for an instant. "Why too much?" she asked.

"Why too much? . . . Well, what do you, what do you feel in your soul, your whole soul – shall I live? What do you think?"

"I am sure of it, sure!" Natasha almost shouted, taking hold of both his hands with a passionate movement.

He remained silent awhile.

"How good it would be!" and taking her hand he kissed it.

Natasha felt happy and agitated, but at once remembered that this would not do and that he had to be quiet.

"But you have not slept," she said, repressing her joy. "Try to sleep . . . please!"

He pressed her hand and released it, and she went back to the candle and sat down again in her former position. Twice she turned and looked at him, and her eyes met his beaming at her. She set herself a task on her stocking and resolved not to turn round till it was finished.

Soon he really shut his eyes and fell asleep. He did not sleep long and suddenly awoke with a start and in a cold perspiration.

As he fell asleep he had still been thinking of the subject that now always occupied his mind – about life and death, and chiefly about death. He felt himself nearer to it.

"Love? What is love?" he thought.

"Love hinders death. Love is life. All, everything that I understand, I understand only because I love. Everything is, everything exists, only because I love. Everything is united by it alone. Love is God, and to die means that I, a particle of love, shall return to the general and eternal source." These thoughts seemed to him comforting. But they were only thoughts. Something was lacking in them, they were not clear, they were too one-sidedly personal and brain-spun. And there was the former agitation and obscurity. He fell asleep.

He dreamed that he was lying in the room he really was in, but that he was quite well and not wounded. Many various, indifferent, and insignificant people appeared before him. He talked to them and discussed something trivial. They were preparing to go away somewhere. Prince Andrei dimly realized that all this was trivial and that he had more important cares, but he continued to speak, surprising them by empty witticisms. Gradually, unnoticed, all these persons began to disappear and a single question, that of the closed door, superseded all else. He rose and went to the door to bolt and lock it. Everything depended on whether he was, or was not, in time to lock it. He went, and tried to hurry, but his legs refused to move and he knew he would not be in time to lock the door though he painfully strained all his powers. He was seized by an agonizing fear. And that fear was the fear of death. It stood behind the door. But just when he was clumsily creeping toward the door, that dreadful something on the other side was already pressing against it and forcing its way in. Something not human – death – was breaking in through that door, and had to be kept out. He seized the door, making a final effort to hold it back – to lock it was no longer possible – but his efforts were weak and clumsy and the door, pushed from behind by that terror, opened and closed again.

Once again it pushed from outside. His last superhuman efforts were vain and both halves of the door noiselessly opened. It entered, and it was death, and Prince Andrei died.

But at the instant he died, Prince Andrei remembered that he was asleep, and at the very instant he died, having made an effort, he awoke.

"Yes, it was death! I died – and woke up. Yes, death is an awakening!" And all at once it grew light in his soul and the veil that had till then concealed the unknown was lifted from his spiritual vision. He felt as if powers till then confined within him had been liberated, and that strange lightness did not again leave him.

When, waking in a cold perspiration, he moved on the divan, Natasha went up and asked him what was the matter. He did not answer and looked at her strangely, not understanding.

That was what had happened to him two days before Princess Marya's arrival. From that day, as the doctor expressed it, the wasting fever assumed a malignant character, but what the doctor said did not interest Natasha, she saw the terrible moral symptoms which to her were more convincing.

From that day an awakening from life came to Prince Andrei together with his awakening from sleep. And compared to the duration of life it did not seem to him slower than an awakening from sleep compared to the duration of a dream.

There was nothing terrible or violent in this comparatively slow awakening.

His last days and hours passed in an ordinary and simple way. Both Princess Marya and Natasha, who did not leave him, felt this. They did not weep or shudder and during these last days they themselves felt that they were not attending on him (he was no longer there, he had left them) but on what reminded them most closely of him – his body. Both felt this so strongly that the outward and terrible side of death did not affect them and they did not feel it necessary to foment their grief. Neither in his presence nor out of it did they weep, nor did they ever talk to one another about him. They felt that they could not express in words what they understood.

They both saw that he was sinking slowly and quietly, deeper and deeper, away from them, and they both knew that this had to be so and that it was right.

He confessed, and received communion. Everyone came to take leave of him. When they brought his son to him, he pressed his lips to the boy's and turned away, not because he felt it hard and sad (Princess Marya and Natasha understood that) but simply because he thought it was all that was required of him, but when they told him to bless the boy, he did what was demanded and looked round as if asking whether there was anything else he should do.

When the last convulsions of the body, which the spirit was leaving, occurred, Princess Marya and Natasha were present.

"Is it over?" said Princess Marya when his body had for a few minutes lain motionless, growing cold before them. Natasha went up, looked at the dead eyes, and hastened to close them. She closed them but did not kiss them, but clung to that which reminded her most nearly of him – his body.

"Where has he gone? Where is he now? . . ."

When the body, washed and dressed, lay in the coffin on a table, everyone came to take leave of him and they all wept.

Nikolushka cried because his heart was rent by painful perplexity. The countess and Sonya cried from pity for Natasha and because he was no more. The old count cried because he felt that before long, he, too, must take the same terrible step.

Natasha and Princess Marya also wept now, but not because of their own personal grief; they wept with a reverent and softening emotion which had taken possession of their souls at the consciousness of the simple and solemn mystery of death that had been accomplished in their presence.

✦ ✦ ✦

When seeing a dying animal a man feels a sense of horror: substance similar to his own is perishing before his eyes. But when it is a beloved and intimate human being that is dying, besides this horror at the extinction of life there is a severance, a spiritual wound, which like a physical wound is sometimes fatal and sometimes heals, but always aches and shrinks at any external irritating touch.

After Prince Andrei's death Natasha and Princess Marya alike felt this. Drooping in spirit and closing their eyes before the menacing cloud of death that overhung them, they dared not look life in the face. They carefully guarded their open wounds from any rough and painful contact. Everything: a carriage passing rapidly in the street, a summons to dinner, the maid's inquiry what dress to prepare, or worse still any word of insincere or feeble sympathy, seemed an insult, painfully irritated the wound, interrupting that necessary quiet in which they both tried to listen to the stern and dreadful choir that still resounded in their imagination, and hindered their gazing into those mysterious limitless vistas that for an instant had opened out before them.

Only when alone together were they free from such outrage and pain. They spoke little even to one another, and when they did it was of very unimportant matters.

Both avoided any allusion to the future. To admit the possibility of a future seemed to them to insult his memory. Still more carefully did they avoid anything relating to him who was dead. It seemed to them that what they had lived through and experienced could not be expressed in words, and that any reference to the details of his life infringed the majesty and sacredness of the mystery that had been accomplished before their eyes.

Continued abstention from speech, and constant avoidance of everything that might lead up to the subject – this halting on all sides at the boundary of what they might not mention brought before their minds with still greater purity and clearness what they were both feeling.

17.

The Repentant Sinner

A Story

And he said, "Jesus, remember me when you come into your kingdom." And Jesus said to him, "Truly, I say to you, today you will be with me in Paradise." —Luke 23:42–43

THERE WAS ONCE A MAN who lived for seventy years in the world, and lived in sin all that time. He fell ill but even then did not repent. Only at the last moment, as he was dying, he wept and said, "Lord! Forgive me, as you forgave the thief upon the cross."

And as he said these words, his soul left his body. And the soul of the sinner, feeling love towards God and faith in his mercy, went to the gates of heaven and knocked, praying to be let into the heavenly kingdom.

Then a voice spoke from within the gate: "What man is it that knocks at the gates of Paradise and what deeds did he do during his life?"

And the voice of the Accuser replied, recounting all the man's evil deeds, and not a single good one.

And the voice from within the gates answered, "Sinners cannot enter into the kingdom of heaven. Go hence!"

Then the man said, "Lord, I hear thy voice, but cannot see thy face, nor do I know thy name."

The voice answered, "I am Peter, the Apostle."

And the sinner replied, "Have pity on me, Apostle Peter! Remember man's weakness, and God's mercy. Weren't you a disciple of Christ? Didn't you hear his teaching from his own lips, and didn't you have his example before you? Remember then how, when he sorrowed and was grieved in spirit, and three times asked you to keep awake and pray, you slept, because your eyes were heavy, and three times he found you sleeping. So it was with me. Remember, also, how you promised to be faithful unto death, and yet denied him three times when he was taken before Caiaphas. So it was with me. And remember, too, how when the cock crowed you went out and wept bitterly. So it is with me. You cannot refuse to let me in."

And the voice behind the gates was silent.

Then the sinner stood a little while, and again began to knock, and to ask to be let into the kingdom of heaven.

And he heard another voice behind the gates, which said, "Who is this man, and how did he live on earth?"

And the voice of the Accuser again repeated all the sinner's evil deeds, and not a single good one.

And the voice from behind the gates replied, "Go hence! Such sinners cannot live with us in Paradise."

Then the sinner said, "Lord, I hear your voice, but I do not see you, nor do I know your name."

And the voice answered, "I am David, king and prophet."

The sinner did not despair, nor did he leave the gates of Paradise, but said:

"Have pity on me, King David! Remember man's weakness, and God's mercy. God loved you and exalted you among men. You had everything: a kingdom, and honor, and riches, and wives, and children; but you saw from your housetop the wife of a poor man, and sin entered into you, and you took the wife of

Uriah, and slew him with the sword of the Ammonites. You, a rich man, took from the poor man his one ewe lamb, and killed him. I have done likewise. Remember, then, how you repented, and how you said, 'I acknowledge my transgressions: my sin is ever before me.' I have done the same. You cannot refuse to let me in."

And the voice from within the gates was silent.

The sinner having stood a little while, began knocking again, and asking to be let into the kingdom of heaven. And a third voice was heard within the gates, saying, "Who is this man, and how has he spent his life on earth?"

And the voice of the Accuser replied for the third time, recounting the sinner's evil deeds, and not mentioning one good deed.

And the voice within the gates said, "Depart hence! Sinners cannot enter into the kingdom of heaven."

And the sinner said, "I hear your voice, but I do not see your face, neither do I know your name."

Then the voice replied, "I am John the Divine, the beloved disciple of Christ."

And the sinner rejoiced and said, "Now surely I shall be allowed to enter. Peter and David must let me in, because they know man's weakness and God's mercy; and you will let me in, because you love much. Was it not you, John the Divine, who wrote that God is Love, and that he who loves not, knows not God? And in your old age did you not say to the people: 'Brethren, love one another'? How, then, can you look on me with hatred, and drive me away? Either you must renounce what you have said, or loving me, must let me enter the kingdom of heaven."

And the gates of Paradise opened, and John embraced the repentant sinner and took him into the kingdom of heaven.

Living Simply

*No one can serve two masters; for either he will hate
the one and love the other, or he will be devoted to
the one and despise the other. You cannot serve
God and mammon.* —Matthew 5:24

The Labor Cross

18.

A Grain as Big as a Hen's Egg

A Story

ONE DAY some children found, in a ravine, a thing shaped like a grain of corn, with a groove down the middle, but as large as a hen's egg. A traveler passing by saw the thing, bought it from the children for a penny, and taking it to town sold it to the king as a curiosity.

The king called together his wise men, and told them to find out what the thing was. The wise men pondered and pondered and could not make head or tail of it, till one day, when the thing was lying on a windowsill, a hen flew in and pecked at it till she made a hole in it, and then everyone saw that it was a grain of corn. The wise men went to the king and said:

"It is a grain of corn."

At this the king was much surprised; and he ordered the learned men to find out when and where such corn had grown. The learned men pondered again, and searched in their books, but could find nothing about it. So they returned to the king and said:

"We can give you no answer. There is nothing about it in our books. You will have to ask the peasants; perhaps some of them may have heard from their fathers when and where grain grew to such a size."

So the king gave orders that some very old peasant should be brought before him; and his servants found such a man and brought him to the king. Old and bent, ashy pale and toothless, he just managed with the help of two crutches to totter into the king's presence.

The king showed him the grain, but the old man could hardly see it; he took it, however, and felt it with his hands. The king questioned him, saying:

"Can you tell us, old man, where such grain as this grew? Have you ever bought such corn, or sown such in your fields?"

The old man was so deaf that he could hardly hear what the king said, and only understood with great difficulty.

"No!" he answered at last, "I never sowed nor reaped any like it in my fields, nor did I ever buy any such. When we bought corn, the grains were always as small as they are now. But you might ask my father. He may have heard where such grain grew."

So the king sent for the old man's father, and he was found and brought before the king. He came walking with one crutch. The king showed him the grain, and the old peasant, who was still able to see, took a good look at it. And the king asked him:

"Can you not tell us, old man, where corn like this used to grow? Have you ever bought any like it, or sown any in your fields?"

Though the old man was rather hard of hearing, he still heard better than his son had done.

"No," he said, "I never sowed nor reaped any grain like this in my field. As to buying, I never bought any, for in my time money was not yet in use. Everyone grew his own corn, and when there was any need we shared with one another. I do not know where corn like this grew. Ours was larger and yielded more flour than present-day grain, but I never saw any like this. I have, however, heard my father say that in his time the grain grew larger and yielded more flour than ours. You had better ask him."

So the king sent for this old man's father, and they found him too, and brought him before the king. He entered walking easily and without crutches: his eye was clear, his hearing good, and he spoke distinctly. The king showed him the grain, and the old grandfather looked at it, and turned it about in his hand.

"It is long since I saw such a fine grain," said he, and he bit a piece off and tasted it.

"It's the very same kind," he added.

"Tell me, grandfather," said the king, "when and where was such corn grown? Have you ever bought any like it, or sown any in your fields?"

And the old man replied:

"Corn like this used to grow everywhere in my time. I lived on corn like this in my young days, and fed others on it. It was grain like this that we used to sow and reap and thresh."

And the king asked:

"Tell me, grandfather, did you buy it anywhere, or did you grow it all yourself?"

The old man smiled.

"In my time," he answered, "no one ever thought of such a sin as buying or selling bread; and we knew nothing of money. Each man had corn enough of his own."

"Then tell me, grandfather," asked the king, "where was your field, where did you grow corn like this?"

And the grandfather answered:

"My field was God's earth. Wherever I plowed, there was my field. Land was free. It was a thing no man called his own. Labor was the only thing people called their own."

"Answer me two more questions," said the king. "The first is, Why did the earth bear such grain then and has ceased to do so now? And the second is, Why does your grandson walk with two crutches, your son with one, and you yourself with none? Your eyes are bright, your teeth sound, and your speech clear and pleasant to the ear. How have these things come about?"

And the old man answered:

"These things are so, because people have ceased to live by their own labor, and have taken to depending on the labor of others. In the old time, people lived according to God's law. They had what was their own, and coveted not what others had produced."

19.

Ivan the Fool

A Fairy Tale

The Story of Ivan the Fool, and of His Two Brothers, Simon the Soldier and Tarás the Stout; and of His Dumb Sister Martha, and of the Old Devil and the Three Little Imps

I

ONCE UPON A TIME, in a certain province of a certain country, there lived a rich peasant, who had three sons: Simon the Soldier, Tarás the Stout, and Ivan the Fool, besides an unmarried daughter, Martha, who was deaf and dumb. Simon the Soldier went to the wars to serve the king; Tarás the Stout went to a merchant's in town to trade, and Ivan the Fool stayed at home with the lass, to till the ground till his back bent.

Simon the Soldier obtained high rank and an estate, and married a nobleman's daughter. His pay was large and his estate was large, but yet he could not make ends meet. What the husband earned his lady wife squandered, and they never had money enough.

So Simon the Soldier went to his estate to collect the income, but his steward said, "Where is any income to come from? We have neither cattle, nor tools, nor horse, nor plow, nor harrow. We must first get all these, and then the money will come."

Then Simon the Soldier went to his father and said: "You, father, are rich, but have given me nothing. Divide what you have, and give me a third part, that I may improve my estate."

But the old man said: "You brought nothing into my house; why should I give you a third part? It would be unfair to Ivan and to the girl."

But Simon answered, "He is a fool; and she is an old maid, and deaf and dumb besides; what's the good of property to them?"

The old man said, "We will see what Ivan says about it."

And Ivan said, "Let him take what he wants."

So Simon the Soldier took his share of his father's goods and removed them to his estate, and went off again to serve the king.

Tarás the Stout also gathered much money, and married into a merchant's family, but still he wanted more. So he, also, came to his father and said, "Give me my portion."

But the old man did not wish to give Tarás a share either, and said, "You brought nothing here. Ivan has earned all we have in the house, and why should we wrong him and the girl?"

But Tarás said, "What does he need? He is a fool! He cannot marry, no one would have him; and the dumb lass does not need anything either. Look here, Ivan!" said he, "Give me half the corn; I don't want the tools, and of the livestock I will take only the grey stallion, which is of no use to you for the plow."

Ivan laughed and said, "Take what you want. I will work to earn some more."

So they gave a share to Tarás also, and he carted the corn away to town, and took the grey stallion. And Ivan was left with one old mare, to lead his peasant life as before, and to support his father and mother.

II

Now the old Devil was vexed that the brothers had not quarreled over the division, but had parted peacefully; and he summoned three imps.

"Look here," said he, "there are three brothers: Simon the Soldier, Tarás the Stout, and Ivan the Fool. They should have quarreled, but are living peaceably and meet on friendly terms. The fool Ivan has spoilt the whole business for me. Now you three go and tackle those three brothers, and worry them till they scratch each other's eyes out! Do you think you can do it?"

"Yes, we'll do it," said they.

"How will you set about it?"

"Why," said they, "first we'll ruin them. And when they haven't a crust to eat we'll tie them up together, and then they'll fight each other, sure enough!"

"That's capital; I see you understand your business. Go, and don't come back till you've set them by the ears, or I'll skin you alive!"

The imps went off into a swamp, and began to consider how they should set to work. They disputed and disputed, each wanting the lightest job; but at last they decided to cast lots which of the brothers each imp should tackle. If one imp finished his task before the others, he was to come and help them. So the imps cast lots, and appointed a time to meet again in the swamp to learn who had succeeded and who needed help.

The appointed time came round, and the imps met again in the swamp as agreed. And each began to tell how matters stood. The first, who had undertaken Simon the Soldier, began: "My business is going on well. Tomorrow Simon will return to his father's house."

His comrades asked, "How did you manage it?"

"First," says he, "I made Simon so bold that he offered to conquer the whole world for his king; and the king made him his general and sent him to fight the King of India. They met for battle, but the night before, I dampened all the powder in Simon's camp, and made more straw soldiers for the Indian king than you could count. And when Simon's soldiers saw the straw soldiers surrounding them, they grew frightened. Simon ordered them to fire; but their cannons and guns would not go off. Then Simon's soldiers were quite frightened, and ran like sheep, and the Indian king slaughtered them. Simon was disgraced. He has been deprived of his estate, and tomorrow they intend to execute him. There is only one day's work left for me to do; I have just to let him out of prison that he may escape home. Tomorrow I shall be ready to help whichever of you needs me.

Then the second imp, who had Tarás in hand, began to tell how he had fared. "I don't want any help," said he, "my job is going all right. Tarás can't hold out for more than a week. First I caused him to grow greedy and fat. His covetousness became so great that whatever he saw he wanted to buy. He has spent all his money in buying immense lots of goods, and still continues to buy. Already he has begun to use borrowed money. His debts hang like a weight round his neck, and he is so involved that he can never get clear. In a week his bills come due, and before then I will spoil all his stock. He will be unable to pay and will have to go home to his father."

Then they asked the third imp (Ivan's), "And how are you getting on?"

"Well," said he, "my affair goes badly. First I spat into his drink to make his stomach ache, and then I went into his field and hammered the ground hard as a stone that he should not be able to till it. I thought he wouldn't plow it, but like the fool that he is, he came with his plow and began to make a furrow. He groaned with the pain in his stomach, but went on plowing. I broke his plow for him, but he went home, got out another, and again started plowing. I crept under the earth and caught hold of the plowshares, but there was no holding them; he leant heavily upon the plow, and the plowshare was sharp and cut my hands. He has all but finished plowing the field, only one little strip is left. Come brothers, and help me; for if we don't get the better of him, all our labor is lost. If the fool holds out and keeps on working the land, his brothers will never know want, for he will feed them both."

Simon the Soldier's imp promised to come next day to help, and so they parted.

III

Ivan had plowed up the whole fallow, all but one little strip. He came to finish it. Though his stomach ached, the plowing must be done. He freed the harness ropes, turned the plow, and began to work. He drove one furrow, but coming back the plow began to drag as if it had caught in a root. It was the imp, who had twisted his legs round the plowshare and was holding it back.

"What a strange thing!" thought Ivan. "There were no roots here at all, and yet here's a root."

Ivan pushed his hand deep into the furrow, groped about, and, feeling something soft, seized hold of it and pulled it out. It was black like a root, but it wriggled. Why, it was a live imp!

"What a nasty thing!" said Ivan, and he lifted his hand to dash it against the plow, but the imp squealed out:

"Don't hurt me, and I'll do anything you tell me to."

"What can you do?"

"Anything you tell me to."

Ivan scratched his head.

"My stomach aches," said he; "can you cure that?"

"Certainly I can."

"Well then, do so."

The imp went down into the furrow, searched about, scratched with his claws, and pulled out a bunch of three little roots, which he handed to Ivan.

"Here," says he, "whoever swallows one of these will be cured of any illness."

Ivan took the roots, separated them, and swallowed one. The pain in his stomach was cured at once. The imp again begged to be let off; "I will jump right into the earth, and never come back," said he.

"All right," said Ivan; "begone, and God be with you!"

And as soon as Ivan mentioned God, the imp plunged into the earth like a stone thrown into the water. Only a hole was left.

Ivan put the other two pieces of root into his cap and went on with his plowing. He plowed the strip to the end, turned his plow over, and went home. He unharnessed the horse, entered the hut, and there he saw his elder brother, Simon the Soldier and his wife, sitting at supper. Simon's estate had been confiscated, he himself had barely managed to escape from prison, and he had come back to live in his father's house.

Simon saw Ivan, and said: "I have come to live with you. Feed me and my wife till I get another appointment."

"All right," said Ivan, "you can stay with us."

But when Ivan was about to sit down on the bench the lady disliked the smell, and said to her husband, "I cannot sup with a dirty peasant."

So Simon the Soldier said, "My lady says you don't smell nice. You'd better go and eat outside."

"All right," said Ivan; "anyway I must spend the night outside, for I have to pasture the mare."

So he took some bread, and his coat, and went with the mare into the fields.

IV

Having finished his work that night, Simon's imp came, as agreed, to find Ivan's imp and help him to subdue the fool. He came to the field and searched and searched; but instead of his comrade he found only a hole.

"Clearly," thought he, "some evil has befallen my comrade. I must take his place. The field is plowed up, so the fool must be tackled in the meadow."

So the imp went to the meadows and flooded Ivan's hayfield with water, which left the grass all covered with mud.

Ivan returned from the pasture at dawn, sharpened his scythe, and went to mow the hayfield. He began to mow but had only swung the scythe once or twice when the edge turned so that it would not cut at all, but needed re-sharpening. Ivan struggled on for a while, and then said: "It's no good. I must go home and bring a tool to straighten the scythe, and I'll get a chunk of bread at the same time. If I have to spend a week here, I won't leave till the mowing's done."

The imp heard this and thought to himself, "This fool is a tough 'un; I can't get round him this way. I must try some other dodge."

Ivan returned, sharpened his scythe, and began to mow. The imp crept into the grass and began to catch the scythe by the heel, sending the point into the earth. Ivan found the work very hard, but he mowed the whole meadow, except one little bit which was in the swamp. The imp crept into the swamp and thought to himself, "Though I cut my paws I will not let him mow."

Ivan reached the swamp. The grass didn't seem thick, but yet it resisted the scythe. Ivan grew angry and began to swing the scythe with all his might. The imp had to give in; he could not keep up with the scythe, and, seeing it was a bad business, he scrambled into a bush. Ivan swung the scythe, caught the bush, and cut off half the imp's tail. Then he finished mowing the grass, told his sister to rake it up, and went himself to mow the rye. He went with the scythe, but the dock-tailed imp was there first, and entangled the rye so that the scythe was of no use. But Ivan went home and got his sickle and began to reap with that, and he reaped the whole of the rye.

"Now it's time," said he, "to start on the oats."

The dock-tailed imp heard this, and thought, "I couldn't get the better of him on the rye, but I shall on the oats. Only wait till the morning."

In the morning the imp hurried to the oat field, but the oats were already mowed down! Ivan had mowed them by night, in order that less grain should shake out. The imp grew angry.

"He has cut me all over and tired me out – the fool. It is worse than war. The accursed fool never sleeps; one can't keep up with him. I will get into his stacks now and rot them."

So the imp entered the rye, and crept among the sheaves, and they began to rot. He heated them, grew warm himself, and fell asleep.

Ivan harnessed the mare, and went with the lass to cart the rye. He came to the heaps, and began to pitch the rye into the cart. He tossed two sheaves and again thrust his fork – right into the imp's back. He lifts the fork and sees on the prongs a live imp; dock-tailed, struggling, wriggling, and trying to jump off.

"What, you nasty thing, are you here again?"

"I'm another," said the imp. "The first was my brother. I've been with your brother Simon."

"Well," said Ivan, "whoever you are, you've met the same fate!"

He was about to dash him against the cart, but the imp cried out: "Let me off, and I will not only let you alone, but I'll do anything you tell me to do."

"What can you do?"

"I can make soldiers out of anything you like."

"But what use are they?"

"You can turn them to any use; they can do anything you please."

"Can they sing?"

"Yes, if you want them to."

"All right; you may make me some."

And the imp said, "Here, take a sheaf of rye, then bump it upright on the ground, and simply say:

> O sheaf! my slave
> This order gave:
> Where a straw has been
> Let a soldier be seen!"

Ivan took the sheaf, struck it on the ground, and said what the imp had told him to. The sheaf fell asunder, and all the straws changed into soldiers, with a trumpeter and a drummer playing in front, so that there was a whole regiment.

Ivan laughed.

"How clever!" said he. "This is fine! How pleased the girls will be!"

"Now let me go," said the imp.

"No," said Ivan, "I must make my soldiers of thrashed straw, otherwise good grain will be wasted. Teach me how to change them back again into the sheaf. I want to thrash it."

And the imp said, "Repeat:

Let each be a straw
Who was soldier before,
For my true slave
This order gave!"

Ivan said this, and the sheaf reappeared.

Again the imp began to beg, "Now let me go!"

"All right." And Ivan pressed him against the side of the cart, held him down with his hand, and pulled him off the fork.

"God be with you," said he.

And as soon as he mentioned God, the imp plunged into the earth like a stone into water. Only a hole was left.

Ivan returned home, and there was his other brother, Tarás, with his wife, sitting at supper.

Tarás the Stout had failed to pay his debts, had run away from his creditors, and had come home to his father's house. When he saw Ivan, "Look here," said he, "till I can start in business again, I want you to keep me and my wife."

"All right," said Ivan, "you can live here, if you like."

Ivan took off his coat and sat down to table, but the merchant's wife said: "I cannot sit at table with this clown, he smells of perspiration."

Then Tarás the Stout said, "Ivan, you smell too strong. Go and eat outside."

"All right," said Ivan, taking some bread and going into the yard. "It is time, anyhow, for me to go and pasture the mare."

V

Tarás's imp, being also free that night, came as agreed to help his comrades subdue Ivan the Fool. He came to the cornfield, looked and looked for his comrades – no one was there. He only found a hole. He went to the meadow, and there he found an imp's tail in the swamp, and another hole in the rye stubble.

"Evidently, some ill-luck has befallen my comrades," thought he. "I must take their place and tackle the fool."

So the imp went to look for Ivan, who had already stacked the corn and was cutting trees in the wood. The two brothers had begun to feel crowded, living together, and had told Ivan to cut down trees to build new houses for them.

The imp ran to the wood, climbed among the branches, and began to hinder Ivan from felling the trees. Ivan undercut one tree so that it should fall clear, but in falling it turned askew and caught among some branches. Ivan cut a pole with which to lever it aside, and with difficulty contrived to bring it to the ground. He set to work to fell another tree – again the same thing occurred; and with all his efforts he could hardly get the tree clear. He began on a third tree, and again the same thing happened.

Ivan had hoped to cut down half a hundred small trees, but had not felled even half a score, and now the night was come and he was tired out. The steam from him spread like a mist through the wood, but still he stuck to his work. He undercut another tree, but his back began to ache so that he could not stand. He drove his axe into the tree and sat down to rest.

The imp, noticing that Ivan had stopped work, grew cheerful.

"At last," thought he, "he is tired out! He will give it up. Now I can take a rest myself."

He seated himself astride a branch and chuckled. But soon Ivan got up, pulled the axe out, swung it, and smote the tree from the opposite side with such force that the tree gave way at once and came crashing down. The imp had not expected this, and had no time to get his feet clear, and the tree in breaking gripped his paw. Ivan began to lop off the branches, when he noticed a live imp hanging in the tree! Ivan was surprised.

"What, you nasty thing," says he, "so you are here again!"

"I am another one," says the imp. "I have been with your brother Tarás."

"Whoever you are you have met your fate," said Ivan, and swinging his axe he was about to strike him with the haft, but the imp begged for mercy: "Don't strike me," said he, "and I will do anything you tell me to."

"What can you do?"

"I can make money for you, as much as you want."

"All right, make some." So the imp showed him how to do it.

"Take," said he, "some leaves from this oak and rub them in your hands, and gold will fall out on the ground."

Ivan took some leaves and rubbed them, and gold ran down from his hands.

"This stuff will do fine," said he, "for the fellows to play with on their holidays."

"Now let me go," said the imp.

"All right," said Ivan, and taking a lever he set the imp free. "Now begone! And God be with you," says he.

And as soon as he mentioned God, the imp plunged into the earth, like a stone into water. Only a hole was left.

VI

So the brothers built houses, and began to live apart; and Ivan finished the harvest work, brewed beer, and invited his brothers to spend the next holiday with him. His brothers would not come.

"We don't care about peasant feasts," said they.

So Ivan entertained the peasants and their wives, and drank until he was rather tipsy. Then he went into the street to a ring of dancers; and going up to them he told the women to sing a song in his honor; "for," said he, "I will give you something you never saw in your lives before!"

The women laughed and sang his praises, and when they had finished they said, "Now let us have your gift."

"I will bring it directly," said he.

He took a seed basket and ran into the woods. The women laughed. "He is a fool!" said they, and they began to talk of something else.

But soon Ivan came running back, carrying the basket full of something heavy.

"Shall I give it you?"

"Yes! Give it to us."

Ivan took a handful of gold and threw it to the women. You should have seen them throw themselves upon it to pick it up! And the men around scrambled for it, and snatched it from one another. One old woman was nearly crushed to death. Ivan laughed.

"Oh, you fools!" says he. "Why did you crush the old grandmother? Be quiet, and I will give you some more," and he threw them some more. The people all crowded round, and Ivan threw them all the gold he had. They asked for more, but Ivan said, "I have no more just now. Another time I'll give you some more. Now let us dance, and you can sing me your songs."

The women began to sing.

"Your songs are no good," says he.

"Where will you find better ones?" say they.

"I'll soon show you," says he.

He went to the barn, took a sheaf, thrashed it, stood it up, and bumped it on the ground.

"Now," said he:

> O sheaf! my slave
> This order gave:
> Where a straw has been
> Let a soldier be seen!

And the sheaf fell asunder and became so many soldiers. The drums and trumpets began to play. Ivan ordered the soldiers to play and sing. He led them out into the street, and the people were amazed. The soldiers played and sang, and then Ivan (forbidding anyone to follow him) led them back to the thrashing ground, changed them into a sheaf again, and threw it in its place.

He then went home and lay down in the stables to sleep.

VII

Simon the Soldier heard of all these things next morning, and went to his brother.

"Tell me," says he, "where you got those soldiers from, and to where have you taken them?"

"What does it matter to you?" said Ivan.

"What does it matter? Why, with soldiers one can do anything. One can win a kingdom."

Ivan wondered.

"Really!" said he; "Why didn't you say so before? I'll make you as many as you like. It's well the lass and I have thrashed so much straw."

Ivan took his brother to the barn and said:

"Look here; if I make you some soldiers, you must take them away at once, for if we have to feed them, they will eat up the whole village in a day."

Simon the Soldier promised to lead the soldiers away; and Ivan began to make them. He bumped a sheaf on the thrashing floor – a company appeared. He bumped another sheaf, and there was a second company. He made so many that they covered the field.

"Will that do?" he asked.

Simon was overjoyed, and said: "That will do! Thank you, Ivan!"

"All right," said Ivan. "If you want more, come back, and I'll make them. There is plenty of straw this season."

Simon the Soldier at once took command of his army, collected and organized it, and went off to make war.

Hardly had Simon the Soldier gone, when Tarás the Stout came along. He, too, had heard of yesterday's affair, and he said to his brother:

"Show me where you get gold money! If I only had some to start with, I could make it bring me in money from all over the world."

Ivan was astonished.

"Really!" said he. "You should have told me sooner. I will make you as much as you like."

His brother was delighted.

"Give me three basketfuls to begin with."

"All right," said Ivan. "Come into the forest; or better still, let us harness the mare, for you won't be able to carry it all."

They drove to the forest, and Ivan began to rub the oak leaves. He made a great heap of gold.

"Will that do?"

Tarás was overjoyed.

"It will do for the present," said he. "Thank you, Ivan!"

"All right," says Ivan, "if you want more, come back for it. There are plenty of leaves left."

Tarás the Stout gathered up a whole cartload of money, and went off to trade.

So the two brothers went away: Simon to fight and Tarás to buy and sell. And Simon the Soldier conquered a kingdom for himself; and Tarás the Stout made much money in trade.

When the two brothers met, each told the other: Simon how he got the soldiers, and Tarás how he got the money. And Simon the Soldier said to his brother, "I have conquered a kingdom and live in grand style but I have not money enough to keep my soldiers."

And Tarás the Stout said, "And I have made much money, but the trouble is, I have no one to guard it."

Then said Simon the Soldier, "Let us go to our brother. I will tell him to make more soldiers, and will give them to you to guard your money, and you can tell him to make money for me to feed my men."

And they drove away to Ivan; and Simon said, "Dear brother, I have not enough soldiers; make me another couple of ricks or so."

Ivan shook his head.

"No!" says he, "I will not make any more soldiers."

"But you promised you would."

"I know I promised, but I won't make any more."

"But why not, fool?"

"Because your soldiers killed a man. I was plowing the other day near the road, and I saw a woman taking a coffin along in a cart, and crying. I asked her who was dead. She said, 'Simon's soldiers have killed my husband in the war.' I thought the soldiers would only play tunes, but they have killed a man. I won't give you any more."

And he stuck to it, and would not make any more soldiers.

Tarás the Stout, too, began to beg Ivan to make him more gold money. But Ivan shook his head.

"No, I won't make any more," said he.

"Didn't you promise?"

"I did, but I'll make no more," said he.

"Why not, fool?"

"Because your gold coins took away the cow from Michael's daughter."

"How?"

"Simply took it away! Michael's daughter had a cow. Her children used to drink the milk. But the other day her children came to me to ask for milk. I said, 'Where's your cow?' They answered, 'The steward of Tarás the Stout came and gave mother three bits of gold, and she gave him the cow, so we have nothing to drink.' I thought you were only going to play with the gold pieces, but you have taken the children's cow away. I will not give you any more."

And Ivan stuck to it and would not give him any more. So the brothers went away. And as they went they discussed how they could meet their difficulties. And Simon said:

"Look here, I tell you what to do. You give me money to feed my soldiers, and I will give you half my kingdom with soldiers enough to guard your money." Tarás agreed. So the brothers divided what they possessed, and both became kings, and both were rich.

VIII

Ivan lived at home, supporting his father and mother and working in the fields with his dumb sister. Now it happened that Ivan's yard dog fell sick, grew mangy, and was near dying. Ivan, pitying it, got some bread from his sister, put it in his cap, carried it out, and threw it to the dog. But the cap was torn, and together with the bread one of the little roots fell to the ground. The old dog ate it up with the bread, and as soon as she had swallowed it she jumped up and began to play, bark, and wag her tail – in short became quite well again.

The father and mother saw it and were amazed.

"How did you cure the dog?" asked they.

Ivan answered: "I had two little roots to cure any pain, and she swallowed one."

Now about that time it happened that the king's daughter fell ill, and the king proclaimed in every town and village, that he would reward anyone who could heal her, and if any unmarried man could heal the king's daughter he should have her for his wife. This was proclaimed in Ivan's village as well as everywhere else.

His father and mother called Ivan, and said to him: "Have you heard what the king has proclaimed? You said you had a root that would cure any sickness. Go and heal the king's daughter, and you will be made happy for life."

"All right," said he.

And Ivan prepared to go, and they dressed him in his best. But as he went out of the door he met a beggar woman with a crippled hand.

"I have heard," said she, "that you can heal people. I pray you cure my arm, for I cannot even put on my boots myself."

"All right," said Ivan, and giving the little root to the beggar woman he told her to swallow it. She swallowed it, and was cured. She was at once able to move her arm freely.

His father and mother came out to accompany Ivan to the king, but when they heard that he had given away the root, and that he had nothing left to cure the king's daughter with, they began to scold him.

"You pity a beggar woman, but are not sorry for the king's daughter!" said they. But Ivan felt sorry for the king's daughter also. So he harnessed the horse, put straw in the cart to sit on, and sat down to drive away.

"Where are you going, fool?"

"To cure the king's daughter."

"But you've nothing left to cure her with?"

"Never mind," said he, and drove off.

He drove to the king's palace, and as soon as he stepped on the threshold the king's daughter got well.

The king was delighted, and had Ivan brought to him, and had him dressed in fine robes.

"Be my son-in-law," said he.

"All right," said Ivan.

And Ivan married the Princess. Her father died soon after, and Ivan became king. So all three brothers were now kings.

IX

The three brothers lived and reigned. The eldest brother, Simon the Soldier, prospered. With his straw soldiers he levied real soldiers. He ordered throughout his whole kingdom a levy of one soldier from every ten houses, and each soldier had to be tall, and clean in body and in face. He gathered many such soldiers and trained them; and when anyone opposed him, he sent these soldiers at once, and got his own way, so that everyone began to fear him, and his life was a comfortable one. Whatever he cast his eyes on and wished for, was his. He sent soldiers, and they brought him all he desired.

Tarás the Stout also lived comfortably. He did not waste the money he got from Ivan, but increased it largely. He introduced law and order into his kingdom. He kept his money in coffers, and taxed the people. He instituted a poll tax, tolls for walking and driving, and a tax on shoes and stockings and dress trimmings. And whatever he wished for he got. For the sake of money, people brought him everything, and they offered to work for him – for everyone wanted money.

Ivan the Fool also did not live badly. As soon as he had buried his father-in-law, he took off all his royal robes and gave them to his wife to put away in a chest; and he again donned his hempen shirt, his breeches and peasant shoes, and started again to work.

"It's dull for me," said he. "I'm getting fat and have lost my appetite and my sleep." So he brought his father and mother and his dumb sister to live with him, and worked as before.

People said, "But you are a king!"

"Yes," said he, "but even a king must eat."

One of his ministers came to him and said, "We have no money to pay salaries."

"All right," says he, "then don't pay them."

"Then no one will serve."

"All right; let them not serve. They will have more time to work; let them cart manure. There is plenty of scavenging to be done."

And people came to Ivan to be tried. One said, "He stole my money." And Ivan said, "All right, that shows that he wanted it."

And they all got to know that Ivan was a fool. And his wife said to him, "People say that you are a fool."

"All right," said Ivan.

His wife thought and thought about it, but she also was a fool.

"Shall I go against my husband? Where the needle goes the thread follows," said she.

So she took off her royal dress, put it away in a chest, and went to the dumb girl to learn to work. And she learned to work and began to help her husband.

And all the wise men left Ivan's kingdom; only the fools remained.

Nobody had money. They lived and worked. They fed themselves; and they fed others.

The old Devil waited and waited for news from the imps of their having ruined the three brothers. But no news came. So he went himself to inquire about it. He searched and searched, but instead of finding the three imps he found only the three holes.

"Evidently they have failed," thought he. "I shall have to tackle it myself."

So he went to look for the brothers, but they were no longer in their old places. He found them in three different kingdoms. All three were living and reigning. This annoyed the old Devil very much.

"Well," said he, "I must try my own hand at the job."

First he went to King Simon. He did not go to him in his own shape, but disguised himself as a general, and drove to Simon's palace.

"I hear, King Simon," said he, "that you are a great warrior, and as I know that business well, I desire to serve you."

King Simon questioned him, and seeing that he was a wise man, took him into his service.

The new commander began to teach King Simon how to form a strong army.

"First," said he, "we must levy more soldiers, for there are in your kingdom many people unemployed. We must recruit all the young men without exception. Then you will have five times as many soldiers as formerly. Secondly, we must get new rifles and cannons. I will introduce rifles that will fire a hundred balls at once; they will fly out like peas. And I will get cannons that will consume with fire either man, or horse, or wall. They will burn up everything!"

Simon the King listened to the new commander, ordered all young men without exception to be enrolled as soldiers, and had new factories built in which he manufactured large quantities of improved rifles and cannons. Then he made haste to declare war against a neighboring king. As soon as he met the other army, King Simon ordered his soldiers to rain balls against it and shoot fire from the cannons, and at one blow he burned and crippled half the enemy's army. The neighboring king was so thoroughly frightened that he gave way and surrendered his kingdom. King Simon was delighted.

"Now," said he, "I will conquer the king of India."

But the Indian king had heard about King Simon and had adopted all his inventions, and added more of his own. The Indian king enlisted not only all the young men, but all the single women also, and got together a greater army even than King Simon's. And he copied all King Simon's rifles and cannons, and invented a way of flying through the air to throw explosive bombs from above.

King Simon set out to fight the Indian king, expecting to beat him as he had beaten the other king; but the scythe that had cut so well had lost its edge. The king of India did not let Simon's army come within gunshot, but sent his women through the air to hurl down explosive bombs onto Simon's army. The women began to rain down bombs on to the army like borax upon cockroaches. The army ran away, and Simon the King was left alone. So the Indian king took Simon's kingdom, and Simon the Soldier fled as best he might.

Having finished with this brother, the old Devil went to King Tarás. Changing himself into a merchant, he settled in Tarás's kingdom, started a house of business, and began spending money. He paid high prices for everything, and everybody hurried to the new merchant's to get money. And so much money spread among the people that they began to pay all their taxes promptly, and paid up all their arrears, and King Tarás rejoiced.

"Thanks to the new merchant," thought he, "I shall have more money than ever; and my life will be yet more comfortable."

And Tarás the King began to form fresh plans, and began to build a new palace. He gave notice that people should bring him wood and stone and come to work, and he fixed high prices for everything. King Tarás thought people would come in crowds to work as before, but to his surprise all the wood and stone was taken to the merchant's, and all the workmen went there too. King Tarás increased his price, but the merchant bid yet more. King Tarás had much money, but the merchant had still more, and outbid the king at every point.

The king's palace was at a standstill and the building did not get on.

King Tarás planned a garden, and when autumn came he called for the people to come and plant the garden, but nobody came. All the people were engaged digging a pond for the merchant. Winter came, and King Tarás wanted to buy sable furs for a new overcoat. He sent to buy them, but the messengers returned and said, "There are no sables left. The merchant has all the furs. He gave the best price, and made carpets of the skins."

King Tarás wanted to buy some stallions. He sent to buy them, but the messengers returned saying, "The merchant has all the good stallions; they are carrying water to fill his pond."

All the king's affairs came to a standstill. Nobody would work for him, for everyone was busy working for the merchant; and they only brought King Tarás the merchant's money to pay their taxes.

And the king collected so much money that he had nowhere to store it, and his life became wretched. He ceased to form plans, and would have been glad enough simply to live, but he was hardly able even to do that. He ran short of everything. One after another his cooks, coachmen, and servants left him to go to the merchant. Soon he lacked even food. When he sent to the market to buy anything, there was nothing to be got – the merchant had bought up everything, and people only brought the king money to pay their taxes.

Tarás the King got angry and banished the merchant from the country. But the merchant settled just across the frontier, and went on as before. For the sake of the merchant's money, people took everything to him instead of to the king.

Things went badly with King Tarás. For days together he had nothing to eat, and a rumor even got about that the merchant was boasting that he would buy up the king himself! King Tarás got frightened, and did not know what to do.

At this time Simon the Soldier came to him, saying, "Help me, for the king of India has conquered me."

But King Tarás himself was over head and ears in difficulties. "I myself," said he, "have had nothing to eat for two days."

XI

Having done with the two brothers, the old Devil went to Ivan. He changed himself into a General, and coming to Ivan began to persuade him that he ought to have an army.

"It does not become a king," said he, "to be without an army. Only give me the order, and I will collect soldiers from among your people, and form one."

Ivan listened to him. "All right," said Ivan, "form an army, and teach them to sing songs well. I like to hear them do that."

So the old Devil went through Ivan's kingdom to enlist men. He told them to go and be entered as soldiers, and each should have a quart of spirits and a fine red cap.

The people laughed.

"We have plenty of spirits," said they. "We make it ourselves; and as for caps, the women make all kinds of them, even striped ones with tassels."

So nobody would enlist.

The old Devil came to Ivan and said: "Your fools won't enlist of their own free will. We shall have to make them."

"All right," said Ivan, "you can try."

So the old Devil gave notice that all the people were to enlist, and that Ivan would put to death anyone who refused.

The people came to the General and said, "You say that if we do not go as soldiers the king will put us to death, but you don't say what will happen if we do enlist. We have heard say that soldiers get killed!"

"Yes, that happens sometimes."

When the people heard this they became obstinate.

"We won't go," said they. "Better meet death at home. Either way we must die."

"Fools! You are fools!" said the old Devil. "A soldier may be killed or he may not, but if you don't go, King Ivan will have you killed for certain."

The people were puzzled, and went to Ivan the Fool to consult him.

"A General has come," said they, "who says we must all become soldiers. 'If you go as soldiers,' says he 'you may be killed or you may not, but if you don't go, King Ivan will certainly kill you.' Is this true?"

Ivan laughed and said, "How can I, alone, put all of you to death? If I were not a fool I would explain it to you but as it is, I don't understand it myself."

"Then," said they, "we will not serve."

"All right," says he, "don't."

So the people went to the General and refused to enlist. And the old Devil saw that this game was up, and he went off and ingratiated himself with the king of Tarakán.

"Let us make war," says he, "and conquer King Ivan's country. It is true there is no money, but there is plenty of corn and cattle and everything else."

So the king of Tarakán prepared to make war. He mustered a great army, provided rifles and cannons, marched to the frontier, and entered Ivan's kingdom.

And people came to Ivan and said, "The king of Tarakán is coming to make war on us."

"All right," said Ivan, "let him come."

Having crossed the frontier, the king of Tarakán sent scouts to look for Ivan's army. They looked and looked, but there was no army! They waited and waited for one to appear somewhere, but there were no signs of an army, and nobody to fight with. The king of Tarakán then sent to seize the villages. The soldiers came to a village, and the people, both men and women, rushed out in astonishment to stare at the soldiers. The soldiers began to take their corn and cattle; the people let them have it, and did not resist. The soldiers went on to another village; the same thing happened again. The soldiers went on for one day, and for two days, and everywhere the same thing happened. The people let them have everything, and no one resisted, but only invited the soldiers to live with them.

"Poor fellows," said they, "if you have a hard life in your own land, why don't you come and stay with us altogether?"

The soldiers marched and marched: still no army, only people living and feeding themselves and others, and not resisting, but inviting the soldiers to stay and live with them. The soldiers found it dull work, and they came to the king of Tarakán and said, "We cannot fight here, lead us elsewhere. War is all right, but what is this? It is like cutting pea soup! We will not make war here anymore."

The king of Tarakán grew angry, and ordered his soldiers to overrun the whole kingdom, to destroy the villages, to burn the grain and the houses, and to slaughter the cattle. "And if you do not obey my orders," said he, "I will execute you all."

The soldiers were frightened, and began to act according to the king's orders. They began to burn houses and corn, and to kill cattle. But the fools still offered no resistance, and only wept. The old men wept, and the old women wept, and the young people wept.

"Why do you harm us?" they said. "Why do you waste good things? If you need them, why do you not take them for yourselves?"

At last the soldiers could stand it no longer. They refused to go any further, and the army disbanded and fled.

XII

The old Devil had to give it up. He could not get the better of Ivan with soldiers. So he changed himself into a fine gentleman, and settled down in Ivan's kingdom. He meant to overcome him by means of money, as he had overcome Tarás the Stout.

"I wish," says he, "to do you a good turn, to teach you sense and reason. I will build a house among you and organize a trade."

"All right," said Ivan, "come and live among us if you like."

Next morning the fine gentleman went out into the public square with a big sack of gold and a sheet of paper, and said, "You all live like swine. I wish to teach you how to live properly. Build me a house according to this plan. You shall work, I will tell you how, and I will pay you with gold coins." And he showed them the gold.

The fools were astonished; there was no money in use among them; they bartered their goods, and paid one another with labor. They looked at the gold coins with surprise.

"What nice little things they are!" said they.

And they began to exchange their goods and labor for the gentleman's gold pieces. And the old Devil began, as in Tarás's kingdom, to be free with his gold, and the people began to exchange everything for gold and to do all sorts of work for it.

The old Devil was delighted, and thought to himself, "Things are going right this time. Now I shall ruin the Fool as I did Tarás, and I shall buy him up body and soul."

But as soon as the fools had provided themselves with gold pieces they gave them to the women for necklaces. The lasses plaited them into their tresses, and at last the children in the street began to play with the little pieces. Everybody had plenty of them, and they stopped taking them. But the fine gentleman's mansion was not yet half-built, and the grain and cattle for the year were not yet provided. So he gave notice that he wished people to come and work for him, and that he wanted cattle and grain; for each thing, and for each service, he was ready to give many more pieces of gold.

But nobody came to work and nothing was brought. Only sometimes a boy or a little girl would run up to exchange an egg for a gold coin, but nobody else came, and he had nothing to eat. And being hungry, the fine gentleman went through the village to try and buy something for dinner. He tried at one house, and offered a gold piece for a fowl, but the housewife wouldn't take it.

"I have a lot already," said she.

He tried at a widow's house to buy a herring, and offered a gold piece.

"I don't want it, my good sir," said she. "I have no children to play with it, and I myself already have three coins as curiosities."

He tried at a peasant's house to get bread, but neither would the peasant take money.

"I don't need it," said he, "but if you are begging 'for Christ's sake,' wait a bit and I'll tell the housewife to cut you a piece of bread."

At that the Devil spat, and ran away. To hear Christ's name mentioned, let alone receiving anything for Christ's sake, hurt him more than sticking a knife into him.

And so he got no bread. Everyone had gold, and no matter where the old Devil went, nobody would give anything for money, but everyone said, "Either bring something else, or come and work, or receive what you want in charity for Christ's sake."

But the old Devil had nothing but money; for work he had no liking, and as for taking anything "for Christ's sake" he could not do that. The old Devil grew very angry.

"What more do you want, when I give you money?" said he. "You can buy everything with gold, and hire any kind of laborer." But the fools did not heed him.

"No, we do not want money," said they. "We have no payments to make, and no taxes, so what should we do with it?"

The old Devil lay down to sleep – without supper.

The affair was told to Ivan the Fool. People came and asked him, "What are we to do? A fine gentleman has turned up, who likes to eat and drink and dress well, but he does not like to work, does not beg in 'Christ's name,' but only offers gold pieces to everyone. At first people gave him all he wanted until they had plenty of gold pieces, but now no one gives him anything. What's to be done with him? He will die of hunger before long."

Ivan listened.

"All right," says he, "we must feed him. Let him live by turn at each house as a shepherd does."

There was no help for it. The old Devil had to begin making the round.

In due course the turn came for him to go to Ivan's house. The old Devil came in to dinner, and the dumb girl was getting it ready.

She had often been deceived by lazy folk who came early to dinner – without having done their share of work – and ate up all the porridge, so it had occurred to her to find out the sluggards by their hands. Those who had calluses on their hands, she put at the table, but the others got only the scraps that were left over.

The old Devil sat down at the table, but the dumb girl seized him by the hands and looked at them – there were no hard places there: the hands were clean and smooth, with long nails. The dumb girl gave a grunt and pulled the Devil away from the table. And Ivan's wife said to him, "Don't be offended, fine gentleman. My sister-in-law does not allow anyone to come to table who has no calluses on his hands. But wait awhile – after the folk have eaten you shall have what is left."

The old Devil was offended that in the king's house they wished him to feed like a pig. He said to Ivan, "It is a foolish law you have in your kingdom that everyone must work with his hands. It's your stupidity that invented it. Do people work only with their hands? What do you think wise men work with?"

And Ivan said, "How are we fools to know? We do most of our work with our hands and our backs."

"That is because you are fools! But I will teach you how to work with the head. Then you will know that it is more profitable to work with the head than with the hands."

Ivan was surprised.

"If that is so," said he, "then there is some sense in calling us fools!"

And the old Devil went on. "Only it is not easy to work with one's head. You give me nothing to eat, because I have no hard places on my hands, but you do not know that it is a hundred times more difficult to work with the head. Sometimes one's head almost splits."

Ivan became thoughtful.

"Why then, friend, do you torture yourself so? Is it pleasant when the head splits? Would it not be better to do easier work with your hands and your back?"

But the Devil said, "I do it all out of pity for you fools. If I didn't torture myself you would remain fools forever. But, having worked with my head, I can now teach you."

Ivan was surprised.

"Do teach us!" said he, "so that when our hands get cramped we may use our heads for a change."

And the Devil promised to teach the people. So Ivan gave notice throughout the kingdom that a fine gentleman had come who would teach everybody how to work with their heads; that with the head more could be done than with the hands; and that the people ought all to come and learn.

Now there was in Ivan's kingdom a high tower, with many steps leading up to a lantern on the top. And Ivan took the gentleman up there that everyone might see him.

So the gentleman took his place on the top of the tower and began to speak, and the people came together to see him. They thought the gentleman would really show them how to work with the head without using the hands. But the old Devil only taught them in many words how they might live without working. The people could make nothing of it. They looked and considered, and at last went off to attend to their affairs.

The old Devil stood on the tower a whole day, and after that a second day, talking all the time. But standing there so long he grew hungry, and the fools never thought of taking food to him up in the tower. They thought that if he could work with his head better than with his hands, he could at any rate easily provide him with bread.

The old Devil stood on the top of the tower yet another day, talking away. People came near, looked on for a while, and then went away.

And Ivan asked, "Well, has the gentleman begun to work with his head yet?"

"Not yet," said the people; "he's still spouting away."

The old Devil stood on the tower one day more, but he began to grow weak, so that he staggered and hit his head against one of the pillars of the lantern. One of the people noticed it and told Ivan's wife, and she ran to her husband, who was in the field.

"Come and look," said she. "They say the gentleman is beginning to work with his head."

Ivan was surprised.

"Really?" says he, and he turned his horse round, and went to the tower. And by the time he reached the tower the old Devil was quite exhausted with hunger, and was staggering and knocking his head against the pillars. And just as Ivan arrived at the tower, the Devil stumbled, fell, and came bump, bump, bump, straight down the stairs to the bottom, counting each step with a knock of his head!

"Well!" says Ivan, "The fine gentleman told the truth when he said that 'sometimes one's head quite splits.' This is worse than blisters; after such work there will be swellings on the head."

The old Devil tumbled out at the foot of the stairs, and struck his head against the ground. Ivan was about to go up to him to see how much work he had done – when suddenly the earth opened and the old Devil fell through. Only a hole was left.

Ivan scratched his head.

"What a nasty thing," says he. "It's one of those devils again! What a whopper! He must be the father of them all."

Ivan is still living, and people crowd to his kingdom. His own brothers have come to live with him, and he feeds them, too. To everyone who comes and says, "Give me food!" Ivan says, "All right. You can stay with us; we have plenty of everything."

Only there is one special custom in his kingdom; whoever has calloused hands comes to table, but whoever has not, must eat what the others leave.

20.

What Is the Meaning of Life?

From The Kingdom of God Is within You

In this ringing conclusion to his classic essay, Tolstoy sums up the answers he has found to the questions that have haunted him all his life.

WHATEVER NAMES we dignify ourselves with, whatever uniforms we wear, whatever priests we anoint ourselves before, however many millions we possess, however many guards are stationed along our road, however many policemen guard our wealth, however many so-called criminals, revolutionists, and anarchists we punish, whatever exploits we have performed, whatever states we may have founded, fortresses and towers we may have erected – from Babel to the Eiffel Tower – there are two inevitable conditions of life, confronting all of us, which destroy its whole meaning: (1) death, which may at any moment pounce upon each of us; and (2) the transitoriness of all our works, which so soon pass away and leave no trace.

Whatever we may do – found companies, build palaces and monuments, write songs and poems – it is all not for very long. Soon it passes away, leaving no trace. And therefore, however we may conceal it from ourselves, we cannot help seeing that the significance of our life cannot lie in our personal fleshly existence, the prey of incurable suffering and inevitable death, nor in any social institution or organization. Whoever you may be who are reading these lines, think of your position and of your duties – not of your position as landowner, merchant, judge, emperor, president, minister, priest, soldier, which has been temporarily allotted you by men, and not of the imaginary duties laid on you by those positions, but of your real positions in eternity as a creature who at the will of Someone has been called out of unconsciousness after an eternity of nonexistence to which you may return at any moment at his will. Think of your duties – not your supposed duties as a landowner to your estate, as a merchant to your business, or as emperor, minister, or official to the state, but of your real duties, the duties that follow from your real position as a being called into life and endowed with reason and love.

Are you doing what he demands of you who has sent you into the world, and to whom you will soon return? Are you doing what he wills? Are you doing his will, when as landowner or manufacturer you rob the poor of the fruits of their toil, basing your life on this plunder of the workers, or when, as judge or governor, you ill-treat others, sentence them to execution, or when as soldiers you prepare for war, kill and plunder? . . .

It cannot be.

Even if you are told that all this is necessary for the maintenance of the existing order of things, and that this social order with its pauperism, famines, prisons, gallows, armies, and wars is necessary to society – at the bottom of your heart you know yourself that it is not true, that the existing organization has outlived its time, and must inevitably be reconstructed on new principles, and that consequently there is no obligation upon you to sacrifice your sentiments of humanity to support it. . . . If you did not desire your position, you would not be doing your utmost to retain it. Try the experiment of ceasing to commit the cruel, treacherous, and base actions that you are constantly committing in order to retain your position, and you will lose it at once. Try the simple experiment, as a government official, of giving up lying, and refusing to take a part in executions and acts of violence; as a priest, of giving up deception; as a soldier, of giving up murder; as landowner or manufacturer, of giving up defending your property by fraud and force; and you will at once lose the position which you pretend is forced upon you, and which seems burdensome to you.

A man cannot be placed against his will in a situation opposed to his conscience.

If you find yourself in such a position it is not because it is necessary to anyone whatever, but simply because you wish it. And therefore knowing that your position is repugnant to your heart and your head, and to your faith, and even to the science in which you believe, you cannot help reflecting upon the question whether in retaining it, and above all trying to justify it, you are doing what you ought to do.

✦ ✦ ✦

It would be perfectly simple and clear if you did not by your hypocrisy disguise the truth which has so unmistakably been revealed to us:

Share all that you have with others, do not heap up riches, do not steal, do not cause suffering, do not kill, do not unto others what you would not they should do unto you, all that has been said not eighteen hundred, but five thousand years ago, and there could be no doubt of the truth of this law if it were not for hypocrisy. Except for hypocrisy human beings could not have failed, if not to put the law into practice, at least to recognize it, and admit that it is wrong not to put it into practice. . . .

There is one thing, and only one thing, in which it is granted to you to be free in life, all else being beyond your power: that is to recognize and profess the truth.

And yet simply from the fact that other people as misguided and as pitiful creatures as yourself have made you soldier, emperor, landowner, capitalist, priest, or general, you undertake to commit acts of violence obviously opposed to your reason and your heart, to base your existence on the misfortunes of others, and above all, instead of filling the one duty of your life, recognizing and professing the truth, you feign not to recognize it and disguise it from yourself and others.

And what are the conditions in which you are doing this? You who may die any instant, you sign sentences of death, you declare war, you take part in it, you judge, you punish, you plunder the working people, you live luxuriously in the midst of the poor, and teach weak people who have confidence in you that this must be so, that one's duty is to do this, and yet it may happen at the moment when you are acting thus that a bacterium or a bull may attack you and you will fall and die, losing forever the chance of repairing the harm you have done to others, and above all to yourself, in uselessly wasting a life which has been given you only once in eternity, without having accomplished the only thing you ought to have done.

However commonplace and out-of-date it may seem to us, however confused we may be by hypocrisy and by the hypnotic suggestion which results from it, nothing can destroy the certainty of this simple and clearly defined truth. No external conditions can guarantee our life, which is attended with inevitable sufferings and infallibly terminated by death. Our life therefore can have no significance except through faithfully doing what is demanded by the Power which has placed us in life with a sole certain guide – the rational conscience.

That is why that Power cannot require of us what is irrational and impossible: the organization of our temporary external life, the life of society, or of the state. That Power demands of us only what is reasonable, certain, and possible: to serve the kingdom of God, that is, to contribute to the establishment of the greatest possible union between all living beings – a union possible only in the truth; and to recognize and to profess the revealed truth, which is always in our power.

"But seek first the kingdom of God and his righteousness, and all these things shall be yours as well" (Matt. 6:33).

The sole meaning of life is to serve humanity by contributing to the establishment of the kingdom of God, which can only be done by the recognition and profession of the truth by every human being.

"The kingdom of God is not coming with signs to be observed; nor will they say, 'Lo, here it is!' or 'There!' for behold, the kingdom of God is within you" (Luke 17:20–21).

The Way of the Kingdom

Seek first for the kingdom of God and his righteousness, and all these things will be given to you as well. —Matthew 5:33

Peaceable Kingdom (detail)

21.

A Talk among
Leisured People

An Introduction to the Story That Follows

SOME GUESTS assembled at a wealthy house one day happened
to start a serious conversation about life. They spoke of people
present and absent, but failed to find anyone who was satisfied
with his life. Not only could no one boast of happiness, but not a
single person considered that he was living as a Christian should
do. All confessed that they were living worldly lives concerned
only for themselves and their families, none of them thinking of
their neighbors, still less of God.

So said all the guests, and all agreed in blaming themselves
for living godless and unchristian lives. "Then why do we live
so?" exclaimed a youth. "Why do we do what we ourselves dis-
approve of? Have we no power to change our way of life? We
ourselves admit that we are ruined by our luxury, our deca-
dence, our riches, and above all by our pride – our separation
from our fellow human beings. To be noble and rich we have to
deprive ourselves of all that gives us joy. We crowd into towns,
become decadent, ruin our health, and in spite of all our amusements we die of ennui, and of regrets that our life is not what it
should be.

"Why do we live so? Why do we spoil our lives and all the
good that God gives us? I don't want to live in that old way! I

253

will abandon the studies I have begun – they would only bring me to the same tormenting life of which we are all now complaining. I will renounce my property and go to the country and live among the poor. I will work with them, will learn to labor with my hands, and if my education is of any use to the poor I will share it with them, not through institutions and books but directly by living with them in a brotherly way.

"Yes, I have made up my mind," he added, looking inquiringly at his father, who was also present.

"Your wish is a worthy one," said his father, "but thoughtless and ill-considered. It seems so easy to you only because you do not know life. There are many things that seem to us good, but the execution of what is good is complicated and difficult. It is hard enough to walk well on a beaten track, but it is harder still to lay out a new one. New paths are made only by people who are thoroughly mature and have mastered all that is attainable by humankind. It seems to you easy to make new paths of life only because you do not yet understand life. It is an outcome of thoughtlessness and youthful pride. We old folk are needed to moderate your impulsiveness and guide you by our experience, and you young folk should obey us in order to profit by that experience. Your active life lies before you. You are now growing up and developing. Finish your education, make yourself thoroughly conversant with things, get on to your own feet, have firm convictions of your own, and then start a new life if you feel you have strength to do so. But for the present you should obey those who are guiding you for your own good, and not try to open up new paths of life."

The youth was silent and the older guests agreed with what the father had said.

"You are right," said a middle-aged married man, turning to the youth's father. "It is true that the lad, lacking experience of life, may blunder when seeking new paths of life and his decision cannot be a firm one. But you know we all agreed that our life is contrary to our conscience and does not give us happiness. So we cannot but recognize the justice of wishing to escape from it.

"The lad may mistake his fancy for a reasonable deduction, but I, who am no longer young, tell you for myself that as I listened to the talk this evening the same thought occurred to me. It is plain to me that the life I now live cannot give me peace of mind or happiness. Experience and reason alike show me that. Then what am I waiting for? We struggle from morning to night for our families, but it turns out that we and our families live ungodly lives and get more and more sunk in sins. We work for our families, but our families are no better off, because we are not doing the right thing for them. And so I often think that it would be better if I changed my whole way of life and did just what that young man proposed to do: ceased to bother about my wife and children and began to think about my soul. Not for nothing did Paul say: 'He that is married is anxious how he may please his wife, but he that is unmarried is anxious how he may please the Lord.'"

But before he had finished speaking his wife and all the women present began to attack him.

"You ought to have thought about that before," said an elderly woman. "You have put on the yoke, so you must draw your load. Like that, everyone will say he wishes to go off and save his soul when it seems hard to him to support and feed his family. That is false and cowardly. No! A person should be able to live in godly fashion with his family. Of course it would be easy enough to save your own soul all by yourself. But to behave like that would be to run contrary to Christ's teaching. God bade us love others; but in that way you would in his name offend others. No. A married man has his definite obligations and he must not shirk them. It's different when your family members are already on their own feet. But no one has a right to force his family."

But the man who had spoken did not agree. "I don't want to abandon my family," he said. "All I say is that my family should not be brought up in a worldly fashion, nor brought up to live for their own pleasure, as we have just been saying, but should be brought up from their early days to become accustomed to privation, to labor, to the service to others, and above all to live a brotherly life with all people. And for that we must relinquish our riches and distinctions."

"There is no need to upset others while you yourself do not live a godly life," exclaimed his wife irritably. "You yourself lived for your own pleasure when you were young, then why do you want to torment your children and your family? Let them grow up quietly, and later on let them do as they please without coercion from you!"

Her husband was silent, but an elderly man who was there spoke up for him.

"Let us admit," he said, "that a married man, having accustomed his family to a certain comfort, cannot suddenly deprive them of it. It is true that when you have begun to educate your children it is better to finish it than to break up everything – especially as the children when they grow up will choose the path they consider best for themselves. I agree that for a family man it is difficult and even impossible to change his way of life without sinning. But for us old men it is what God commands. Let me say for myself: I am now living without any obligations, and to tell the truth, simply for my belly. I eat, drink, rest, and am disgusting and revolting even to myself. So it is time for me to give up such a life, to give away my property, and at least before I die to live a while as God bids a Christian live."

But the others did not agree with the old man. His niece and godchild was present, to all of whose children he had stood sponsor and gave presents on holidays. His son was also there. They both protested.

"No," said the son, "You worked in your time, and it is time for you to rest and not trouble yourself. You have lived for sixty years with certain habits and must not change them now. You would only torment yourself in vain."

"Yes, yes," confirmed his niece. "You would be in want and out of sorts, and would grumble and sin more than ever. God is merciful and will forgive all sinners – to say nothing of such a kind old uncle as you!"

"Yes, and why should you?" added another old man of the same age. "You and I have perhaps only a couple of days to live, so why should we start new ways?"

"What a strange thing!" exclaimed one of the visitors who had been silent until now. "What a strange thing! We all say that it would be good to live as God bids us and that we are living badly and suffer in body and soul, but as soon as it comes to practice it turns out that the children must not be upset and must be brought up not in godly fashion but in the old way. A married man must not upset his wife and children and must live not in a godly way but as of old. And there is no need for old men to begin anything: they are not accustomed to it and have only a couple of days left to live. So it seems that none of us may live rightly: we may only talk about it."

22.

Walk in the Light
While There Is Light

A Story of Early Christian Times

IT HAPPENED in the reign of the Roman emperor Trajan a hundred years after the birth of Christ, at a time when disciples of Christ's disciples were still living and Christians held firmly to the Teacher's law, as is told in the Acts:

> Now the company of those who believed were of one heart and soul, and no one said that any of the things which he possessed was his own, but they had everything in common. And with great power the apostles gave their testimony to the resurrection of the Lord Jesus, and great grace was upon them all. There was not a needy person among them, for as many as were possessors of lands or houses sold them, and brought the proceeds of what was sold and laid it at the apostles' feet; and distribution was made to each as any had need (Acts 4:32–35).

I

In those early times there lived in the province of Cilicia, in the city of Tarsus, a rich Syrian merchant, Juvenal by name, who dealt in precious stones. He was of poor and humble origin, but by industry and skill in his business had earned wealth and the respect of his fellow citizens. He had traveled much in foreign countries, and though uneducated he had come to know and understand much, and the townsfolk respected him for his ability and probity. He professed the pagan Roman faith that was held by all respectable citizens of the Roman Empire, the ritual of which had been strictly enforced since the time of the Emperor Augustus and was still adhered to by the present Emperor Trajan. Cilicia was far from Rome, but was ruled by Roman governors, and all that was done in Rome was reflected in Cilicia, whose governors imitated their Emperor.

Juvenal remembered the stories he had heard in childhood of what Nero had done in Rome, and later on he saw how the emperors perished one after another, and being a clever man he understood that there was nothing sacred in the Roman religion but that it was all the work of human hands. But being a clearheaded man he understood that it would not be advantageous to struggle against the existing order of things and that for his own tranquility it was better to submit to it. The senselessness of the life all around him, and especially of what went on in Rome, where he repeatedly went on business, often however perplexed him. He had his doubts, he could not grasp it all, and he attributed this to his lack of learning.

He was married and had had four children, but three of them had died young and only one son, Julius, was left.

To him Juvenal devoted all his love and care. He particularly wished to educate his son so that the latter might not be tormented by such doubts about life as perplexed himself. When Julius had passed his fifteenth year his father entrusted him to a philosopher who had settled in their town and who received youths for their instruction. His father gave his son to this philosopher, together with his comrade Pamphilius, the son of a former slave whom Juvenal had freed.

The lads were friends, of the same age, and both handsome fellows. Both studied diligently and both were well conducted. Julius distinguished himself more in the study of the poets and in mathematics, but Pamphilius in the study of philosophy. A year before the completion of their studies, Pamphilius at school one day informed his teacher that his widowed mother was moving to the town of Daphne, and that he would have to abandon his studies.

The teacher was sorry to lose a pupil who was doing him credit, Juvenal too was sorry, but sorriest of all was Julius. But nothing would induce Pamphilius to remain, and after thanking his friends for their love and care, he took his leave.

Two years passed. Julius had finished his studies and during all that time had not once seen his friend.

One day, however, he met him in the street, invited him to his home, and began asking him how and where he was living. Pamphilius told him that he and his mother were still living in the same place.

"We are not living alone," said he, "but among many friends with whom we have everything in common."

"How 'in common'?" inquired Julius.

"So that none of us considers anything his own."

"Why do you do that?"

"We are Christians," said Pamphilius.

"Is it possible?" exclaimed Julius. "Why, I have heard that the Christians kill children and eat them! Is it possible that you take part in that?"

For to be a Christian in those days was the same thing as in our days to be an anarchist. As soon as someone was convicted of being a Christian he was immediately thrown into prison, and if he did not renounce his faith, was executed.

"Come and see," replied Pamphilius. "We do not do anything strange. We live simply, trying to do nothing bad."

"But how can you live if you do not consider anything your own?"

"We manage to live. If we work for our brethren they do the same for us."

"But if your brethren take your labor and do not give you theirs – how then?"

"There are none of that sort," said Pamphilius. "Such people like to live in luxury and will not come to us. Our life is simple and not luxurious."

"But there are plenty of lazy people who would be glad to be fed for nothing."

"There are such, and we receive them gladly. Lately a man of that kind came to us, a runaway slave. At first, it is true, he was lazy and led a bad life, but he soon changed his habits, and has now become a good brother."

"But suppose he had not improved?"

"There are such, too, and our Elder, Cyril, says that we should treat these as our most valued brethren, and love them even more."

"How can one love a good-for-nothing fellow?"

"One cannot help but love a fellow human being!"

"But how can you give to all whatever they ask?" queried Julius. "If my father gave to all who ask he would very soon have nothing left."

"I don't know about that," replied Pamphilius. "We have enough left for our needs, and if it happens that we have nothing to eat or to wear, we ask of others and they give to us. But that happens rarely. It only once happened to me to go to bed without supper, and then only because I was very tired and did not wish to go to ask for anything."

"I don't know how you manage," said Julius, "but my father says that if you don't save what you have, and if you give to all who ask, you will yourself die of hunger."

"We don't! Come and see. We live, and not only do not suffer want, but even have plenty to spare."

"How is that?"

"Why, this way. We all profess one and the same faith, but the strength to fulfill it differs in each of us. One has more and another less of it. One has advanced much in the true path of life, while another is only just beginning it. In front of us all stands Christ with his life, and we all try to emulate him and see our welfare in that alone. Some of us, like the Elder Cyril and his wife Pelagia, are leaders, others stand behind them, others again are still farther behind, but we are all following the same path. Those in front already approach a fulfillment of Christ's law – self-renunciation and readiness to lose their life to save it. These desire nothing. They do not spare themselves, and in accord with Christ's law are ready to give the last of their possessions to those who ask. Others are feebler, they weaken and are sorry for themselves when they lack their customary clothing and food, and they do not give away everything. There are others who are still weaker – such as have only recently started on the path. These still live in the old way, keeping much for themselves and only giving away their superfluities. And it is these hindmost people who give the largest material assistance to those in the van. Besides this, we are all of us entangled by our relationships with the pagans. One man's father is a pagan who has property and gives to his son. The son gives to those who ask, but then the father again gives to him. Another has a pagan mother who is sorry for her son and helps him. A third is the mother of pagan children, who take care of her and give

her things, begging her not to give them away, and she takes
what they give her out of love for them, but still gives to others.
A fourth has a pagan wife and a fifth a pagan husband. So we
are all entangled, and the foremost, who would gladly give away
their all, are not able to do so. That is why our life does not prove
too hard for those weak in the faith, and why it happens that we
have much that is superfluous."

To this Julius said:

"But if that is so, then you fail to observe Christ's teaching
and only pretend to do so. If you do not give up everything there
is no difference between you and us. To my mind if a person is a
Christian he ought to fulfill Christ's whole law – give up everything and become a pauper."

"That would be best of all," said Pamphilius. "Why do you
not do it?"

"Yes, I will when I see you do it."

"We don't want to do anything for show. And I don't advise
you to come to us and renounce your present way of life for the
sake of appearances. We act as we do not for appearances, but
according to our faith."

"What does 'according to our faith' mean?"

"'According to our faith' means that salvation from the evils
of the world, from death, is only to be found in a life according
to the teaching of Christ. We are indifferent to what people may
say of us. We act as we do not for other people's approval, but
because in this alone do we see life and welfare."

"It is impossible not to live for oneself," said Julius. "The gods
themselves have implanted it in us that we love ourselves more
than others and seek pleasure for ourselves. And you do the
same. You yourself say that some among you have pity on themselves. They will seek pleasures for themselves more and more,

264 ◆ THE WAY OF THE KINGDOM

and will more and more abandon your faith and behave just as we do."

"No," said Pamphilius, "our brethren are traveling another path and will not weaken but will grow ever stronger, just as a fire will never go out when more wood is laid on it. That is our faith."

"I don't understand what this faith of yours is!"

"Our faith consists in this, that we understand life as Christ has explained it to us."

"How is that?"

"Christ once told this parable. Certain men kept a vineyard and had to pay rent to its owner. That is, we human beings who live in the world must pay rent to God by doing his will. But these men, in accord with their worldly belief, considered that the vineyard was theirs and that they need pay no rent for it, but had only to enjoy its fruits. The owner sent a messenger to them to collect the rent, but they drove him away. Then the owner sent his son, but him they killed, thinking that after that no one would disturb them. That is the faith of the world by which all worldly people live who do not acknowledge that life is only given us that we may serve God. But Christ has taught us that this worldly belief – that it is better for a person if he drives the messenger and the owner's son out of the vineyard and avoids paying the rent – is a false one, for there is no avoiding the fact that we must either pay the rent or be driven out of the garden. He has taught us that all the things we call pleasures – eating, drinking, and merry-making – cannot be pleasures if we devote our lives to them, but are pleasures only when we are seeking something else – to live a life in conformity with the will of God. Only then do these pleasures follow as a natural reward of the fulfillment of his will. To wish to take the pleasures without the labor of fulfilling God's will – to tear the pleasures away from duty – is the same as to tear up a flower and replant it without its roots. We believe this, and so we cannot follow error when we see the truth. Our faith is that the good of life is not in its pleasures but in the fulfillment of God's will, without any thought of present or future pleasures. And the longer we live the more we see that the pleasures and the good come in the wake of a fulfillment of God's will, as a wheel follows the shafts. Our Teacher said: 'Come unto me, all ye that labor and are heavy laden, and I will give you rest. Take my yoke upon you and learn of me, for I am meek and lowly in heart, and ye shall find rest unto your souls. For my yoke is easy and my burden is light.'"

So spoke Pamphilius. Julius listened and his heart was touched, but what Pamphilius had said was not clear to him. At first it seemed to him that Pamphilius was deceiving him; but then he looked into his friend's kindly eyes and remembered his goodness, and it seemed to him that Pamphilius was deceiving himself.

Pamphilius invited Julius to come to see their way of life and, if it pleased him, to remain to live with them.

And Julius promised, but he did not go to see Pamphilius, and being absorbed by his own affairs he forgot about him.

II

Julius's father was wealthy, and as he loved his only son and was proud of him, he did not grudge him money. Julius lived the usual life of a rich young man, in idleness, luxury, and dissipated amusements, which have always been and still remain the same: wine, gambling, and loose women.

But the pleasures to which Julius abandoned himself demanded more and more money, and he began to find that he had not enough. On one occasion he asked his father for more than he usually gave him. His father gave what he asked, but reproved his son. Julius, feeling himself to blame, but unwilling to admit it, became angry and was rude to his father, as those who know they are to blame and do not wish to acknowledge it, always do.

The money Julius got from his father was very soon all spent. And just at that time it happened that he and a drunken companion became involved in a brawl and killed a man. The city prefect heard of this and would have had him arrested, but his father intervened and obtained his pardon. Julius now needed still more money for dissipation, and this time he borrowed it from a companion, promising to repay it. Moreover his mistress demanded a present: she had taken a fancy to a pearl necklace, and Julius knew that if he did not gratify her wish she would abandon him and attach herself to a rich man who had long been trying to entice her away.

Julius went to his mother and told her that he must have some money, and that he would kill himself if he could not get what he needed. He placed the blame for his being in such a position not on himself but on his father. He said: "My father accustomed me to a life of luxury and then began to grudge me money. Had he given me at first and without reproaches what he gave me later, I should have arranged my life properly and should not have been in such difficulties, but as he never gave me enough I had to go to the moneylenders and they squeezed everything out of me, and I had nothing left on which to live the life natural to me as a rich young man, and was made to feel ashamed among my companions. But my father does not wish to understand anything of all this. He forgets that he was young once himself. He has brought me to this state, and now if he will not give me what I ask I shall kill myself."

The mother, who spoilt her son, went to his father, and Juvenal called his son and began to upbraid both him and his mother. Julius answered his father rudely and Juvenal struck him. Julius seized his father's arm, at which Juvenal shouted to his slaves and bade them bind his son and lock him up.

Julius was left alone, and he cursed his father and his own life. It seemed to him that the only way of escape from his present position was either by his own or his father's death.

Julius's mother suffered even more than he did. She did not try to understand who was to blame for all this. She only pitied her adored son. She went again to her husband to implore him to forgive the youth, but he would not listen to her, and reproached her for having spoilt their son. She in turn reproached him, and it ended by Juvenal beating his wife. Disregarding this, however, she went to her son and persuaded him to beg his father's pardon and yield to his wishes, in return for which she promised to take the money he needed from her husband by stealth, and give it him. Julius agreed, and then his mother again went to Juvenal and urged him to forgive his son. Juvenal scolded his wife and son for a long time, but at last decided that he would forgive Julius, on condition that he should abandon his dissolute life and marry the daughter of a rich merchant – a match Juvenal was very anxious to arrange.

"He will get money from me and also have his wife's dowry," said Juvenal, "and then let him settle down to a decent life. If he promises to obey my wishes, I will forgive him; but I will not give him anything at present, and the first time he transgresses I will hand him over to the prefect."

Julius submitted to his father's conditions and was released. He promised to marry and to abandon his bad life, but he had no intention of doing so.

Life at home now became a hell for him. His father did not speak to him and quarreled with his mother on his account, and his mother wept.

One day she called him into her apartments and secretly handed him a precious stone which she had taken from her husband's room.

"Go and sell it," she said, "not here but in another town, and then do what you have to do. I shall be able to conceal its loss for the present, and if it is discovered I will lay the blame on one of the slaves."

Julius's heart was pierced by his mother's words. He was horrified at what she had done, and without taking the precious stone he left the house.

He did not himself know where he was going or with what aim. He walked on and on out of the town, feeling that he needed to be alone, and thinking over all that had happened to him and that awaited him. Going farther and farther away at last he reached the sacred grove of the goddess Diana. Coming to a secluded spot he began to think, and the first thought that occurred to him was to seek the goddess's aid. But he no longer believed in the gods, and knew that he could not expect aid from them. And if not from them, then from whom?

To think out his position for himself seemed to him too strange. All was darkness and confusion in his soul. But there was nothing else to be done. He had to listen to his conscience, and began to consider his life and his actions in the light of it. And both appeared to him bad, and above all stupid. Why had he tormented himself like this? Why had he ruined his young life in such a way? It had brought him little happiness and much sorrow and unhappiness. But chiefly he felt himself alone. Formerly he had had a mother whom he loved, a father, and friends. Now there was no one. Nobody loved him! He was a burden to them all. He had been a cause of suffering to all who knew him. For his mother he was the cause of discord with his father. For his father he was the dissipater of the wealth collected by a lifetime of labor. For his friends he was a dangerous and disagreeable rival. They must all desire his death.

Passing his life in review he remembered Pamphilius and his last meeting with him, and how Pamphilius had invited him to go there, to the Christians. And it occurred to him not to return home, but to go straight to the Christians and remain with them.

But could his position be so desperate, he wondered. Again he recalled all that had happened to him, and again he was horrified at the idea that nobody loved him and that he loved no one. His mother, father, and friends did not care for him and must wish for his death. But did he himself love anyone? His friends? He felt that he loved none of them: they were all his rivals and would be pitiless to him now that he was in distress. His father? He was seized with horror when he put himself that question. He looked into his heart and found that not only did he not love his father, he even hated him for the restraint and insult he had put upon him. He hated him, and more than that he saw clearly that his father's death was necessary for his own happiness.

"Yes," he said to himself. "If I knew that no one would see it or ever know of it, what should I do if I could immediately, at one stroke, deprive him of life and free myself?"

And he answered his own question: "I should kill him!" And he was horrified at that reply.

"My mother? I am sorry for her but I do not love her: it is all the same to me what becomes of her. All I need is her help . . . I am a beast, and a wretched, hunted one at that. I only differ from a beast in that I can by my own will quit this false and evil life. I can do what a beast cannot do – I can kill myself. I hate my father. There is no one I love . . . neither my mother nor my friends . . . unless, perhaps, Pamphilius alone?"

And he again thought of him. He recalled their last meeting, their conversation, and Pamphilius's words that, according to their teaching, Christ had said: "Come unto me all ye that labor and are heavy laden, and I will give you rest." Could that be true?

He went on thinking, and remembering Pamphilius's gentle, fearless, and happy face, he wished to believe what Pamphilius had said.

"What indeed am I?" he said to himself. "Who am I? A man seeking happiness. I sought it in my lusts and did not find it. And all who live as I did fail to find it. They are all evil and suffer. But there is a man who is always full of joy because he demands nothing. He says that there are many like him and that all people will be such if they follow their Master's teaching. What if this be true? True or not it attracts me and I will go there."

So said Julius to himself, and he left the grove, having decided not to return home but to go to the village where the Christians lived.

III

Julius went along briskly and joyously, and the farther he went the more vividly did he imagine to himself the life of the Christians, recalling all that Pamphilius had said, and the happier he felt. The sun was already declining towards evening and he wished to rest, when he came upon a man seated by the roadside having a meal. He was a man of middle age with an intelligent face, and was sitting there eating olives and a flat cake. On seeing Julius he smiled and said:

"Greeting to you, young man! The way is still long. Sit down and rest."

Julius thanked him and sat down.

"Where are you going?" asked the stranger.

"To the Christians," said Julius, and by degrees he recounted to the unknown his whole life and his decision.

The stranger listened attentively and asked about some details without himself expressing an opinion, but when Julius had ended he packed the remaining food in his wallet, adjusted his dress, and said:

"Young man, do not pursue your intention. You would be making a mistake. I know life; you do not. I know the Christians; you do not. Listen! I will review your life and your thoughts, and when you have heard them from me, you will take what decision seems to you wisest. You are young, rich, handsome, strong, and the passions boil in your veins. You wish to find a quiet refuge where they will not agitate you and you would not suffer from their consequences. And you think that you can find such a shelter among the Christians.

"There is no such refuge, dear young man, because what troubles you does not dwell in Cilicia or in Rome but in yourself. In the quiet solitude of a village the same passions will torment you, only a hundred times more strongly. The deception of the Christians, or their delusion – for I do not wish to judge them – consists in not wishing to recognize human nature. Only an old man who has outlived all his passions could fully carry out their teaching. But a man in the vigor of life, or a youth like you who has not yet tested life and tried himself, cannot submit to their law, because it is based not on human nature but on idle speculations. If you go to them you will suffer from what makes you suffer now, only to a much greater extent. Now your passions lead you into wrong paths, but having once mistaken your road you can correct it. Now at any rate you have the satisfaction of desires fulfilled – that is life. But among the Christians, forcibly restraining your passions, you will err yet more and in a similar way, and besides that suffering you will have the incessant suffering of unsatisfied desires. Release the water from a dam and it will irrigate the earth and the meadows and supply drink for the animals, but confine it and it will burst its banks and flow away as mud. So it is with the passions. The teaching of the Christians (besides the belief in another life with which they console themselves and of which I will not speak) – their practical teaching is this: They do not approve of violence, do not recognize wars, or tribunals, or property, or the sciences and arts, or anything that makes life easy and pleasant.

"That might be well enough if all people were such as they describe their Teacher as having been. But that is not and cannot be so. Human beings are evil and subject to passions. That play of passions and the conflicts caused by them are what keep people in the social condition in which they live. The barbarians know no restraint, and for the satisfaction of his desires one such man would destroy the whole world if everyone submitted as these Christians do. If the gods implanted in humankind the sentiments of anger, revenge, and even of vindictiveness against the wicked, they did so because these sentiments are necessary for human life. The Christians teach that these feelings are bad, and that without them people would be happy, and there would be no murders, executions, and wars. That is true, but it is like supposing that people would be happy if they did not eat food. There would then indeed be no greed or hunger, or any of the calamities that result from them. But that supposition would not change human nature. And if some two or three dozen people believed in it, and did actually refrain from food and die of hunger, it would still not alter human nature. The same is true of other human passions: indignation, anger, revenge, even the love of women, of luxury, or of the pomp and grandeur characteristic of the gods and therefore unalterable characteristics of humankind too. Abolish what nourishes humankind and humankind will be destroyed. And similarly abolish the passions natural to humankind and humanity will be unable to exist. It is the same with ownership, which the Christians are supposed to reject. Look around you: every vineyard, every enclosure, every house, every donkey, has been produced by human beings under conditions of ownership. Abandon the rights of property and not one vineyard will be tilled or one animal raised and tended. The Christians say that they have no property, but they enjoy the fruits of it. They say that they have all things in common and that everything is brought together into a common pool. But what they bring together they have received from people who owned property. They merely deceive others, or at best deceive themselves. You say that they themselves work to support themselves, but what they get by work would not support them if they did not avail themselves of what those who recognize ownership have produced. Even if they could support themselves it would be a bare subsistence, and there would be no place among them for the sciences or arts. They do not even recognize the use of our sciences and arts. Nor can it be otherwise. Their whole teaching tends to reduce them to a primitive condition of savagery – to an animal existence.

"They cannot serve humanity by our arts and sciences, and being ignorant of them they condemn them. Nor can they serve humanity in any of the ways which constitute humankind's peculiar prerogative and ally humans to the gods. They have neither temples nor statues nor theaters nor museums. They say they do not need these things. The easiest way to avoid being ashamed of one's degradation is to scorn what is lofty, and that is what they do. They are atheists. They do not acknowledge the gods or their participation in human affairs. They believe only in the Father of their Teacher, whom they also call their Father, and the Teacher himself, who they think has revealed to them all the mysteries of life. Their teaching is a pitiful fraud! Consider just this. Our religion says: The world depends on the gods, the gods protect humankind, and in order to live well people must respect the gods, and must themselves search and think. In this way our life is guided on the one hand by the will of the gods, and on the other by the collective wisdom of humankind. We live, think, search, and thus advance towards the truth.

"But these Christians have neither the gods, nor their own will, nor the wisdom of humanity. They have only a blind faith in their crucified Teacher and in all that he said to them. Now consider which is the more trustworthy guide – the will of the gods and the free activity of collective human wisdom, or the compulsory, blind belief in the words of one man?"

Julius was struck by what the stranger said and particularly by his last words. Not only was his intention of going to the Christians shaken, but it now appeared to him strange that, under the influence of his misfortunes, he could ever have decided on such an insanity. But the question still remained of what he was to do now, and what exit to find from the difficult circumstances in which he was placed, and so, having explained his position, he asked the stranger's advice.

"It was just of that matter I now wished to speak to you," replied the stranger. "What are you to do? Your path – in as far as human wisdom is accessible to me – is clear. All your misfortunes have resulted from the passions natural to humankind. Passion has seduced you and led you so far that you have suffered. Such are the ordinary lessons of life. We should avail ourselves of them. You have learned much and know what is bitter and what is sweet, you cannot now repeat those mistakes. Profit by your experience. What distresses you most is your enmity towards your father. That enmity is due to your position. Choose another and it will cease, or at least will not manifest itself so painfully. All your misfortunes are the result of the irregularity of your situation. You gave yourself up to youthful pleasures: that was natural and therefore good. But it was good only as long as it corresponded to your age. That time passed, but though you had grown to manhood you still devoted yourself to the frivolities of youth, and this was bad. You have reached an age when you should recognize that you are a man, a citizen, and should serve the state and work on its behalf. Your father wishes you to marry. His advice is wise. You have outlived one phase of life – your youth – and have reached another. All your troubles are indications of a period of transition. Recognize that youth has passed, boldly throw aside all that was natural to it but not natural for a human being, and enter upon a new path. Marry, give up the amusements of youth, apply yourself to commerce, public affairs, the sciences and arts, and you will not only be reconciled to your father and friends, but will yourself find peace and happiness. You have reached manhood, and should marry and be a husband. So my chief advice is: accede to your father's wish and marry. If you are attracted by the seclusion you thought to find among the Christians, if you are inclined to philosophy and not towards an active life, you can with advantage devote yourself to it only after you have experienced the real meaning of life. But you will know that only as an independent citizen and the head of a family. If afterwards you still feel drawn to solitude, yield to that feeling. It will then be a true desire and not a mere flash of vexation such as it is now. Then go!"

These last words persuaded Julius more than anything else. He thanked the stranger and returned home.

His mother welcomed him with joy. His father, too, on hearing of his intention to submit to his will and marry the girl he had chosen for him, was reconciled to his son.

IV

Three months later the marriage of Julius with the beautiful Eulampia was celebrated. The young couple lived in a separate house belonging to Julius, and he took over a branch of his father's business which was transferred to him. He had now changed his way of life entirely.

One day he went on business to a neighboring town, and there, while sitting in a shop, he saw Pamphilius passing by with a girl whom Julius did not know. They both carried heavy baskets of grapes which they were selling. On seeing his friend, Julius went out to him and asked him into the shop to have a talk.

The girl, seeing that Pamphilius wished to go with his friend but hesitated to leave her alone, hastened to assure him that she did not need his help, but would sit down with the grapes and wait for customers. Pamphilius thanked her, and he and Julius went into the shop.

Julius asked the shopkeeper, whom he knew, to let him take his friend into a private room at the back of the shop, and having received permission they went there.

The two friends questioned each other about their lives. Pamphilius was still living as before in the Christian community and had not married, and he assured his friend that his life had been growing happier and happier each year, each day, and each hour.

Julius told his friend what had happened to himself, and how he had actually been on his way to join the Christians when an encounter with a stranger cleared up for him the mistakes of the Christians and showed him what he ought to do, and how he had followed that advice and had married.

"Well, and are you happy now?" inquired Pamphilius. "Have you found in marriage what the stranger promised you?"

"Happy?" said Julius. "What is happiness? If you mean the complete satisfaction of my desires, then of course I am not happy. I am at present managing my business successfully, people begin to respect me, and in both these things I find some satisfaction. Though I see many others richer and more highly regarded than myself, I foresee the possibility of equaling or even surpassing them. That side of my life is full, but marriage, I will say frankly, does not satisfy me. More than that, I feel that it is just my marriage – which should have given me happiness – that has failed. The joy I at first experienced gradually diminished and at last vanished, and instead of happiness came sorrow. My wife is beautiful, clever, well-educated, and kind. At first I was perfectly happy. But now – not having a wife you will not have experienced this – differences arise, sometimes because she desires my attentions when I am indifferent to her, and sometimes for the contrary reason. Besides this, for passion novelty is essential. A woman less fascinating than my wife attracts me more when I first know her, but afterwards becomes still less attractive than my wife: I have experienced that. No, I have not found satisfaction in marriage. Yes, my friend," Julius concluded, "the philosophers are right. Life does not afford us what the soul desires. I have now experienced that in marriage. But the fact that life does not give the happiness that the soul desires does not prove that your deception can give it," he added with a smile.

"In what do you see our 'deception'?" asked Pamphilius.

"Your deception consists in this: that to deliver people from the evils connected with life, you reject all life – repudiate life itself. To avoid disenchantment you reject enchantment. You reject marriage itself."

"We do not reject marriage," said Pamphilius.

"Well, if you don't reject marriage, at any rate you reject love."

"On the contrary, we reject everything except love. For us it is the basis of everything."

"I do not understand you," said Julius. "As far as I have heard from others and from yourself, and judging by the fact that you are not yet married though you are the same age as myself, I conclude that your people do not marry. Those who are already married continue to be so, but the others do not form fresh marriages. You do not concern yourself about continuing the human race. And if you were the only people the human race would long ago have died out," he concluded, repeating what he had often heard said.

"That is unjust," replied Pamphilius. "It is true that we do not set ourselves the aim of continuing the human race, and do not make it our concern in the way I have often heard your philosophers speak of it. We suppose that our Father has already provided for that. Our aim is simply to live in accord with his will. If it is his will that the human race should continue, it will do so, if not it will end. That is not our affair, nor our care. Our care is to live in accord with his will. And his will is expressed both in our teaching and in our revelation, in which it is said that a husband shall cleave unto his wife and they twain shall be one flesh.

"Marriage among us is not only not forbidden, but it is encouraged by our elders and teachers. The difference between marriage among us and marriage among you consists only in the fact that our law reveals to us that every lustful look at a woman is a sin, and so we and our women, instead of adorning ourselves to stimulate desire, try so to avoid it that the feeling of love between us as between brothers and sisters, may be stronger than the feeling of desire for a woman which you call love."

"But all the same you cannot suppress admiration for beauty," said Julius. "I feel sure, for instance, that the beautiful girl with whom you were bringing the grapes evokes in you the feeling of desire – in spite of the dress which hides her charms."

"I do not yet know," said Pamphilius, blushing. "I have not thought about her beauty. You are the first to speak to me of it. To me she is as a sister. But to continue what I was saying about the difference between our marriages and yours, that difference arises from the fact that among you lust, under the name of beauty and love, and the worship of the goddess Venus, is evoked and developed in people. With us on the contrary lust is considered, not as an evil – for God did not create evil – but as a good which begets evil when it is out of place: a temptation as we call it. And we try by all means to avoid it. And that is why I am not yet married, though very possibly I may marry tomorrow."

"But what will decide that?"

"The will of God."

"How will you know it?"

"If you never seek its indications you will never discern it, but if you constantly seek them they become clear, as divinations from sacrifices and birds are for you. And as you have your wise ones who interpret for you the will of the gods by their wisdom and from the entrails of their sacrificed animals and by the flight of birds, so we too have our wise ones who explain to us the will of the Father according to Christ's revelation and the promptings of their hearts and the thoughts of others, and chiefly by their love of others."

"But all this is very indefinite," retorted Julius. "Who will indicate to you, for instance, when and whom to marry? When I was about to marry I had the choice of three girls. Those three were chosen from among others because they were beautiful and rich, and my father was agreeable to my marrying any one of them. Of the three I chose Eulampia because she was the most beautiful, and more attractive to me than the others. That is easily understood. But what will guide you in your choice?"

"To answer you," said Pamphilius, "I must first tell you that as by our teaching all people are equal in our Father's eyes, therefore they are also equal in our eyes both in their station and in their spiritual and bodily qualities, and consequently our choice (to use a word we consider meaningless) cannot in any way be limited. Anyone in the whole world may be the husband or wife of a Christian."

"That makes it still more impossible to decide," said Julius.

"I will tell you what our Elder said to me about the difference between the marriage of a Christian and a pagan. A pagan such as yourself chooses the wife who in his opinion will give him the greatest amount of personal enjoyment. In such circumstances the eye wanders and it is difficult to decide, especially as the enjoyment is to be in the future. But a Christian has no such choice to make, or rather, when choosing, his personal enjoyment occupies not the first but a secondary place. For a Christian the question is how not to infringe the will of God by his marriage."

"But in what way can there be an infringement of God's will by marriage?"

"I might have forgotten the Iliad which we used to read and study together, but you who live among sages and poets cannot have forgotten it. What is the whole Iliad? It is a story of the infringement of God's will in relation to marriage. Menelaus and Paris and Helen; Achilles and Agamemnon and Chryseis – it is all a description of the terrible ills that flowed and still flow from such infringements."

"But in what does the infringement consist?"

"In this: that a man loves a woman for the enjoyment he can get by connection with her and not because she is a human being like himself. He marries her solely for his own enjoyment. Christian marriage is possible only when a man loves his fellow human beings, and when the object of his carnal love is first of all an object of this brotherly love. As a house can only be built rationally and durably when there is a foundation, and a picture can be painted only when something has been prepared on which to paint it, so carnal love is only legitimate, reasonable, and permanent when it is based on the respect and love of one human being for another. Only on that foundation can a reasonable Christian family life be established."

"But still," said Julius, "I do not see why such a Christian marriage, as you call it, excludes the kind of love for a woman that Paris experienced . . ."

"I do not say that Christian marriage does not admit of any exclusive feeling for one woman: on the contrary, only then is it reasonable and holy. But an exclusive love for one woman can arise only when the previously existent love for all people is not infringed.

"The exclusive love for one woman which the poets sing, considering it as good in itself without being based on the general love of humanity, has no right to be called love. It is animal lust and very often changes into hatred. The best examples of how such so-called love (eros) becomes bestial when it is not based on brotherly love for all men are cases like this: the very woman the man is supposed to love is violated by him; he causes her to suffer and ruins her. In such violence there is evidently no brotherly love, for the man torments the one he loves. In unchristian marriage there is often a concealed violence – as when a man who marries a girl who does not love him, or who loves another, compels her to suffer, and has no compassion for her, using her merely to satisfy his 'love'."

"Granted that that is so," said Julius, "but if the maiden loves him there is no injustice and I don't see the difference between Christian and pagan marriage."

"I do not know the details of your marriage," replied Pamphilius, "but I know that every marriage based on nothing but personal happiness cannot but result in discord, just as among animals, or people differing little from animals, the simple act of taking food cannot occur without quarreling and strife. Each wants a nice morsel, and as there are not enough choice morsels for all, discord results. Even if it is not expressed openly it is still there secretly. The weak man desires a dainty morsel but knows that the strong man will not give it to him, and though he knows it is impossible to take it away directly from the strong man, he watches him with secret and envious malice and avails himself of the first opportunity to take it from him by guile. The same is true of pagan marriage, but there it is twice as bad because the object of desire is a human being, so that the enmity arises between husband and wife."

"But how can married couples possibly love no one but each other? There will always be some man or woman who loves the one or the other, and then, in your opinion, marriage is impossible. So I see the justice of what is said of you – that you deny marriage. That is why you are not married and probably will not marry. It is not possible for a man to marry a woman without ever having aroused the feeling of love in some other woman, or for a girl to reach maturity without having aroused any man's feeling for herself. What ought Helen to have done?"

"Our Elder Cyril speaks thus about it: In the pagan world men, without thinking of loving their brethren – without cultivating that sentiment – think only of arousing in themselves passionate love for a woman, and they foster that passion in themselves. And so in their world Helen, and every woman like her, arouses the love of many men. Rivals fight one another and strive to surpass one another, as animals do to possess a female. And to a greater or lesser extent their marriage is an act of violence. In our community we not only do not think about the personal enjoyment a woman's beauty may afford, but we avoid all temptations which lead to this – which in the pagan world is regarded as a merit and an object of worship. We, on the contrary, think of those obligations of respect and love of our neighbor which we feel for all people, for the greatest beauty and the greatest deformity. We cultivate them with all our might, and so the feeling of brotherly love supplants the seduction of beauty, vanquishes it, and eliminates the discords arising from sexual intercourse. A Christian marries only when he knows that his union with the woman will not cause pain to anyone."

"But is that possible?" rejoined Julius. "Can men control their passions?"

"It is impossible if they are allowed free play, but we can prevent their awakening and being aroused. Take, for example, the relations of a father and his daughter, a mother and her son, or of brothers and sisters. However beautiful she may be, the mother is for her son an object of pure love and not of personal enjoyment. And it is the same with a daughter and her father, and a sister and her brother. Feelings of desire are not awakened. They would awaken only if the father learned that she whom he considered to be his daughter was not his daughter, and similarly in the relation of a mother and son, and a brother and sister. But even then the sensation would be very feeble and easily suppressed, and it would be in the man's power to restrain it. The feeling of desire would be feeble because at its base would lie the sentiment of maternal, paternal, or fraternal love. Why do you not wish to believe that such a feeling towards all women – as mothers, sisters, and daughters – may be cultivated and confirmed in men, and that the feeling of conjugal love could grow up on the basis of that feeling? As the brother will only allow a feeling of love for her as a woman to arise in himself after he has learned that she is not his sister, so also a Christian will only allow that feeling to arise in his soul when he feels that his love will cause pain to no one."

"But suppose two men love the same girl?"

"Then one will sacrifice his happiness for that of the other."

"But how if she loves one of them?"

"Then the one whom she loves less will sacrifice his feeling for her happiness."

"And if she loves both of them and they both sacrifice themselves, she will not marry at all?"

"No, in that case the elders will look into the matter and advise so that there may be the greatest good for all with the greatest amount of love."

"But you know that is not done! It is not done because it would be contrary to human nature."

"Contrary to human nature? What human nature? A man is a human being besides being an animal, and while it is true that such a relation to a woman is not consonant with man's animal nature, it is consonant with his rational nature. When man uses his reason to serve his animal nature he becomes worse than an animal, and descends to violence and incest and to things no animal would do. But when he uses his reason to restrain his animal nature, then that animal nature serves his reason, and only then does he attain a happiness that satisfies him."

V

"But tell me about yourself," said Julius. "I see you with that lovely girl, it seems that you live near her and help her. Is it possible that you do not wish to become her husband?"

"I do not think about it," said Pamphilius. "She is the daughter of a Christian widow. I serve them as others do. You ask whether I love her so that I wish to unite my life with hers? That question is hard for me to answer, but I will do so frankly. That thought has occurred to me but I dare not as yet entertain it, for there is another young man who loves her. That young man is a Christian and loves us both, and so I cannot do anything that would cause him pain. I live without thinking of it. I seek only one thing: to fulfill the law of love of humankind. That is the one thing needful. I shall marry when I see that it is necessary."

"But it cannot be a matter of indifference to her mother to get a good industrious son-in-law. She will want you and not someone else."

"No, it is a matter of indifference to her, because she knows that we are all ready to serve her, as we would anyone else, and that I should serve her neither more nor less whether I became

286 + THE WAY OF THE KINGDOM

her son-in-law or not. If it comes about that I marry her daughter, I shall accept it gladly, as I should do her marriage with someone else."

"That is impossible!" exclaimed Julius. "What is so terrible about you is that you deceive yourselves and so deceive others. What that stranger told me about you was correct. When I listen to you I involuntarily yield to the beauty of the life you describe, but when I reflect I see that it is all a deception leading to savagery, to a coarseness of life resembling that of the animals."

"In what do you see this savagery?"

"In this, that supporting yourselves by labor, you can have neither leisure nor opportunity to occupy yourselves with the sciences and arts. Here you are in ragged garments, with coarsened hands and feet; and your companion, who could be a goddess of beauty, resembles a slave. You have neither songs to Apollo, nor temples, nor poetry, nor games – none of the things the gods have given for the adornment of human life. To work, to work like slaves or like oxen, merely to feed coarsely – is not this a voluntary and impious renunciation of human will and of human nature?"

"Again 'human nature'!" said Pamphilius. "But in what does this nature consist? In tormenting slaves to work beyond their strength, in killing one's brothers and enslaving them, and making women into instruments of pleasure? All this is needed for that beauty of life which you consider natural for human beings. Is that man's nature? Or is it to live in love and concord with all people, feeling oneself a member of one universal brotherhood?

"You are much mistaken, too, if you think that we do not recognize the arts and sciences. We value highly all the capacities with which human nature is endowed, but we regard all the inherent capacities of human beings as means for the attainment of one and the same end, to which we consecrate our lives, namely the fulfillment of God's will. We do not regard art and science as an amusement, of use only to while away the time of idle people. We demand of science and art, as of all human occupations, that in them should be realized that activity of love of God and of our neighbors which should be the aim of all Christian activities. We regard as true science only such knowledge as helps us to live a better life, and we esteem as art only what purifies our thoughts, elevates our souls, and strengthens the powers we need for a life of labor and love. Such knowledge we do not fail to develop in ourselves and in our children as far as we can, and to such art we willingly devote our leisure time. We read and study the works bequeathed to us by the wisdom of those who lived before us. We sing songs and paint pictures, and our poems and pictures brace our spirit and console us in moments of grief. That is why we cannot approve of the applications you make of the arts and sciences. Your learned ones employ their mental capacities to devise new means of injuring others. They perfect methods of warfare, that is, of murder. They contrive new methods of gain, by getting rich at the expense of others. Your art serves for the erection and adornment of temples in honor of gods in whom the more educated among you have long ceased to believe, but whom you encourage others to believe in, in order by such deception the better to keep them in your power. You erect statues in honor of the most powerful and cruel of your tyrants, whom none respect but all fear. In your theaters performances are given extolling guilty love. Music serves for the delectation of your rich, who glut themselves with food and drink at their luxurious feasts. Painting is employed in houses of debauchery to depict scenes such as no sober person, no one who is not stupefied by animal passion, could look at without blushing. No, not for such ends have those higher capacities which distinguish him from the animals been given to humankind. They must not be employed for bodily gratification. Devoting our whole lives to the fulfillment of God's will, we employ our highest faculties especially in that service."

"Yes," said Julius. "All that would be excellent if life were possible under such conditions, but one cannot live so. You deceive yourselves. You condemn our laws, our institutions, and our armies. You do not recognize the protection we afford. If it were not for the Roman legions could you live at peace? You profit by the protection of the state without acknowledging it. Some of your people, as you told me yourself, have even defended themselves. You do not recognize the right of private property, but you make use of it. Our people have it and give to you. You yourself do not give away your grapes, but sell them and buy other things. It is all a deception! If you did what you say that would be all right, but as it is you deceive yourselves and others!"

He spoke heatedly and said all that he had in his mind. Pamphilius waited in silence, and when Julius had finished, he said:

"You are wrong in thinking that we avail ourselves of your protection without acknowledging it. Our welfare consists in not requiring defense, and this no one can take from us. Even if material things which in your eyes constitute property pass through our hands, we do not regard them as our own, and we give them to anyone who needs them for their sustenance. We sell the grapes to those who wish to buy them, not for the sake of personal gain, but solely to acquire necessities for those who need them. If someone wished to take those grapes from us we should give them up without resistance. For the same reason we are not afraid of an incursion of the barbarians. If they began to take from us the product of our toil we should let them have it, and if they demanded that we should work for them, we should also do that gladly; and they would not merely have no reason to kill or ill-treat us, but it would conflict with their own interests to do so. They would soon understand and learn to love us, and we should have less to suffer from them than from the civilized people who now surround us and persecute us.

"You say that the things necessary for existence can only be produced under a system of private property. But consider who really produces the necessaries of life. To whose labor do we owe all these riches of which you are so proud? Were they produced by those who issued orders to their slaves and workers without themselves moving a finger, and who now possess all the property; or were they produced by the poor slaves who carried out their masters' orders for their daily bread, and who now possess no property and have barely enough to supply their daily needs? And do you suppose that these slaves, who expend all their strength in executing orders often quite incomprehensible to them, would not work for themselves and for those they love and care for if they were allowed to do so – that is to say, if they might work for aims they clearly understood and approved of?

"You accuse us of not completely achieving what we strive for, and for taking advantage of violence and property even while we do not recognize them. If we are cheats, it is no use talking to us and we are worthy neither of anger nor of exposure, but only of contempt. And we willingly accept your contempt, for one of our precepts is the recognition of our insignificance. But if we sincerely strive towards what we profess, then your accusation of fraud is unjust. If we strive, as I and my brethren do, to fulfill our

Master's law and to live without violence and without private property – which is the result of violence – we do so not for external ends, riches or honors – we account these as nothing – but for something else. We seek happiness just as you do, only we have a different conception of what it is. You believe that happiness is to be found in wealth and honors, but we believe it is found in something else. Our belief shows us that happiness lies not in violence, but in submissiveness; not in wealth, but in giving everything up. And we, like plants striving towards the light, cannot help but press forward in the direction of our happiness. We do not accomplish all that we desire for our own welfare. That is true. But can it be otherwise? You strive to have the most beautiful wife and the largest fortune. But have you, or has anyone else, ever attained them? If an archer does not hit the mark will he cease to aim at it because he often fails? So it is with us. Our happiness, according to Christ's teaching, lies in love. We seek our happiness, but attain it far from fully and each in his own way."

"Yes, but why do you disbelieve all human wisdom? Why have you turned away from it? Why do you believe only in your crucified Master? Your slavish submission to him – that is what repels me."

"There again you are mistaken, and so is anyone who thinks that we hold our faith because we were bidden to do so by the man in whom we believe. On the contrary, those who with their whole soul seek a knowledge of the truth and communion with the Father – all those who seek for the good – involuntarily come to the path which Christ followed, and so cannot but see him before them, and follow him! All who love God will meet on that path, and you will, too! Our master is the son of God and a mediator between God and humankind, not because someone has said so and we blindly believe it, but because all who seek God find his son before them on the path, and involuntarily come to understand, to see, and to know God, only through him."

Julius did not reply, and they sat in silence for a long time.

"Are you happy?" he asked.

"I wish for nothing better. More than that, I generally experience a feeling of perplexity and am conscious of a kind of injustice that I am so tremendously happy," said Pamphilius with a smile.

"Yes," said Julius, "perhaps I should be happier if I had not met that stranger and had come to you."

"If you think so, what keeps you back?"

"How about my wife?"

"You say that she is inclined towards Christianity – so she might come with you."

"Yes, but we have already begun a different kind of life. How can we break it up? As it has been begun we must live it out," said Julius, picturing to himself the dissatisfaction of his father, his mother, his friends, and above all the effort that would have to be made to effect the change.

Just then the maiden, Pamphilius's companion, came to the door accompanied by a young man. Pamphilius went out to them, and in Julius's presence the young man explained that he had been sent by Cyril to buy some hides. The grapes were already sold and some wheat purchased. Pamphilius proposed that the young man should go with Magdalene and take the wheat home, while he would himself buy and bring home the hides. "It will be better for you," he said.

"No, Magdalene had better go with you," said the young man, and went away.

Julius took Pamphilius into the shop of a tradesman he knew, and Pamphilius poured the wheat into bags, and having given Magdalene a small share to carry, took up his own heavy load, bid farewell to Julius, and left the town with the maiden. At the turning of the street he looked round and nodded to Julius with a smile. Then, with a still more joyous smile, he said something to Magdalene and they disappeared from view.

"Yes, I should have done better had I then gone to them," thought Julius. And in his imagination two pictures alternated: the kindly bright faces of the lusty Pamphilius and the tall strong maiden as they carried the baskets on their heads; and then the domestic hearth from which he had come that morning and to which he must soon return, where his beautiful, but pampered and wearisome wife, who had become repulsive to him, would be lying on rugs and cushions, wearing bracelets and rich attire.

But Julius had no time to think of this. Some merchant companions of his came up to him, and they began their usual occupations, finishing up with dinner and drinking, and spending the night with women.

VI

Ten years passed. Julius had not met Pamphilius again, and the meeting with him had slowly passed from his memory, and the impression of him and of the Christian life wore off.

Julius's life ran its usual course. During these ten years his father had died and he had taken over the management of his whole business, which was a complicated one. There were the regular customers, salesmen in Africa, clerks, and debts to be collected and paid. Julius found himself involuntarily absorbed in it all and gave his whole time to it. Besides this, new cares presented themselves. He was elected to a public office, and this new occupation, which flattered his vanity, attracted him. In addition to his business affairs he now attended to public matters also, and being capable and a good speaker he began to distinguish himself among his fellows, and appeared likely to reach high public office. In his family life a considerable and unpleasant change had occurred during these ten years. Three children had been born to him, and this had separated him from his wife. In the first place she had lost much of her beauty and freshness, and in the second place she paid less attention to her husband. All her tenderness and endearments were devoted to her children. Though according to the pagan custom the children were handed over to wet-nurses and attendants, Julius often found them with their mother, or found her with them instead of in her own apartments. For the most part Julius found the children a burden, affording him more annoyance than pleasure.

Occupied with business and public affairs, he had abandoned his former dissipated life, but considered that he needed some refined recreation after his labors. This, however, he did not find with his wife, the more so as during this time she had cultivated an acquaintance with her Christian slave girl, had become more and more attracted by the new teaching, and had discarded from her life all the external, pagan things that had attracted Julius. Not finding what he wanted in his wife, Julius formed an intimacy with a woman of light conduct, and passed with her the leisure that remained after his business.

Had he been asked whether he was happy or unhappy during those years he would have been unable to answer.

He was so busy! From one affair or pleasure he passed to another affair or pleasure, but not one of them was such as fully to satisfy him or make him wish it to continue. Everything he did was of such a nature that the quicker he could free himself from it the better he was pleased, and his pleasures were all poisoned in some way, or the tedium of satiety mingled with them.

In this way he was living when something happened that came near to altering his whole manner of life. He took part in the races at the Olympic Games, and was driving his chariot successfully to the end of the course when he suddenly collided with another which was overtaking him. His wheel broke, and he was thrown out and broke his arm and two ribs. His injuries were serious, though they did not endanger his life, and he was taken home and had to keep to his bed for three months.

During these three months of severe physical suffering his mind worked, and he had leisure to think about his life as if it were someone else's. And his life presented itself to him in a gloomy light, the more so as during that time three unpleasant events occurred which much distressed him.

The first was that a slave, who had been his father's trusted servant, decamped with some precious jewels he had received in Africa, thus causing a heavy loss and a disorganization of Julius's affairs.

The second was that his mistress deserted him and found herself another protector.

The third and most unpleasant event for him was that during his illness there was an election, and his opponent secured the position he had hoped to obtain.

All this, it seemed to Julius, came about because his chariot wheel had swerved a fingerbreadth to the left.

Lying alone on his couch he began involuntarily to reflect on the fact that his happiness depended on such insignificant happenings, and these thoughts led him on to others, and to the recollection of his former misfortunes, of his attempt to go to the Christians, and of Pamphilius, whom he had now not seen for ten years. These recollections were strengthened by conversations with his wife, who was often with him during his illness and told him everything she had learned about Christianity from her slave girl.

This slave girl had at one time been in the same community with Pamphilius, and knew him. Julius wished to see her, and when she came to his couch, questioned her about everything in detail, and especially about Pamphilius.

Pamphilius, the slave girl said, was one of the best of the brethren, and was loved and esteemed by them all. He had married that same Magdalene whom Julius had seen ten years ago, and they already had several children.

"Yes, anyone who does not believe that God has created human beings for happiness should go to see their life," concluded the slave girl.

Julius let the slave girl go and remained alone, thinking of what he had heard. It made him envious to compare Pamphilius's life with his own, and he did not wish to think about it.

To distract himself he took up a Greek manuscript which his wife had left by his couch, and began to read as follows:

There are two ways: one of life and the other of death. The way of life is this: First, you shall love God who has created you, secondly, you shall love your neighbor as yourself; and you shall do to no one what you would not have him do to you.

Now this is the meaning of these words: Bless them that curse you, pray for your enemies and for those that persecute you. For what merit have you if you love only those who love you? Do not the heathen so? Love them that hate you, and you shall have no enemies. Put away from you all carnal and worldly desires. If a man smites you on the right cheek, turn to him the other also, and you shall be perfect. If a man compels you to walk a mile with him, go with him two. If he takes what belongs to you, demand it not again, for this you shall not do; if he takes your outer garment, give him your shirt also. Give to everyone that asks of you, and demand nothing back, for the Father wishes that his abundant gifts should be received by all. Blessed is he who gives according to the commandment!

The second commandment of the teaching is this: Do not kill, do not commit adultery, do not be wanton, do not steal, do not employ sorcery, do not poison, do not covet your neighbor's goods. Take no oath, do not bear false witness, speak no evil, do not remember injuries. Shun duplicity in your thoughts and be not double-tongued. Let not your words be false nor empty, but in accord with your deeds. Be not covetous, nor rapacious, nor hypocritical, nor ill-tempered, nor proud. Have no evil intention against your neighbor. Cherish no hatred of any man, but rebuke some, pray for others, and love some more than your own soul.

My child! Shun evil and all appearance of evil. Be not angry, for anger leads to murder. Be not jealous, nor quarrelsome, nor passionate, for of all these things comes murder.

My child! Be not lustful, for lust leads to wantonness, and be not foul-mouthed, for of this comes adultery.

My child! Be not untruthful, for lying leads to theft; neither be fond of money, nor vain, for of all these comes theft also.

My child! Do not repine, for that leads to blasphemy; neither be arrogant, nor a thinker of evil, for of all these things comes blasphemy also. Be humble, for the meek shall inherit the earth. Be long-suffering, merciful, forgiving, humble, and kind, and take heed of the words that you hear. Do not exalt yourself, and yield not your soul to arrogance nor let your soul cleave to the proud, but have converse with the humble and just. Accept as a blessing all that befalls you, knowing that nothing happens without God's will . . .

My child! Do not sow dissensions, but reconcile those that are at strife. Stretch not out your hand to receive, nor hold it back from giving. Be not slow in giving, nor repine when giving, for you shall know the good Giver of rewards. Turn not away from the needy, but in everything have communion with your brother, and call not anything your own, for if you are partakers in that which is incorruptible, how much more so in that which is corruptible. Teach your children the fear of God from their youth. Deal not with your slave in anger, lest he cease to fear God who is above you both, for he is no respecter of persons but calls those whom the Spirit hath prepared.

But this is the way of death: First of all it is wrathful and full of curses; here are murder, adultery, lust, wantonness, theft, idolatry, sorcery, poisoning, plundering, false witness, hypocrisy, deceitfulness, insidiousness, pride, malice, arrogance, avarice, obscenity, envy, insolence, presumption, and vanity. Here are the persecutors of the righteous, haters of the truth, lovers of falsehood, who do not acknowledge the reward for righteousness nor cleave to what is good or to righteous judgments, who are vigilant not for what is good but for evil, from whom meekness and patience are far removed. Here are those that love vanity, who follow after rewards, who have no pity for their neighbors and do not labor for the oppressed or know their Creator. Here are the murderers of children, destroyers of God's image, who turn away from the needy. Here are the oppressors of the oppressed, defenders of the rich, unjust judges of the poor, sinners in all things. Beware, children, of all these!

Long before he had read the manuscript to the end, Julius had entered with his whole soul into communion with those who had inspired it – as often happens to people who read a book (that is, another person's thoughts) with a sincere desire to discern the truth. He read on, guessing in advance what was coming, and not only agreed with the thoughts expressed in the book but seemed to be expressing them himself.

He experienced that ordinary, but mysterious and significant phenomenon, unnoticed by many people: of a man, supposed to be alive, becoming really alive on entering into communion with those accounted dead, and uniting and living one life with them.

Julius's soul united with him who had written and inspired those thoughts, and in the light of this communion he contemplated himself and his life. And it appeared to him to be all a terrible mistake. He had not lived, but had only destroyed in himself the possibility of living by all the cares and temptations of life.

"I do not wish to ruin my life. I want to live and to follow the path of life!" he said to himself.

He remembered all that Pamphilius had said to him in their former conversations, and it all now seemed so clear and unquestionable that he was surprised that he could have listened to the stranger and not have held to his intention of going to the Christians. He remembered also that the stranger had said to him: "Go when you have had experience of life!"

"I have now had experience of life, and have found nothing in it!" thought Julius.

He also recalled the words of Pamphilius: that whenever he might go to the Christians, they would be glad to receive him.

"No, I have erred and suffered enough!" he said to himself. "I will give up everything and go to them and live as it says here!"

He told his wife of his plan, and she was delighted with it. She was ready for everything. The only difficulty was to decide how to put the plan into execution. What was to be done with the children? Were they to be taken with them or left with their grandmother? How could they be taken? How, after the delicacy of their upbringing, could they be subjected to all the difficulties of a rough life? The slave girl proposed to go with them, but the mother was afraid for the children, and said that it would be better to leave them with their grandmother and to go alone. And to this they agreed.

All was decided. Only Julius's illness delayed the execution of their plans.

VII

In that state of mind Julius fell asleep. In the morning he was told that a skillful physician was visiting the town and wished to see him, promising him speedy relief. Julius willingly consented to see him, and the physician proved to be none other than the stranger whom he had met when he started to join the Christians. Having examined his injuries the physician prescribed certain potions of herbs to strengthen him.

"Shall I be able to work with my hands?" inquired Julius.

"Oh yes! You will be able to write and to drive a chariot."

"But hard work – digging?"

"I was not thinking of that," said the physician, "because it cannot be necessary for someone in your position."

"On the contrary, it is just what is wanted," said Julius, and he told the physician that since he had last seen him he had followed his advice and had experienced life; and that life had not given him what it promised, but on the contrary had disillusioned him, and that he now wished to carry out the intention he had then spoken of.

"They have evidently employed all their deceptions and have enchanted you so that in spite of your position and the responsibilities that rest upon you – especially in regard to your children – you still do not see their error."

"Read that!" was all Julius said in reply, handing him the manuscript he had been reading.

The physician took the manuscript and looked at it.

"I know this," he said. "I know this deception, and am surprised that someone such as you should be caught by such a snare."

"I don't understand you. Where is the snare?"

"It is all tested by life! These sophists and rebels against humanity and the gods propose a way of life in which all people will be happy, and there will be no wars or executions, no poverty or depravity, no strife or anger. And they insist that this condition will come about when all people fulfill the law of Christ – not to quarrel, nor yield to lust, nor take oaths, nor do violence, nor take arms against another nation. But they deceive themselves and others by taking the end for the means.

"Their aim is not to quarrel, not to bind themselves by oaths, not to be wanton, and so forth, and this aim can only be attained by means of public life. But what they say is as if a teacher of archery should say: 'You will hit the target when your arrow flies to it in a straight line.' The problem is how to make it fly straight. And that result is attained in archery by having a taut bowstring, a flexible bow, and a straight arrow. It is the same in life. The best life, in which people have no need to quarrel, to be wanton, or to commit murder, is attained by having a taut bowstring (the rulers), a flexible bow (the power of government), and a straight arrow (the justice of the law). But they, under pretext of living a better life, destroy all that has improved or does improve it. They recognize neither government, nor the authorities, nor the laws."

"But they say that if people fulfill the law of Christ, life will be better without rulers, authorities, and laws."

"Yes, but what guarantee is there that people will fulfill it? None! They say: 'You have experienced life under rulers and laws, and life has not been perfected. Try it now without rulers and laws and it will become perfect. You cannot deny this, for you have not tried it.' But this is the obvious sophistry of these impious people. In saying that, is it not in effect as though someone should say to a farmer: 'You sow your seed in the ground and cover it up, and yet the harvest is not what you would wish. I advise you to sow in the sea. It will be better like that – and you cannot deny my proposition, for you have not tried it'?"

"Yes, that is true," said Julius, who was beginning to waver.

"But that is not all," continued the physician. "Let us assume the absurd and impossible. Let us assume that the principles of the Christian teaching can be poured into people like medicine, and that suddenly all will begin to fulfill Christ's teaching, to love God and their fellows, and to fulfill his commandments. Even assuming all that, the path of life inculcated by them would still not stand examination. Life would come to an end and the race would die out. Their Teacher was a young vagabond, and such will his followers be, and according to our supposition such would the whole world become if it followed his teaching. Those living would last their time, but their children would not survive, or hardly one in ten would do so. According to their teaching all children should be alike to every mother and to every father, whether they are their own children or not. How will these children be looked after, when we see that all the devotion and all the love implanted in mothers hardly preserves their own children from perishing? What will happen when this devotion is replaced by a compassion shared by all children alike? Which child is to be taken and preserved? Who will sit up at night with a sick (and malodorous) child except its own mother? Nature has provided a protection for the child in its mother's love, but the Christians want to deprive it of that protection, and offer nothing in exchange! Who will train a son, who will penetrate into his soul like his father? Who will defend him from dangers? All this they reject! All life – that is, the continuation of the human race – is made away with."

"That also is true," said Julius, carried away by the physician's eloquence.

"Yes, my friend, have nothing to do with these ravings. Live rationally, especially now that you have such great and serious and pressing responsibilities. It is a matter of honor for you to fulfill them. You have reached the second period of your doubts, but go on and your doubts will vanish. Your first and evident duty is the education of your children, which you have neglected. You must train them to be worthy servants of their country. The existing political structure has given you everything you have, and you must serve it yourself and give it worthy servants in the persons of your children, on whom you will thereby also confer a benefit. Another obligation you have is the service of the community. You are mortified and discouraged by your accidental and temporary failure. But nothing is achieved without effort and struggle, and the joy of triumph is great only when the victory has been hardly won. Leave it to your wife to amuse herself with the babble of the Christian writers. You should be a man, and bring up your children to be men. Begin to live with the consciousness of duty, and all your doubts will fall away of themselves. They were caused by your illness. Fulfill your duty to the state by serving it and by preparing your children for its service. Set them on their feet, so that they may be able to take your place, and then peacefully abandon yourself to the life which attracts you. Till then you have no right to do so, and were you to do so you would encounter nothing but suffering."

VIII

Whether it was the effect of the medicinal herbs or the advice given him by the wise physician, Julius speedily recovered, and his plans of adopting a Christian life now appeared to him like raving.

After staying a few days the physician left the city. Soon afterwards Julius left his sick bed and began a new life in accord with the advice he had received. He engaged teachers for his children and supervised their studies himself. He spent his own time on public affairs and soon acquired great influence in the city.

So a year passed, and during that time Julius did not even think about the Christians. But at the end of the year a legate from the Roman Emperor arrived in Cilicia to suppress the Christian movement, and a trial was arranged to take place in Tarsus. Julius heard of the measures that were being undertaken against the Christians, but he paid no attention to them, not thinking that they related to the commune in which Pamphilius was living. But one day as he was walking in the forum to attend to his duties, a poorly dressed elderly man approached him whom he did not at first recognize. It was Pamphilius. He came up to Julius leading a child by the hand, and said:

"Greetings, friend! I have a great favor to ask of you, but now that the Christians are being persecuted I do not know whether you will wish to acknowledge me as your friend, or whether you will not be afraid of losing your post if you have anything to do with me."

"I am not afraid of anyone," replied Julius, "and as a proof of it I ask you to come with me to my house. I will even neglect my business in the forum to have a talk with you and help you. Come with me. Whose child is that?"

"He is my son."

"I need not have asked. I recognize your features in him, and I also recognize those light-blue eyes, and need not ask who your wife is. She is the lovely girl I saw you with several years ago."

"You have guessed right," replied Pamphilius. "She became my wife soon after you saw us."

On reaching the house, Julius called his wife and handed the boy over to her, and then led Pamphilius to his luxurious private room.

"You can speak freely here," he said. "No one will hear us."

"I am not afraid of being heard," replied Pamphilius. "My request is not that the Christians who have been arrested should not be judged and executed, but only that they should be allowed to announce their faith in public."

And Pamphilius told how the Christians who had been seized by the authorities had succeeded in sending word from their prison to the community telling of their condition. Cyril the Elder, knowing of Pamphilius's relations with Julius, had sent him to intercede for the Christians. They did not ask for mercy. They looked upon it as their vocation to testify to the truth of Christ's teaching, and they could do this equally well by suffering martyrdom as by a life of eighty years. They would accept either fate with equal indifference, and physical death, which must inevitably overtake them, was as welcome and void of terror now as it would be fifty years hence. But they wished by their death to serve their fellow human beings, and therefore Pamphilius had been sent to ask that their trial and execution should be public.

Julius was surprised at Pamphilius's request, but promised to do all in his power to aid him.

"I have promised to help you," he said, "out of friendship, and because of the particular feeling of tenderness you have always aroused in me, but I must say that I consider your teaching most senseless and harmful. I can judge of this because some time ago, when I was ill, disappointed, and low-spirited, I myself once again shared your views and came very near to abandoning everything and joining your community. I know now on what your error is based, for I have myself experienced it. It is based on love of self, weakness of spirit, and sickly enervation. It is a creed for women, not for men."

"But why?"

"Because, while you recognize the fact that discord lies in human nature and that strife results therefrom, you do not wish to take part in that strife or to teach others to do so; and without taking your share of the burden you avail yourselves of the organization of the world, which is based on violence. Is that fair? Our world owes its existence to the fact that there have always been rulers. Those rulers took on themselves the trouble and all the responsibility of defending us from foreign and domestic foes, and in return for that we subjects submitted to them and rendered them honor, or helped them by serving the state. But you, out of pride, instead of taking your part in the affairs of the state and rising higher and higher in the regard of others by your labors and to the extent of your deserts – you in your pride at once declare all people to be equal, in order that you may consider no one higher than yourself, but may reckon yourself equal to Caesar. That is what you yourself think and teach others to think. And for weak and idle people that is a great temptation! Every slave, instead of laboring, at once considers himself Caesar's equal. But you do more than this: you deny taxes, and slavery, and the courts, and executions, and war – everything that holds people together. If people listened to you, society would fall to pieces and we should return to primitive savagery.

"Living under a government you preach the destruction of government. But your very existence is dependent on that government. Without it you would not exist. You would all be slaves of the Scythians or the barbarians – the first people who happened to hear of your existence. You are like a tumor which destroys the body but can only nourish itself on the body. And a living body resists that tumor and overcomes it! We do the same with you, and cannot but do so. And in spite of my promise to help you obtain your wish, I look upon your teaching as most harmful and despicable: despicable because I consider it dishonorable and unjust to gnaw the breast that feeds you – to avail yourselves of the advantages of governmental order, and to destroy that order by which the state is maintained, without taking part in it!"

"If we really lived as you suppose there would be much justice in what you say," replied Pamphilius. "But you do not know our life, and have formed a false conception of it. The means of subsistence which we employ are obtainable without the aid of violence. It is difficult for you, with your luxurious habits, to realize on how little a person can live without privation. A healthy man is so constituted that he can produce with his hands far more than he needs for his subsistence. Living together in a community we are able by our common work to feed without difficulty our children, our old people, and the sick and weak. You say of the rulers that they protect people from external and internal enemies – but we love our enemies, and so we have none. You assert that we Christians stir up in the slave a desire to be Caesar, but on the contrary, both by word and deed we profess one thing: patient humility and labor, the humblest of labor, that of a worker. We neither know nor understand anything about political matters. We only know one thing, and we know that with certainty, that our welfare lies solely in the good of others, and we seek that welfare. The welfare of all human beings lies in their union with one another, and union is attained not by violence but by love. The violence of a brigand inflicted on a traveler is as atrocious to us as the violence of an army to its prisoners, or of a judge to those who are executed, and we cannot intentionally participate in the one or the other. Nor can we profit by the labor of others enforced by violence. Violence is reflected on us, but our participation in violence consists not in inflicting it but in submissively enduring its infliction on ourselves."

"Yes," said Julius, "you preach about love, but when one looks at the results it turns out to be quite another thing. It leads to barbarism and a reversion to savagery, murder, robbery, and violence, which according to your doctrine must not be repressed in any way."

"No, that is not so," said Pamphilius, "and if you really examine the results of our teaching and of our lives carefully and impartially, you will see that not only do they not lead to murder, robbery, and violence, but on the contrary those crimes can only be opposed by the means we practice. Murder, robbery, and all evils, existed long before Christianity, and people have always contended with them, but unsuccessfully, because they employed means that we deplore, meeting violence by violence; and this never checks crime, but on the contrary provokes it by sowing hatred and exasperation.

"Look at the mighty Roman Empire. Nowhere else is such trouble taken about the laws as in Rome. Studying and perfecting the laws constitutes a special science. The laws are taught in the schools, discussed in the Senate, and reformed and administered by the most educated citizens. Legal justice is considered the highest virtue, and the office of Judge is held in peculiar respect. Yet in spite of this it is known that there is now no city in the world so steeped in crime and corruption as Rome. Remember Roman history: in olden times when the laws were very primitive the Roman people possessed many virtues, but in our days, despite the elaboration and administration of law, the morals of the citizens are becoming worse and worse. The number of crimes constantly increases, and they become more varied and more elaborate every day.

"Nor can it be otherwise. Crime and evil can be successfully opposed only by the Christian method of love, and not by the heathen methods of revenge, punishment, and violence. I am sure you would like people to abstain from evil voluntarily and not from fear of punishment. You would not wish people to be like prisoners who only refrain from crime because they are watched by their jailers. But no laws or restrictions or punishments make people averse to doing evil or desirous of doing good. That can only be attained by destroying evil at its root, which is in the human heart. That is what we aim at, while you only try to repress the outward manifestations of evil. You do not look for its source and do not know where it is, and so you can never find it.

"The commonest crimes – murder, robbery, and fraud – are the result of people's desire to increase their possessions, or even to obtain the necessaries of life which they have been unable to procure in any other way. Some of these crimes are punished by the law, but the most important and far-reaching in their consequences are perpetrated under the wing of the law, as, for instance, the huge commercial frauds and the innumerable ways in which the rich rob the poor. Those crimes which are punished by law may indeed to a certain extent be repressed – or rendered more difficult of execution – and the criminals for fear of punishment become more prudent and cunning and invent new forms of crime which the law does not punish. But by leading a Christian life a person preserves himself from all these crimes, which result on the one hand from the struggle for money and possessions, and on the other from the unequal concentration of riches in the hands of the few. Our one way of checking theft and murder is to keep for ourselves only as much as is indispensable for life, and to give to others all the superfluous products of our toil. We Christians do not lead others into temptation by the sight of accumulated wealth, for we rarely possess more than enough for our daily bread. A hungry man, driven to despair and ready to commit a crime for a piece of bread, if he comes to us will find all he wants without committing any crime, because that is what we live for – to share all we have with those who are cold and hungry. And the result is that one sort of evildoer avoids us, while others turn to us, give up their criminal life, and are saved, and gradually become workers laboring for the good of all.

"Other crimes are prompted by the passions of jealousy, revenge, carnal love, anger, and hatred. Such crimes cannot be suppressed by law. A person who commits them is in a brutal state of unbridled passion; he is incapable of reflecting on the consequences of his actions, opposition only exasperates him, so the law is powerless to restrain these crimes. We however believe that people can find satisfaction and the meaning of life only in the spirit, and that as long as they serve their passions they can never find happiness. We curb our passions by a life of love and labor, and develop in ourselves the power of the spirit, and the more deeply and widely our faith spreads the rarer will crime inevitably become.

"A third class of crime," Pamphilius continued, "arises from the desire to help humankind. Some people – revolutionary conspirators – are anxious to alleviate the people's lot, and kill tyrants, imagining that they are thereby doing good to the majority of the people. The origin of such crimes is the belief that one can do good by committing evil. Such crimes, prompted by an idea, are not crushed out by legal punishments: on the contrary they are inflamed and evoked by them. In spite of their errors the ones who commit them do so from a noble motive – a desire to serve humankind. They are sincere, they readily sacrifice themselves, and they do not shrink from danger. And so the fear of punishment does not stop them. On the contrary, danger stimulates them, and sufferings and executions exalt them to the dignity of heroes, gain sympathy for them, and incite others to follow their example. We see this in the history of all nations. But we Christians believe that evil will only pass away when people understand the misery that results from it both for themselves and for others. We know that brotherhood can only be attained when we are all brothers – that brotherhood without brothers is impossible.

"And though we see the errors of the revolutionary conspirators, yet we appreciate their sincerity and unselfishness, and are attracted by the good that is in them.

"Which of us then is more successful in the struggle with crime and does more to suppress evil – we Christians, who prove by our life the happiness of a spiritual existence from which no evil results and whose means of influence are example and love; or you, whose rulers and judges pass sentences in accord with the dead letter of the law, ruin their victims, and drive them to the last extremity of exasperation?"

"When one listens to you," said Julius, "one almost begins to think that you may be right. But tell me, Pamphilius, why are people hostile to you? Why do they persecute you, hunt you down, and kill you? Why does your teaching of love lead to discord?"

"The reason of that lies not in us but outside us. Till now I have been speaking of crimes which are regarded as such both by the state and by us. These crimes constitute a form of violence which infringes the temporary laws of any state. But besides these there are other laws implanted in man – laws that are eternal, common to all human beings, and written in their hearts. We Christians obey these divine, universal laws, and find their fullest, clearest, and most perfect realization in the words and life of our Master, and we regard as a crime any violence that transgresses the commands of Christ, because they express God's law. We consider that to avoid discord we must also obey the laws of the country we live in, but we regard the law of God, which governs our conscience and reason, as supreme, and we can only obey those human laws which do not conflict with the divine Law. 'Render unto Caesar the things that are Caesar's, and unto God the things that are God's.' Our struggle against crime is therefore both deeper and wider than the state's, for while we avoid transgressing the laws of the particular country we happen to live in, we seek above all not to infringe the will of God – the law common to all human nature. And because we regard the law of God as the highest law, people hate and fear us, for they consider some particular laws as supreme – the legislation of their own country, for instance, or even very often some custom of their own class. They are incapable of becoming, or unwilling to become, real human beings, in the sense of Christ's saying that 'The truth shall make you free.' They are content with their position as subjects of this or that state or as members of society, and so they naturally feel enmity towards those who see and proclaim the higher destiny of humanity. Incapable of understanding, or unwilling to understand, this higher destiny for themselves, they are unwilling to admit it for others. It was of such that Christ said: 'Woe to you, Pharisees! for you take away the key of knowledge; you do not enter yourselves, and you hinder those that are entering.' They are the authors of those persecutions which raise doubts in your mind.

"We have no enmity towards anyone, not even towards those who persecute us, and our life brings harm and injury to no one. If others are irritated against us and even hate us, the reason can only be that our life is a thorn in their side, a constant condemnation of their own life which is founded on violence. We are unable to prevent this enmity against us, which does not proceed from us, for we cannot forget the truth we have understood, and cannot begin to live contrary to our conscience and our reason. Of this hostility which our belief provokes against us in others our Teacher said: 'Think not that I come to bring peace upon earth. I come not to bring peace, but a sword!' Christ himself experienced this hostility, and he warned us, his pupils, of it more than once. He said: 'The world hates me, because its deeds are evil. If you were of the world, the world would love its own; but because you are not of the world, but I chose you out of the world, therefore the world hates you. The hour is coming when whoever kills you will think he is offering service to God.'

"But we, like Christ, fear not them that kill the body and then can do nothing more to us. Sufferings and the death of the flesh will not pass any person by, but we live in the light and therefore our life does not depend on the body. It is not we who suffer from the attacks upon us, but our persecutors and enemies, who suffer from the feeling of enmity and hatred they nurse like a serpent in their breasts. 'And this is the condemnation, that light is come into the world, and men loved darkness rather than light, because their deeds were evil.' There is no need to be disconcerted about this, for the truth will prevail. The sheep hear the voice of the shepherd and follow him, because they know his voice. And Christ's flock will not perish, but increase, drawing new sheep to itself from all the countries of the earth, for the wind blows where it wills, and you hear the sound of it, but you do not know whence it comes or whither it goes."

"Yes," Julius interrupted him, "but are there many among you who are sincere? You are often accused of only pretending to be martyrs and glad to die for the truth, but the truth is not on your side. You are proud madmen, destroying all the foundations of social life!"

Pamphilius made no reply, and looked sorrowfully at Julius.

IX

Just then Pamphilius's little son ran into the room and pressed close to his father's side.

Despite the caresses Julius's wife had bestowed upon him, he had run away from her to find his father. Pamphilius sighed, caressed the child, and got up to go, but Julius detained him, asking him to stay to dinner and have a further talk.

"It surprises me," he said, "to see that you are married and have children. I cannot understand how you Christians can bring up a family while having no property. How can the mothers among you live at peace, knowing that their children are not provided for?"

"Why are our children less provided for than yours?"

"Because you have neither slaves nor property. My wife is much inclined to Christianity. She even at one time wished to give up our way of life, and I intended to go away with her. But she feared the insecurity and poverty she foresaw for the children, and I could not but agree with her. That was at the time of my illness. My whole way of life was repulsive to me just then and I wished to abandon it. But my wife's fears, and the explanation given me by the physician who was treating me, convinced me that though a Christian life as you live it may be right and possible for people who have no family, it is impossible for family people, or for mothers with children: that with your outlook life itself – the human race – would cease to exist. And it seems to me that that is quite correct. So your appearance with a son greatly surprised me."

"Not only a son – there is also one at the breast and a three-year-old girl, who have remained at home."

"But I don't understand it! Not so long ago I was ready to give up everything and become one of you. But I had children, and it was clear to me that, however good your life might be for myself, I had no right to sacrifice my children. So for their sake I remained here, living as before, that they might be brought up in the conditions in which I myself grew up and have lived."

"It is strange how differently we look at things," said Pamphilius. "We say that if adults live in the worldly way it may be excused, for they are already spoiled, but for children it is terrible. To bring them up in worldly fashion and expose them to temptation! 'Woe to the world for temptations to sin! For it is necessary that temptations come, but woe to the man by whom the temptation comes!' So says our Teacher, and I repeat it to you not as a retort, but because it is really true. The chief necessity for us to live as we do comes from the fact that there are children among us; those children of whom it is said: 'Unless you become like little children, you will never enter the kingdom of heaven.'"

"But how can a Christian family manage to live without definite means of livelihood?"

"According to our belief there is only one means – that of loving work for others. Your method is violence. But that method may fail and be destroyed, as riches are destroyed, and then only work and the love of others is left. We consider that love is the basis of all, and should be firmly held to and increased. And when that is so, families live and prosper. No," continued Pamphilius, "if I doubted the truth of Christ's teaching, or hesitated to follow it, my doubts and hesitations would vanish when I thought of the fate of children brought up among the pagans in the conditions in which you and your children have been and are being brought up. Whatever arrangement of life some people may make, with palaces, slaves, and the imported produce of other lands, the life of the majority of humankind will remain as it should be. And the security for that life will always be the same – brotherly love and labor. We wish to exempt ourselves and our children from these conditions, and make others work for us by means of violence and not by love, and strange to say the more we apparently secure ourselves thereby, the more do we actually deprive ourselves of the true, natural, and reliable security – that of love. The greater a ruler's power the less he is loved. It is the same with the other security – labor. The more a person frees himself from labor and accustoms himself to luxury, the less capable of work he becomes and the more he deprives himself of true and reliable security. And yet when people have placed their children in these conditions they say they have 'provided for them!' Take your son and mine and send the two of them to find their way anywhere, to transmit instructions, or to do some necessary thing, and you will see which of the two will do it better. Or offer them for education, and you will see which of the two would be accepted the more readily. No! Do not make that terrible statement that a Christian life is only possible for the childless. On the contrary, it might be said that a pagan life may be pardonable only for those who have no children. 'But woe unto him that shall cause one of these little ones to stumble.'"

Julius was silent for some time.

"Yes," he said at last. "Perhaps you are right. But my children's education has been begun, they have the best teachers. Let them learn all we know – there can be no harm in that. There is time enough both for me and for them. They can come to you when they are grown up if they find it necessary. And I can do the same when I have set them on their feet and am left free."

"Know the truth, and the truth shall make you free," said Pamphilius. "Christ gives perfect freedom at once: the world's teaching will never give it. Farewell!" And Pamphilius called his son and went away.

The Christians were condemned and executed publicly, and Julius saw Pamphilius with other Christians clearing away the bodies of the martyrs.

He saw him, but from fear of the higher authorities did not approach him or invite him to his house.

X

Another twenty years passed. Julius's wife died. His life flowed on in public activity and in efforts to obtain power, which sometimes seemed within his reach and sometimes eluded him. His wealth was great and continued to increase.

His sons had grown up; and the second, especially, began to lead an extravagant life. He made holes in the bottom of the bucket which held his father's wealth, and in proportion as that wealth increased so did the rapidity of the outflow through those holes. And here began for Julius a conflict with his sons such as he had had with his father – anger, hatred, and jealousy.

About this time a new Prefect was appointed and deprived Julius of favor. His former flatterers abandoned him, and he was in danger of banishment. He went to Rome to explain matters but was not received, and was ordered to return.

On reaching home he found his son carousing with dissolute companions. A report had spread in Cilicia that Julius was dead, and the son was celebrating his father's death! Julius lost control of himself and felled his son to the ground. He then retired to his wife's rooms. There he found a copy of the Gospels, and read:

"Come unto me, all ye that labor and are heavy laden, and I will give you rest. Take my yoke upon you, and learn of me; for I am meek and lowly in heart; and ye shall find rest unto your souls. For my yoke is easy, and my burden is light."

"Yes," thought Julius, "he has long been calling me. I did not believe him but was refractory and wicked, and my yoke was heavy and my burden grievous."

He sat there for a long time with the open Gospel on his knee, thinking over his whole past life and remembering all that Pamphilius had said to him at different times. At last he rose and went to his son. To his surprise he found him on his feet, and was inexpressibly glad to find that he had sustained no injury.

Without saying a word to his son Julius went out into the street and set off towards the Christian settlement. He walked all day, and in the evening stopped at a villager's for the night. In the room which he entered lay a man, who got up at the sound of footsteps. It was his acquaintance the physician.

"No, this time you shall not dissuade me!" cried Julius. "This is the third time I have started to go thither, and now I know that only there shall I find peace of mind."

"Where?" asked the physician.

"Among the Christians."

"Yes, perhaps you may find peace of mind, but you will not have fulfilled your duty. You lack manliness: misfortunes crush your spirit. Not so do true philosophers behave! Misfortunes are only the fire in which gold is tried. You have passed through a test. And now that you are wanted you run away! Now is the time to try people and yourself. You have acquired true wisdom and should employ it for the good of your country. What would happen to the people if all who have learned to know human-kind, its passions, and its conditions of life, were to bury their knowledge and experience in their search for peace of mind, instead of sharing them for the benefit of society? Your experience of life was gained among human beings and you ought to use it for their benefit."

"But I have no wisdom at all! I am altogether sunk in error! My errors have not become wisdom because they are ancient, any more than water becomes wine because it is stale and foul."

And seizing his cloak Julius hastily left the house and set out to walk farther, without staying to rest. By the close of another day he reached the Christian settlement.

They received him gladly, though they did not know that he was a friend of Pamphilius, whom they all loved and respected. At the refectory Pamphilius, seeing his friend, ran to him gladly and embraced him.

"At last I have come," said Julius. "Tell me what I am to do and I will obey you."

"Don't trouble about that," said Pamphilius. "Come with me." And he led Julius into the guesthouse, and showing him a bed, said:

"When you have had time to observe our life you will see for yourself how you can best be of use to humankind. But I will show you something to do tomorrow to occupy your time for the present. We are gathering grapes in our vineyards. Go there and help. You will see yourself what you can do."

Next morning Julius went into the vineyards. The first was of young vines which were loaded with clusters. Young people were plucking and gathering them. The places were all occupied and Julius, having walked about for some time, found no place for himself. He went on farther and came to an older vineyard where there was less fruit. But here also there was nothing for him to do; the gatherers were all working in pairs and there was no place for him. He went still farther and entered a very old, deserted vineyard. The vine stocks were gnarled and crooked and Julius could see no grapes.

"There, that is like my life," he said to himself. "Had I come the first time, it would have been like the fruit in the first vineyard. Had I come when I started the second time, it would have been like the fruit in the second vineyard. But now here is my life – like these useless superannuated vines, only fit for fuel!" And Julius was terrified at what he had done, terrified at the

320 + THE WAY OF THE KINGDOM

320 ✦ THE WAY OF THE KINGDOM

punishment awaiting him for having uselessly wasted his life. And he became sad and said aloud:

"I am no longer good for anything and can now do nothing!" And he sat down and wept because he had wasted what he could never recover. Suddenly he heard the voice of an old man calling him:

"Work, brother!" said the voice.

Julius looked round and saw an old man, gray and bowed by age and scarcely able to move his feet. He was standing by the vines and gathering the few sweet bunches that still remained here and there. Julius went up to him.

"Work, dear brother! Work is joyous!" And the old man showed him where to look for bunches of the grapes that still remained. Julius began to look for them, and finding some, brought them and laid them in the old man's basket. And the old man said to him:

"Look, in what way are these bunches any worse than those they are gathering in the other vineyards? 'Walk while you have the light!' said our Teacher. 'The will of him who sent me is that everyone who sees the Son and believes in him should have eternal life; and I will raise him up at the last day. For God sent the Son into the world, not to condemn the world, but that the world might be saved through him. He who believes in him is not condemned; he who does not believe is condemned already, because he has not believed in the name of the only Son of God. And this is the judgment, that the light has come into the world, and men loved darkness rather than light, because their deeds were evil. For everyone who does evil hates the light, and does not come to the light, lest his deeds should be exposed. But he who does what is true comes to the light, that it may be clearly seen that his deeds have been wrought in God.' My son, be not unhappy! We are all sons of God and his servants! We are all one army! Do you think that he has no servants besides you, and that if you had devoted yourself to his service with your whole strength you could have done all that he needs – all that is needful for the establishment of his kingdom? You say you would do twice, ten times, a hundred times, more than you did. But if you did ten thousand times ten thousand more than all people have done, what would that have been in the work of God? A mere nothing! God's work, like himself, is infinite. God's work is you. Come to him, and be not a laborer but a son, and you will become a partner of the infinite God and of his world. In God's sight there is neither small nor great, there is only what is straight and what is crooked. Enter into the straight path of life and you will be with God and your work will be neither small nor great, it will be God's work. Remember that in heaven there is more joy over one sinner than over a hundred just persons. The world's work – all that you have neglected to do – has only shown you your sin, and you have repented. And when you repented you found the straight path. Go forward and follow it, and do not think of the past nor of what is great or small. All people are equal in God's sight! There is one God and one life!"

And Julius was comforted, and from that day he lived and worked for the brethren according to his strength. And so he lived joyfully for another twenty years, and did not notice how death took his body.

Afterword

Finding the Gospel in Tolstoy

Eberhard Arnold*

Translated by Hugo Brinkmann

EARLY IN TOLSTOY'S spiritual development, while he was living in the Caucasus, he came strongly under the influence of Jean-Jacques Rousseau. There in that mountainous region, Tolstoy found joy at being far away from the city, from the corruption of body and soul, and he sought God in nature. Over the course of his later life, it became increasingly clear to him that the ultimate mystery of nature – that which nature and humankind have in common – is summarized in Jesus' command: "Love your enemies!" To Tolstoy, such love meant dedicated service to humankind.

It must be admitted, of course, that Tolstoy was not permeated by the freely working grace of the cross of Christ; he had not, through rebirth, won through to the freedom of the spirit, and he therefore remained mired in legalism. As regards the Sermon on the Mount, he focused on what he called the "five laws" of Jesus (Matthew 5), and especially on the command "Do not resist one who is evil!" Here two things stand out: (1) Tolstoy's legalistic formulation of Jesus' commands and (2) the fact that what he picked out as important in the Sermon on the Mount was a *negative* sentence. This fully corresponds to his

---

* This essay is taken from Eberhard Arnold's lecture "Nature and Evil," dated November 28, 1922.

stage of inner development. In his published writings and letters he never progressed beyond this legalism and kept on stressing the one extreme: Do not resist one who is evil; do not use weapons; live only for the will to fellowship!

Such an approach is not only one-sided – it can also be destructive. Not by coincidence did destructive powers intrude into Tolstoy's own life. This finds its most shaking expression in his dramatic work *The Light Shines in the Darkness,* where he presents a picture of his immediate family's experience. The wife, faced with a husband intent on taking principle to its extreme, refuses to follow him; the son and daughter are left engulfed in despair. We are left to ask: is this what redemption looks like? Surely not!

Tolstoy's biography illustrates why legalistic obedience to Jesus' command must result in error and torment. To rigidly implement the principle of loving one's enemies would be tantamount to a support of evil – for example, to abolish the police force would allow the worst elements in society to gain the upper hand. Such "obedience" would result in destroying large swathes of human society. It is no coincidence that the victorious Bolsheviks set up a monument to Tolstoy.

If someone were to demand: "Lay down your weapons, abolish the military, do not obey armed powers, set up a communist regime with no private property, issue a new legal code to implement the Sermon on the Mount down to every detail, including in foreign and economic policy" – to take such a path would result in calamity. In essence, it would be little different from other past failed attempts to use the word of God as a blueprint for running a state; history gives us examples such as the sixteenth-century Reformers in Switzerland or Oliver Cromwell's Puritan republic in England. The idea of a Christian

Europe – of a Christianity allied with the state – is a basic root of corruption, a fundamental error. Only by making a sharp separation between the *life of nature,* such as it is in a fallen world, and a *life of grace,* as vouchsafed to us by Christ, will our ship be steered through all the distress of our life without foundering.

Having said this, Christians must join Tolstoy in confronting humankind with the witness to a life without private property and without weapons. The possibility that our testimony to such a way might be misused by evil forces must not deter us.

In humankind's present condition, a *normative* precept for the orderly function of society and the state remains necessary. But as Christians, we know that this can only represent a very relative truth. Accordingly, we need an ongoing new *corrective* that is set up and against the "normal" human condition – a corrective that lives and works in a way totally different from the world around it, including the state. This corrective is destined to be the normative order of the future, one that is in harmony with justice, love, and genuine community.

This corrective – what is it? It is the kingdom of God! From above, God's rulership has to make peace between all the groups fighting each other; it has to set up great new orders in politics and economics, has to bring forth here on earth concrete effects of God's will.

When Jesus came into the world, he bore witness to a new kind of "state" for all humankind. He brought into being genuine fellowship – the community of his church. He lived with his disciples in a fellowship that comprised everything. Roaming about in an itinerant community of goods, he had his mind on just one goal: to establish the communal church as a rock amid the storms of history. The message was to go out to all nations.

The disciples were to proclaim everything he had confided to them. And then, after the death of Jesus and his resurrection and the outpouring of the Holy Spirit, who gave strength to the witnesses, a communal church did come into being (Acts 2). This first, original church community was the grain of seed for humankind's future; it proved strong in the mystery of God: in love, in the Spirit.

The love of the early church manifested itself outwardly by miracles of healing, inwardly by the members' becoming "of one heart and one soul" (Acts 4:32). What this church community bore witness to was God's very heart, which is present in the Spirit poured out by the Risen One. Where this heart of God is, there is love, there are the riches of God:

> Therefore, if anyone is in Christ, he is a new creation; the old has passed away, behold, the new has come. All this is from God, who through Christ reconciled us to himself and gave us the ministry of reconciliation; that is, in Christ God was reconciling the world to himself, not counting their trespasses against them, and entrusting to us the message of reconciliation. So we are ambassadors for Christ, God making his appeal through us. We beseech you on behalf of Christ, be reconciled to God. (2 Cor. 5:17–20)

In the communal church of Jesus Christ, the new nature for which Tolstoy longed becomes a reality.

Note on the Translations

TRANSLATING TOLSTOY is a matter that continues to spark passionate debate. With one exception (see below), this volume uses English versions either by Constance Garnett or by Louise and Aylmer Maude, who were friends and collaborators of Tolstoy. These translators' works are in the public domain and are widely available online. As classic texts loved by generations of readers, the Garnett and Maude versions have many strengths but do occasionally betray their age; accordingly, for the sake of clarity they have been lightly revised to reflect today's standard American style and punctuation, spelling, and usage. Similarly, Scripture quotations for which the translators originally used the King James Version are now given using the Revised Standard Version.

Translations by Louise and Aylmer Maude include: "The Three Hermits" (1); "The Death of Ivan Ilyich" (3); "Three Questions" (5); "Where Love Is, God Is" (6); "Master and Man" (7); "What Men Live By" (8); "The Empty Drum" (9); "Nikolai Meets the Enemy" (10) and "What Pierre Learned from Platon the Peasant" (12), from *War and Peace*; "God Sees the Truth, but Waits" (13); "A Spark Neglected Burns the House" (14); "Nekhlyudov Seeks Redemption" (15), from *Resurrection*; "The Healing of Prince Andrei," from *War and Peace* (16); "The Repentant Sinner" (17); "A Grain as Big as a Hen's Egg" (18); "Ivan the Fool" (19); and "A Talk among Leisured People" and "Walk in the Light While There Is Light" (21 and 22).

Translations by Constance Garnett include: "Levin Looks for Miracles," from *Anna Karenina* (2); and "How to Resist Evil" (11) and "What Is the Meaning of Life?" (20) from *The Kingdom of God Is within You.*

Translation by David Patterson: "My Way to Faith" (4) from *Confession* (New York: W. W. Norton, 1983). Used with permission.

Other Titles from Plough

The Gospel in Dostoyevky: Selections from His Works. Passages from Dostoyevsky's greatest novels explore the devastating, yet ulitmately healing, implications of the Gospels.

Provocations: The Spiritual Writings of Kierkegaard. Introduces a man whose writings pare away the fluff of modern spirituality to reveal the basics of the Christ-centered life: decisiveness, obedience, and recognition of the truth.

Tidings: A Novel by Ernst Wiechert. A concentration camp survivor's classic novel of guilt and redemption. First published in 1950, it deserves is place among the masterpieces of European literature.

Salt and Light: Living the Sermon on the Mount by Eberhard Arnold. Unlike dozens of other books on the "Great Teaching" of Jesus, this one not only interprets it, but says that it ought to be put into practice.

My God and My All: The Life of Saint Francis of Assisi by Elizabeth Goudge. The ever-fascinating life of Saint Francis, retold for today's readers by one of the great novelists of our time.

Plough Publishing House
www.plough.com
PO Box 398, Walden, NY 12586, USA
Robertsbridge, East Sussex TN32 5DR, UK
4188 Gwydir Highway, Elsmore, NSW 2360, AU